Mr E Entertainment
Independently publishing the crime novels of Mr GS
Revel Burroughs

A Recipe for Murder
ISBN 978-1-3999-8783-7

First published September 2024

1

No generative AI has been used in the writing of this book.

All enquiries

gary@wasteground.co.uk

www.garyburroughs.co.uk

Amuse Bouche

"Something to get your teeth into while the starter gets its boots on."

Shimonoseki, Honshu, Japan.

Gemma Collis sat in the corner of a large warehouse, dropped headphones over her ears, and watched the monitor in front of her. The camera crew had set up their primary camera to film a long-range shot as the host of "Wilde in Japan" made his entrance. They hadn't long come in from filming drone shots outside, and the warehouse was beginning to come alive with traders and buyers.

'Okay, Max, hold it there. We'll come in for the close-up and your piece to camera.' The director, a thin, wiry man from Manchester, spoke into his walkie-talkie. He handed his radio to a runner and got up from where he sat. Gemma watched as he glided across the warehouse floor to where a make-up artist was attending to Max Wilde.

Gemma had been on set at every one of Max's food tours worldwide, and the director was the only other crew member who could say the same. She had watched them film the experimental "Wilde in Africa" and then joined them on "Wilde in Australia," "Wilde in America," "Wilde in Vietnam," and "Wilde in China". Next year, they would film "Wilde in South America," but Japan had caught Gemma's heart.

Gemma's story was now forever linked to Max's. They were bound together by bonds stronger than love, and it was a friendship that had grown and matured over the years and had been further cemented by Max's meteoric rise to stardom. He had been nothing more than a chef, to begin with, somewhat eclipsed by his older brother, Robert, who was the undoubted talent of the two. What that man couldn't do with food wasn't worth doing. But Max had the personality and the flair and could charm anything and anyone. Following a brief stint on a television cooking show, something Robert had declined to do, Max was given his own cooking show, followed by a daytime quiz show, "Wilde at Five", where Gemma, a contestant, first met Max.

It had been love at first shag, but, like all explosive passions, their romance had cooled. Max wasn't the sort to limit himself to just one person, and Gemma wasn't about to let go of a good thing when she found it. Besides, they had something in common that would tie them together for the rest of their lives.

Crime.

Not actual crime, of course, but crime fiction. Agatha Christie, Ngaio Marsh, Raymond Chandler, Francis Iles et al. Gemma had written her first detective novel and self-published it on Amazon, where, like many books, it simply vanished, barely registering one hundred sales, a single five-star review and a one-star review that bit harder than she had expected.

She showed the book to Max, who showed it to his publicist and a publisher friend who made a few suggestions. Gemma was pleased to admit not many, but one vitally important one that had changed her world. Put Max's name on the cover and watch it fly.

So they did, and several million copies later, a multi-million-pound book deal for five more, a movie deal and an unbreakable contract that made Gemma Collis the powerhouse behind the legend that had become Max Wilde, and the Wilde phenomenon seemed unlikely ever to end.

'Okay, Max,' the Director began, holding five fingers in the air and dropping them as he counted back, 'five, four, three, two, one and go..'

Gemma watched Max's face on the monitor as he switched it on. She didn't know what "it" was, but Max had it in bucket loads. He was warm, friendly, knowledgeable and approachable, the latter being responsible for many broken hearts along the way and one or two divorces. She watched as he gave his piece to the camera. Whatever "it" was, he still had it.

Max held his hands out. 'This is one of the largest fish markets in Japan,' he said as he walked slowly toward a fish seller. The cameraman walked backwards, equally slowly, being guided by the director as he did so. 'Nothing special there, I hear you say, and quite right, too. Fish markets are ten-a-penny and exist in every single corner of the globe. But,' he paused, 'they're not quite like this one.' He waved at the camera, engaging the audience directly. It was a nice touch, Gemma thought. 'Come with me. Let me show you something very special.'

Gemma watched the monitor as the cameraman followed Max into a room stacked with tanks of water filled with fish. There were dozens of them in each tank, seemingly oblivious to their fate. She watched a young Japanese man dressed in an all-white coat reach into a net and pick up a fish. He handed the live fish to Max, who turned and held it up to the camera.

'This is Takifugu Rubripes, or what the Japanese call Torafugu. To you and me, it's plain old tiger pufferfish, and it contains one of the most deadly poisons known to man, tetrodotoxin, a poison so toxic that the Japanese government strictly controls the sale and preparation of this fish. Chefs who wish to prepare and sell this delicacy must study for over three years before gaining their licence, and even then, poisonings happen. As recently as 2020, three people died from eating Fugu, the delicacy made from this fascinating creature.

'But, as with many fishery products, there was a danger that the pufferfish would be fished to the brink of extinction, so, in early spring, the spawn of this fish is caught and held in cages in the Pacific before being brought to places like this, up and down the country. Their numbers are strictly controlled.'

Max turned and handed the now swollen pufferfish back to the man who had given it to him, who bowed respectfully and dropped it back into the tank.

'But we're not going to buy one of these fish.' Max smiled and shook his head. 'The really sought-after tiger pufferfish is wild-caught, and this is Wilde in Japan, so that's exactly what we're going to do, and tomorrow night I'm going to give it to a gentleman called Kaito Fukushima, a world-renowned fugu specialist who will prepare fugu sashimi for me, and I am going to experience my first ever fugu..'

The director looked up and said, 'Okay, cut there.' He looked over the cameraman's shoulder at Max and said, 'You're going to do what now?'

'I'm going to eat fugu,' Max declared brightly.

'Are you fucking mad? You've just told everyone how poisonous this stuff is, and you want to eat some?'

'Of course.'

'What about the dead people?'

'That was actually in the Philippines. No one has died in Japan for ages. Not from properly licensed restaurants.'

The director turned as Gemma walked in. 'Tell him he's fucking mad.'

'You're fucking mad,' Gemma said, smiling. She had half suspected Max would want to try it. 'You've met the chef, Mr Fukushima. He can't be a day under 84.'

'He's 79,' Max countered. 'And what's more, he eats the stuff every day.'

The director shook his head. He glanced at his watch and said, 'We'll discuss this later. Our fishing trip departs in thirty minutes. We need to get the equipment on board now.'

Gemma waited until the director and the cameraman had left the building. 'I think you've scared him.'

'I'm a chef, Gem. I can't travel the world talking about exotic foods and not try them. My audience expects it.'

'I don't disagree.' Gemma said. 'I still think you're mad, though.'

***

It took forty minutes for the crew to load the necessary equipment onto the small fishing vessel that bobbed gently in the harbour. The Japanese captain, a small, round little man with a distinct lack of care for foreigners who couldn't follow a simple timetable, paced back and forth on the boat's deck, mumbling under his breath.

Finally, Max and Gemma climbed aboard the small vessel, and the captain set off, away from the harbour and out into the Sea of Japan. Before them, the ocean spanned out as far as the eye could see, interspersed here and there by small islands shrouded in an early morning mist.

Gemma sat admiring the view while Max and the crew filmed a dozen set pieces to camera. The director threw suggestions around in his carefree Manc accent, to which Max instinctively objected, and the two men then entered into a brief discussion as to whose ideas were the best. The crew waited patiently as this tradition played out before them, a tradition created over the years in every corner of the world that led to the "Wilde in" franchise becoming the most successful food series the network had ever had. The last series, "Wilde in China", had surpassed all expectations and was even gaining traction in the US, where the careers of many British celebrity chefs had been left wanting. It was a hard market to crack, but Max's flair and personality, along with America's love of a good British crime novel, had increased his visibility. It had started to prove to be a very lucrative market indeed. How Max and the director reached an agreement always amazed Gemma, but in the end, they always did, and the resulting compromise always worked.

In the distance, Gemma saw a small island break out of the low mist and loom large before her. She heard the Captain shout something to his crew and looked at Max enquiringly.

The Japanese fixer the network had hired to manage the day-to-day details of the show translated for her. He was a friendly young man, around thirty years old, with striking black hair, deep brown eyes and a flawless complexion.

'This is the spot,' he said, in patchy, though understandable, English. 'The captain says that even the worst fishermen catch the puffer here!'

She felt the engines of the boat take on a different timbre, and the movement of the craft over the crystal blue waters slowed. It took a dozen minutes or so for the crew to drop anchor and set up the various lines that were subsequently cast out into the sea. Gemma watched with keen interest. Everything she hadn't seen before was potential material for Max's next book, and she wrote her observations in a small notepad that was never far from her hands. Every detail, every nuance and interaction between the various people on the boat was subject to her minute observations. Very little got past her, and much of it found its way into her little notepad.

The director set up the camera and filmed all over the boat from multiple angles. He and Max spent an hour filming filler, and in that time, the fishermen managed to catch absolutely nothing.

The heat rose with the hour, and before long, Gemma felt the press of the humidity as it closed in around her.

'I'm going below to keep cool.' She declared to no one in particular and dropped down into the belly of the boat.

It wasn't a big boat, but it wasn't exactly small, either, she thought as she passed through the galley and into an air-conditioned room with comfortable chairs and a fridge. She opened the fridge, grabbed a bottle of beer, and dropped onto a small couch. She drank the cooling liquid and closed her eyes. She often worked best with her eyes closed, which seemed to help her visualise her characters as they formed in her imagination. It wasn't a perfect system as she often fell asleep on the cusp of a brilliant idea only to wake up with absolutely no clue what that brilliant idea was. Right now, the fugu thing was dominating her thoughts. Had it been used before? It must have been. She'd need to research that. She didn't want to rehash an old plotline. Did everyone who ate contaminated fugu die? Were there any survivors? If there were, Japan would be the place to find them. Could you deliberately poison someone with fugu, and how would it manifest itself? What would the autopsy show? How could a murderer employ fugu as a weapon and not kill everyone around the table? Was there an antidote?

She sat up, opened her notepad and began scribbling. She opened her phone and started to scroll through Wikipedia. She hadn't expected to find much signal but was pleasantly surprised that it was as strong in the middle of the ocean as she had found it anywhere in Japan. But then, she mused, that was Japan all over!

She scrolled and made notes for a couple of hours. It passed in the blink of an eye. She was interrupted in her research by Max, who had come down into the boat for some beers.

'There you are. I wondered where you had gone.'

'It was getting too hot.' Gemma declared. 'Have you caught anything yet?'

Max shook his head. 'Not a bloody thing. Doug's still giving me earache about eating fugu. He reckons I probably wouldn't be insured if anything happened, and the network would fire him and sue him for everything he has for letting me do it.'

'Make him eat some then.' Gemma said. 'If the fugu is poisoned and you die, he'll probably die too. You can't sue a dead man.'

Max paused. Then he smiled. 'Gem, you're a fucking genius.'

'I know. Would you like to know what else I know?'

Max sighed. Gemma sometimes knew more than was good for her.

'I know that if you eat poisoned fugu as an evening meal, the chances are you'll be in bed, alone, when the poison begins to take effect. It paralyses you while keeping you perfectly aware of what is happening but incapable of raising the alarm. Eventually, your lungs stop working, and you die. It's horrible.'

'It won't happen, Gem. I promise. But, just to be sure, you could stay with me? You know, to tend to my needs..'

Gemma watched Max's expression as a wicked look crossed his eyes.

'I know perfectly well what needs you are referring to, so I shall gracefully pass on the invitation. Perhaps the pretty young waitress you were flirting with last night would be up to the job? I assume it was her knocking on your hotel room door at 1 o'clock this morning?'

Max laughed. 'You don't miss a thing, do you? What's all this,' he asked, indicating the notes she had been writing, 'book stuff?'

'Hopefully. I have a few ideas. I need to pin them down.'

She was about to go into more detail when she heard a commotion on deck. A few seconds later, several voices were calling Max back up on deck. Gemma followed him up and back out into the heat and humidity.

On the port side, one of the Japanese fishermen was gently tugging back on his rod and slowly reeling in his line. A child-like grin stretched across his face.

'Come on, Max,' Doug, the director, cried. 'Take over quickly, and we'll get a good shot of you reeling the thing in.'

'Is it a pufferfish?' Max asked.

'Yes, yes,' the fixer shouted excitedly. 'Quickly, come.'

Max was guided over to the beaming fisherman, who handed over the rod. He stepped back proudly and watched as Max took control.

'Gently, now, Max. Don't let her go!' Doug cried.

Max slowly retrieved most of the line and hauled an impressive-looking fish over the side. The cameraman caught it all. Max worked on removing the hook from the fish's mouth and then held it up to the camera.

'There she is,' he began, 'a wild caught tiger pufferfish. A much sought-after delicacy. Isn't she beautiful?'

It wasn't beautiful, Gemma thought. It had puffed itself up and looked ridiculous. She was surprised anyone wanted to eat it.

'We'll keep the fish alive in one of these small tanks and deliver it to Mr Fukushima later,' Max said, giving his pitch directly to the lens. 'I can't wait to see how a master of his art prepares such a wonderful-looking fish and creates his world-renowned fugu sashimi.'

Max beamed. Doug looked worried.

Max turned and dropped the fish into the tank specially designed to carry the live fish to Mr Fukushima's restaurant.

'Right then,' Max declared, 'let's eat fugu!'

***

That evening, Max, Gemma, and the film crew boarded an overnight train bound for Tokyo. The pufferfish had been securely loaded into the cargo hold, and the train slowly departed from Shimonoseki precisely on time.

Gemma sat with Max and Doug and watched as the day slowly faded to night beyond the rapidly changing landscape outside the train's window. She let her mind wander, picking at ideas as they came and went and finishing conversations her characters had in her head so that an imperfectly formed idea began to develop. It was an exciting idea, founded in the conversations about deadly poisons that Max and Doug were having. She had found their musings trivial and wearying. One way or another, Max would get his way. He always did. She knew it, Max knew it, and so did Doug. Doug's acceptance of that fact was the only thing that separated the three of them.

The quiet monotony of the train's motion tugged at her consciousness, and her eyes became heavy. They had eaten a large dinner before boarding the train and had opened a bottle of wine as the train departed. Gemma drained the liquid from her glass and stood to leave.

'I'm going to bed.' She declared. 'I'm tired.'

The two men stopped bickering, and Max glanced at the expensive Breitling strapped to his wrist.

'Only another five hours to go!' He grinned and raised his glass. 'See you in Tokyo.'

Gemma said her goodnights to the other film crew, who had taken seats behind them, and made her way to the sleeper carriage. She found her room and crept inside.

It took a few minutes to undress and brush her teeth. She stood in the small bathroom and admired the figure that looked back. Not bad for a thirty-something, she mused. She still held on to her youthful looks; bright green eyes sparkled behind an olive-skinned face.

She climbed into her bed and turned off the light. She stared into space for some time before the hypnotic rumble of the carriage tipped her over the edge, and she began to drift asleep.

Plot lines shot across her consciousness and balanced her on the edge of sleep. She considered them and weighed them up. Some were quite good, and others not so much, but her mind would not settle. Her characters began talking again, holding entire conversations while she tried to control their direction. And then an idea. A wonderful idea, but only if….

Like all good ideas, Gemma woke the following morning unable to recall what it was, exactly, that she had considered to be a good idea. Still, if it were a good idea, she'd think of it again, but in her experience, sleep ideas were akin to drunk ideas - not so good in the cold, hard light of day.

Tokyo was, without doubt, the most amazing, awe-inspiring and phenomenal city Gemma had ever visited. The crew alighted in the early morning, long before the great mass of humanity that was Tokyo came to life. It was a wonderful time of day, Gemma thought. The city had an altogether different vibe. It smelt different. It *looked* different.

Mr Fukushima's restaurant had opened early for the television crew, who set about filming background shots to accompany the series. Max and Gemma left them to it and checked into their hotel.

'One more night and then home.' Max said as the receptionist handed over their digital keys.

'I think I'm going to work on the next book for a couple of hours,' Gemma said. 'Then I may freshen up and go for a wander.'

Max had been on one of Gemma's wanders before. Bangkok, if he remembered rightly. The bloody women could wander aimlessly for hours. In the end, he'd grabbed a tuk-tuk and found a hostess bar where he wiled away a lazy day in the company of some beautiful young women and lost several hundred dollars in the process. Perhaps that's what he'd do today but in a more salubrious establishment.

'Have fun,' he said drily.

Gemma smiled. 'See you at the restaurant later. What time do you plan to film?'

Max shrugged. He left that sort of thing to Doug. 'About five o'clock, I think. Doug wants to film a bit before evening service.'

'See you then.'

***

She was dressed in a light grey mini dress, the hem of which hovered delicately above her knees. Smart-looking but comfortable shoes graced her feet, and she carried a small bag.

'There you are,' Max exclaimed as Gemma walked through the front door of Mr Fukushima's restaurant. 'Come on, we're about to film the fugu being prepared.'

Gemma followed the excitable Max Wilde through the small restaurant and into the kitchen. Two cameras had been set up in the kitchen, and Doug stood behind one of them, looking apprehensive. Crew members were to be found vying for room in the tiny space. The kitchen was small. Max took his place in front of the cameras next to an old man with a long grey beard that Gemma took to be Mr Fukushima. Next to him was a pretty little Japanese girl around twenty years old. She was elegantly dressed in a blouse and short skirt. She had the darkest hair that Gemma had ever seen. It sparkled under the lights.

'Everyone ready?' Doug asked, not expecting an answer. 'Okay, Max, you're up.'

Max turned it on. He oozed charm and knowledge and carefully weaved a quick piece to camera. Mr Fukushima listened attentively as the young Japanese girl translated Max's words. Max gushed platitudes on the old man, and Gemma could see they were having the desired effect. Mr Fukushima was beaming and slowly becoming a member of Max Wilde's global fan club.

'And this is Sakura Fukushima, Mr Fukushima's granddaughter.' Max turned to the young girl, bowed, and said hello in Japanese. Sakura visibly melted, and her dark skin glowed with red.

Max turned and opened the crate which had been transported from Shimonoseki and lifted the pufferfish. He held it to the camera and then to Mr Fukushima.

'What do you think? She's a beauty, isn't she?'

Mr Fukushima took the fish and smiled. He said something which Sakura translated.

'He says it is a beautiful fish.'

Mr Fukushima placed the fish on a specially prepared board, picked up a wooden hammer, and hit the fish over the head.

'The first thing Mr Fukushima must do,' Max explained to the camera, 'is render the fish unconscious.

A swift blow to the head achieves this in the most efficient and humane way.'

Everyone watched as Mr Fukushima then grabbed a large knife from nearby and sliced the fish's head off. He placed the head into a bowl.

Max explained: 'Every part of the fish that isn't used for eating must be separated from the rest and securely bagged up and sent to a licensed facility for disposal. The entrails, skin and, most importantly, the liver will go into that bowl. The liver was once considered the most delicious part of the fish, and even today, it is still sought after. However, it is also deliciously deadly, containing most of the tetrodotoxin within the fish. A simple mouthful could kill you.'

Mr Fukushima started talking as he began to gut the fish.

'This is the most important part,' Sakura translated. 'The poisonous parts of the fish must be removed carefully and delicately. A cut in the wrong place could cause the deadly poison to infect the parts of the fish that we are to eat. There is no way to tell if this happens. We must trust the chef.'

Max watched in awe as the elderly Mr Fukushima deftly prepped the fish with steady hands. When he had finished preparing the fish, an airtight lid was placed on the bowl, and the contents were removed.

Mr Fukushima was then left with the fillets. He opened an elaborately decorated box and removed a knife.

'My grandfather says that this knife was once owned by his father and before that, his father. It is an ancient knife and very sharp.'

Slowly, Mr Fukushima began to slice the fish into incredibly thin strips.

'This is called Usuzukuri,' Sakura explained. 'The fish is sliced so thin that it becomes translucent.'

As if to prove the point, Mr Fukushima began laying the fish slices onto a brightly painted dish. It was a dish of multiple colours: greens, reds, and blues, all combined to give a definitive Japanese feel. The colours were clearly visible through the fish. When Mr Fukushima had finished, the fish slices were fanned out on the plate and ready to eat.

He held the plate out to Max, who took it and held it to one of the cameras. 'And there you have it. Fugu Sashimi. Doesn't it look wonderful?' There was a long pause as Max looked directly into the lens. 'Let's eat.'

Max sat next to Mr Fukushima and his granddaughter as the plate of fugu sashimi was laid out on the table before them. A bottle of fugu saki was brought out. Sakura explained that the drink was made from the dried fins of the pufferfish and was completely safe.

The film crew took a while to relocate, but before long, they were recording and watching in silence as Max took a small piece of fugu sashimi and swallowed it.

'There are no words….' Max said. 'It is easily the finest fish I have ever eaten. There's something indescribable about its flavour.'

The crew watched as Max took another piece and ate it. Doug's face dropped.

'There's always that knowledge, too, that you could be eating your last meal. This,' he said, taking another piece of fugu, 'is the ultimate thrill. How can something so delicious be so deadly?'

Sakura had been translating Max's words to her grandfather. He spoke rapidly and passionately. Max waited while Sakura translated.

'He says you will ruin his reputation. Not once in his whole life has my grandfather served spoiled fugu. Not once.'

Sakura looked serious.

Max adopted his placating voice and took another piece of fugu. 'It is because of my dearest respect for your grandfather that I am eating it. I would trust no other chef.'

Mr Fukushima nodded and smiled.

'In fact,' Max went on, 'I'm so confident in the quality of this fugu that I think our dear leader ought to try some. What do you think, Doug?'

One of the cameramen turned and filmed Doug. Doug looked stunned.

'Well, I… I'm not sure. I'm not a fan of fish.'

'Nonsense.' Max declared firmly. 'This is a food show. *Your* food show, in fact. And it would be rude to Mr Fukushima here if the man who makes all this possible didn't at least try some.'

Everyone waited. Gemma grinned. Max always got what he wanted. Mr Fukushima listened as his granddaughter translated. He nodded and said something back to her.

'My grandfather would consider it a great compliment if you tried his fugu sashimi.'

Max could barely control his glee as he swept another piece of fugu into his mouth.

'Well, when you put it like that…'

Reluctantly, Doug picked up some chopsticks, guided a piece of fugu between them, and dropped it into his mouth. He held it there for a few seconds before swallowing it.

'That's actually very nice..'

Max pushed the plate forward. 'Would you like some more?'

'Do you know, I think I will,' Doug said, much to Max's displeasure. He reached over and took another piece of fugu. 'It really is bloody good.'

Mr Fukushima beamed. Max looked cross. Gemma marvelled at how skilfully Doug was able to reign Max back in. Max's little joke hadn't worked.

They filmed a few more scene shots and one or two pieces to camera, but it was clear that Max had lost his enthusiasm for it. The crew dismantled their equipment and began loading it back into their vans.

Gemma sat at the table with Max, Mr Fukushima and his granddaughter as more food was brought to the table. Gemma avoided the fugu but dived into the other pieces of sushi and sashimi with relish. She was going to miss Japan.

Max looked across at Mr Fukushima and said. 'This has been one of my favourite dining experiences of all time.'

He waited as Sakura translated.

'And I was wondering,' Max went on, slowly, 'whether this is something you would be prepared to travel to England to recreate…'

Mr Fukushima shook his head sadly as Sakura said, 'My grandfather has much love for your country. He has been there many times, but he fears he is getting too old for the journey.'

Max was undeterred.

'I'm a very wealthy man, Mr Fukushima, and you would be paid handsomely for your time. All your expenses would be taken care of. I will fly you and your granddaughter, first class. Your every need would be taken care of.'

Max waited as Sakura translated.

Before she could reply, Max said, 'You see, I'm a celebrity at home. I have my own TV shows and quizzes.

We film a Sky TV breakfast show from my home every Saturday morning. I would love for you to be on it if that can be arranged.

'I'm also something of a crime writer. You may have seen some of my work.'

Gemma said nothing. She tucked into a mouthful of salmon roe.

'My grandfather knows all about you. Your reputation extends to the Far East. He regrets that he has not read your books but knows you are well respected in that field.'

'Once a year,' Max continued, 'I host a bit of a dinner at my home in the Cotswolds. Nothing too fancy,' he lied, 'but my guests are some of the most revered and respected crime writers of this generation. Richard Osman came once, you know. And I invite a few up-and-coming writers to give them a lift up in what is quite a difficult world.'

Mr Fukushima nodded appreciatively.

'I'm holding my next dinner at the end of summer and would very much like you to serve your fugu sashimi to my guests.'

Sakura smiled. Mr Fukushima had taken that as a great compliment. 'My grandfather says he is tempted but fears that fugu is illegal in Europe.'

Max nodded. 'It is. But Great Britain is not in Europe. And, besides, I know of a way in which we can, how should I put it... circumnavigate the rules.'

Gemma watched as Max's eyes twinkled. What was he up to?

'My grandfather says that if you can assure him that he will not be involved in anything illegal, he would be delighted to come. We would be delighted to come.'

'Excellent.' Max stood up as if to leave. 'I'll leave you in Gemma's capable hands. She sorts all this stuff out for me.'

Mr Fukushima stood and bowed respectfully. Max took his hand and shook it warmly.

'I look forward to welcoming you to England.'

***

Lilac Cottage, Wiltshire, England.

Patricia Hemshaw sat on her patio in the afternoon sun and gently turned the page of the latest Sanjay Chakrabati novel set in Colonial India. He had a delicate hand, she mused and touched on the delicacies of the human condition without ever going into much detail. There was violence, of course. He was India's premier crime writer. One doesn't get crime without violence, but Mr Chakrabati had a unique talent that allowed the reader to form the images in their minds without him ever having to describe them. It was the same with the romantic angle, which he always managed to slip into his books, but never once was the physical act described. Of course, they were all at it, but it was always implied and suggested. Pat nodded appreciatively.

She glanced at the table where the latest Margaret Hemshaw novel sat and grimaced. They weren't bad books - in fact, Pat had been the driving force behind her mother's crime novels for over ten years. As she had recently drifted unceremoniously into her seventieth year, her mother's novels had become more graphic. The violence was gory and precisely detailed, and Pat had learnt more about the workings of the male sexual organ than she cared for. The latest review for the Sunday

Times had described the book as: "a perfect storm of sex and violence, written by your grandmother."

It had become an instant bestseller, as they all did, and the latest book, 'Death of a Highwayman,' had been snapped up by a Hollywood studio. Plans were afoot for Pat and her mother to move to California for six months to oversee production.

'Pat!'

Her mother's voice bellowed out of the house behind her, abruptly smashing the peace. Pat thought she had a voice that could start engines and, given the right weather conditions, could easily knock a small child off their feet.

'Pat!' She boomed again.

'Yes, mother?'

'Come here.' She ordered.

Pat got up and walked across the small patio and in through a set of French windows. On the mantelpiece proudly stood the latest offering from the Crime Writer's Association. A Gold Dagger with "Margaret Hemshaw" etched into the silver plate. Mother was rightly proud of her achievement, even though much of the research and editing had been done by Pat.

'Mother?'

Mother was sat at the centre of a large oak table, surrounded on nearly all sides by reams of paper. Behind her, thirty-two books in hardback and in mint condition sat in tribute to a lifetime's work. Margaret had a cigarette burning in an ashtray nearby. Pat walked over and stubbed it out.

'I do wish you'd stop. It's bad for your health.'

Margaret reached for her packet of cigarettes and lit another.

'I do wish you'd stop complaining.'

'You summoned me?' Pat said.

'I did not summon you.' Margaret argued. 'I called for you. You're my editor and researcher, and I require you to do your job.'

Margaret took a sheet of paper from the table before her and launched it at Pat. Pat took the paper and looked at it. It was littered with Pat's corrections and suggestions.

'What's wrong with it?' Pat asked.

'Third paragraph down. Why can't I have people "welshing" on an agreement?'

'Our Welsh sensitivity readers may find the term offensive.' Pat said.

Margaret paused. Pat waited for the onslaught.

'I don't see why we need bloody sensitivity readers. Or bloody trigger warnings. It's a crime novel, for god's sake. They should expect a bit of crime. The giveaway's in the title.'

'It's a different world from the one you started writing in,' Pat explained.

'It's a bloody stupid one,' Margaret countered. 'People are offended by the most ridiculous things. What's wrong with "welshing"? Why is it offensive?'

'Perhaps if you were Welsh, you would understand.'

'Perhaps,' Margaret said. 'But it's an eighteenth-century crime novel. It has highwaymen violently taking the maidenheads of young women. Buccaneers raping and pillaging and captain's buggering the cabin boys, and I need to be careful about a single word?'

'Yes.' Pat said. 'You do. Or at least, I do. Besides, "welshing" didn't exist in the written form until the 1850s. It was likely used in conversation before that, but certainly not in 1734.'

Margaret looked at her daughter. 'Well, why didn't you bloody say that in the first place? Take the word out. Do you know, I think you do things like that to get a rise out

of me. You can be very snide, young lady. I thought I
had brought you up better than that.'

"Brought up" was certainly not how Pat described her
upbringing. When she was five, she was shipped off to
boarding school, where she was held prisoner, as she
thought it, until she turned eighteen. Holidays were spent
following her mother on her book tours, where Pat was
tended to by various nannies. She went to university and
studied history, for which she received a first, and
English, for which she received a second, much to her
mother's eternal disappointment. She had been her
mother's assistant ever since.

Margaret looked up as her letterbox clattered at the
front of the house.

'That would be the post.' She said.

Pat took the hint, collected the letters, and dropped
them in front of her mother.

'Is there anything else?' She asked.

'I don't think so. Not just at the moment.' Margaret
said as she leafed through the pile of letters. 'Ah,' she
said, holding a single envelope in the air. It had a crest on
the reverse, stamped onto the envelope. 'The annual
summons!'

Margaret slipped a knife into the envelope and
carefully opened it. Pat looked on expectantly. She eyed
the pile of letters nearby, carefully looking for another
envelope of the same design. She couldn't see one.

'Max Wilde, Burnham Manor, Burnham-on-the-Wold.

*You are hereby cordially invited to Max's annual dinner party
at Burnham Manor on the last Friday of August of this year. We
look forward to yet another Murderously Mischievous dinner party
where you will be able to enjoy some of Max's criminally good food.
RSVP by 1st August.'*

Pat waited expectantly.

'Is it an invite for one?' Pat asked.

'Of course it is,' Margaret said, and Pat sensed her tone.

'There's only one letter?' Pat asked, despite every bone in her body suggesting that perhaps she shouldn't.

'Yes.' Margaret said firmly. She never looked at the pile of letters, but she knew there wasn't one for Pat. She had firmly instructed Max not to invite Pat again. Not after last time.

Pat looked crestfallen.

'I daresay Max will accommodate again. It doesn't say on the invite,' Margaret said, ignoring her daughter, 'perhaps I'll give that assistant of his a ring. She seems to do all his planning. Now, what was her name?'

'Gemma.' Pat said. 'Gemma Collis. Her number's in your phone. Would you like me to call her?'

'No.' Margaret said abruptly. 'I'll do it. I shall go down on the Friday afternoon. I'll be back early on Saturday. I trust you'll be able to stay out of trouble while I'm away?'

Pat didn't reply.

'Good. That's settled then.' Slowly, she said, 'It's for your own good. You're quite a naive young girl. You need looking after.'

Pat took that to be her mother's final words on the matter, and she turned and left the room. She returned to the patio, her emotions inflamed. Young girl, indeed! Naive! She sat and fumed. She was thirty bloody years old, and she still treated her like a child! Sometimes, her mother could be quite intolerable.

***

Waterstones The Bookseller, Piccadilly, London.

Sydney Fletch opened the front cover of her bestselling novel, "The Last Hangman", turned to a blank page and looked up at the elderly lady who hovered expectantly in front of her.

'Who should I address it to?' She asked softly.

The old lady beamed. 'Hattie, my dear. As in Jacques,' and then, as an afterthought, 'Oh, but you're so young, you probably don't even know who Hattie Jacques is..'

Sydney was young. At just twenty-eight years old, she was one of the youngest crime writers to have ever had her novel sit for several weeks on both the New York Times and UK Times Bestseller lists. Not bad for a debut book. And, of course, she knew who Hattie Jacques was. She was young, not stupid.

She wrote: 'To Hattie, as in Jacques, best wishes, Sydney, as in bridge.'

She passed the book back to the old lady who was ushered aside by Sydney's agent, the equally young and simply brilliant Emily, and then found herself looking up at an old man with a crooked nose and yellow teeth, who smelt of week-old tobacco. That was the problem, Sydney thought, of meeting and greeting the great unwashed. Some of them were literally unwashed.

'Could you make it out to my wife,' he asked in an accent that reminded Sydney of an old black-and-white movie. 'To Betty..'

'As in Spencer?' Sydney asked drily.

She watched as her attempt at humour sailed past her intended victim and out into the street, never to be seen again.

'Who?' The old man asked.

'Never mind,' Sydney said, sweetly, dutifully signing the book to "Betty" before handing it back to the old man, who bared his teeth in an attempt at a smile before Emily came along and ushered him away.

'Gregg,' the next one said, whose eyes lingered far too long on Sydney's body. She could almost smell the Rohypnol hidden about his person. Sydney had often wondered how some criminals managed to look exactly that. Like criminals. Gregg looked like a criminal. He looked exactly like the sort of person who might carry a vial of Rohypnol with him on a night out. She was prejudiced. She knew that. Gregg may well have been a perfectly lovely person, albeit odd-looking. But she was a crime writer. It was her job to see the darkness in people.

Emily came and dealt with Gregg, and the next person in line stood forward. And so the day continued until the line ended a couple of hours later.

Sydney stood up and stretched like a domestic cat rising from its slumber. She stood for a minute, massaging her right hand. Emily bounded over with a coffee.

'Thank you,' Sydney said. 'How many did we do?'

'They're still counting,' Emily replied. 'But it was good. The manager reckons it was one of the best this year.'

Sydney had been Emily's first signing. The two of them were new at the publishing game, and Sydney's phenomenal rise had shocked them both. It had also shocked the more senior agents at Woodhouse Literary Agents, who had all declined Sydney's manuscript and handed it to Emily as a starting project. Emily's tenaciousness and obvious talent had worked wonders on a very good book and turned it into something special. When Charles Woodhouse invited Sydney and Emily into a meeting where he declared his intention, as senior agent, to remove Emily and take control of the Sydney Fletch phenomenon, Sydney politely, yet firmly, pointed out which orifice he could kindly shove his offer.

Furthermore, she had declared that if Woodhouse Literary Agents didn't like it, they could lump it. Charles Woodhouse was no fool. He knew a good thing when he saw it, and he wasn't about to lose Sydney or Emily and gracefully relented. He was also slightly terrified of Sydney.

'There's a few more books to sign,' Emily continued. 'Actually, there's about three hundred. Do you mind?'

Sydney minded deeply. Her wrist hurt. 'Of course not,' she lied, and the two young women followed a staff member into the back of the bookstore where several hundred more copies of "The Last Hangman" were stacked up.

The staff member offered refreshments, which were declined, and Sydney sat in front of the large pile of books. Emily sat next to her and took her pen.

'I'll sign them,' she said, 'you finish your coffee. I don't want my leading writer to get RSI!'

Emily sat and signed the remaining books while Sydney sat and watched. When they had finished, Sydney said, 'I need a drink. What about you?'

The black cab flitted about the streets of London before depositing them in Covent Garden.

'Come on,' Sydney said, 'I know where we can get a bloody good cocktail.'

Ten minutes later, they sat in a small booth in the corner of what Sydney would later describe in one of her books as a British take on a speakeasy. They drank cocktails from treacle cans adorned with freshly cut fruit and ordered a ridiculously expensive bottle of fizz. After drinking most of it, they ordered a large sharing plate of Italian meats, breads, and olives.

'We need to talk about Max Wilde.' Emily said, dropping an olive into her mouth and washing it down with a swig of champagne.

'Why?' Sydney asked.

Emily reached into her bag and pulled out an envelope. She handed it to Sydney, who opened it and read the contents aloud.

'To the managing agent of Sydney Fletch, Woodhouse Lit. Ag., London

Max Wilde, Burnham Manor, Burnham-on-the-Wold.

Sidney Fletch is hereby cordially invited to Max's annual dinner party at Burnham Manor on the last Friday of August of this year. We look forward to yet another Murderously Mischievous dinner party where you will be able to enjoy some of Max's criminally good food. RSVP by 1st August.'

'What's there to talk about?' Sydney asked. 'I'm not going.'

'You *do* know who Max Wilde is?' Emily asked.

Of course, she knew. Who didn't? Max Wilde, celebrity chef, Michelin Star holder, quiz show host and internationally acclaimed bestselling crime writer. Few people were unaware of Max Wilde.

'He's a powerful man.' Emily explained. 'A difficult man, too, at times. He's certainly not the sort of man who sends out invitations to his world-famous gatherings without careful thought or the sort of man who would take kindly to his invitation being rejected. Being at one of his gatherings would open a world of opportunities. He wants you to go on his Saturday morning breakfast show. They film it on-site at Burnham Manor. You'll attend the dinner party the evening before, stay overnight at the Manor, and go on the show in the morning. He has more viewers than ITV, you know.'

'Sounds like a blast,' Sydney said, her tongue dulled somewhat by the fizz but still sharp enough for Emily to note the hint of sarcasm.

'Once you've been on his show, the offers will flood in. Max will probably get you on his quiz show. From there, you could be doing The Chase Celebrity Special, Celebrity Family Fortunes, Celebrity Masterchef…'

That would be fun, Sydney thought. Her family were a mixed bag of villains, convicts, scumbags and scroungers. She had grown up on an estate in Coventry and had run away when she was fifteen. Life had been tough for a while, but her tenacity and strength of spirit had lifted her out of her life of hell to the one she was living now.

'Celebrity Catchphrase, House of Games, even,' Emily paused, as if the thought had only just come to her, 'I'm a Celebrity Get Me Out Of Here.'

She looked so excited. Sydney felt bad, wanting to let her down. She was a writer, not a celebrity. She preferred anonymity and solitude. The idea of munching on kangaroo testicles did not fill her with joy.

'Look,' she said at last, 'I'll do the dinner thing. I agree. It can't do me any harm. As for the TV stuff, we'll cross those bridges as and when they come in.'

Emily beamed. Then, a frown crossed her face. 'Which is why we need to talk about Max Wilde.'

'I thought we just did?'

'No. I mean, actually, about Max. About the sort of man he is.'

Sydney was intrigued. 'Tell me more!'

'Well,' Emily began, carefully marshalling her thoughts. 'Max is something of a player. You know, with women. It's not necessarily a bad thing. He's not predatory or anything like that. He likes women, and he likes sleeping with them, but he doesn't stay around for much longer than that. There's a wake of broken hearts behind him. And it's not like he uses his fame or power or anything like that. He's almost hypnotic. He's hard to resist.'

'You sound like you're speaking from experience!' Sydney joked, and Emily turned red.

'Oh my god! You are!' Sydney leant forward in the booth in a conspiratorial fashion. 'Tell me all about it!'

Emily looked around her to ensure no one was listening, then leant forward. She told Sydney everything, leaving no detail or body parts unexplained.

'The next morning, he got up and left, and I haven't spoken to him since. I can't lie, Syd. It was the best night of my life.'

Sydney nodded in appreciation. Why were the good lovers such shits and the good men such bad lovers?

'And I didn't want you to, you know, fall for it. You're far too good for him. You deserve better.'

Sydney thought about that for a long minute. She also deserved to experience the best night ever, something she had yet to find.

She said, 'You're a good friend, Emily. But I'm stronger than you think. I'm more than a match for the likes of Max Wilde. Trust me.'

'Oh, I trust *you*.' Emily said. 'It's Max Wilde I don't trust.'

*****

Film City, Mumbai, India.

Sanjay Chakrabati sat in the lee of a small copse of Banyan trees that served as the backdrop for the last scene they were filming that day. Set designers from the BBC and several Indian productions had worked their magic and turned this quiet corner of the vast Film City estate into 19th-century Colonial India. Local Indian actors milled about the set alongside several British actors dressed in typical Colonial dress of that period.

The production of "Death in the Raj" had become famous for its historical accuracy and attention to detail. Little wonder it had become one of the BBC's flagship shows.

There had been some criticism, of course. Every aspect of colonial rule in India was emotive and controversial. Still, Sanjay had penned his novels carefully and built a world that touched on sensitive issues but dealt with them in a reasoned and educated way.

Sanjay himself was a product of Colonial India. His great-great-grandparents had been servants to an English landowner who had sent his great-grandparents to England for a better education. The landowner had been a typical Victorian gentleman who believed firmly in Justice, fair play and tolerance and had ruled his house similarly. Several generations of the Chakrabati family had benefitted from British rule and had become landowners, lawyers and politicians. Sanjay's Grandfather had been a tireless campaigner for Indian independence and proudly took his place in government when the British finally left in 1946.

This understanding of Victorian India allowed Sanjay to write such powerful crime novels. Men could be evil, Sanjay knew, and that evil knew no nationality. Men could also be kind, and that, too, knew no borders. In his novels, everyone, Indian or British, was capable of great evil and great love. His criminals came from all parts of the social spectrum, which had a clear definition in those days within the British and Indian hierarchies. His heroes also came from both sides. No one group of people were ever held to be better or worse than the other, each with their own issues and complexities that Sanjay touched on lightly in his books. Perhaps that was why they had become so successful, he wondered. They rose high on the bestseller lists in the UK and India.

Sanjay watched as a pompous-looking Englishman with an extravagant-looking Victorian moustache entered the set, wielding a fearsome-looking cane. It must have been a hundred degrees in the sun, Sanjay mused, yet the actor was fully adorned in a bright 19th-century suit and hat. He was coping well, he noted.

Detective Inspector William Shakleton-Mills was the star of several of Sanjay's books and had been the lead in the BBC/Indian production of "Death in the Raj." He was so English, Sanjay thought, as the actor ran through his lines. You could almost hear the history in his words and smell the tea and cakes.

Sanjay watched as a handsome young Indian actor approached and spoke his words. Sanjay was proud of this creation. He enjoyed writing about his adventures and misadventures and was delighted that the British and Indian public had so well received him. He was the star of the show and had done much to bring a sense of authenticity to Sanjay's script.

Daksh Patel played the role to perfection. He played it so well that Sanjay couldn't get his voice out of his head as he wrote new editions of his novels. The character of Detective Sergeant Johan Maharaj was definitively Daksh's.

The director hovered nearby, watching a monitor closely. The directors for this, the fourth "Death in the Raj" series, had been chosen carefully. Each was selected by a panel of Indian and British producers, including Sanjay, and consisted of an even split of nationalities. This helped bring perspective to the series and worked incredibly well. The director for the last episode of series four was a hard-working Scot who had been instrumental in filming episodes of some of the BBC's other flagship dramas, such as "Death in Paradise." He brought with him a fresh element and a unique manner.

Sanjay had thought he worked well. The rushes had certainly indicated as much.

'Okay, that will do,' the director said softly, in gentle Scottish tones. 'Everyone happy?'

He looked at the crew, who all smiled, and then back at the actors, who waited patiently for his next words.

'Okay then, that's a wrap. Well done, everybody. Let's go celebrate.'

There was a ripple of applause and a round of back-slapping. Sanjay closed the last page of his script and watched as everyone began the shutdown. He was filled with conflicting emotions. Ending a long project was a joyous moment, but it was tinged with a sense of emptiness. He would now not see many people around him for many months while the next series was scripted and put into production. He was a writer and liked his own company, but he was very proud of his achievements on "Death in the Raj" and couldn't wait to get back at it.

A runner hovered at his shoulder. He turned and looked at her.

'The men from the BBC are here.' She said.

Sanjay smiled. 'Make sure they are well looked after,' he instructed. 'They are very important people.'

The runner nodded and disappeared.

Rumours had been floating about the industry that the BBC, in association with an Indian film company, was about to embark on producing a film version of "Death in the Raj." Sanjay had been waiting patiently to hear which of his novels was in line for the movie and was quietly preparing a treatment for each book. With any luck, he'd get to write the script, too.

Sanjay got up from his spot in the shade and rode back to the studios in an old golf cart. He could feel his heart thumping in his chest and the adrenaline pumping through his veins. Since he had first heard that the head of BBC Drama was flying into Mumbai for a meeting with him and the other show producers, Sanjay had felt the fluttering in his chest. It could only mean good things. He was riding high on his successes and felt confident that bigger and better things were ahead.

He found the delegation from the BBC in one of the boardrooms hired out to the show's makers. It was often used as a place where the cast and crew could do read-throughs of the script and where the actors were encouraged to offer suggestions and improvements. Today, it was used to entertain the guests who sat around the table and looked very serious.

Sanjay looked at them and felt the first pangs of doubt. Two men and two women were dressed in business suits and looked like they didn't have a sense of humour to share. More importantly, Sanjay noted, the head of BBC Drama wasn't there.

'There you are, Sanjay,' one of Sanjay's co-producers stood and pulled a chair for him. He mouthed something to him and threw his eyes back at the Brits, but Sanjay couldn't make out what he was trying to say.

Sanjay sat. 'I was expecting Mr Okenshaw…'

One of the men opposite fidgeted, which drew Sanjay's attention. He had clearly been elected as spokesperson. He was a grey-looking man in his thirties with dull, grey eyes and a sense of eternal doom that sat on his face and dragged him down.

'I'm afraid Mr Okenshaw has other priorities. He sends his apologies..'

The young man looked at his colleagues, who all avoided eye contact. They all looked somewhere else but nowhere in particular.

'Well, there's no point beating about the bush,' the grey man said, 'so I shall come straight to it. The BBC has decided not to renew "Death in the Raj" for a fifth season. We're terribly sorry, but we're pulling out.'

Sanjay couldn't believe the words he was hearing. Everyone sat in stunned silence. No one saw this coming.

'But I don't understand,' Sanjay said. 'It's one of the most successful BBC dramas. It even has better ratings than "Death in Paradise."'

The grey man fiddled with his fingers. 'That's not entirely true,' he said slowly. 'Once or twice, the ratings have been better, but on the whole, not so much. I'm afraid it's a question of budgets. Money's tight, as you know. There isn't the money for another series.'

Sanjay's shoulders dropped. '"Death in the Raj" is dead in the water..' he said solemnly.

'Not necessarily,' the grey man said, 'other networks may be interested in commissioning another series.'

Sanjay doubted it. Regardless of its success, it was rare for a network to take on another's project. Netflix, Amazon and Sky were proud of their "Originals" tag. Somehow, he didn't think "Death in the Raj" fitted their future plans. There was ITV, of course, but Sanjay was well aware that they had already started filming a project in Film City to try and capture some of the enthusiasm the viewing public had for Colonial India. No, "Death in the Raj" was done.

'You owe us at least one more series,' Sanjay said, more in hope than conviction. 'Let us finish the series properly…'

The grey man threw his hands out in a sign of exasperation. 'There's no money.' He said firmly. 'Next year's budget has already been spent. A decision has been made. There will be no more "Death in the Raj."'

The finality cut through the air like a scythe. Sanjay looked at his fellow producers and saw the realisation in their expressions.

The grey man and his colleagues murmured together in a small huddle before the grey man rose from his chair.

'We have some work to do here,' he said slowly. 'The BBC has some investment in this studio, which it is keen to protect. There will be some paperwork to take care of. Accounts to settle, that sort of thing.'

That was why he was so grey, Sanjay thought. He was an accountant.

Sanjay sat, dejected and depressed, as the grey cloud left the room. Slowly, Sanjay's colleagues rose from their chairs without saying a word and left him all alone. There were wounds to be licked, he thought. It was better done alone.

He rose slowly and wandered over to the window. Below him, life continued. People's work continued. Their dreams survived while his lay ruined, shattered and broken at the foot of the BBC's budget. He could write more "Death in the Raj" books, but that didn't seem enough. He was on the cusp of becoming a famous film and TV executive, but now he was pulled back from success and handed a morsel of mediocrity for his troubles.

He sighed deeply. What on earth would come next?

***

Private residence, West London.

Lottie Chamberlain carefully applied a deep rouge to her lips. She looked at her mirror, and a face she had known her entire life stared back. There were some differences, she had to admit. Her twenties were long behind her, her thirties were rattling by in a hurry, and age was beginning to touch the corners of her eyes. Her hair, which had once floated effortlessly down to her hips, was now gathered more sensibly (and manageably) about her shoulders. There were no greys. She was pleased with that. She didn't like grey, not in women. For some reason, it aged women where it didn't for men. Salt and pepper for men, hair dye for women. It was ridiculous, really. Men who dyed their hair to hold back the years looked older for their troubles, and women who didn't dye their hair looked equally old. Silly.

She caught the sound of a motorcycle entering her street, and caught sight of it as it pulled into her drive. It was huge, yet moved gracefully and purred like a big cat. She watched as the rider dismounted and removed his helmet.

It was her first time seeing him, and she wasn't disappointed. He had black hair, unfettered with grey or hair dye, and he had the hint of a five o'clock shadow about his face. His face was lean, much like the figure beneath it. Her eyes wandered the length of the man's body, and she smiled appreciatively.

'He's here!' Her husband cried as she heard the front door being opened.

She reached for a small bottle of expensive perfume and sprayed it lightly onto her neck. It was always worth laying the extra foundation.

'Mr Black.' Lottie said as she held her hand out in front of her.

Lottie's husband had guided the motorcyclist through their spacious home and into a custom-built recording studio in the garden. She found him slipping out of his motorcycle jacket and accepting a cold can of cola her husband had pulled from a nearby fridge.

'Please, call me Gareth.'

Gareth Sebastian Black. Self-published and fully independent author, writer of six books and currently the "next big thing" in the literary world.

Gareth reached out and shook Lottie's hand warmly.

'Gareth it is,' she said, and Gareth caught the faint aroma of something sweet and sickly assail his nostrils.

He was even more handsome up close and smelt delicious, Lottie thought as she held his hand a little longer than usual.

Lottie and her husband, Jack, ran a hugely successful Podcast, "Lottie Loves Books," out of the studio her husband had built in the garden. They had over three million followers, a massive Instagram following and a rapidly growing Facebook presence. In the last two years, Lottie's book recommendations had started gaining traction and became the 'go-to' podcast for the latest news and recommendations. Publishers were queuing around the street to get their new and existing authors onto her podcast. It was easily worth an extra two hundred thousand sales. Equally, it had made Lottie and Jack incredibly wealthy.

'Please, take a seat.'

Lottie indicated a comfortable sofa in the corner of the recording studio. This was where she recorded her podcasts and conversations with writers. An expensive camera was set up in front of it, behind which her husband took up position.

'Do you mind if we film?' Lottie asked.

Gareth minded a great deal, but he shook his head instead. 'Not at all.'

He sat on one side of the sofa, and Lottie sat beside him. Her husband fiddled with equipment and started turning things on.

Lottie edged closer to Gareth and placed her hand on his knee.

'It's so kind of you to agree to do this,' she gushed.

Gareth smiled. 'I couldn't say no. Not after everything you have done for me.'

It had been a lot, too. After five books, he was barely scraping a living. His Amazon advertising bill cost more than his total sales. He had tried everything. He had literally sold his soul to the Devil trying to promote his books to the general public and was on the verge of giving it all up when Lottie happened.

She had been in the midst of a hugely successful podcast with the inimitable Max Wilde when she spoke of Gareth's latest book, "Murder on Five-Mile Drive," which instantly propelled his book to the top of the Amazon bestseller list. A week later, Gareth Black had knocked Max Wilde's latest offering off the number-one bestseller position and made him a household name.

Gareth was no idiot. He always said be kind on the way up, even if he had never been on the way up, and karma will take care of you. He held to that today, so he wasn't objecting to being the subject of Lottie's latest podcast. Any other day, and he'd rather stick needles in his eyes.

Lottie's husband looked up from behind the camera and said, 'We're good to go when you are, Lottie.'

Lottie's hand lingered on Gareth's leg.

'Okay, shall we do this?'

Gareth smiled the best smile he could manage. Lottie paused as she gathered her thoughts. Then, looking directly at the camera lens, she began her introduction.

'Today, we will speak to Gareth Sebastian Black about his journey through the self-publishing mine-field, his rise to the top of the bestseller lists, and what the future holds. Welcome, Gareth.'

'Thank you for having me. It's a pleasure to be here.'

Lottie withdrew her hand slowly, but not before making a slight detour up Gareth's leg. Gareth was painfully aware of Lottie's husband watching the proceedings through a top-quality video camera lens, but, surprisingly, he made no sound.

'Let's start with you, Gareth,' Lottie continued, 'tell us about yourself.'

Gareth spoke quietly yet firmly. He had a well-educated voice, even if his education was lacking. Most, if not all, of what he had learnt in life had come from inside the pages of a book. He touched briefly on his happy childhood, his problematic teenage years, and his fall into a deep depression. They spoke about mental health for some time before they moved on.

'What brought you into the Crime Fiction world?' Lottie asked.

'Agatha Christie did,' Gareth said warmly. 'Like a lot of people, I suppose. I was deep into my depression at the time, and I remember watching an episode of "Poirot" on the TV and becoming utterly beguiled by it. It was the one moment in that period of my life where I could escape. I felt a connection. I felt joy, and let me tell you, that was in short supply at the time. The next day, I wandered into my local library and picked up my first "Christie."'

'Do you remember which one it was?' Lottie asked.

'I do. It was "Murder in Mesopotamia."'

Lottie smiled. 'It's a good one, even if the solution is hard to swallow.'

'It didn't matter.' Gareth went on. 'It saved my life. It shone a small beacon of light where once there was only darkness. I returned to the Library, borrowed what they had left, and devoured them. I had to buy the others. A year or so later, I'd read them all. I still read them today.'

'There is something quite special about them.' Lottie agreed. 'Is that what made you want to become a writer?'

'No. I always knew I was going to be a writer. I didn't know what I was going to write. Finding Agatha Christie focussed my attention.'

'But that was your late teens, wasn't it? And now you are in your late forties? Why did you wait so long?'

'Thirty-year writer's block!' Gareth chuckled. 'Actually, it was a bit of that and a bit of a hangover from my struggles. When I was at school, I said I wanted to be a writer, and my career advisor suggested I work at my local factory and gain life experience. When I overcame my struggles, my Job Centre advisor suggested that we all have 'pipe dreams' and perhaps I should get a job. Everywhere I turned, everyone I spoke to suggested writing novels was for old people and that I should concentrate on living my life. So that's what I did. I got a job - several, in fact, and the years just fell away. I wrote my first crime novel in my forties and thoroughly enjoyed the process.'

'So why self-publish? Did you not want to go the traditional route of finding an agent and publisher?'

'Of course I did. That's the dream. I polished my book until it shone, wrote a cracking introduction letter, and sent it to over thirty agents. Three replied instantly with 'a thanks, but no thanks' e-mail, and four took nearly four months to say the same thing. I'm still waiting for the other twenty-seven or so to reply.'

'What do you think went wrong?'

'I'm too old.' Gareth said. 'Rather ironic. But publishers don't want people like me at my age. I'm too working class, too uneducated, and I have no contacts in the industry. I'm not what the publishing world wants.'

'And yet your latest book has sold over a million copies?'

'Readers don't care what the publishing world thinks they want to read. The struggle is getting to them in a world dominated by celebrity writers.'

Lottie smiled. Her podcast was dominated by semi-famous celebrities becoming multi-million-selling crime novelists. Crime writing had become the domain of the rich and famous.

'What do you say to people who say self-published authors aren't proper writers? That self-published work is inferior?'

'It can be of inferior quality,' Gareth admitted. 'Some of it. But not all. I've read as many traditionally published books that weren't worth the paper they were printed on as I have self-published books. Dreadful books are not the sole domain of indy writers! Most self-published writers go to extraordinary lengths to put out the best they can manage, often with a limited budget. We don't have a team of designers working on the cover or a crack team of editors working on the text. We do it all ourselves. And yes, sometimes there are mistakes, and sometimes we get things wrong. It's raw and from the heart. We write while holding down a job because no self-published author is rich. We plot in the evenings and write on weekends; when we're finished, we have to do everything else. We have to be the graphic designer, the copywriter, the accountant, the advertising executive and the marketing bod. And I'll tell you what you get for that. You get something pure. It's unfiltered and genuine. You get the stories the publishers think you don't want, and I *know* they're wrong. You get to read about worlds, events, and dramas from various people from all walks of life, and it comes to you straight from the heart.'

'A heartfelt sentiment,' Lottie said, 'but does that hold true for you now? Publishers must be fighting amongst themselves for your next book?'

'It's true, they are. I've had some excellent offers but don't need them now. The self-publishing world is very sophisticated. All I needed to crack it was money, and last month, I got that thanks to your podcast.'

Lottie beamed.

Gareth continued, 'And now I have a lot of the stuff. I can afford to employ a graphic designer, a proofreader and an editor. I can afford to employ social media experts and advertising geniuses. My books can stand shoulder to shoulder with mainstream books, and I don't need a publisher to do that for me.'

'So let's talk about your books. Shall we start with your latest? "Death on Five Mile Drive."'

Gareth and Lottie sat and chatted like old friends, with Lottie's hand stroking Gareth's leg occasionally. They spoke about books, plotting novels, the mechanics of crime and Gareth's preferred method of writing.

'Do you have a special place where you like to write?' Lottie asked.

'No. I write where I'm most comfortable, usually on the sofa. But, actually, anywhere the mood takes me. I plot all the time while at work, driving or in the shower. I get my best ideas as I fall asleep, and I'm afraid most have been lost to the gods of sleep!'

Lottie chuckled. 'Just about every writer tells me that. So what about your plots? Where do they come from?'

'Anywhere and everywhere.' Gareth said. 'I've spent the last thirty years writing books in my head. There's a bit of a queue! Ideas can come from the most mundane of situations.'

'Your book, "Murder on Five Mile Drive" has been phenomenally successful, not just for a self-published author. Very few mainstream writers get the same level of sales as you have. As a consequence of that success, your novel knocked Max Wilde off the top spot, something no other crime novelist has been able to do when their books are released at the same time as his. Max Wilde has strong market dominance. How do you feel knowing your book has come ahead of his?'

Gareth chose his words carefully.

'Obviously, I'm delighted my book has done so well, particularly after all the hard work I've put into it. But I don't consider myself in competition with other crime writers. Max's book and mine have stayed constantly at the top for several weeks. It doesn't mean fewer people have bought Max's book. It just means they've bought mine as well. It can only be a good thing for crime writing in general. Plurality in the crime writing world benefits the readers.'

Lottie nodded. 'Has Max Wilde reached out to you?'

'Gareth shook his head. 'No. We've not spoken.'

Lottie pushed on. 'It's coming up to that time of year when Max Wilde invites the best writers in the crime writing world to his house for dinner. We outsiders know very little about what goes on at these gatherings. Everyone remains tight-lipped about them. We know Richard Osman and the Reverend Richard Coles have been in the past. Margaret Hemshaw was there last year with her daughter Pat, and if I'm right, Harlan Coben was there the year before. No one has uttered a single word about what has occurred at the dinner parties.

'We think that Margaret Hemshaw has been invited again this year, and I'm guessing that Sydney Fletch is likely to be on the list, given the awards she has won from the Crime Writers Association.'

Gareth nodded. He had read ''The Last Hangman'' and couldn't wait to read more from the young Sydney Fletch.

'And given that you have knocked the old master off his throne, we wondered whether you've been invited this year?'

Gareth smiled. 'Like I said,' he began, 'we've not spoken.'

He felt Lottie search his eyes for the truth, and he was worried his poker face wasn't up to the job.

'Is that a yes or a no?' Lottie pressed.

'It's a no.' Gareth lied. He could feel the envelope in his back pocket as he said so. Like in "Fight Club," no one talked about Max Wilde's little gatherings. It had become an industry secret, shared only by those invited.

The conversation went on for another hour. Lottie knew her stuff, and her passion for books shone through. Gareth could see why she had become one of the world's pre-eminent book reviewers.

When they had finished, Lottie took Gareth's hand and led him out of the studio and back into the kitchen. She opened a fridge, opened a bottle of beer, and handed it to Gareth. She took one for herself and drank a large mouthful.

'Sorry that took so long,' Lottie said. 'We don't usually get that much out of writers! Jack will be in the studio for hours getting that lot edited.'

'It's been my pleasure.' Gareth replied.

'Do you know,' Lottie continued, 'I don't review self-published books on my blogs. Perhaps I should. Maybe you could recommend some?'

'Of course. I'd be delighted.'

'Did you mean what you said,' Lottie asked, 'about publishing your own work? You're not going to sign with a publishing house?'

Gareth laughed. 'God no! I couldn't think of anything I'd want to do less than publish my own work! I'm a writer, and a bit of a romantic one, at that. I want to write. I'm quite happy to let other people do the rest!'

Lottie looked at Gareth with a quizzical expression. 'Then why say you were going to pursue that route?'

'Because, at the moment, I'm nose-deep in negotiations. As soon as the publishers hear your podcast, which they will, they'll up their offers.'

It was Lottie's turn to laugh. She edged closer to Gareth. 'You're quite the manipulator!'

Lottie dropped her bottle on the kitchen worktop and leaned forward until her lips touched Gareth's. A second later, her tongue was pressing at his.

For a moment, Gareth reciprocated. It felt like the natural thing to do, and then he remembered Lottie's husband less than fifty yards away. He pushed Lottie back.

'Are you okay?' Lottie asked. She seemed genuinely surprised to have been rebuffed.

'What about your husband?'

Lottie's face looked surprised as if it had only just been pointed out to her that she was married.

'Oh, Jack?' She exclaimed. 'I can ask him to join us if that's your thing?'

'I meant, won't he mind? What if he saw us?'

'Oh, I see. Jack won't mind at all. He's as happy as a pig in you know what when he's editing. He'll be in his little shed for most of the night. Besides, we have a liberal attitude when it comes to sex. If you're still here in the morning, he'll probably make you breakfast.'

Lottie took Gareth's hand and led him out of the kitchen and up their lavishly decorated staircase to the first floor. By the time they reached the bedroom, Lottie was wearing nothing but a skimpy black thong, and Gareth was slowly discarding his clothes as he walked.

Three hours later, Gareth opened the taps on his Suzuki GSX 1300 and felt the beast surge beneath him. Open skies and an open road stretched before him, and he embraced them both eagerly. He was still reeling from the last few hours and relishing in the steamy memory as the pictures played out again in his head. Lottie had been a passionate lover and pressed all the right buttons, even a few he didn't know he had. He had left her bed reluctantly, but he couldn't quite come to terms with the fact her husband was a few yards away. He certainly wasn't going to stay for breakfast.

Still, he mused, being a famous writer was coming with many unexpected bonuses.

***

The Larches, Burnham-on-the-Wold, Gloucestershire

Former Detective Inspector John Finney, known to his friends and former colleagues as the "Man Who Grew Vegetable Marrows," sat in his garden on the edge of the Cotswold village of Burnham-on-the-Wold and afforded himself a smile.

His garden was laid out before him, and he was pleased. It had been a labour of love, and he had thrown himself into it with all the enthusiasm of a man more used to spending his time chasing ne'er-do-wells. His borders were a wonderful display of different colours, pinks, reds, blues, and yellows. It had taken some time to get used to the different pace of life, but he had settled into it as though he had been born into it.

His greatest pride lay at the bottom of his garden, just behind the greenhouse and just before the fence that separated his garden from the farmland beyond. Three giant marrows lay sheltered from the sun under several large umbrellas. He had grown several in the last few years, but they had been quite different from the ones that had appeared this year. They must have been two hundred pounds apiece, and he didn't care to try and work that out in modern parlance. He was getting old and perfectly content to live in the old way. The future was for the young - he wanted nothing to do with it.

'Morning, Jack.' A voice said from behind.

He turned and smiled at his neighbour, the elderly Mrs Sloame, who beamed at him from beyond a small fence that separated their gardens.

'Good morning, Grace,' Jack said, smiling. He had moved into the Larches just over three years ago, and Grace and her husband Arthur had embraced their new neighbour with all the love and attention usually reserved for family. They had no family, so they adopted Jack, who was just a few years short of their own age. Arthur had succumbed to cancer barely eight months ago, and Jack had stepped up and dealt with the formalities and difficulties that death brings with it. He and Grace shared the grief that had visited upon them both, and they found comfort in each other's company. Loneliness and despair were not allowed to thrive.

'How are the marrows doing?' Grace asked.

'Come and see.' Jack said, standing up as he did so.

Further along the garden, where the borders ended, and Jack's allotment began, a small gate opened, allowing the neighbours easy access to each other's gardens. Since Arthur's death, Grace had suffered considerably from arthritis and rheumatism, and her garden had become a burden to her. Jack had willingly stepped in and took over Arthur's work, keeping Grace's flowers and borders looking as good as they had ever done.

Grace walked slowly, aided by a walking stick, and the two gathered at the foot of Jack's small vegetable patch and marvelled at the size of his marrows.

'Goodness!' Grace exclaimed. 'Whatever have you been feeding them?'

Jack tapped his nose conspiratorially and said, 'I'm afraid there are only two people who know the secret, and I promised Arthur I wouldn't say a word to another living soul.'

Grace smiled. She enjoyed hearing Arthur spoken about like that. She remembered many evenings when Arthur and Jack would sit amongst the marrows, carrots, and potatoes, chatting about nothing in particular. Jack had a habit of enjoying a drink or two, and Arthur was never one to refuse.

'Will you be showing them this year?' Grace asked.

'I hope so.' Jack said. 'I need to find a young man to help me get them to the Manor.'

Burnham Manor had hosted the village fête and vegetable growing contest for fifty years. The famous crime writer Simon Delancey had been quite the philanthropist when it came to the lives of Burnham-on-the-Wold villagers. He opened his house and gardens every year and had become the village's favourite resident of the Manor. Max Wilde, the latest incumbent, maintained the tradition, if not the village's respect. Max had grown up in Burnham-on-the-Wold. His parents had been the proprietors of The Marlborough Hotel in the village. Everyone knew very well who Max Wilde was.

'I should think Mr Fenwick has a fight on his hands this year.' Grace continued.

Jack pondered John Fenwick. His marrows had won the competition for the last ten years and were widely expected to win again this year. He had been Delancey's gardener and ground's keeper for as long as anyone

could remember and had been bequeathed the
Gamekeeper's Cottage, deep inside the grounds of the
Manor, on Delancey's death. When Max Wilde
purchased Burnham Manor, he acquired John Fenwick at
the same time.

'I hope so,' Jack replied. 'I'd certainly like to rub that
smug grin off his face this year.'

'I rather think it would please Mr Wilde,' Grace said.
'And Arthur would be terribly proud!'

He would, Jack agreed. After several failed attempts at
growing competition marrows, Arthur supplied Jack with
some marrow seeds and a few trade secrets to get him
underway. They had proved to be extremely good seeds
(from a marrow planted in 1988, Arthur would often
remind him) and excellent advice.

Jack reached into his jacket pocket and pulled out a
small, round tin. He opened it carefully, selected a mint,
and popped it into his mouth before closing the tin and
dropping it back into his pocket. It was a curious habit
that he had acquired a few years back when he had given
up smoking. He had never been quite able to ween
himself off the mints, but he surmised it was the lesser
of the evils. Grace watched the little act as she had done
so many times. It was a curious quirk, she thought. And
he had never once offered a sweet to anyone else. She
never thought it rude, just peculiar, and that's just how
folk were, and she wouldn't have changed it for the
world.

'What about you, Grace? Can we be assured of a slab
of your finest lardy cake at the fête this year?'

'Oh, yes!' She said firmly. 'I have a few secrets up my
sleeve. There will not be a repeat of last year,' she added
portentously.

Jack smiled at the recollection. Grace's efforts had
come second place to the efforts of Niki Latham, a stay-

at-home mother of twins who had, in Grace's opinion, swayed the judges by the fortuitous position of her breasts rather than her cakes. Jack wondered what secrets Grace had devised to counter Niki's ample bosom. Jack had worked the tough streets of Gloucester for nearly thirty years, from Bobby to CID, and he had never found as much sex and intrigue as he had in Burnham-on-the-Wold.

The village fête was a little over a week away.

Jack smiled. He had no doubt it would be a good one this year.

***

Robert Wilde stood at the foot of a large allotment and addressed the sea of little faces that looked up at him. There were at least thirty of them, he thought, all dressed in a bright red school uniform largely covered by hideous-looking hi-vis vests.

Their teacher, Miss Lewis, also adorned in a hi-vis vest and a white flowery dress, had led the children in a small convoy from the gates of their Junior school along the main road in Burnham-on-the-Wold, past The Marlborough Hotel and through a large cast-iron gate that led into the grounds of Burnham Manor. The gate was usually locked, but the pretty young teacher had played Max like a cheap violin and persuaded him to open some of his private grounds to the local school's children to be taught the delights of growing their own food. Max had suggested that his brother, Robert, would be the one to show the kids the ropes, and Max had disappeared like he usually did, with Robert literally holding the baby.

Fortunately, it had been no hardship for Robert. As part owner of The Marlborough Hotel with Max, they had grown a business so successful that they could employ some incredibly talented chefs to maintain the single Michelin Star they had been awarded. He also liked children mostly, and their teacher was flirty and attractive. He had come to look forward to a couple of hours each week when they would join him on his allotment.

'Right then. Any questions?'

Fifteen dirty little hands shot into the air. Miss Lewis pointed to one.

'Archie?'

A small, round little boy of about eight years of age said, 'I need the toilet.'

'Can you hold it?' Miss Lewis asked. Archie had a habit of always needing the toilet, even when he didn't.

'I think so.'

Another hand shot up. A small girl with heavy-framed pink glasses said, 'Miss. I think I've been bitten.'

Several more hands shot up.

'And me!'

'Me too. Miss, it hurts.'

After a few minutes of tending to a few insect bites and one or two that looked barely like freckles, the children ran off in various directions, tending to their plants and pulling up weeds.

Miss Lewis wandered over to where Robert was helping a small child identify a plant.

'You're very good with them. Have you ever considered becoming a teacher?'

Robert shook his head. 'No chance. It was bad enough looking after Max when we were kids. I'm not sure I could look after a whole herd of the little darlings.'

'You sell yourself short,' Miss Lewis said. 'You're a natural.'

Miss Lewis was very pretty, Robert noted. She made a particular effort on Wednesday mornings when she brought her train of little darlings to the community allotment. Her hair was well tended, and her make-up done in such a way as to highlight her deep brown eyes, which, in Robert's opinion, were her best feature.

'Excuse me, mister,' a small hand tugged at Robert's trousers.

'It's Mr Wilde, George,' Miss Lewis corrected.

'Excuse me, Mr Wilde,' George asked again, 'is this edible?'

He held out a bunch of what looked like parsley. On multiple occasions, all the children had been told never to eat anything until it had been positively identified by an adult. Robert reached out and took the parsley from the boy.

'Where did you find this?' Robert asked.

The boy pointed to where more of it grew.

'Did you eat any of it?' Robert asked, more forcibly than he intended.

George sensed that he was about to get in trouble. Adults always sounded like that just before they started shouting at him. He looked down at the floor and shook his head.

Robert crouched down in front of him and raised his chin. 'You're not in trouble, George, but you must tell me the truth. It's vitally important, do you understand?'

George nodded.

'Did you eat any, George?'

'No, sir.'

'Good lad.' Robert stood up.

'Is everything okay?' Miss Lewis asked.

'I think that's enough for today,' Robert said, glancing at his watch. They had almost had their time, anyway.

'Make sure you wash his hands. Do you have any alcohol gel?'

Miss Lewis always had alcohol gel. Children could get very messy. She applied the gel to George's hands and gathered the children around. 'Come on, children, it's almost time for lunch. What do we say to Mr Wilde?'

There was a chorus of 'Thank you, Mr Wilde,' then the chain gang of small children in hi-vis vests followed Miss Lewis out of the allotment and back up the road to school.

Robert waited until the last child had gone through the gate before closing and locking it behind them.

He stormed out of the community allotment and into the allotment that supplied The Marlborough Hotel with fresh produce. The allotment was huge and covered land the size of a football pitch. Large greenhouses stood at the furthest end.

'Where's Fenwick' Robert demanded of the young man digging on the allotment.

'Where he usually is,' the young man replied in a deep Gloucestershire accent. He nodded to where an old brick shed still stood as a tribute to early twentieth-century architecture. It was covered in ivy, and Robert saw the open front door. He stormed through the door and slammed it shut behind him. He threw the plant the small boy had picked onto the table in front of John Fenwick.

'What the fuck is that?'

John Fenwick had the weather-beaten face of an old man who had spent his years outside. He had white whiskers that struck out untidily from his chin and, oddly, deep black eyebrows beneath a shock of unkempt white hair. He sat in a beaten-up old armchair, drinking beer from a bottle and listening to the radio. Calmly, he sat up, placed his beer on the side, and turned the radio down. He looked at the plant in front of him.

'Hemlock.' He answered.

'Yes, it is.' Robert yelled. 'Fucking poison Hemlock. Why the fuck is it growing on my allotments?'

'It's a native plant,' Fenwick replied. 'It grows everywhere.'

'Really?' Robert said, holding on to his fury. 'You think I don't know that.'

Fenwick sat back in his chair. 'I'll get one of the lads to sweep the grounds and remove it all.'

'It's that fucking Poison Garden. I told Max he should have burnt the fucking thing to the ground when he bought the house, but no. Max knows better. Max always thinks he knows better.'

'I shouldn't think it came from the Poison Garden,' Fenwick said quietly. 'Like I said, the stuff grows freely round here. I'll get it sorted.'

Robert turned to leave, his fury still raging fiercely within him. He turned back to Fenwick. 'Yes, do that, would you? Ensure none of the stuff is growing in amongst the kitchen allotments. God forbid we would serve Fool's Parsley to a customer. Can you imagine the scandal?'

Fenwick could, but he knew of no cases where Hemlock had been served accidentally in a professional kitchen. He had heard of a few cases involving the Wildes, where customers had been served food they had been allergic to. In the early days of their business, Max had almost shut them down when he served a nut dish to an allergic young girl. The girl had died, and it took most of Robert's money and some successful lawyers to make the thing go away.

Robert opened the door as if to leave. 'I still think we should burn the Poison Garden down. Who on earth thinks it's a good idea to grow the world's deadliest plants in a garden in the Cotswolds?'

He left the question unanswered and left Fenwick to his thoughts.

Fenwick remembered the day that Simon Delancey had conceived the idea for the Poison Garden. He had it built in the grounds of Burnham Manor, hemmed in on all sides by a ten-foot Cotswold stone wall. Inside that wall, Delancey grew some of the most fearsome plants known to mankind. Ironically, many grew wild in the UK.

Delancey had been a peculiar man, but Fenwick had liked him. He had strange habits and weird tastes, but these had inspired and created some of his finest works. He saw a little of the oddity in Max Wilde.

There was a reason Max Wilde had never burnt down the Poison Garden and why he never would. That kind of thing burned his imagination and fired his creativity. He was a man who liked to live dangerously.

Fenwick was interested to see what would happen next.

***

Gemma Collis missed Japan. There was something about the country she couldn't quite articulate. It was special. The people were special. It had made an indelible impression on her, and she itched to return and see more. But life got in the way, as usual, and she had thrown herself into her work in the usual Gemma-like way. Full on.

She crossed the hallway of Burnham Manor with her hands full of paperwork and emails. She found Max in the library, standing by a set of open French windows and clutching a glass of amber liquid.

'It's a bit early for that, isn't it?' Gemma asked as she entered the room and laid the papers on Max's desk.

Max disagreed. 'It's never too early.' He turned and looked back out of the windows.

Outside, a dozen men and women milled about installing and fitting a huge marquee. Across the length and breadth of Max's large front garden, the fixtures and fittings for the forthcoming fête were being laid out.

Max sighed.

'Do we have to do this every year?' He asked.

'Yes. It's a yearly summer fête. The clue's in the title.'

'Why can't they do it on the common?' Max asked. 'Why do they have to do it in my garden?'

'Because Simon Delancey started it fifty years ago, and now it's part of village tradition.'

'It's a bloody annoying one.'

Gemma agreed. It was annoying and very disruptive. But it came with a significant amount of goodwill from the community, and she was inclined to keep it that way. She reached out for a sheet of paper that she had laid on the table and passed it over to Max.

'Schedule for this weekend's show.'

Max read the sheet and placed it back on the table.

'Who's Anne Marie?' He asked.

Gemma sighed. 'She's a singer—a very good and successful one. You'll like her. She's quirky.' As an afterthought, she added, 'Try not to sleep with her, like you did with the last one.'

Max smiled. The memory was still fresh.

Gemma handed over another piece of paper. This one was an email stamped "Urgent".

Max ignored it. 'Just tell me,' he said, taking a large mouthful of whiskey.

'Agatha Christie Ltd have sent a cease and desist letter via their lawyer.'

Max turned with a quizzical expression on his face. 'What for?'

'Your recipe for "Delicious Death" that you had on last week's show. They have the trademark for chocolate cakes with that name.'

'Really?' He said. 'The same people who are happy to fuck up a good Christie novel for money, and throw Miss Marple into a perfectly good Poirot story, think I'm damaging her reputation?'

'Exactly.'

'Fine. Take it off the website. Call it something else.'

Gemma already had. The recipe for Deliciously Dreamy Chocolate Cake had already been updated.

'Anything else?' Max asked.

Gemma held up a handful of papers. 'There's a shooting schedule for your quiz show. It starts in four weeks. Then there's a producer of "House of Games" asking if you'd like to appear. That's in three months if you agree. I think they film in Glasgow.'

Max nodded. He had longed to get on that show.

'Anything else?'

'An email from your solicitor regarding The Marlborough Hotel.'

There was a long pause while Gemma waited for Max to turn around. He didn't. It was clear he had no intention of showing her his face.

'Why didn't you tell me you were selling your share of the hotel?' Gemma asked.

'I wasn't sure I was going to. I was weighing up my options.'

'Does Robert know?'

Max turned and drained his glass. He looked Gemma square in the eye. 'No, he doesn't. Not yet. And you're not to tell him, either.'

'But Max, Robert's a friend. He's your brother!'

'It's nothing personal. I think it's time I moved on. There's no point standing still in life. You must keep pressing forward.'

'I think you should tell Robert.' Gemma insisted.

'I will.' Max assured her. 'As soon as I've found a buyer.'

'I think you should tell him now.'

'No.' Max said firmly. 'I'll do it when I'm ready and not before.'

Max turned back to the open window. The conversation was over.

Gemma let her anger subside before she continued. There was no point in pushing Max when he was in that sort of mood. She'd come back to it later.

'Proofs for "Tea in the Sahara" are in.' Gemma continued. 'I think they're rather good. Probably one of the best yet.'

'Leave them on my desk.' Max said. 'I'll look at them later.'

Gemma felt deflated. She had put so much work into the new book. All she wanted was a simple "well done". Anything. Some sort of acknowledgement would be nice. It was beginning to pain her seeing Max's name emblazoned across the book cover when he did so little towards it.

'I have some ideas for the next one. Perhaps we could discuss them?' Gemma asked.

Max poured himself another glass of whiskey and stared out the window. 'Later, perhaps.' He said.

'I'll leave everything right here, then.' Gemma said. She turned and walked out of the library without looking back. Sometimes, Max could be quite unbearable.

She walked along the long sweeping drive that wound its way from the front door of Burnham Manor and left the cloying atmosphere behind her. She wandered slowly along the gravel drive, between borders in full bloom and underneath several large oak trees that straddled the driveway. Summer had finally got its boots on, and the heat was oppressive. Even in the shadow of the great oaks, Gemma felt the heat. She stopped at Honeysuckle Cottage, at the far end of the drive and just before the large cast iron gates that marked the end of the vast grounds of Burnham Manor. She let herself into her small home, poured herself a large glass of white wine, and sat in the corner of her garden, sheltered from the sun by a large awning that protruded from the building.

Sometimes, when devising the many and varied ways in which she murdered her characters, she thought of Max. Just then, she thought of him lying over that great antique desk of his, with the back of his head missing and a large hammer casually discarded on the floor nearby. Perhaps the door and the French windows were locked? Interesting. She began to wonder how she would go about making that work.

***

John Fenwick grabbed another beer from his small fridge and cracked it open. He wandered out into the late afternoon sun and walked amongst his crops. At the far end of his small patch, generously gifted to him by the late Simon Delancey, he opened the door of his greenhouse. He turned on the taps at the front of the greenhouse, and water began to trickle onto the roots of a hundred different plants.

He was most proud of his marrows. They were prize-winning marrows, no less. Fenwick was the current holder of the Gold Cup, awarded to the best marrows produced each year and awarded to contestants at the Burnham fête. Fenwick had won the contest for the last ten years. Looking at this year's crop, he was quietly confident of a record-breaking eleventh year.

They were massive, even by Fenwick's standards. He had never seen marrows like it. His only issue now was getting them across to the marquee intact. He did not doubt that the lads who worked the gardens of Burnham Manor could carry them there, but he was equally in no doubt about their clumsiness and carelessness. Still, they needed to get there. He didn't have much choice.

He returned to his little brick hut, sat on his ageing armchair, and finished his beer. He drifted asleep, dreaming of the Gold Cup.

***

Burnham Manor Fête, Burnham Manor.

At approximately the same time and in different locations within Burnham-on-the-Wold, two carefully planned missions to carry giant marrows to the grounds of Burnham Manor were well underway.

Jack Finney carefully supervised loading his marrows onto a wheelbarrow, which had been modified to ensure the prime specimens could be transported undamaged. Sam Holt, an enthusiastic, if somewhat overweight, fourteen-year-old nephew of Mrs Sloame, had been employed for the task. Grace had quietly slipped the young man a twenty-pound note while his mother wasn't watching, and Jack had done the same, unaware that Grace had already paid him. Sam pushed the wheelbarrow along the small lanes with a contented smile and into the grounds of Burnham Manor. Stewards pointed the young man to the correct location, and between him and Jack, they managed to lift the vegetables into position.

John Fenwick had employed several of the groundsmen at Burnham Manor for the same job. They entered the marquee and gently arranged Fenwick's marrows next to Finney's.

Grace moved beside Finney and said, 'I think you've got it this year, Jack. They are by far and away the best specimens!'

Finney agreed, but judges could be fickle. He was painfully aware that Fenwick was Max Wilde's gardener, and no one wanted to upset the host.

As the morning drew on, more and more visitors appeared at the fête. By lunchtime, Burnham Manor was buzzing.

Niki Latham, last year's controversial winner of the Cake Off, had lavishly laid out a stall at the far end of the marquee. Grace pointed her out to Finney.

'Has she no shame?' She asked. 'I mean, look at her. She's practically in her underwear!'

Finney looked. She had a good figure, he admitted. And while her clothing lacked substance, he thought it was a little unfair to say it was practically underwear. All young women wore the same sort of thing these days, he pondered. There was no harm in it if it made them feel good. And Niki Latham was undoubtedly enjoying the attention.

'The proof is in the pudding,' Finney said. 'I'm sure your cakes will do fine.'

Grace snorted. She didn't believe that for a second.

'Ooh, here he is!' Grace said suddenly, pointing to a man who had just entered the tent. 'I suppose judging is about to get underway.'

Finney watched Max Wilde stroll nonchalantly around the tent, chatting amicably with locals and shaking hands furiously. He was followed in his wake by Gemma, who had an excellent talent for deflecting certain villagers from Max while introducing the important ones and remembering their names to boot. She rubbed people's egos while Max added the polish.

There were several rounds of judging to be had across several different plots around the grounds. Pets and animals were judged first, followed by paintings, photographs and cakes. Grace beamed as the Gold award was handed to her for her Lardy cake. Niki Latham and her ample breasts came second. Max consoled her while Gemma handed Grace her cup.

The decision for best marrow, the judges admitted, had split the panel. It had been a hard choice, but John Fenwick crossed the line ahead of Finney. Max handed the Gold Cup to Fenwick, who bared his discoloured and uneven teeth in what amounted to a smile.

Gemma commiserated with Finney.

'They do look very good,' she enthused. 'I've often wondered,' she said, 'what they're like to eat? I mean, do they taste the same as normal marrows.'

Finney leant forward and said, 'Better, in my opinion. I would be happy to let you have some.'

'That would be lovely,' Gemma said. 'Max, may I introduce you to Mr Jack Finney?'

Max turned and shook Finney's hand. He was about to turn away when he stopped and looked Finney in the eye.

'Do I know you?' He asked. 'That's a familiar name. Are you famous for anything?'

'Nothing at all.' Finney said. 'I don't think we've ever met.'

'Of course, you know him', Grace said, butting into the conversation and not wasting an opportunity to meet the famous Max Wilde. 'This is former Chief Inspector Jack Finney. He cracked the Painswick Poisoning case a few years ago.'

Gemma looked at Finney with renewed interest. '*That's* where I know you. I thought you were familiar.'

'What brings you to quiet old Burnham-on-the-Wold?' Max asked.

'Retirement.' Finney said. 'And oversized marrows.'

Max laughed. 'Look, I've just had a wonderful idea. I've got a dinner party in a few weeks. You may have heard of it. The gossip rags love it. I do it every year. I invite some of the best crime writers in the world to my home for an evening of good food, good wine, and even better company. Now and then, I invite a special guest. I want to invite you along if you're interested. My guests will probably bore you to bits, mining you for information and details. Crime writers are like that, I'm afraid. But I can promise you a good meal.'

For a moment, Grace Sloame thought Finney was about to decline and was preparing to whack him on the shins with her walking stick.

''That would be lovely,' Finney said, to Grace's surprise. 'I'd be honoured to be your guest.'

Grace released the firm grip on her stick.

'Good. That's settled, then. I'll leave you in Gemma's capable hands. She does all the arranging.'

Niki Latham hovered nearby with a handful of her cakes. She caught Max's eye, and Max was quickly lured away.

Gemma asked. 'You live at The Larches, don't you?'

Finney nodded. It was a small village. It was hard to be anonymous.

'I'll have an invitation sent to you. You'll need to bring it; otherwise, you'll never get past security.' Gemma held out her hand, and Finney took it gently.

'We look forward to seeing you then. By the way, it's black tie.'

A secret location somewhere in the UK

A gloved hand moved across the harsh white light and dropped the leaves into a container of boiling water. The container was placed directly under an array of copper pipes and tubes which collected the steam. It rose up the pipes before cooling, then dropped down the other side as a clear liquid. After an hour, they had accumulated a vial of the stuff. With gloved hands, they carefully pressed a cork stopper into the glass. They affixed a white label to the front and placed the vial inside a glass cabinet with several other such bottles.

They were all labelled in black ink.

Aconite. Hemlock. Ricin. Arsenic. Cyanide. Eserine. Belladonna. Strychnine. Opium. Datura. Digitalis. Nicotine.

The list was endless.

For someone, it was going to be an endless night.

Starter

A soupçon of Suspicion
Creamy Tomato Soup with carrots, celery and basil

Murderous Mushrooms
Fresh garlic mushrooms in a dry white wine, garlic, single
cream, topped with cheese, served with granary bread

Red Herring
Sous vide pickled Herring in a parsnip cream with apple
and radish Dashi

Margaret Hemshaw sat on her patio, shaded from the summer sun by a large umbrella, and opened her newspaper. She had no time for the modern way of doing things, preferring the written word to be delivered to her within the pages of actual paper rather than the less intimate realm of electronics. It felt so much more real, more physical. As much as she found computers, tablets, and mobile phones useful, she felt a greater connection with the world when she could connect with it. She enjoyed nothing more than sitting down with her broadsheet on a sunny Friday morning beneath a huge umbrella, sipping at a steaming cup of coffee, and reading about the world burning around her.

She turned to the entertainment page and began a careful read. A new Netflix drama had just been released, and she found the review considered and well-constructed. She turned the page again, and the headline caught her attention.

"Max Wilde signs six-figure deal with the BBC."

She turned as Pat stepped out of the French windows and sat beside her.

'Have you seen this?' Margaret asked.

Pat leant over and read the headline.

'Yes. I caught snippets of it on Twitter. The news is trending at the minute.'

Margaret sighed. It annoyed her that people's interest in news items was based on the item's popularity rather than its actual newsworthiness. The news was not supposed to be popular or judged as such. The human race was seemingly striving for the greatest level of stupidity, and Margaret often consoled herself in the knowledge that she was old enough to no longer care.

'I wonder if that's why Mr Chakrabati's show was cancelled?' She pondered out loud.

'Sanjay certainly seems to think so,' Pat said, realising her mistake as the words left her mouth.

Margaret looked up slowly. Her brow furrowed, and Pat saw the questions form an orderly queue behind her mother's eyes.

'You've spoken to Mr Chakrabati? When? How long has this been going on for?'

'Since last year, mother. We met at Max's dinner, remember?'

'I didn't know you had become…. friends.'

'We exchanged emails. We're mutual friends on Twitter and Instagram. We don't really talk. We send one another messages from time to time. We have much in common.'

Margaret snorted. 'Much in common, indeed! He's a grown man from India. You're a child from England. What on earth could you possibly have in common?'

'Sanjay has a fondness for history, as do I—and crime writing, of course. And I'm not a child, mother. I'm thirty years old!'

'You don't write, Pat. I do. And you're very naive. You don't know the world like I do. I disapprove. I really do. You're to stop communicating with the man at once. Men can't be trusted.'

'You can trust Sanjay. He's a perfect gentleman.'

Margaret snorted again. Such a thing no longer existed, if it ever did.

'I wonder if he'll be there this year?' Margaret asked.

'He landed in London a couple of hours ago. He's driving up to Max's later this afternoon. Speaking of which, what time is your taxi due?'

Margaret glanced at her watch. 'About half an hour.'

'I think it would be better if I drove you,' Pat said.

Margaret didn't think so. She said, 'No,' firmly, and Pat knew better than to push the issue.

'I'll only be gone for the night. I'll be back after breakfast tomorrow.'

'You don't have to rush back. I'll be fine.'

'Nonsense. I don't like leaving you on your own. I shall be calling you at regular intervals. On the house phone. Make sure you answer.'

'What if I'm in the bath?'

'It's a cordless handset. Take it with you.'

'You don't have to worry about me, mother. I'm a grown woman.'

'That's what worries me. Ensure you answer the phone, or I shall come straight back.'

Pat smiled. She had grown accustomed to her mother's controlling personality. She had been forced to commute to university from home so that her mother could keep an eye on her. She felt she had lost out on so much because of it, but she had learned a few things, too. One of the things she had learned was how to divert a call from the house phone to her mobile so that she could go where she pleased. The fact that she had such an older mother played to her advantage. Her mother had given up trying to understand technology, whereas Pat hadn't.

The still summer air was suddenly filled with the noise of a car's tyres on the gravel drive.

Pat stood. 'That must be your taxi.'

'He's early. Send him away.'

'Don't be silly, mother. We'll never get another taxi at this late hour, and then I shall have to drive you.'

'Very well,' Margaret relented. 'My bags are in the porch.' Then, looking Pat up and down, she added. 'Put a coat on. You can't be seen in public like that.'

Pat had dressed that morning in a small summer skirt and a bikini top, over which she had draped a linen poncho. She felt unusually pretty in it—her mother's words bit at her confidence.

'All the girls are wearing this sort of thing, Mother. There's no harm.'

'You are not all the girls, Pat. You are my daughter, and you will not be ogled at by strange men while in your underwear.'

Pat reached the front door as the driver rang the bell. She grabbed a thin summer coat that hung on a hook at the entrance and opened the door, drawing the coat around her front as the door swung open.

'You're not Mr Ince,' she said.

'No, I'm not. That's my dad. He's retired.'

He stood at the door looking awkward before offering his hand and saying, 'Martin. You must be Pat.'

Pat took his hand and squeezed it gently. He was cute, she thought. Late twenties, she guessed, with a full mop of blonde hair, a square jaw gently covered in a hint of a five o'clock shadow, and the most piercing green eyes she had ever seen. Yes, very cute.

'Mother won't be pleased.'

She watched as the young man screwed up his face. 'Yeah. Dad warned me.' He looked over Pat's shoulder and into the house. 'Is your mother coming?'

Pat heard her mother's footsteps as she approached. She stepped aside as she drew near.

'You're not Mr Ince. Where's Mr Ince? I always have Mr Ince.'

'This is Martin Ince, Mother. Mr Ince's son. Mr Ince has retired.'

Margaret sniffed. 'Well, this is most irregular. And quite dishonest. I should have been told it wasn't Mr Ince when I booked. I would have gone elsewhere.'

'I could always drive you, mother.'

Margaret looked at her daughter and then at the young man who waited patiently at the door. 'Well, you're here now. My bags are there. Put them in the car and wait for me there.'

Martin stepped inside the porch and grabbed Margaret's bags. He smiled at Pat as he turned and walked back to his car. Pat had a feeling she might need a taxi later.

'Now, look here.' Her mother said. 'It's just for one evening, and I shall be back early tomorrow. Answer the phone when I ring.'

Pat leaned over and kissed her mother on the cheek. She gave the driver a look and a smile and a cheeky wink. Martin blushed.

'Go, mother. Have a good time. Tell me all about it tomorrow.'

Margaret sat in the taxi and watched as her home disappeared behind her. She felt anxious leaving Pat alone. She was a funny child. She didn't want to leave her behind, but she couldn't very well take her with her, not after last year.

No. Not after last year.

***

Gemma watched a shiny red car pull up the long sweeping drive to Burnham Manor and pull in alongside Max's Range Rover. A young woman of no more than thirty years of age, Gemma guessed, stepped out of the car and smiled at her.

'Is it okay to park this here?' She asked sweetly.

'Of course.' Gemma replied, walking over to where the young woman stood, her arm outstretched. 'You must be Sydney.'

Sydney Fletch shook the proffered hand. 'I suppose I must be.'

Of course she was Sydney Fletch, Gemma mused. The only other female guest that evening was the awful Margaret Hemshaw, who bore no resemblance to the beautiful young woman before her. She felt suddenly old in her presence. She had the most delectable blonde hair that fell about her shoulders as though it had only just that minute been washed. Her skin was flawless. Not a mark on it anywhere, and no hint of heavily applied makeup or Botox. Her brown eyes sparkled in the summer sun, and there was no faking the warmth and kindness in the smile she wore. Not only was she beautiful, Gemma mused, but she was incredibly talented. Her debut crime novel was flying off the shelves. Max was going to enjoy this one.

'Welcome to Burnham Manor,' Gemma said. 'Max is in rehearsals for tomorrow's show.' She handed Sydney a sheet of paper. 'These are some of the questions Max will likely ask you during the show. Do you have any allergies?'

Sanjay Chakrabati had been Max's guest on his Saturday morning cooking show the previous year. This year, it was Sydney's turn.'

'Sydney shook her head. 'No.'

'Good. Max will be tied up until this evening. He likes to make an entrance! Come, let me show you to your room.'

Sydney followed Gemma through the large oak doors of Burnham Manor and into the entrance hall. It was a grand affair, largely untouched from the early twentieth century. Ancient pictures of the great and good, and some of the not-so-good, hung on the walls and gave the house a brooding, melancholy feel. Sydney felt a shiver run down her spine.

'It's intimidating, isn't it?' Gemma remarked as she watched Sydney's expression closely.

'It is. It really is! If it was my house, I think I'd have remodelled it by now.'

Gemma laughed. 'Believe me, I've tried. Max loves it. He thinks it's atmospheric. Moody. I think it's evil.'

Sydney felt the word as Gemma spoke it.

'The house has had a colourful history almost from the moment it was built.' Gemma said. 'It's had nearly four hundred years of intrigue and drama. The man who had it built was a particularly unpleasant slaver. About a year after the building was finished, he was murdered in the East Indies. They cut off his head and displayed it on a pole.'

'That's awful.' Sydney said.

'Not nearly as awful as he was,' Gemma remarked. 'Since then, the house has been owned by a series of pirates, privateers, criminals, murderers and several men of extremely low moral fibre. The last incumbent was Simon Delancey. He was quite weird, too.'

'I've read some of his books.' Sydney said.

'He was quite the writer, for sure.' Gemma nodded as she led Sydney through the hallway and up the staircase. 'He was a complicated man with complicated interests. Some strange things went on in this house when he lived here. You get a sense of it in his novels.'

Sydney had read a biography of Simon Delancey some years ago. He had been a heavy drinker and smoker and enjoyed the company of young women right up until his death. He also enjoyed the delights of a few young men, which, during his lifetime, had remained a tightly guarded secret. After he died, all the stories poured out.

'Max loves a character.' Gemma went on. 'I suppose that's why he bought the Manor when Delancey died. Max grew up in the village. His mum and dad owned

The Marlborough Hotel, which Max now owns with his brother, Robert. He grew up listening to the stories and rumours about this place.'

Gemma reached the top of the staircase and led Sydney down a long corridor. The decor had changed from the mauling and claustrophobic atmosphere of the hallway to something much more homely and welcoming. Modern paintings adorned the walls, and brightly coloured antiques furnished every nook and corner. The floor was softly carpeted, and a gentle, bright light swathed everything in an ethereal glow.

'We've put you in the Blue room.'

Gemma opened a door on her right and stepped inside. Sydney followed.

'Please, make yourself at home. Feel free to take a tour of the house. The gardens are particularly lovely, though I should warn you about Fenwick.'

'Fenwick?'

'He's the gardener. He's a grumpy old sod who likes to complain a lot. About everything. Unfortunately, he came with the house, so we tolerate him.'

'I'll look out for him.'

'You won't see him. Not until it's too late. He's a sneaky old man and moves like a cat. If you stand on a piece of grass you shouldn't be standing on or pick a flower while you think no one's watching, he'll appear by your side and shout at you.'

'You sound like you speak from experience!' Sydney joked.

Gemma raised her eyes. 'I do! But take little notice of him. He's a bit like the hallway. Dark and malevolent but tolerated. He adds atmosphere to the place.'

Sydney wandered over to the large windows that looked down on the front of the house and watched as a

motorbike pulled up next to her car and the rider
dismounted.

Gemma joined her at the window.

'That must be Gareth Black.' She said.

They watched as the rider removed his helmet and
slipped his heavy jacket off his shoulders.

'He's pretty.' Gemma said.

Sydney looked the man up and down and disagreed
with her summation. Not pretty, she thought, although
there was something attractive about the man. He had
chiselled looks and a warm smile. She had read all of his
books and had been something of a fan before his latest
one had gone viral and pushed him into the bestseller
lists. She knew nothing about him or what he looked like
and wasn't entirely disappointed. There was something
about men who rode motorbikes that was strangely
attractive.

'I should go and introduce myself.' Gemma said. 'I've
put him in the Green room next to yours. I've put
Margaret Hemshaw in the Yellow room and Mr
Chakrabati in the Orange room.'

'Sanjay Chakrabati?' Sydney asked.

'Yes. Have you met him?'

'No, but I love his books.'

'Me too. And you'll love Sanjay even more. He's such
a lovely man.' Gemma turned and opened the door to
Sydney's room. 'There'll be many people around the
house and gardens later. Max has hired staff for the
dinner this evening. Given the weather, Max has decided
to eat outside. They're building a thing for it now. Drinks
at seven-thirty in the drawing room. Dinner at eight.'

Gemma closed the door behind her.

Sydney remained at the window and watched as
Gemma reappeared on the driveway, her arm
outstretched, bearing down on Gareth Black. They

engaged in standard pleasantries for a few moments before Gareth unstrapped a bag from the back of his bike and followed Gemma into the house.

She heard voices in the corridor and then the door next to her room being opened. A few minutes later, she heard Gemma say, 'Drinks in the drawing room at seven-thirty. Dinner at eight.' Then the door closed.

Sydney opened her door and stepped out into the corridor. She walked up to the Green room and knocked. The door opened a few seconds later.

She changed her mind. He was pretty, in a handsome way. She held out her hand. 'Sydney Fletch.'

Gareth Black stood before Sydney in black leather trousers and a crisp white t-shirt.   'Hello.'

'My friends call me Syd or Fletch.' She said and walked into the room. 'What should I call you?'

'I don't have any friends. You can call me whatever you like.'

Sydney walked over to the side of the bed and sat down. 'Then I shall call you Gareth.'

Gareth closed the door and turned to look at the pretty young woman who had barged her way into his room. She had the face and figure of a twenty-something but the air of a mature young woman. She had confidence, too. He liked that.

'I was just about to get changed…' Gareth said.

Sydney leant back on her elbows and said, 'Don't let me stop you.'

Gareth smiled. He grabbed his bag and entered his ensuite bathroom, closing the door behind him.

'I read you books.' Sydney said. 'You're very good.'

The door opened, and Gareth stuck his head around. 'Really? You've read my books? As in plural? Not just the last one?'

'Nope. I've read them all. I follow you on Twitter. Sadly, you have not returned the compliment.'

'Then I shall remedy that at once.' His head slipped back inside the bathroom. Sydney heard water running. 'I've also read "The Last Hangman."' Gareth said above the noise. His head appeared from behind the door again. 'You're remarkably clever for such a young thing. I didn't see the end coming at all.'

'Thank you. You weren't supposed to. That's rather the trick, isn't it?'

Gareth stepped out of the bathroom, having changed out of his motorcycling clothes into something more comfortable. He was wearing light grey slacks and a blue t-shirt.

Sydney approved.

She got up and held out her hand for Gareth's. 'I want to explore. We are to be partners in crime.'

'Do I have a choice?' Gareth asked.

'Nope. Come on. It'll be fun.'

Sydney took Gareth's hand and stepped out of his room and into the corridor. 'It's a big house,' she declared, 'where should we start?'

'Let's start at the top and filter down.'

The tour of the house took an hour. They opened doors, explored corridors, opened cupboards and generally familiarised themselves with the entire building.

'They say the house has a colourful past.' Sydney declared as they wandered into the hallway, with its old pictures and gloomy presence. 'A dark past. I wonder how many people have died within its walls?'

'That's a very dark imagination you have, Fletchy.'

'It's the nature of my business, I'm afraid. One must consider the worst in people and places. If only the walls could talk.' She was about to say something about being called "Fletchy" and then changed her mind. She liked the way he said it. 'I'm hungry,' she declared and headed towards what she thought must be the kitchen.

It was a large kitchen and immaculately laid out, with all the modern tech you would expect from a Television chef. Sydney wandered over to the fridges and started rifling through the food.

'Do you think we should ask?' Gareth asked, not wanting to insult his host before having met him.

'Max's secretary said I should make myself at home. So I am.'

'Gemma Collis?' Gareth asked. 'She's more than his secretary, you know.'

Sydney took a bite out of an apple. 'Is she? Are they doing it, do you think?'

'Not like that,' Gareth explained. 'She writes his books. It's just his name on the cover.'

Sydney was shocked. 'No! Really? She writes them?'

Gareth was about to expand on his topic when they heard voices approaching. Sydney grabbed his hand and pulled him into a pantry.

'What are you doing?' He asked.

'Hiding.' Sydney declared.

'But why?'

'Why not?' Sydney asked.

Sydney cracked the door to the pantry open a few centimetres and watched as Gemma walked into the kitchen with an arm full of papers and laid them down on the kitchen table. She was followed into the kitchen by a man neither of them had seen before. He certainly wasn't Max Wilde.

'What time are the staff arriving?' Gemma asked.

'About six. We'll start preparing dinner around seven o'clock.'

'Is everything ready?'

'We've done most of the prep at The Marlborough. You've outdone yourself on the menu. Very clever.'

'It was Max's idea.' Gemma said. 'He thought last year was a bit off-topic.' She picked up a copy of the menu from the table. 'The Poisoned Quail. Red Herring. Murderous Mushrooms. I rather enjoyed coming up with the names for the courses. We even have a bottle or two of Sparkling Cyanide. Max had some labels specially made. I think the guests will love it.'

'Is Pat Hemshaw coming this year?'

Gemma giggled. 'Stop it, Robert! You know full well she isn't invited. Can you imagine it?'

'That's Robert Wilde,' Sydney whispered. 'Max's brother.'

Robert laughed at the memory. 'Poor Pat. She was mortified. Caught by her mother too!'

Robert stood next to Gemma and pulled her closer to him. His hands explored her back. Sydney held her breath.

'Not here, Robert. Max would be angry.'

'I thought he was in rehearsals?'

'He is,' Gemma said, resisting her body's urge to respond.

'You know what he's like. He's a perfectionist. He'll be there hours.' He leaned in and kissed her neck. He knew which buttons to press.

Gemma melted and let him explore her neck. 'What about the guests?'

'There's only two at the minute. The others haven't arrived. They'll be out in the gardens enjoying the sun.'

'Be quick, then.' Gemma said, throwing caution to the wind.

Robert stood up and turned Gemma around. His hands felt for the hem of her skirt and lifted it up past her thighs. His fingers gently pulled at her knickers until they were around her ankles. He fumbled at his belt for a few seconds before they fell to the ground.

From their hiding spot in the pantry, Sydney and Gareth watched as the two lovers went at it over the kitchen table. When they had finished, they quickly put their clothes back on, and Gemma picked up her papers from the table. Her face was flushed, and she was breathing heavily. She reached up and kissed Robert.

'Come to mine after the dinner. You can take your time then.'

Gemma disappeared out through the kitchen door. Robert took a minute to compose himself before leaving the same way.

Sydney and Gareth stepped out from the pantry.

Gareth felt a little awkward. 'Well, that was interesting, if a little unhygienic.'

Sydney smiled. She didn't feel awkward at all. 'Isn't it funny how you find the best stories when you hide?' She took Gareth's hand and urged him on. 'Come on. Let's go and explore some more!'

***

Sydney was still clutching Gareth's hand as they made their way through the manor and out a set of French windows that led to the rear garden. Beyond, a large, well-manicured lawn stretched almost as far as the eye could see, bordered by great oaks and horse chestnut trees. In the centre of the lawn stood an imposing cedar tree that rose splendidly into the sky before its branches folded down on themselves like a natural umbrella.

Between the patio, where Sydney and Gareth stood, and the large cedar tree, half a dozen men were erecting what looked like a stage. A huge canopy had been erected above it, which struck down into the lawn at five different places, making it appear like an alien craft coming into land. Sydney pulled Gareth behind her and approached the stage. One of the young men, stapling carpet to the structure, watched Sydney approach. His eyes never left her figure.

'What's that?' Sydney asked, walking up to a worker who was lifting a glass unit into place.

The worker stopped and drew his sleeve across his brow. He looked at the young woman and smiled.

'It's a fish tank, miss.'

Sydney scrunched her face in confusion. 'A fish tank?'

'So I'm told.' The worker replied.

'For decoration or consumption?' Sydney asked.

Now, it was the worker's turn to look confused.

Gareth said, 'I think my friend is wondering whether the fish will be for us to look at or to eat.'

The worker shrugged. 'No idea. I just install the things.'

Sydney wondered.

She took Gareth's hand and led him away from the stage and across the lawn. Half a dozen pairs of eyes followed the young woman's form as it walked away, and half a dozen men felt a degree of envy for the man who held her hand.

They crossed under the shadow of the large cedar tree and walked towards the great oaks that bordered the lawn. Beyond the border, the land changed into something quite different. Here were acres of land turned over to growing food. More young men could be seen tending to the crops.

Sydney and Gareth walked through the grounds, staying on the walkways that criss-crossed the allotments. At the far edge, the allotments stopped, and they entered a small wooded area.

'Where are we going?' Gareth asked.

'I want to find the Poison Garden.' Sydney declared brightly.

'The what?'

'Surely you must have heard of it?' Sydney asked. 'Old Simon Delancey built it years ago to grow some of the world's most dangerous plants. He used his knowledge of them to great effect in his novels. I read somewhere that Max Wilde has kept it.'

Sydney strode with purpose along a nicely maintained path that meandered through the trees. Gareth followed.

As they turned a corner, a cast-iron gate barred their way. A simple skull and crossbones made of cast iron had been welded to the gate.

'This must be it.' Sydney declared, reaching out and trying the handle.

'Do you think we should?' Gareth asked.

The gate swung open and creaked as it did so.

Without replying, Sydney disappeared inside. Gareth shook his head and followed. He had a feeling he was going to enjoy Fletch's company.

The gardens were kept in excellent condition. Plants of all shapes and sizes and all the colours of the rainbow thrived there. The only way into the gardens was through the cast iron gate, and a six-foot wall ran the entire length, keeping interlopers out. In the centre of the gardens, they found a glass greenhouse and, within its centre, some very odd and exotic-looking plants.

'They don't look particularly dangerous.' Sydney said, disappointed. She reached down to a plant that was barely three feet tall, with nondescript leaves that fanned out from its base.

'I wouldn't touch that if I were you, miss.'

Sydney jumped, and Gareth felt his heart miss a beat.

Sydney pulled her hand back and stood up. 'You made us jump.'

'You shouldn't be in here.' The man said.

He had broken, discoloured teeth, dirty grey hair that stuck to his head, and large, filthy hands with nicotine stains along his index finger. He had approached so quietly that neither she nor Gareth had heard him.

'You must be Mr Fenwick.' Sydney smiled her most flirtatious smile and looked the old man directly in the eye. She watched his stern manner falter. 'Is it terribly dangerous?' She asked. 'It doesn't look like much.'

'Dendrocnide Moroides.' Fenwick said. 'Known as the Gympie Gympie plant to the natives or the Australian Stinging Tree to you and me. They say its sting is like having acid poured over you while being electrocuted. The effects can last for months. It's not nice.'

Sydney looked back at the plant she had almost touched and felt grateful for Mr Fenwick's sudden appearance.

'You shouldn't judge a plant by its looks.' Fenwick said. 'Just about every plant here can kill or maim or at least make you regret touching them. Take a look at this one.'

Fenwick wandered over to where an ordinary-looking plant grew and removed a black bean. He handed it to Sydney, who smelt it and then handed it to Gareth.

'It doesn't smell of anything,' Gareth remarked. 'What does it taste like?'

'That's not something you ever want to find out,' Fenwick said ominously. 'That's a Calabar bean, *physostigma venenosum,* one of the deadliest beans known to mankind. They used it in the old days to prove witchcraft. It was known as the Ordeal Bean of Old Calabar. If you ate it and lived, you were innocent of witchcraft. If you died, you died a horrible, agonising death.'

'Sounds horrible.' Sydney shivered.

'Not as horrible as its effects on the body.' Fenwick went on. 'It's like a nerve gas. It shuts down your central nervous system, causing seizures. You lose control of your bodily functions before eventually your lungs stop working, and you suffocate to death.'

It was Gareth's turn to shiver.

'That's why you shouldn't be in here.' Fenwick declared. 'You should leave.'

'What are these?' Sydney asked, ignoring Mr Fenwick's insistence that they leave. He turned as if to usher them from the building, but Sydney had turned to face an old wooden cabinet with a glass front, criss-crossed with lead trim. Inside were a collection of old looking medicine bottles, or vials, with faded labels. Sydney went to open the door but found it locked. She peered through the glass.

The labels were written in neat handwriting, in black ink. She read: *Hemlock, Cyanide, Aconite, Erserine.*

There were others, too, but their labels were too faded or obstructed to read.

'Poisons, Miss.' Fenwick said. The way he said it made Sydney shudder.

'Are they real?' She asked.

'They are.' Fenwick admitted. 'Mr Delancey and me made them years ago, from the plants that grow in here.'

'How do you know they're effective?' Sydney continued. 'I mean, how do you know they work?'

'They work.' Fenwick said mysteriously. 'Come on, Miss. You need to go.'

Sydney and Gareth allowed themselves to be escorted from the garden. Every few yards or so, Sydney would stop and ask a question about a plant. Despite his annoyance, Sydney realised that Mr Fenwick was an expert on his subject. Experts loved to be quizzed. It was half an hour before they were outside the gates, and the metalwork was being closed behind them.

'Keep following the path.' Fenwick said. 'There's a small maze at the end and some nicer plants to admire.'

Fenwick bared his teeth in an attempt at a smile and disappeared back inside the Poison Garden.

'He was fun.' Gareth remarked. 'Do you think his mouth has ever seen a toothbrush?'

'Don't be mean.' Sydney teased. 'I thought he was interesting. I shall put him into my next book. I shall have him trying out his deadly poisons on unsuspecting runaways!'

Gareth thought about that for a moment.

'How can you be sure that's not how he knows they work?'

Sydney turned and looked at Gareth.

'Hmm. Interesting. It appears your imagination is as twisted as mine. I think we'll be friends.'

Gareth followed Sydney until the path led them out of the small wooded area into a secluded yet well-maintained part of the garden. There was a small pond, several benches laid out around it, and several neatly manicured borders that gave the gardens a warm, comfortable feel. Beyond the pond, Sydney saw the entrance to what she guessed was the maze. It was made of a tall, well-trimmed hedge that dwarfed the pair as they strolled through the opening.

Sydney let go of Gareth's hand, turned to the left and ran off, declaring her intention to race Gareth to the centre. Gareth tried to follow, but she moved like a nymph and vanished into the maze.

He hated mazes. He had got lost in one once, as a child, and vowed never to step inside one again. They were confusing and disorientating, and they made him feel dizzy. He wandered aimlessly for an hour before giving up and slumping to the ground. It was hot, and he was sweating, and he felt that it was time for a stiff drink, and he had absolutely no idea how to get out. Within a few minutes, he had resolved to die there and for the guilt to sit firmly on Fletch's conscience for the rest of her life.

As he came to terms with his impending doom, he heard voices. Strange voices, but voices nonetheless. He rose to his feet and followed the noise. As he turned a corner, he realised he had made it to the maze's centre, which was considerably bigger than he had imagined. There was a fountain at its heart and a bench, upon which sat the frame of a man. An older woman was standing nearby, brandishing a stick. He was about to introduce himself when he felt a pair of hands grab his arms and pull him to one side. He turned to see Fletchy, a single finger pressed tightly against her lips. Gareth moved closer, and the two of them knelt on the floor.

'Where have you been?' He asked in a whisper, his voice edged in annoyance.

'Waiting for you! You're rubbish at mazes!'

'Why are we hiding?' He asked.

Sydney gave him a look that said if he didn't know, then they probably weren't going to be friends, when she said, 'because I like hiding. Besides, they won't continue their argument if we're there!'

Gareth gave his attention to the two people in the epicentre of the maze. He recognised Margaret Hemshaw. She was waving her stick at the man on the bench like a wild thing.

'Who's the man?' Gareth asked.

'That's Max Wilde.' Sydney whispered. 'I saw him come into the maze, and I hid here. I don't want to meet him on my own. He has a bit of a reputation.'

Gareth knew of Max's reputation. Women were seemingly unable to resist his boyish charms. 'Don't you trust yourself?'

Sydney shot him a warning look that missed. 'I don't want to break the man's nose on our first meet.' She said.

Gareth looked at her and realised she was being deadly serious. He put any thoughts of making a play for her affections to the back of his mind. He didn't want a broken nose, either.

The two of them looked back at Mrs Hemshaw, who had suddenly raised her voice.

'I told you I wanted you to stay well away from Pat!' She said, poking her stick at Max.

'And I have.'

'Do you expect me to believe that?' She screamed. 'I know what you men are like. You're all the same. You think with your dicks. You're pathetic.'

Max seemed unmoved. 'I really don't care what you believe. I haven't spoken to Pat since you were here last. I didn't invite her at your request. I thought you'd be happy.'

'Happy? *Happy?* You've sullied my little girl's reputation, and you think I'd be happy?'

'Damn it, Margaret, she's in her thirties. She's not a little girl.'

'Not anymore, she isn't. Not after she's had your dirty hands on her. Who's going to want her now, knowing that?'

They watched as Max threw his head back and laughed. 'For fuck's sake, this isn't the seventeen hundreds. Do you know, I think you're losing the plot!'

'Why invite me this year, hmm?' Margaret asked. 'What do you want from me? Or are you just revelling in your smut?'

'I Invited you because I respect you. I shan't do it again. And, if you're that angry and upset with me, why are you even here?'

'I wanted to see what game you're playing. Because you're up to something, I can feel it.'

Max stood up. He towered over the elderly Mrs Hemshaw. 'You really are a miserable old woman, do you know that?'

Margaret jammed the tip of her walking stick into Max's chest. 'One of these days, someone's going to do us all a good deed and turn your lights out.'

She put her stick to the ground and began to walk out of the middle of the maze.

'Maybe one day someone will.' Max laughed. 'But it won't be you, Margaret. You're not clever enough and you haven't got it in you.'

Margaret Hemshaw turned at the exit and faced Max Wilde. From their hiding spot, Sydney and Gareth saw a change come over her. There was a look on her face that spoke volumes.

She smiled. 'Don't be so sure, Mr Wilde. Never underestimate people. It could end up getting you killed.'

And with that, she turned purposefully away and left.

Gareth made as if to move but was held back by Sydney.

'Where are you going?' She asked.

'To introduce myself to my host. I've never met him.'

'Just wait,' Sydney whispered.

Gareth relented and returned to his hiding spot. He didn't mind so much. It was a tight little hiding place, and he could feel Sydney push up close next to him. He thought she smelt almost as beautiful as she looked, and he resisted the urge to reach over and kiss her.

Gareth looked up as a phone rang nearby. Max looked annoyed and answered the call.

'What is it?' He asked abruptly. 'I'm in the maze, going through some last-minute changes for tomorrow. I was hoping to get some peace. Can it wait? Okay, then, I'll wait here. Be quick, though. I have things to do.'

They watched as Max threw his phone onto the bench and sighed deeply. Gareth felt Sydney squeeze his hand tightly as another figure approached and entered the centre of the maze.

Max looked up and beamed.

'Sanjay, my old friend, how are you?'

Max bounced over to Sanjay Chakrabati, his hand outstretched and a warm smile across his face.

Sanjay did not hold out a hand in reply, and from the way he stood, the two spies deduced that he was not a happy bunny. He held his arms tightly behind his back and puffed out his chest.

Max looked awkward and slowly dropped his hand. 'Is everything okay, old boy?'

'Don't "old boy" me, you old snake.'

Gareth and Sydney exchanged looks. Sydney raised her eyebrows.

Max sighed. His pleasantness evaporated. He knew full well what it was about but asked anyway. 'What is it, Sanjay?'

'They've cancelled "Death in the Raj."' He said.

Max nodded. 'I heard.'

'Of course you bloody heard,' Sanjay spat. 'They cancelled it because of you.'

'Don't be ridiculous, Sanj. I don't own the BBC. I can't control their decisions.'

'But you can ask for a ridiculous sum of money and effectively close the door to the rest of us. You've demanded the kind of money the rest of us can only dream about. Three shows have gone to the wall so the BBC can pay you. One of those shows was mine.'

Max shrugged. 'I never made any demands. The BBC made their offers based on the commercial viability of my books. They made a commercial decision that had nothing to do with me.'

'That's always the way with you, isn't it, Max? You leave a trail of broken hearts and ruined lives behind you and never take responsibility. It's just a game to you. You don't care who you hurt or who you have to destroy, just so long as you're at the top. And the real irony is that you don't even create anything that you've become famous for. You ride off other people's talent.'

Max straightened up. 'All right, Sanj, that's enough. If that's how you feel about me, why are you here? Why come tonight?'

'Because I am a gentleman. When I have an issue with another man, I come to him, face to face.'

'Well, you've had your say. Do you feel better?'

Sanjay felt the patronising tone the moment the words left Max's mouth. He smiled and turned to walk away. Then he stopped and looked back at Max.

'Sooner or later, actions have consequences. I used to like you, Max. I respected you. You're a clever man. But one day, your cleverness will catch up with you. There'll be a price to pay. I wonder, Max, whether you are ready to pay it?'

Sanjay calmly walked past Gareth and Sydney's hiding spot. Sydney held her breath, fearing that they would be discovered. As Sanjay left, Robert Wilde came thundering past. He held a letter in his hand and waved it above his head. His face was red, and his eyes burned with venom.

'What the fuck is this?' He screamed at Max.

Max watched as his brother approached him. Calmly, he said, 'I don't know. I haven't read it, have I?'

Robert pushed the letter into Max's chest with some force.

'Fucking read it then.'

Max took the letter and removed its contents. He looked abashed.

'Ah, I see. They've sent the notice to you already. They weren't supposed to do that until next week.'

'So it's real? You're really doing it? You're selling your share of The Marlborough?'

Max placed the letter back in its envelope and dropped it on the bench.

'Yes. I have a buyer already in place.'

'Why, Max? It's a successful business. It's *our* successful business. Mum and Dad made it their own place. We grew up there!'

'I don't live by sentimentality.'

'Then what about loyalty?' Robert said.

'A sentimentality based on familiarity.' Max answered. 'It's nothing personal, Robert. It's time I moved on.'

Sydney and Gareth watched as conflicting emotions engulfed Robert. His anger would barely let him stand still. He moved around, agitated.

'Max, you own sixty per cent of The Marlborough. If you sell your share, I'll be forced out. It won't be my place anymore. You'll destroy me!'

'Have you forgotten why I own the controlling share?' Max asked, stoking Robert's anger.

'Of course, I haven't forgotten. How could I? You've never let me forget.'

'So I'm quite within my rights to sell my share. I have the paperwork to prove it.'

'Then let me buy you out. Let me buy your share.'

Max laughed. 'God, no. You're terrible with money. There's no way you could afford the sixty per cent.'

'Then sell me my ten per cent back,' Robert pleaded.

Max bit his lip. 'I can't. My buyer wants the controlling stake. He has plans for The Marlborough.'

Robert's fury intensified. He walked over to where Max stood and punched him square in the face. Max tumbled backwards, clutching a bloody nose.

Robert towered over him. 'After everything I ever did for you, this is how you treat me. You're no brother of mine.'

He stormed out of the centre of the maze without looking back. Max stayed on the floor for some time, clutching his nose. He stood up uneasily and moved over to the bench. He drew a hanky from his pocket, tipped his head back, and tried to stem the bleeding. Sydney and Gareth waited, unsure whether to chance their luck at trying to leave or to stay hidden.

She floated in like a butterfly, and had it not been for the bright yellow dress, neither Sydney nor Gareth would have seen her. She fluttered over to where Max was clutching a hanky to his bloody nose and starting fussing. She took the hanky from Max and dabbed away some of the blood and tears.

'Let me see,' she said. 'I don't think it's broken. Who did this to you, Max?'

Max looked at the young woman. 'What the hell are you doing here?' He asked gruffly.

'I wanted to see you.'

Max took back his hanky. 'I thought I made myself clear. I didn't want to see you again.'

'I know what you said, Max, but I didn't believe your words. They weren't your words; they were other people's. You said what other people wanted you to say. I shan't believe them until you tell me to my face.'

She looked longingly into Max's eyes.

'I don't want you,' Max began. 'It was just a bit of fun. It was one night. I didn't mean for you to get hurt.'

'I know,' the young woman said. 'I only wanted to hear it from you, face to face. Besides, we have unfinished business.'

Sydney and Gareth watched as the young woman knelt before Max, reaching for his belt and slowly unbuckling it. Her fingers hovered over the button that sealed his trousers and then slowly undid it. She gripped the zip gently and drew it down. In the blink of an eye, Max's trousers were around his ankles, and the young woman was face down in his lap. Sydney and Gareth watched, unable to draw their eyes away. It was a sordid yet curiously erotic scene, and Gareth felt his blood surge. He felt Sydney's arm grip his even tighter.

It was a few minutes before Max sighed deeply, and the young woman stopped moving. She stood up and looked down at Max.

'It's fine if you don't want me,' she declared. 'I'm over you. You showed me something I hadn't seen before. I wanted to finish what I had started.' She leaned down and kissed Max on the cheek. 'Goodbye, Max.'

With that, the yellow butterfly left the maze.

Sydney and Gareth waited as Max dressed. His face was bloodied and flushed, but he was smiling. He looked around to see if he had been watched and then slowly followed the young woman out of the Maze.

Sydney climbed out of her hiding spot, followed by Gareth.

'See!' Sydney declared. 'It's amazing what you can learn when you hide.'

Gareth agreed. 'Yes, it is. I've learned that some people get a lot more sex than me and in much stranger places!'

Sydney giggled, and Gareth moved in to kiss her.

Sydney pushed him away. 'What are you doing?' She asked.

'Making a fool of myself,' Gareth said, fearing he had overstepped the mark.

'Some people might call that an unwelcome sexual advance.' Sydney said.

'Yes, I suppose they might.'

'Some may call it sexual harassment.'

Gareth nodded. 'I suppose they might.'

'Do you think I'm that easy?' Sydney asked.

Gareth began to feel a little deflated. His passion ebbed away. It was one thing to be rejected, but another thing entirely for the rejector to enjoy it quite so much.

'Look, I meant no harm….' he stuttered.

Sydney turned with a flourish and made to leave the maze. Then she turned slowly to face Gareth, a wicked grin on her face.

'Mr Black. I never said *I* would call it an unwelcome sexual advance, nor that *I* would call it sexual harassment. I prefer my suitors to make a little more effort. The rewards more than make up for it. Please try again if you wish.'

With that, she left.

Gareth found himself slowly falling in love with the dangerous Miss Fletch. He also suddenly realised that he was alone in the centre of a large maze, with no idea how to get out.

It was going to be a long afternoon.

***

Max Wilde looked every bit the quintessential English gentleman. He wore a ridiculously expensive-looking suit from Saville Row that had been specifically tailored to his needs. He wore a crisp, white shirt that stretched out from the end of his sleeves, folded into neat cuffs adorned with gold links. A paisley bow tie circled his neck and sat neatly beneath a crisp white collar. He wore an expensive Breitling on his right wrist and a silver bracelet on his left. A single silver ring adorned his little finger. His hair was gelled neatly to the top of his head, and his face was clean-shaven and moisturised. He cared greatly about his appearance and was particularly satisfied with tonight's look. He had an air of a man of substance and great worth, and he carried the look like he was born to it.

He strolled purposefully through the corridors of his Manor House and down the great staircase. He went directly to the kitchens and was pleased to see that it was a hive of activity. Young men and women went about their tasks without so much as glancing up. They were directed in their activities by a formidable-looking man in chef's whites who, now and then, delivered a sharp rebuke or considered praise without ever raising his voice above a whisper. Everyone seemed to be in awe of the man, and they followed his instructions without complaint.

Max made a beeline for him. He was one of the head chefs at The Marlborough, and he knew his business.

'Where's Rob?' Max asked.

The softly-spoken giant looked at Max and said. 'I don't know.'

'What do you mean, you don't know? He's supposed to be here. Who's looking after The Marlborough?'

The chef shrugged his shoulders. 'I haven't seen Rob all day. We were supposed to have a meeting at two, but he never showed up. I called Gemma, and she asked me to cover here while she looked for him. The Marlborough is in good hands.'

The chef had heard the rumours about The Marlborough. Bad news travels fast in villages like Burnham-on-the-Wold. He had already sent tentative feelers to several restaurants in London and Europe. It wouldn't take him long to find another place.

Max pulled out his phone.

'Where are you?' He asked, speaking into his phone. 'Right. Do you know where Rob is? Okay. Meet me in the library in five.'

Max closed his phone and slipped it into a trouser pocket.

'Is everything on target here?' He asked.

The chef nodded. 'It's all good. We'll be on time.'

'Be sure that you are.'

Max left the kitchen behind him and made his way to the library. It was no longer a library in the strictest sense, although the walls were still overflowing with books. Most of the great and good had long been lost to book dealers from all over the world on Delancey's passing. He had been an ardent collector and had one of the most valuable collections in Europe. The vultures did their work with incredible efficiency, and by the time Max acquired the library, the very best had gone. He had tried to re-supply it, but it was an expensive hobby. Many first editions from the twentieth century, mostly crime, sat on shelves behind sun-protective glass.

Gemma was stood at the French windows looking out over the gardens. The work on the stage had been completed, and now a great oak table stood at the centre with seven chairs around it. It had already been laid for dinner.

She turned as Max walked in. She wore a blue sequinned dress that fell just short of her knees. Her shoulders were bare, and her neck had a simple silver chain across it. She was drinking from a champagne flute.

'Can I get you one?'

'No. Where the fuck's Rob?'

Gemma took a sip of her champagne and watched Max carefully. She knew Max well, and could tell when his mood was a bit spikey.

'I don't know.' She lied.

'Yes, you do. I know you're fucking him. Where is he Gemma?'

Words of denial gathered on her lips, but she pulled them back in. Of course he knew. Max knew everything.

'We're seeing one another if that's what you mean. At least we were. He's pissed that I didn't tell him you were selling The Marlborough. We had a row, and he took off. That was a few hours ago. I haven't seen him since, and I don't know where he went.'

Max walked over to a decanter of rusty-looking liquid and poured himself three fingers of the stuff. He knocked it back in one go and grimaced.

'If he fucks tonight up for me, I'll never speak to him again.'

Gemma smiled. Rob had said something similar about Max.

'I've taken care of everything, Max.' Gemma said. 'You don't have anything to worry about. I've spoken to the chef. He's been a part of creating the menu, so he knows what to do. The waiting staff are here and getting ready.' She glanced at a small watch that graced her delicate wrist. 'I should go and put them in place. Your guests will be convening soon. I've set up the old drawing room. They can take drinks on the verandah first.'

Gemma emptied her glass and laid it on a table.

'Relax, Max. It's going to be a wonderful evening.'

***

'Gemma said I might find you in here.'

Sanjay Chakrabati wore a fine-looking dinner suit and a heavily polished pair of black shoes. He closed the library door behind him as he walked in.

Max had poured himself another glass of the rusty liquid and took his time over it. He was surprised to see Sanjay.

'I wanted to apologise,' Sanjay began, gathering the words carefully in his mind before speaking them. 'About earlier. I'd rather worked myself up into a bit of a frenzy. These things play on your mind. I'm sure you know how it is. Before long, it becomes an obsession, and you stop thinking clearly. I realise now that it's not your fault. Not really. I was angry, you see. Film is my passion. I'd hoped that "Death in the Raj" would be the making of me. But there we are. I still have my books.'

'Your books are what make you who you are, Sanjay.' Max said. 'And for what it's worth, I'm sorry your show's been cancelled. I have some contacts at Netflix; perhaps I could put a good word in for you?'

Sanjay smiled, and the effort almost choked him. He didn't want hand-me-downs from Max Wilde. After tonight, he didn't care if he never saw the man again.

'No, that's okay, Max. I have a few books in mind. A couple of new projects to get stuck into.'

'Well, the offer's always there, Sanj. Whenever you need it. You only have to ask.'

Sanjay bowed slightly. He would never ask. Not of Max Wilde. Never.

'They're having drinks in the drawing room before dinner.' Max said. 'I'll see you there.'

Sanjay smiled, turned, and left the library. Max watched him go and wondered.

***

'Young man! Come here!'

Gareth Black was unused to being summonsed in such a forthright manner and, for a moment, considered a witty response that would have laid the old woman out in its ferocity. However, realising that the old woman was Margaret Hemshaw, he held his tongue and graciously went over to see what was wrong.

'I'm afraid I'm getting too old for stairs,' she said as she teetered on the top step of the staircase with one hand on the bannister and the other on her walking stick. She held her arm aloft and said, 'Grab on, would you?'

Gareth obliged and held his arm out for the old woman to grip onto.

'You look very smart for staff.' Margaret said, disguising her remark as a question.

Gareth stepped down and felt Margaret bear down on his arm for support.

He agreed, he did look smart. He had spent a worthwhile hour in front of the mirror perfecting his look. Fletchy was getting the full treatment.

'That's because I'm not staff,' he replied.

Margaret looked at him and said, 'I don't recognise you. Who are you?'

She had a bluntness about her that Gareth liked. There was no beating about the bush. She was all-in, feet first.

'Gareth Black. It's an honour to finally meet you, Mrs Hemshaw.'

'Don't go starting on that Mrs Hemshaw business. It's Margaret, or Peggy. I don't mind which.' She paused as she thought about something. 'Oh, you're Gareth Sebastian Black. The Indy one.'

'I am, yes. At least in part. Don't tell anyone, but I signed with one of the Big Five just the other day.'

'Good. I've read your work. You deserve that, at the very least. Particularly after knocking that obnoxious fraud off the top of the bestseller list.'

Gareth chuckled. 'You don't mean our esteemed host, do you?'

'Esteemed my arse.' Margaret spat. 'That man's never created a thing in his life. You should watch him, you know. Be careful. He wouldn't have taken it so kindly to be out-sold by someone like you. It will have irked him.'

'I'll bear that in mind,' Gareth replied.

They reached the bottom of the stairs, and Margaret held onto Gareth's arm. They walked together to the drawing room and were ushered in by a slim girl in her late teens dressed in a waitress outfit from the 1920s. She had an Art-Deco-styled hairband that held her dark hair above her eyes.

Gemma greeted the two with a warm smile.

'Margaret. So lovely to see you again. You look lovely! Mr Black. My, you do scrub up well!'

Gareth took the compliment and returned it.

'You look stunning, Miss Collis,' he said as he leant over and kissed her on the cheek.

'Excellent,' Margaret declared as the formalities came to an end. 'We all look lovely. Shall we have a drink?'

A waiter, similarly dressed to the young waitress at the door, except in black chequered trousers and a crisp white shirt and braces, opened a bottle of champagne from an ice bucket.

'A glass of Sparkling Cyanide, Margaret?' Gemma asked as the waiter poured several glasses and held them out for the guests.

Margaret took one. Gemma handed another to Gareth.

'Max had the labels specially printed by the producer in France. I daresay they will become collectables.'

'There you are, Sanjay? May I offer you a glass of bubbly?'

Sanjay took a glass from Gemma and joined the gathering as they stepped out onto the verandah.

'Sanjay, may I introduce Mr Gareth Black?'

The two men shook hands.

'Good work on your latest novel,' Sanjay said, gripping Gareth's hand firmly. 'Glad to see you knocked you know who off the top spot!'

Gemma ignored the slur. It pained her to feel that her books were becoming a target because of who Max Wilde was.

'Good to see you again, Sanjay,' Margaret said, allowing her cheeks to be gently kissed.

'You too, Margaret. How's Pat getting on?'

Gareth felt the cold air emanate from Margaret.

'She's fine.' She said abruptly. 'It's a beautiful summer we're having, isn't it?'

Sanjay took the lifeline.

'Very warm for the time of year.'

The two drifted sideways, and Margaret took a chair. Their conversation stayed on topic for some time, and Pat was quickly forgotten.

***

She wore a simple red dress that ended just above her knees. It was a deep, ruby red, flecked with silver sparkles, and she glistened as she walked out of the French windows and onto the verandah. Understated silver earrings hung from her ears, and she wore several rings on her fingers. Gareth was the first to rise and offer a glass of freshly poured champagne.

'You look absolutely stunning.' He said quietly.

Sydney accepted the compliment graciously and took the glass.

'You don't look too bad yourself,' she replied, under-egging the pudding as best she could. As she stepped outside, her first look at Gareth was met with a missed heartbeat. She took a long moment to savour his classic good looks and how he held himself in his crisp evening suit. Not bad at all.

Gemma bounded over.

'I see you have a glass.' She said, shooting Gareth a quizzical look. She felt the sparks coming off them and had to admit that they'd probably make pretty children. 'Let me introduce you to the others. That's an amazing dress, by the way. Where did you get those legs?'

Sydney laughed. 'Same place as you, by the look of it.'

Gemma hooked an arm through Sydney's and drew her away from Gareth.

'Mrs Hemshaw. May I introduce you to Miss Sydney Fletch?'

Margaret turned and looked the young woman up and down.

'You're far too young and pretty to be so successful.' Margaret said, smiling. 'I read your book. I was very impressed.'

'Thank you.' Sydney leant over in a conspiratorial fashion. 'I'm a massive fan, Mrs Hemshaw. I've read all your books. Please tell me there's another one coming soon!'

Gemma watched as Sydney's charm washed over the elderly woman.

'As I told the young man earlier, it's Margaret or Peggy. I don't care which. And I believe the next one's out next month. Pat deals with all that sort of thing.'

'Is Pat your daughter?' Sydney asked.

'She is.' Margaret said. Then, turning to Sanjay, she said, 'Have you met Mr Chakrabati?'

Sanjay rose, and the two exchanged pleasantries.

They were interrupted by the young waitress, who topped their glasses up and returned back inside the house. She returned a few seconds later with another bottle and refilled Gareth's glass. Gareth said something to the waitress that Sydney failed to hear, and she watched as the young girl giggled and looked demure. Sydney felt an emotion rise up within her and suppressed it with all her might. She was unused to such emotions, particularly those caused by a man. He was beginning to get under her skin, and it annoyed her and entertained her in equal measure.

'Excellent. You're all here!'

Everyone turned as Max Wilde made his entrance. He stood at the doorway in a deep blue dinner suit and gold bow tie.

'Actually, not everyone,' he said, glancing around the verandah. He looked at his watch. 'There's still time.' He took a glass from the waitress, who shrunk in Max's presence, and waited while she filled his glass. As she was about to walk back into the house, he grabbed her arm and pulled her gently towards him. 'No one's glass is to be left to get empty.'

The girl nodded, still in awe at having met the famous Max Wilde, and hurried back inside the house.

Gemma had been braced to intervene should Max make a play for the girl, something he was known to do, but was relieved to see her pass almost unnoticed. Max had his eye on someone else.

He walked right over to Sydney, took her hand, and kissed it gently. It was an old-fashioned thing to do, and every time Gemma saw Max do it, she witnessed yet another of his conquests. This time, however, it looked as if Sydney's underwear was staying in place, at least for the foreseeable future, as she merely said, 'Thank you for inviting me to your home, Mr Wilde. I feel privileged to be here,' and removed her hand from his mouth.

Gemma glanced across at Gareth, who looked relieved, and Max, who looked confused. He rarely had to work for his conquests. They usually fell at his feet, but Sydney Fletch was a different kind of woman. The rebuff had been firm yet polite, but it had left Max knowing exactly where he stood. Gemma hoped Max wouldn't realise that he stood metaphorically about two metres behind Gareth, who walked over and introduced himself.

'Gareth Black. Very pleased to meet you.'

Max recovered his composure, drew a smile upon his face, and turned to the rest of his guests, looking at the beautiful young Sydney Fletch from time to time but each time being disappointed to find that she wasn't looking at him.

Max looked at his watch. They had one more guest to arrive, and then they could begin. The question was, where was he?

***

Grace had just finished tying Finney's bow tie when the latter said, 'No, I don't want to go. I think I'll stay at home.'

'You'll do no such thing,' Grace said, smoothing the arms of Finney's jacket. 'They're expecting you. It wouldn't be the done thing to cancel at this late hour.'

Grace looked at the clock on Finney's mantelpiece. It was fifteen minutes to eight, and the walk to Burnham Manor was at least five minutes.

'I'm not sure I care.' Finney said.

'I'll walk with you.' Grace said, ignoring him.

'I just don't think it's my thing. I'd rather stay at home. It was stupid of me to agree to go in the first place… I think…'

'Now look at me, Jack Finney!' Grace interrupted. 'The last time you were at a social gathering was at my late husband's wake. Before that, your poor wife's. It's time you started being sociable again. Come. I'll walk with you.'

Jack Finney doubted if he had ever been sociable, even when his wife was still alive. Caroline had been the sociable one.

'What will I talk about?' Finney asked. 'I'm not very good at making small talk.'

Grace led Finney to the front door of his cottage and bundled him out into the street. It was a warm summer evening. The sun had lost some of its bite and was slowly descending into the western sky. A few cotton wool clouds drifted between the vapour trails left behind by passing aircraft.

'You won't need to find anything to say,' Grace said, closing the door behind her. 'They are crime writers. As soon as they discover what you used to do for a living, they'll pump you for information. You won't have a quiet second to yourself.'

Finney wondered if that was true. It's not like how it's portrayed in the movies. Policing could be a dull and tedious information-gathering exercise, with a five-minute climax, followed by another dull and tedious information-gathering exercise to get a case to court, which was, more often than not, another dull and tedious exercise.

Grace held on to Finney's elbow as they walked through the small village. They passed The Marlborough Hotel, whose bar was beginning to heave with Friday night drinkers, and on towards The Manor.

'Good evening.' Fenwick declared as his form appeared in a doorway leading to the grounds of Burnham Manor.

'Good evening, John.' Grace replied brightly.

Finney nodded, and Fenwick returned the gesture.

'You were robbed,' Grace said, looking back to ensure Fenwick was out of earshot. She watched as he crossed the road and entered The Marlborough. 'He really is a very unpleasant man.'

They continued walking until the main entrance to Burnham Manor loomed large ahead of them. Their way was blocked by a pair of impressive black gates and a man in a suit standing in front of them.

'This is private property.' He declared politely but firmly as they approached.

'He's expected.' Grace said.

The guard looked at Grace as she said the words. Then he looked at Finney. 'You must be Mr Finney, then?'

Finney said he was, and the guard pushed one of the gates back far enough to allow him to pass. 'Follow the drive up. Someone at the front door will show you where to go.'

Finney turned to Grace. 'I shan't stay long.' He declared.

Grace disagreed. 'You will stay until midnight. I don't want to hear you return before then, or I shall be cross.'

'But that's *four* hours!' Finney exclaimed.

'That's agreed, then. Four hours at least.' Grace herded Finney towards the gates. 'And not before!'

***

Max beamed as his surprise guest was shown through the drawing room and onto the patio.

'Mr Finney! I'm so glad you could make it. A drink?'

Finney took a glass of champagne from a young girl who hovered nearby and let himself be drawn towards the other guests.

'Ladies and gentlemen, may I introduce my guest, former Detective Chief Inspector Jack Finney.' Max declared brightly.

Margaret was the first to speak.

'A detective? A real detective?'

'Indeed, madam. Twenty-five years with Gloucester Constabulary.' Finney said.

'I'm no madam,' Margaret declared, 'although it feels like I've sold myself often enough. Call me Margaret or Peggy.'

'Margaret Hemshaw?' Finney asked.

Margaret nodded graciously. She enjoyed being recognised.

'I've read some of your books. My late wife was a big fan.'

'You're too kind, I'm sure.'

Max turned and introduced Sanjay to Finney. The two men shook hands.

Finney said, 'I don't watch much television, but I do watch your show. It's probably the only thing worth watching these days. Shame it got cancelled.'

Sanjay threw Max a look that went unnoticed by the others, but Finney had seen it. His old eyes didn't miss a thing.

'That's very kind of you to say,' Sanjay replied, 'but these things have a natural life span. "Death in the Raj" had come to the end of its natural course. One must look forward, never back.'

Finney felt the truth in the words but detected the undercurrent that flowed beneath them.

'Mr Gareth Black.' Max said.

Gareth stood forward and gripped Finney's hand firmly.

'Pleased to meet you.'

'Gareth's one of the new breed.' Max said sharply. 'One of Amazon's little fishes that has swum into the open sea.'

Finney nodded. He had already done his homework, thanks to Grace's nosiness. The village had been rife with the gossip of Max's invitees to his annual gathering, and Finney had googled them all. Knowledge was power.

'I believe your book is number one on the bestseller lists?' Finney remarked. 'I haven't read it yet, but I intend to.'

Gareth smiled as Max wilted.

'I shall send you a copy.' Gareth said. 'It will be my pleasure.'

Max moved on.

'May I introduce Miss Sydney Fletch..'

Sydney stepped into Finney's line of sight with an outstretched hand. She was quite beautiful, Finney mused. Elegant and graceful, yet understated. She reminded him a little of his daughter, and the memory pained him.

'You're not by any chance the DCI Finney who cracked the Painswick Poisoning case a few years ago, are you?' Sydney asked.

Finney looked at the young woman in amazement. He had come to Burnham-on-the-Wold to be anonymous and to fade into the background. In this, he had mostly succeeded, but every now and then, someone would surprise him. Sydney surprised him.

'I am indeed.' Finney admitted. 'I'm surprised you've even heard of it.'

'I hate to be the one to break it to you, Mr Finney,' Sydney said, 'but you're surrounded by crime writers. We don't know much, but we do know crime.'

'You're *that* Finney,' Margaret exclaimed.

'I remember the case,' Sanjay said. 'An inscrutable case solved by a brilliant detective.'

'It was some disgruntled old woman, wasn't it?' Gareth asked. 'Exacting revenge on those she thought had slighted her somehow. You must tell us all about it.'

Finney braced himself. Grace had been right.

'I'm afraid detective work isn't quite how it's portrayed in fiction.' Finney began. 'I was the leading edge of a large team of people who all came together to solve the case. At one point, almost two hundred people were working on it. Each had their own skill set and talents, which, individually, amounted to little but, taken as a whole, helped us solve the case. The idea that all the information and clues are gathered by a single person who solves the puzzle in a moment of clarity, is entirely your domain.'

Margaret laughed.

'Our way is so much more fun!' She declared.

'Well, I don't disagree with that. Proper policing is hard graft.'

'I'm afraid you're in for it, Mr Finney.' Sydney said. 'Crime writers have a single factor in common. An inexhaustible desire for knowledge.'

Gemma stepped up. She had been left out of the introductions.

'Hello again, Mr Finney.' She said sweetly. 'I'm so glad you could make it.'

Finney remembered Max's pretty young PA. He shook her hand gently.

'I'm very grateful for the invitation.'

'I'm afraid Sydney's quite right. You're not going to get a moment's peace!'

Finney started to relax. He drained his glass and found it almost immediately refilled.

'Then I think a few more of these will be in order.' He said. 'If only to lubricate the throat!'

The small gathering of crime writers chatted for some time, never following any particular topic for longer than a minute. Each manoeuvred around Finney, vying for the best spot to drain the poor man of his knowledge. Finney stood in the centre, not giving too much away, while the questions came at him relentlessly.

Max stood and watched. He watched as the insidious Margaret Hemshaw interrupted the younger ones with her overpowering and demanding voice that cut through the talk like a power saw. She demanded attention and showed her displeasure when it wasn't given.

He watched Sanjay slip to the periphery and take a small role in the inquisition of his guest. Sanjay had a melancholy about him that showed in his expression. He was unhappy, and Max thought his apology earlier was little more than smoke. It didn't bother him a great deal. He doubted that Sanjay would be a guest at any of his future gatherings. Sanjay's star was on the wane. He would be quickly forgotten.

He watched as Gareth held Margaret's arm for support and watched as he and Sydney exchanged knowing glances when they thought no one was watching. Gareth was a character he couldn't place. He was different. Not your normal writer type. He was old-school polite with an obvious talent for crime writing, which Max had begrudgingly admitted. But there was something about him that Max didn't like, but he couldn't put his finger on it.

He watched as the delightful Sydney Fletch stood opposite Gareth and flirted with him with her eyes. Max traced her figure from her feet to her head, delighting in every gentle curve. He could almost taste the desire as it burned through his veins, but he was no fool. Sydney had little interest in him, and he, oddly, felt nothing more than a simple sexual attraction for her. He had much more in life to enjoy than anyone knew, and he wasn't about to spoil it for a quick shag.

Then there was Gemma and his hatred for her burned his soul. When he found out that she was sleeping with his brother, he set his plans in motion for selling The Marlborough. No one cheated on Max Wilde. He knew full well that it would ruin Robert, but he didn't care. He had plans for Gemma, but she was a little more difficult. Gemma was undeniably the brains behind his empire, but she had too much power. He needed to cut her down. He had already found a replacement to write his novels, and his publishers had agreed. Cutting her off without losing too much money was all that held him back for now.

He glanced across the lawn to where Mr Fukushima and his granddaughter stood. They had prepared a table at the foot of where his guests would be eating, and they waited patiently.

'Ladies and gentlemen.' Max spoke loudly, bringing the conversation to an end. 'Let's eat.'

***

The small procession went from the patio across the neatly manicured lawn to where Max had built the shelter. It glowed under a hundred lights secured beneath the cover. A single chandelier hung from the centre and came to rest six feet from the middle of the great oak dining table. One by one, the guests entered the dining area and took their seats.

'This is amazing, Max.' Margaret said. She wasn't one for platitudes, particularly where Max was concerned, but she couldn't help but admire the lengths her host had gone to to create such a luxurious setting. Crystal wine glasses were slowly filled with an amber liquid before the waiting staff withdrew to a discreet distance.

'This does look wonderful.' Sydney agreed. She eyed the label on one of the wine bottles that a young waitress held. It read, "Malevolent Muscadet." She gathered her glass and tasted it. She watched as the others did the same. It was good wine.

Max remained standing at the head of the table, holding his own glass of wine. He watched as his guests settled into their seats and admired the view around them. One by one they noticed the additional table at the foot of theirs and the elderly Japanese gentleman who stood there, watching them. In front of him was a white chopping board and a selection of serious-looking knives. Behind him was a small Japanese woman in her twenties who stood quite still, with her arms folded behind her back.

Sydney took it all in and relished the experience. Even if she was never invited back, she was tonight, at least, one of a very few select members of a hugely desired cliqué. She was among some of the greatest living exponents of her trade on the grounds of what was once the home of one of the greatest British Crime writers of the 20th Century. She almost couldn't believe it was real.

'Ladies and gentlemen,' Max began, 'it gives me immense pleasure to welcome you to my home. Some of you are old friends, and some, I hope, will become new ones.' He glanced at Sydney, who smiled. 'This is now the tenth year that I have hosted my little event, and I hope it has become something of a badge of honour to be invited here. With the exception of Mr Finney, we are all crime and mystery writers, and we ply our trade not as rivals or competitors but as colleagues and co-conspirators. For us, it is not the thrill of the bestseller lists or the grand advances the public thinks we are paid, nor is it the awards or the recognition. For us, it is the thrill of the chase. We follow in the footsteps of some of the greatest crime writers in the world in an effort to create and produce some of the finest works of mystery. It is, for us, like setting a crossword puzzle. Each clue must be engineered perfectly to entice and amuse the reader while giving them a fair chance at deciphering it, but not so much as they come to the correct conclusion. We are the magicians of the writing world, where sleight of hand rules supreme, and we are never more than a thousand words away from pulling the rabbit out of the hat. For us, it is like the hunt for the Holy Grail, to produce that one book that pitches our claim to the title of King or Queen, that forever ties our name alongside the greats that have gone before us. We are, each of us, looking to write our own Roger Ackroyd mystery that bends the conventions without breaking them but which sets us apart from the others.

'Our small party consists of what I believe to be some of the best proponents of our trade, writing today. We have the wonderful Mrs Hemshaw, whose forays into seventeenth-century England have kept us amused, entertained and astonished over several decades. I speak no word of a lie when I tell you that even I have learned a thing or two from her books. My bedroom activities have been somewhat enhanced by carefully re-reading some of Margaret's scenes!'

A cautious chuckle rose from the party. They had all read Margaret's books and knew fully what Max suggested. For an older lady, neither her morals nor her imagination knew any limit.

Max continued his little speech.

'And I am proud to call Sanjay a friend and a colleague. His books, set in British India, set him far above others in his field. He mixes historical accuracy and fiction like an old weaver. As we all know, history is never black and white. It is multi-faceted and complex, and Sanjay finds a fine balance that embraces the colonial spirit of the day with love and concern for his own countrymen that looks far deeper than a simple right and wrong.'

Sanjay took a long, considered sip of his wine and nodded graciously.

'And we have the new breed.'

Max paused as everyone looked across at Sydney and Gareth.

'Welcome both. P G Wodehouse once wrote, "It has been well said that an author who expects results from a first novel is in a position similar to that of a man who drops a rose petal down the Grand Canyon of Arizona and listens for the echo." I cannot tell you what Sydney's rose was made of, but its echo has resounded across the world. She possesses a flower that every man desires! Congratulations, Miss Fletch, you must tell us what your secret is!'

Sydney blushed as Max made his awkward compliment. In one sentence, he had managed to reduce her to the component parts of her body. In normal circumstances she would have left, but she was surrounded by the great and good of the crime writing world, and suddenly felt very small amongst them.

She glanced at Gareth who looked as though he were about to say something, but Max had seen it too.

'And of course, finally, Mr Gareth Sebastian Black, who, finding the conventional route into publishing closed to him, set about blowing a Gareth-sized hole in the building and coming in anyway. You are the first crime writer to have successfully knocked my book off the top spot while it was still at its peak. Well done. I'm going to make sure that never happens again!'

A nervous laugh rose from the table and was joined by Max, who patted Gareth on the shoulder.

'And now to dinner.'

They watched as Max laid his glass of wine onto the table and went to where Sydney and Gareth had seen a fish tank being installed. It was still there but covered with a large blue cloth. Max approached it and cast the cover aside like a showman revealing his trick. He turned and watched the expressions on his guests' faces.

'It's a fish.' Margaret said disappointedly.

'It's an ugly one.' Gareth remarked.

'We're not going to eat it, are we?' Sydney asked.

'I hope not.' Finney said quietly.

One by one, the guests turned to Finney. Max beamed. Gemma, slighted by the lack of a mention in Max's speech, sat quietly with her arms folded.

'It's a puffer fish.' Finney explained to the inquisitive faces that looked across at him. 'It's a delicacy in Japan and deadly if it's been prepared badly.'

Finney pulled his small tin from his pocket, selected a single sweet, and popped it into his mouth.

'And that is why I have brought Mr Fukushima and his granddaughter here, especially for the occasion.'

Max nodded at the waiting staff, who lingered nearby. They filed into the dining area carrying plate upon plate of carefully prepared sushi and laid them across the oak table. Each guest was handed a small, carefully prepared menu that detailed what they were about to eat.

Fugu sashimi; Salmon and tuna nigiri; salmon sashimi; Dragon roll; Truffle roll; hamachi.

It was a long list that included a brief description of the contents of the sushi. Sydney salivated at the thought and then looked across at the puffer fish.

'That's not a real puffer fish, is it?' She asked cautiously.

'It is.' Max said. He nodded to another waiting staff member, who walked over to Max with a net. Max held the net into the tank and scooped up the fish. As they watched, the fish blew itself up to twice its normal size. Max took the fish and handed it to Mr Fukushima. The old man carefully retrieved the fish from the net and laid it on a chopping board. Before anyone could look away, he stunned the fish with a mallet before swiftly removing its head. He threw all the parts of the fish that wouldn't be eaten into a bowl next to him, which had been labelled with a skull and crossbones.

Gareth looked to see if Sydney was still watching and was amazed to find her glued to the spectacle. On the other hand, Margaret had taken to searching for something in her bag, while Sanjay found himself unusually intrigued. They watched on as Mr Fukushima worked his skills on the fish, and before long, some thin slices of fugu sashimi were laid out on a plate before them.

Max held the plate aloft and marvelled at the incredibly thin strips of fish that were fanned out in a circle. He turned to Mr Fukushima and bowed respectfully. Mr Fukushima beamed and bowed back.

'I believe you have excelled yourself, Mr Fukushima. My guests and I are extremely grateful.'

The young Japanese girl translated, and Mr Fukushima bowed to them all. Everyone waited as Mr

Fukushima gathered his tools, and the young girl took his arm and led him away.

Max laid the plate at the centre of the table and returned to his seat.

'So, then. Who's going to try some with me?'

Max leant forward and selected several slices and placed them on his plate, followed by a few more pieces from the sushi platter. Everyone watched and waited.

'Is it very poisonous?' Sydney asked.

Finney smiled. 'It is. It contains one of the deadliest poisons known to man. There is no antidote.'

Sydney looked across at Max.

'Do you mind if I don't? I don't care much for raw fish.' She lied.

'Not at all.' Max said. 'That's why I laid on some sushi.'

'I think I'll pass, too, Max.' Sanjay said, following Sydney's lead.

Gareth leaned over, grabbed several fugu sashimi slices, and laid them on his plate. He gathered one slice between his fingers and slipped it into his mouth.

'Bloody hell, that's delicious.' He said. 'I'll try anything once. Except death. That can wait.'

Max copied Gareth and swallowed a slice.

'How long will it be before they die?' Sydney asked, directing her question at Finney.

Finney shrugged.

'I'm afraid I don't know. Given its exotic nature, the poison wasn't part of the Painswick Poisonings, so I had no cause to find out. I can tell you a lot about thallium or arsenic or strychnine.'

Gemma roused herself from her mood.

'If the fish hasn't been prepared properly and the flesh is poisoned,' she said, 'and if there are sufficient quantities of tetrodotoxin, then death will most likely occur a few hours later. They will both be in bed, alone, when the poison works its magic.'

Max laughed.

'Come now, Gemma,' Max said, 'you know me better than that. I am rarely alone at night!'

Everyone watched as Max's eyes landed on Sydney. Sydney felt distinctly uncomfortable under his glare. She shivered. She watched as Gareth tucked into the rest of the fugu and put more sushi on his plate. She felt the anxiety tug at her stomach. She then looked on in amazement as Finney reached over and placed three slices of fugu on his plate. She hadn't expected that.

Finney dropped a slice into his mouth and relished the flavour. He took a second slice between his fingers and swallowed that.

'I must congratulate Gareth on his description. It really is bloody delicious.'

Slowly, the table tucked into the rest of the sushi, and before too long, most of it had been demolished. Gareth and Finney returned for more fugu sashimi, much to Sydney's displeasure. As they ate, the waiting staff returned to the table and refilled everyone's glasses with Malevolent Muscadet. It was the perfect accompaniment to the delicate sushi. Max certainly knew his stuff.

When they had finished and the table had been cleared, two waitresses returned and dropped another menu in front of each guest. Sydney picked hers up and read it.

To start:

A Soupçon of Suspicion. Creamy tomato soup with carrots, celery and basil.

Murderous Mushrooms. Fresh garlic mushrooms in a dry white wine, garlic and single cream, topped with cheese and served with granary bread.

Red Herring. Sous vide pickled herring in a parsnip cream with white radish and an apple dashi.

'I'm beginning to see the theme, Max.' Sydney said. 'It all looks rather delicious.'

'I'm somewhat partial to a good mushroom starter.' Gareth said, reading the menu. 'No Death Cap in there, is there?'

'Not to my knowledge,' Max laughed, 'but I can't be entirely sure. Robert grew them.'

Gemma shot Max a look and decided against the mushrooms.

'I'm going for the soup.' She declared.

'What about you, Margaret?' Max asked.

'I'm more of a pudding girl myself. But I think I shall have the fish.'

'Mr Finney?'

'The soup for me, please.'

Sanjay agreed.

'Absolutely. No chance of a deadly poison being snuck in there accidentally!'

'Which is why I went for the fish!' Margaret said, draining her glass of wine and holding it aloft for a waitress to refill.

'Actually,' Finney began. 'The tomato is part of the Deadly Nightshade family, as are potatoes. I believe it does, actually, contain a poison in small doses.'

'Not enough to kill.' Gemma added. 'I believe it's called tomatine and is abundant in the leaves and stems and the green fruit, but not so much the red fruit. I think you'll also find that wild parsnip is extremely poisonous. It's part of the hemlock family.'

Finney raised his glass in tribute.

'You know your stuff.'

Gemma smiled.

'Research for Max's next novel.' Gemma explained.

'Fascinating,' Sanjay interrupted. He turned to Max and said: 'Perhaps you could tell us more about your new book, Max? I promise your secrets will be safe with us.'

Max saw the trap coming.

'I never discuss my plots before they're fully formed in my head and down on paper. I find the idea diminishes in the light of day.'

Sanjay caught the expression on Max's face as he spoke. There was some truth to that. Long ago, he found that talking about a plotline tended to ruin it. It lost its magic. In this case, he knew that the reason Max didn't know much about it was because Gemma hadn't told him yet. He was nothing more than a fraud.

'I suppose you must be something of an expert on poisons yourself, Mr Finney.' Margaret said. 'What with the Painswick Poisoning case.'

'I must admit, I learned an awful lot. The poisoner used a variety of toxins which made it quite difficult to pin down.'

'You must tell us all about it!' Margaret declared.

'Yes, please do.' Sydney joined in. 'Poisoning cases seem so rare these days. I think our modern-day murderers have lost their class. They seem to be running around, stabbing and shooting people. There's no flair.'

'I believe it was a woman, wasn't it?' Gareth asked. 'Some old dear with too much time on her hands.'

'Very much a woman's crime,' Sanjay added.

'You'd think,' Finney began slowly. 'But one must always keep an open mind. Men have been some of the worst poisoners in the last one hundred and fifty years. It wasn't a safe assumption to make.'

'There was that fella in the fifties who poisoned his workmates, wasn't there?' Gareth asked. 'Got the idea from an Agatha Christie book, didn't he?'

Finney was about to reply when a waiter appeared and took everyone's food request. A waitress followed and topped everyone's wine up.

'Graham Young.' Finney declared when the waiting staff had once again withdrawn to a discreet distance. 'The Teacup poisoner. A very unique individual with a penchant for poisons and poisoning people. I believe the novel you are referring to is The Pale Horse, although Young denied having ever read it. Because of Mr Young and Agatha Christie, the government created The Poisons Act, bringing to an end several fruitful years for poisoners, which is why, I suppose, so few people engage in it these days. It's much harder to acquire, or so I thought.

'I'm afraid I have a rather sad part to play in acquiring the knowledge I have, which is why I was brought onto the Painswick case. My dear young daughter, Sarah, died on her twelfth birthday after eating a meal containing peanuts. We knew she was allergic and were extremely careful to avoid any chance of contamination. I suppose we wrapped her up in cotton wool a bit. Anyway, we made a reservation at a restaurant in Gloucester and gave them all the relevant information, but for some reason, a menu change was instigated at the last minute, and my daughter was served a meal containing nuts. Despite everyone's best attempts, we were unable to save her.'

'My god, that's awful.' Sydney said. 'I'm so sorry.'

'My dear man, that's awful to have happened.' Margaret said.

'Awful.'

'That's shocking.'

'It's unlikely that could happen today.' Max said. 'Restaurants go to great lengths to prevent it.'

Finney nodded.

'Indeed. I like to think my wife and I were some small part of that. We campaigned tirelessly for a change in the law. As you say, it is unlikely to happen today. I dearly hope my daughter's death was not in vain. But, you see, I was able to look at the Painswick case a little differently. Initially, it was unclear if a crime had even been committed. People die. It's a fact of life. In some regions, more people die than in others, but in Painswick, a town of no more than three thousand souls, there seemed to be an unusually large death rate. The percentages didn't make sense. An initial investigation found nothing to work with, and the case was given to me to look at.

'I at once began to study poisons. There was no proof that anything like that was happening as most of the bodies had been cremated, and very few had been autopsied. But I was painfully aware that if someone had wished to murder my daughter, then all they would have to do would be to add nuts to something she was about to eat. So I began to look at some of the people who had died, shall we say, prematurely, and began to dig around in their lives. In this case, knowledge was a dangerous weapon.

'I found a couple of people who had serious heart conditions, whose deaths aroused no suspicion. I found that adding digitalis to their food and drink could have had devastating consequences. Everywhere I looked in Painswick, I found foxgloves growing in abundance. It would be simple to extract the poison and administer it without anyone thinking to look for it.

'The problem I faced was twofold. Motive and connection. From the outside, looking in, I could see no motive. And there was no connection. Some of the victims I potentially identified didn't know each other, and the victims were of all age groups, sexes and races, although they were predominantly white. So we had to wait. Murder, unfortunately, begets murder. Murderers are vain and arrogant and apt to kill again. I had no choice but to wait for another victim, and because most of the victims weren't *seen* to have been murdered, we investigated every death in the town and within a ten-mile radius. It was all done very quietly. We stayed under the radar. The last thing we wanted was to alert the killer that we were onto them.

'Then we hit gold. Or rather, Aconitine. A fifty-two-year-old male was found dead in his garden, having suffered what we suspected was a heart attack. He was alone at the time, and we had no first-hand account of his symptoms. The initial post-mortem showed signs of asphyxia, which is not uncommon, and serious heart failure. His family had a history of heart failure and were quite happy to accept that as his cause of death. But we did a full tox-screen and found aconite, a deadly alkaloid found in the common garden plant, Monkshood.'

Gemma nodded. She had not long finished researching aconite.

'It grows in our garden.' She said.

'I know. I saw it as I walked up the drive. It is a beautiful plant. But it is quite deadly. As we were hunting for a poisoner, I had every foodstuff in this gentleman's house bagged and tested. We found large amounts of aconite in a beer bottle in his greenhouse. We suspect he had not long drunk out of it and, after beginning to feel unwell, was returning to his house. He was found there by a neighbour sometime later.'

'A horrible way to die.' Sydney remarked.

'As poisons go, there are much worse.' Finney continued. 'I began researching the kind of poisons that could be readily acquired and easily cultivated. I have to admit my findings shocked me. If I wanted cyanide, I could find it inside the seeds of an apple. I grant you, a single apple core would do you little harm, but the contents of five apples, ground to a powder, could do a person some serious mischief.'

'We have a Cassava Plant in the poison garden.' Gemma added.

'Cassava Plant?' Gareth asked.

'It's a common plant in South America,' Gemma explained, 'and is cultivated for its edible tubers. Unfortunately, it is deadly in its raw form because of the high quantity of cyanide it contains.'

Finney paused his little lecture as the waiting staff returned bearing the starters. Plates were placed in front of the guests and glasses were topped up.

'Feel free to talk as you eat, Mr Finney.' Max said. 'You have us gripped.'

Finney spooned some soup into his mouth and dabbed at his lips with a napkin.

'We were still without a motive or a suspect,' Finney continued, taking small mouthfuls of his food as and when he could. 'We researched as many poisons that could be cultivated with a small amount of knowledge and tried to link them with some of the deaths that had gone before. We were quite keen to prevent this person, whoever it was, from striking again. We extracted Belladonna from a Deadly Nightshade plant that grew quite happily in my garden. We cultivated Hemlock from the wild plant on our roadsides, and deadly ricin from a Castor Oil Plant. We could produce as many as twenty deadly poisons without ever having to make a purchase that could be traced and we gained our knowledge from information readily available on the internet. We slowly began to link certain poisons with certain deaths. In one case, a lorry driver fell asleep at the wheel of his truck and died in the crash that ensued along with two other people. We believed that a poison was added to his food that induced a somnolent effect quite quickly, but as he was cremated long before our investigation began, we were never able to prove this comprehensively.

'After several months, we were still unable to find a motive or a link between the victims.'

He paused as he finished his soup.

'How on earth did you catch the killer?' Sydney asked.

'Luck.' Finney said. 'And some clever planning. We had instructed medical centres and A&E departments to be on the lookout for patients who came from the Painswick area. We were hoping to catch a victim before the autopsy and perhaps save a life. A young woman in her twenties showed up at Cheltenham A&E displaying signs of acute gastroenteritis and muscle spasms. As we tried to interview her she began to display signs of strychnine poisoning, and we were able to control her seizures and help her breathe as the toxin moved through her body. I must take my hat off to the men and women in our health service. Their knowledge and experience were vital in keeping this young woman alive. It took some time, but we were able to manage the poisoning successfully, and she made a full recovery. She also provided us with a suspect and motive.'

'It was an old woman, wasn't it?' Gareth asked.

'It was.' Finney admitted. 'The young woman, whose life we had just saved, had recently moved into a new house in Painswick and had, unfortunately for her, fallen out with her neighbour, a sixty-nine-year-old woman called Julia Edwards. It was nothing much, just a simple disagreement over noise, the usual neighbour complaint.

But it turns out that Mrs Edwards was not a woman to be scorned. She held grudges. She complained a lot about a lot of things and about a lot of people. I believe young people label this type of woman as a "Karen"; unfortunately, she more than lived up to the stereotype.

'As we had no proof, we could obtain no warrant to search her property, where we felt certain we would find evidence to link her to some of the deaths. Magistrates don't like policemen going on fishing trips, so we had to work smarter. I gathered a small task force of officers to start digging, albeit very quietly. We couldn't afford to let Mrs Edwards get wind of our investigation for fear that she might destroy any compelling evidence before we could search her home. It was my considered opinion that while she believed that no one was looking at her for these deaths, she would have been taking few precautions. I had to hope that she was as arrogant as most murderers are.

'After a short while, we could link nearly all the victims we had identified to Mrs Edwards. All of them, in one way or another, had crossed paths with her. We had the connection we were after and the motive. Each of the victims we were looking at had, in some way, upset or offended Mrs Edwards. She was exacting a vicious and devastating revenge.'

Finney paused as the waiting staff cleared the plates. When they had retired from the table, he continued.

'But we still had no proof or chance of a warrant to search her home. And then, during an interview with one of the alleged victim's relatives, we heard someone refer to Mrs Edwards as a Black Widow.

'As it turned out, Mrs Edwards had been married twice, and both men had died during the marriage. Only one of the men had been cremated. Unbeknownst to Mrs Edwards, her first husband had left provision in his will for his body to be interred next to his young brother, who had been killed during the first Iraq campaign. When he buried his brother, he bought the plot next to him, so, in layman's terms, we had him dug up.'

'Did she poison him?' Sydney asked.

'Yes. With arsenic. We could prove it conclusively, and the Magistrate signed off on the search warrant.'

Margaret waved her empty glass in the air, and a young waiter glided up to her and refilled it. He disappeared into the shadows.

'I don't remember the court case?' Margaret said.

'There wasn't one.' Finney replied. 'As I believed, Mrs Edwards had made no effort to hide evidence. We found enough evidence in her home to send her to prison for the rest of her life. She confessed her crimes quite readily. She bore no resentment at being caught and almost delighted in regaling her crimes to us. But, in one respect, I was quite wrong. She did expect to be caught one day, so she made little effort to cover her tracks. In fact, she knew exactly what she would do if, and when, that time arrived. A young constable was charged with sitting with Mrs Edwards as we conducted our investigation and dutifully handed her some medication that she was taking for her heart. Unfortunately for us, she had replaced one of the pills with a lethal dose of cyanide and died almost instantly. The families of the victims were deprived of their day in court. My heart bled for them.'

***

'Have you ever thought of writing your adventures down, Mr Finney?' Margaret asked. 'You have a natural gift for storytelling.'

'Good God, no!' Finney joked. 'I'm retired. I grow marrows. That's more than enough for me.'

'Perhaps you will let one of us write them for you?' Sydney suggested.

'What a fantastic idea, Sydney.' Sanjay said. 'What do you think, Max? Do you reckon you'd be up for the job? You'd be a guaranteed bestseller with your name on the cover.

Max sighed. Sanjay was becoming tiresome. Finney watched as Max's expressions gave himself away.

As Finney watched Max, Sydney watched Finney. He didn't miss a thing, the wily old dog, she thought. Perhaps good detectives never retired?

Gareth watched as Sydney watched Finney. His desire for her was growing by the minute. The more time he spent in her company, the more he fell desperately in love.

Gemma watched no one in particular. She was absorbed entirely by her melancholy.

From her position, Margaret watched them all. She watched the all-seeing Mr Finney, the resentful Sanjay, the lovestruck Gareth, and beautiful Sydney Fletch, the apparent cause of his malady. She watched Max, too, and quietly despised the man. Gemma sat opposite him, and Margaret saw the same emotion writ large across her face. She resolved then and there to have a quiet word with Miss Collis. There were a few things she needed to know. Now was the time to tell her.

Max raised his hand, and the waiting staff gathered around the table. They removed the old wine glasses, much to Margaret's dismay, and replaced them with new ones that were deeper and more rounded across the top. They returned with bottles of red wine with "Murderous Merlot" stamped on the label. Slowly, they filled everyone's glasses. When they had finished, they returned with the next menu.

'Just two items on this one.' Max declared. 'But I'm sure you'll find them equally delicious.'

Sydney raised her menu.

The Poisoned Quail. Breast of Quail, pea purée, pancetta and a marjoram jus.

Bella-doner Kebab. Japanese Wagyu beef, Morel mushrooms, 25-year-old Italian vinegar, milk-fed lamb, goat, Turkish basil, Jerusalem artichokes with La Vallée des Beaux olive oil.

'This looks amazing.' Sydney declared. 'I'm a kebab girl all day long.'

Margaret tasted her wine.

'The Quail, for me, I think. Why is it called The Poisoned Quail?'

Max looked around the table and beamed. Sparking people's imaginations and firing their taste buds was all he ever really cared about.

'Anyone care to answer that? Mr Finney?' Max asked.

'I don't know. It's not something I've ever come across. Is it a thing?'

'It is.' Max declared. 'It's been a thing across most of human history. The ancients knew of it, and I believe the most recent case of Quail poisoning happened in the 50s in France. Many people died.'

'I'll have the kebab, then.' Finney joked, and a laugh made its way around the table.

'You have my word, Mr Finney, that nothing upon this table will harm you.'

'What about the fugu?' Sydney asked.

Max smiled.

'Smoke and mirrors, Sydney. Smoke and mirrors.'

'I'll have the Quail,' Gareth said.

'Me too.' Sanjay said.

'Are you not afraid of being poisoned?' Max asked.

'Not from Quail, no.' Sanjay replied.

'Then I shall have Quail, too.' Max declared brightly. 'Coturnism be damned.'

Once again, the table looked at Max for clarification. Gemma sighed. She hated it when Max knew something others didn't, and she particularly hated it because the Quail had been her idea. Max had never heard of Coturnism before she told him about it.

'The Quail's a clever little thing,' Max began. 'It is seemingly impervious to some poisons that would kill another creature. It is believed that the bird feeds upon the seeds of the Hemlock plant, quite without risk to themselves, while simultaneously poisoning the bird's flesh, thus killing whoever eats it.'

'Perhaps I should have the kebab?' Margaret said. 'Is it too late to change my mind?'

'It's perfectly safe, Margaret.' Gemma said. 'Most Quail is harmless. It affects mostly migratory Quail from the east that nest in Central Europe, hence why the last serious case was in France. Our Quail is bred locally with no access to Hemlock.'

'Or is it?' Max teased. 'You must remember that Hemlock grows quite freely in our hedgerows.'

'I can assure you, Margaret, the Quail is safe. I've tasted it myself.' Gemma added. 'And it is disputed whether the Quail is poisoned by Hemlock at all.'

Max chuckled.

'No need to spoil a good story!' He laughed.

'So what does poison the Quail then?' Finney asked.

Gemma shrugged her shoulders.

'There is no definitive answer, but tests have shown that a plant in the Labiata family may be responsible.'

'And what plant is that?' Finney asked. 'I've never heard of it.'

Gemma sighed. She had feared someone would ask. She half expected one of the inquisitive writers around the table to ask the question, but Finney had got there first.

'It's part of the mint family.' She answered reluctantly.

'And does it grow in this country?' Max teased.

'Yes. But not on the farm where we breed the Quail.' Gemma replied.

'Then I shall have the kebab.' Margaret resolved. 'I'm too old and have survived enough bad dinners to be seen off by a bloody bird.'

'Shame!' Max declared. 'I have to say, it's one of my favourite dishes. At least I shall have more of it to eat!'

Orders for food were given and relayed back to the kitchen. The guests sat around the table, discussing nothing in particular and drinking wine. As the evening wore on, a veil of darkness began to descend. It came in slowly at first, but before long, those within the dining area could no longer focus on those outside. They sat in a small oasis of light, laughter, and good food.

The dinner was presented to the guests at the same time. Sydney's mouth salivated at the sight of her kebab, and Margaret looked on in envy as a plate of delicious-looking Quail was set down in front of the person next to her. For several long minutes, the table descended into silence. Nothing could be heard but for the scraping of knife across plate, and the gentle tinkle of glass as wine was laid onto the table.

When they had finished, the table was quickly cleared, and a dessert menu was laid in front of them.

Sydney picked hers up eagerly. Diet be damned. Tonight she was eating lavishly.

Delicious Death. Indulgent and luxurious sticky chocolate pudding lavishly draped in a chocolate sauce.

Coffin Cake. Cherry and almond loaf cake presented in coffin-shaped loaf tin.

A selection of I-Screams. A selection of luxury sorbets from around the world.

Rancid Rhubarb and Custard. Our not-so rancid rhubarb grown on the estate and served with locally produced custard.

Guilty Pleasure. Sticky date pudding with salted caramel sauce and pistachio praline.

Gareth felt his taste buds tingle. As he was now a man of a certain age, he found that weight was easy to acquire and difficult to lose. He had a relatively toned figure and was rightly proud of it, and he wanted to keep it that way, at least as long as it took for him to turn Sydney's attention his way.

'I think I want it all.' He remarked. A long sigh followed it.

'It's a no-brainer for me.' Sydney declared. 'Delicious Death all the way!'

Gareth was torn. He enjoyed chocolate and had no reason to believe it would be anything but the most incredible chocolate pudding he had ever eaten. Max's reputation in this matter was legendary. He was, however, partial to cherry and almond. He also enjoyed ice creams. They were a perfect palate cleanser. Rhubarb was also a firm favourite, and if puddings didn't come lavished in creamy custard, they weren't, in his opinion, puddings. And sticky dates! It was like he was stuck in a pudding-themed maze with no clue how to get out.

'Ice cream for me.' Margaret decided.

'Coffin Cake.' Sanjay declared.

'The rhubarb for me.' Finney joined in.

'Guilty Pleasure.' Gemma said.

Max joined Gemma in declaring his attention to have the Guilty Pleasure. It was, by far and away, his favourite dish.

Everyone looked at Gareth.

'I think I might have to have it all.' He said. 'I can't decide.' He looked up at Sydney. 'Decide for me.'

Sydney smiled and glanced at the menu.

'He'll have a Delicious Death.' She said and wondered, for a second, what a delicious death would taste like, and images of an x-rated disposition filled her mind's eye. She shook the feeling off. Why did this man make her feel this way? It annoyed her.

'That's settled then,' Gareth agreed. 'I look forward to a delicious death!'

He smiled at her, and she wobbled again.

The puddings came swiftly and were demolished similarly. Max stood and tapped a spoon on the side of his glass.

'I'm not of one for speeches,' he declared and everyone braced themselves for a speech. 'So I won't give one. Suffice to say that I hope one and all have enjoyed their meals, and there is a large selection of petit fours and cocktails on the verandah, should anyone wish to get horribly twisted with me!'

Max followed a path across his lawn that was lit on either side with a hundred low-level solar lights. Sanjay followed a dozen paces behind, chatting amicably with Finney and Gareth, his arm suitably entwined in Sydney's, a yard or two behind them.

'My dear, I wonder if you wouldn't mind helping me across the lawn,' Margaret said, addressing Gemma. 'My eyesight is much like my legs, I'm afraid. I find it's much worse at night.'

Gemma happily assisted Margaret from her chair and to the steps that led to the lawn. As they began the slow march across the lawn, Margaret slowed and gripped Gemma's arm firmly.

'There is something I think you should know, dear.' She began. 'I'm not one for telling tales, or spreading gossip, but I've grown rather fond of you over the last couple of years, and I know how much you do for that ungrateful bastard.'

Gemma smirked. Margaret's lack of love for Max in recent months was well known.

'I'm intrigued.' She said.

'As you know,' Margaret said, 'Max and I have the same publisher. Both in this country and the States, and recently, I've been getting wind of something that I think you ought to know. Pat tells me that I should say nothing. She has an unhealthy liking for the man I can't fathom, and I fear her judgement is somewhat impaired.'

Gemma smiled again. She had been witness to Pat's unhealthy liking for Max.

Margaret stopped and faced Gemma.

'You should know that Max has employed a ghostwriter for his next three books. He intends to get rid of you.'

Gemma felt the cold as it swept up the small path.

'That.. that can't be true..' She stuttered. 'I write Max's books. He's nothing without me. They're *my* books!'

'Yes, my dear, I know. But they're not your books; they're Max's. It's his name on the cover and his copyright.'

Gemma shook her head.

'He can't do that. We have a contract.' She said.

Margaret turned and continued the slow walk to where the other guests gathered.

'Contracts can be broken. Loopholes found. I trust you had it inspected by a contract lawyer?'

Gemma felt her heart miss a beat. Max had absorbed her at the time, and she had been so in love and so caught up in the thrill of it all that she had mostly taken it on trust. It was a contract. Max wouldn't have cheated her. Would he?

As they approached the verandah, Margaret said softly, 'I think you should get yourself a good lawyer. Call me tomorrow, and I'll give you the number of mine.'

Gareth enjoyed the walk across the lawn and delighted in the sweet smell of the beautiful young woman on his arm.

'I must say that's one of the most interesting meals I've ever had.' He declared. 'Deadly fugu, Poisoned Quail and a large dollop of Delicious Death!'

Sydney didn't find it particularly funny.

'It worries me that you ate the fugu. I intend to stay up with you until I'm certain you're not going to die.'

'Worried eh?' Gareth teased. 'Now that is interesting. I think, perhaps, I shall retire to bed early. You wouldn't want me to die alone, now would you?'

Sydney smiled.

'I admire your persistence, Mr Black, but it will take more than that to lure me to your bed. I will pull up a chair next to you, and sit there until the early hours, just to be sure.'

'I sleep naked, you know.'

'Then I shall close my eyes and listen for your breathing.'

Gareth admitted defeat.

'Very well, then your services will not be required this evening. If I die, I shall die alone, and it will all be your fault.'

'Oh, don't say that!.' Sydney stopped just as they reached the verandah. She had a genuine look of concern on her face.

Gareth took her hand and looked into her eyes. They were a deep, luscious brown, and he felt himself drawn to them.

''It's an illusion.' He said calmly. 'There was no more poison in that fish than there was hemlock in that Quail. You have nothing to worry about, I promise.'

'You can't promise that. You can't know that. Not for sure.'

'I can, Sydney.' Gareth assured her. 'Max is an illusionist. We all are, I suppose. As he said, it's smoke and mirrors. It's not real. Nothing about Max is genuine.'

'There you are.' Max declared as his name caught his ears. 'Come on. It's cocktail time.'

The small party gathered on the verandah. Margaret sat on a comfortable chair near the lawn, and Gemma sat beside her. Gareth and Sydney hovered at the far end of the verandah, which had been converted into an outside bar. Sanjay sat on a bar stool, and Max had gone to the other side of the bar and mixed various drinks into a shaker.

'I can make pretty much any drink you can think of.' Max declared. 'But I've created a few of my own cleverly themed drinks if anyone dares try one.'

Another glossy menu lay on the bar, and Sydney passed two across to Margaret and Gemma.

Cocktails.

Arsenic and Old Spice

Red Rum
Death on the Beach
A Very Bloody Mary
Crème de passion
Malignant Mojito

Max shook his drink and gently poured it into a frosted martini glass. He held it out for Sydney, who took a sip.

'My God, that's fiery.' She said. 'What is it?'

Max poured a second glass and held it out for Gareth.

'It's my signature cocktail. Arsenic and Old Spice. It's a secret combination of gin, tequila, and spices from the east, with a hint of chilli.'

'That's some hint!' Gareth choked.

'What can I get you, Sanjay?' Max asked.

Sanjay perused the menu and selected a Red Rum. Gemma asked for a glass of champagne and was given a bottle to share with Margaret.

'Mr Finney?'

Finney had never been much of a drinker. He tolerated champagne, but rarely drank it, and he was occasionally partial to a glass of red.

'I don't suppose you have whiskey?' He asked.

Max beamed.

'Wait there.'

He left the bar and disappeared through the French windows, returning a few minutes later carrying a bottle of Scotch and two glasses.

'I've been saving this for a special occasion. I bought a crate of the stuff a few years ago at auction. Cost me a pretty penny, I can tell you.'

He opened the bottle and smelt the aroma that escaped.

'How do you take it?' He asked.

'Neat. No ice.' Finney replied.

'A man after my own heart!'

Max poured two heavy measures and handed a glass to Finney. The two embraced the drink like it was some special event, and Finney gave an appreciative nod as the amber liquid burned his throat.

They played music from a hidden speaker connected to a smart device that was hidden somewhere on the verandah. It amused Max that no one could find it, but as soon as it received a request for a song, it began playing it.

Sanjay commanded it to play a selection of popular Indian music, which Sydney found alluring. She laid her drink on the bar and pulled Gareth onto the lawn, where the two moved rhythmically to the sound.

'I'm not much of a dancer,' Gareth pleaded but his cries went unheeded.

'I can tell,' Sydney joked, 'you're very wooden.'

Max selected some traditional Western music, and Gareth and Sydney were joined on the lawn by Gemma and Sanjay. Margaret looked on from her seat and was joined by Finney. They watched as Max walked down onto the lawn and approached Sydney. Max had put on a slow song and he gently pushed Gareth to one side.

'May I?'

Gareth stepped back politely, despite Sydney's look of protest, and Max slipped his arms around Sydney's waist, and began to move in time to the music.

'It's been a lovely evening.' Sydney said. 'I've enjoyed myself very much.'

She felt Max push his body close to hers and tried to step back, but he placed his hand in the small of her back and pulled her in.

'The night is young,' he leered.

Sydney smiled awkwardly. She felt his hand rub her back and begin a slow descent.

Politely, Sydney pushed Max away.

'I think I need a drink.' She exclaimed.

Gemma had watched the interaction and had moved to intervene. She grabbed Sydney's hand.

'Let's go make cocktails!'

Max smiled. Sydney was cute, but he'd had a hundred Sydneys. It was the thrill of the chase he revelled in. The fox didn't always catch its prey.

'I was never a good dancer,' Finney remarked as he watched the scene play out. 'Caroline was the dancer. I used to sit in the corner and be jealous of the men who could dance. I'm afraid I move like a duck on ice.'

'But I bet she always used to go home with you,' Margaret said, and Finney found the years fall away in his imagination. 'I used to dance,' Margaret said, 'but the old pins have other ideas!'

Finney looked up as Max approached. He had the bottle of whiskey in his hands and quickly refilled Finney's glass.

The night drew on, and the air was filled with laughter and music. As legs grew tired, the small party gathered in a circle next to Margaret, drank cocktails, and rambled on about nothing in particular.

Margaret stood and leant on her stick for support.

'I think that's enough for me.' She said. 'I'm not one for staying up late these days.' She turned and addressed Max directly. 'Thank you, Max, it's been a wonderful evening. You have certainly excelled yourself this year.'

'Can I walk you to your room?' Gareth said taking to his feet and stumbling.

'I think it would be safer if I took myself,' she joked, 'and that's not something I would have said forty years ago!'

Finney rose respectfully. 'I think it's time I went home, too. Perhaps I could take you to your room, Mrs Hemshaw?'

Margaret agreed, and the two said goodnight and left the party. Finney held Margaret's arm as they climbed the staircase to the first floor.

'This is me.' Margaret declared at her door. 'You'll forgive me, Mr Finney, but I won't invite you in for a nightcap. At my age, going to bed means exactly that. The spirit is willing, but the body, unfortunately, is not.'

Finney smiled.

'It's been a pleasure to have met you, Margaret. Good night.'

Finney waited as Margaret closed the door.

He returned via the large staircase and headed out the front door into the evening air. The great oaks that lined the driveway creaked and swayed in a light breeze that brought a fresh feel to the evening. As he walked down the drive, he heard voices and laughter behind him, interspersed with the faint throb of modern music being played. The large gate at the entrance was no longer manned, and he let himself out through the pedestrian gate. He closed it behind him and stepped into the lane, feeling suitably full and light-headed.

The party continued for some time on the verandah. Drinks were poured, dances were danced, and stories were told. Max stood up suddenly at around one in the morning and swayed unsteadily on his feet.

'I must away to bed!' He slurred, and for a moment, it looked as if his feet had no intention of joining him.

'Are you okay, Max?' Gemma asked as he stumbled towards the French windows.

'I'll be fine!' He declared, gripping the door frame for support. 'I can't feel my feet!'

He giggled like a drunk schoolboy and disappeared into the drawing room. There was the sound of something being walked into, followed by an 'Ouch!' and the sound of something crashing to the floor.

'Should we help him?' Sydney asked.

Gemma stood up and looked surprisingly firm on her feet.

'I'll go.' She declared. 'I know what he's like.' She added, giving Sydney a knowing look.

She returned ten minutes later.

'He does that.' Gemma said, opening another bottle of champagne and pouring four glasses. 'He gets to a stage where he can't take any more and just goes to bed. It seems rude, but it isn't. It's just a thing he does. He usually manages to get there by himself, though! Last year he left early and, well, let's just say we all saw more of Max than we were expecting.'

'Ooh. Is this about Pat?' Sydney asked. 'Do tell.'

'I don't think we need to gossip.' Sanjay said, shooting Gemma an icy look. Gemma was undeterred.

'We caught them at it last year. Poor Pat, her mother was apoplectic with rage! She bullies that girl. She bullies her terribly. And there was her precious daughter on her knees in the hallway, giving Max a you-know-what when we all piled in on them. God, it was funny!'

Sanjay was more circumspect.

'Max took advantage. She's a naive young woman. Her mother wrapped her in cotton wool all her life. She's had a miserable time since that night. I feel for her.'

'She's a grown woman, Sanjay. If her mother is so cruel, she can leave. No one forces her to stay.'

'That's not strictly true, though, is it?' Sydney said. 'I mean, controlling personalities can be very shrewd. Her daughter may not even know the extent of how much she is controlled. She may not see it. But she may believe that she has to stay with her mother, that she would have no life without her. She may not even believe that she *can* leave.'

Gemma thought about that for a second and realised there was more to Sydney than she realised.

They sat and chatted until the champagne ran dry, and Sydney got up, declaring her intention to go to bed.

'I'm exhausted,' she said. 'I must be up early tomorrow for Max's show. I wouldn't want to be hungover for it!'

Sanjay rose.

'Yes, I think I've had enough. I'll walk with you.'

'Well, I suppose that's us then,' Gareth said, rising to his feet. 'Wait for me, you two. It's a big house, and I'm not entirely sure where my room is!'

Gemma followed them into the drawing room and closed the French windows behind her. Most of the glasses and plates from the dinner had been cleared and washed earlier before the waiting staff had gone home. The rest could wait until the morning. She watched the three guests climb the staircase and disappear at the top. She turned to the front door and stepped outside, ensuring the door was locked behind her.

Sanjay opened the door to his room and said goodnight. Sydney opened hers and felt Gareth's presence nearby. His door was next to hers, and he was almost halfway through it when she said, 'Goodnight, Mr Black.'

Gareth stepped back out into the corridor. Sydney walked up to him and kissed him gently on the cheek.

'I've had fun.' She said.

Gareth leant in for another kiss, but Sydney stepped back.

'That's enough for now, Mr Black.' She teased. 'Sleep well.'

With that, she turned and disappeared into her room. Gareth stood momentarily, thinking of all the wonderful things he'd like to do to Miss Fletch, sighed, and stepped into his bedroom.

Gemma strolled down the drive beneath the great oaks until she arrived at her small cottage. She felt a presence and turned to see Fenwick standing behind her.

'Mr Fenwick, you startled me!'

'I'm sorry,' he said. 'I didn't mean to. I was just on my way home.'

Gemma could smell the beer on him. For an old man, he drank a lot. She wondered why he was so late, and then remembered that The Marlborough was a country pub. They had probably turned off all the lights and stayed for a lock-in.

'Goodnight Fenwick.'

'Goodnight, miss.'

Gemma let herself into her cottage and collapsed on her sofa, where she fell instantly asleep.

Main Course

Poisoned Quail
Breast of Quail with a pea puree, pancetta and a
marjoram jus

Bella Donna Kebab
Japanese Wagyu beef, Morel mushrooms, 25-year-old
Italian Vinegar, milk-fed lamb, goat, Turkish Basil,
Jerusalem artichokes and La Valée des Beaux olive oil

Detective Inspector Sarah Davenport showed her ID at the gate and was shown through. She strolled up the long, sweeping drive beneath the great oaks that lined it and met her Sergeant at the front door to Burnham Manor.

'Morning guv'.' He said brightly.

Davenport disliked good moods in her sergeants, particularly on Saturday mornings. Her head throbbed.

'Morning Tom. What have we got?' She asked.

'Deceased is Max Wilde. He was due to film his live show this morning but never showed up for rehearsals. His PA went to rouse him and found him dead in bed.'

'Any signs of foul play?'

'No. Nothing.'

Davenport stroked her temples. She had taken the Chief Constable's call at six thirty that morning, and he emphasised the need for a senior officer to attend.

'It's Max Wilde,' he said as if that was good enough reason to interrupt her hang-over. And you're the closest. Go and make sure it's done correctly.'

'How many people were in the house last night?' Davenport asked.

'Five. Including the deceased. The PA,' he consulted his notes, 'Gemma Collis, lives in the cottage by the front gate. There's a gardener on the estate, too.'

'Five?' Davenport asked.

'There was a dinner party last night. It's a yearly thing that Max Wilde does. All the other guests are crime writers.'

Davenport threw her sergeant a look.

'Who?'

'Margaret Hemshaw and Sanjay Chakrabati.' He glanced at his notes again. 'The other two, I don't know. Gareth Sebastian Black and Sydney Fletch.'

Davenport had heard of them. She was a big fan of Margaret Hemshaw. A copy of Sydney Fletch's book was sitting on her coffee table.

'This should be interesting.'

Her sergeant smiled.

'There was someone else there, too,' he added. 'Jack Finney.'

Davenport turned and looked at her sergeant.

'Former DCI Jack Finney?' She asked.

He nodded.

'Curiouser and curiouser! Well, if there's anything sinister here, at least we have a professional witness!'

'Wait until you see this.' He said, handing Davenport several slips of glossy paper.

'What is it?'

'Last night's menu. You should read it.'

Davenport paused as she was about to climb the large steps to the Manor. She read the menus and then reread them.

'That is interesting,' she said. 'Is fugu legal in this country? Where do you even get it from?'

'I don't know. I've made a few calls. We should find out soon enough.'

'Any chance Max was accidentally poisoned?'

Her sergeant shook his head.

'That was my first thought. I've spoken to everyone, but they all ate the same things, and no one feels unwell. Max's local Doctor is here. Miss Collis called him after finding Mr Wilde's body.'

They found Dr Harris in the drawing room.

'DI Davenport,' she said, introducing herself, 'this is Sergeant Graves.'

Dr Harris nodded a silent good morning.

'A DI? That's a big egg for sudden death, isn't it? He asked.

'Not really,' Davenport suggested. 'Max Wilde is a big name in the village and an important figure in the county. We want to make sure everything is done by the book. We always investigate sudden death.'

'Of course. In my experience, though, it's usually uniformed officers.'

'As I say, it's out of respect for who Max Wilde was. I understand you are Max's doctor. Have you known him long?'

'I've been a doctor in the village for thirty years. I've known Max since he was a boy.'

'Anything in his medical history we should know about? Any heart conditions, recent surgeries, family risks, allergies?'

Dr Harris shook his head.

'Nothing. Max was in the prime of his life. I rarely knew him to be ill. As part of his contracts with his publishers and management company, he visits me twice yearly for a health check. On the last check, he was perfectly well.'

'Thank you, Doctor. I understand you were called here this morning by Miss Collis. What time was that?'

'She called around five-thirty. I was here a few minutes later. I confirmed that Max was dead at five forty-eight this morning.'

'How long had he been dead?'

'I don't know. A few hours, at least. The autopsy should give you a more accurate time.'

'Did you see any indication of what may have caused his death?'

'Nothing at all, I'm afraid. Nothing immediately struck me. I shouldn't wonder if it turns out to be a rare case of Sudden Adult Death Syndrome. Rare, but not unheard of.'

'Thank you, Doctor Harris. We'll be in touch.'

Doctor Harris took his cue to leave and left the room.
'Let's see the body.'

Max's room was luxuriously decorated. Soft, grey carpet lay beneath their feet, and at every point where it met a wall, antique bedroom furniture stood in quiet testament to his wealth. Max's bed was a vast, bespoke piece of furniture, almost twice the size of the largest bed Davenport had ever slept in. Max lay to the right side, looking up at the ceiling, his arms down by his side but above the bedsheets. A bedside table was illuminated to his right, and a half-drunk glass of liquid sat there.

'How was he found?' Davenport asked.

Sergeant Graves checked his notes.

'He was lying on his right side, with his legs drawn up to his chest in the foetal position. Miss Collis remarked that he looked peaceful.'

Death was peaceful, Davenport thought. It didn't mean the dying was. She paid particular attention to the glass of liquid on the bedside table.

'Have the liquid bagged and checked.' Then, as it occurred to her, 'What happened to the dishes and drinks served at the dinner?'

'None of the leftover food was thrown away. We can take samples of everything eaten and drunk at the dinner party.'

'Good. See if we can get it fast-tracked. They owe me a favour at the lab. Drop my name.'

Davenport walked over to the side of the bed and looked down at the famous Max Wilde.

'You can release the body to the undertakers.' She said solemnly. 'Take him to the mortuary. The coroner will want to conduct an autopsy as quickly as possible.' She paused and looked up at Sergeant Graves. 'I suppose we ought to interview the guests.'

Max had an office on the ground floor of Burnham Manor that looked out across the lawn to where last night's dinner was held. It was an airy room. The curtains had been drawn back fully, and the windows opened. Bookcases ran across several walls and, in the centre of the room, sat a squat-looking log burner beneath a massive mantelpiece. There was a picture on the mantelpiece of Max Wilde with Richard Osman standing in front of that very log burner. The two were chatting amicably. Over the mantelpiece was a large, framed print that declared, "Ten Commandments of Detective Fiction, by Ronald Knox." The print was signed.

Davenport took a chair next to a corner sofa and waited while Sergeant Graves brought in Gemma Collis. She sat on the couch and dabbed at her eyes. They were puffy and red.

'I understand you were Max Wilde's assistant?'

Gemma sniffed. Through the tears, she said: 'Yes. I've been with him for years.'

'This must be very difficult for you,' Davenport said in her most soothing and reassuring voice. 'You understand in the case of sudden and unexplained death, we have to investigate?'

'Of course.'

'Tell me about last night.'

Quietly and in considerable detail, Gemma relayed the events of the previous evening.

'How was Max when you took him to bed?' Davenport asked.

'He was very drunk. Unsteady on his feet.'

'Did he get into bed, or did you help him?'

'I helped him. He fell asleep almost right away.'

'And you returned to your guests?'

Gemma nodded.

'Who poured the glass of water by his bedside?'

'I don't know. I suppose Max must have got up for a drink in the middle of the night.'

'You didn't pour it for him?'

'No.'

'Tell me about the menu.' Davenport asked. 'Whose idea was it? Who sourced the ingredients? Who cooked it? Do you remember who ate what?'

It had been Max's suggestion. He designed the menu with his brother, Robert. They sourced the ingredients together. She didn't know where the fugu came from. The chef from The Marlborough cooked the food last night, apart from the fugu, which Mr Fukushima prepared. As best she could, Gemma listed what everyone had eaten last night and the drinks they consumed.

'Thank you, Miss Collis. Would you send Robert Wilde to see us?'

***

Robert Wilde strode purposefully into the office and closed the door behind him. He sat on a chair, as indicated by Sergeant Graves.

'My condolences for your loss, Mr Wilde.'

Robert bowed his head, but beyond that, he betrayed little emotion.

'I understand you and your brother were partners?' Davenport asked.

'In some of his affairs, yes.' Robert agreed. 'We run several successful restaurants in the country. We have a kitchen in Burnham, one in Edinburgh and two in London. I have very little to do with his other ventures.'

'Max hosted an event last night for some of his crime writing colleagues. I believe you, and he designed the menu.'

Davenport laid out the glossy menus in front of Robert.

'That's right.'

'But you didn't cook them? I understand a chef from The Marlborough came over for that.'

'That's correct. I had business in London. We have rooms above one of our restaurants. I stayed there overnight and rushed back first thing this morning after I learned of my brother's death.'

Sergeant Graves made a few notes. Davenport waited until his pen had stopped scratching the paper before continuing.

'We were wondering about the fugu. How did you source it, and who prepared it? Whether or not it's even legal to serve in the UK?'

She looked for some sign of anxiety on Robert's face but found only amusement.

'You should know,' Robert said, 'that nothing on last night's menu was poisonous or illegal. There's a fugu club in London which, for a hefty sum, will import and serve fugu to their members. It's a sought-after delicacy.'

'As I understand it, the fugu wasn't imported. An alleged Japanese fugu expert prepared and served it here at Burnham Manor. You should know that our lawyers are currently looking at the legality of it.'

'The fish served at dinner last night wasn't poisonous.' Robert said. 'It was theatre, nothing more.'

'But the fish is poisonous?' Davenport asked. 'It was a genuine puffer fish?'

'It was.' Robert admitted. 'But the fish itself isn't poisonous. It contains no naturally occurring poisons. The fish acquires the tetrodotoxin by consuming other

153

fish and sea-life with it, and that's how it comes to contain it. Pufferfish bred in captivity, fed on a diet which does not contain the poison, are not poisonous. There's a whole industry in Japan that specialises in non-toxic fugu.'

Graves wrote it down. Davenport raised an eyebrow. Robert smiled.

'That's detective writers for you,' he said. 'They can be quite devious. You shouldn't trust them.'

Davenport watched as Robert spoke the words. Four of the dinner guests were celebrated crime writers. She sincerely hoped that it would turn out that Max Wilde had died of natural causes.

'Thank you, Mr Wilde. As soon as we discover your brother's cause of death, we'll be in touch. I assume you are his next of kin? He wasn't married, was he?'

'No, he wasn't. And yes, unless he's stipulated otherwise in his will, I'm his next of kin.'

Robert rose and bade them goodbye. It was interesting, she thought, how Robert Wilde had tactfully, yet discreetly, pointed at an alibi and told her simultaneously that he didn't know the contents of his brother's will. He also suggested several suspects, all of whom should not be trusted. She rubbed her temples. It was a hazard of the job that she always saw the worst in people.

***

Davenport looked across at Graves.

'Get statements from the chef who did the cooking last night and the Japanese chef who prepared the fugu.'

Graves nodded and left the room, returning a few minutes later with Margaret Hemshaw close behind.

'I would very much like to go home,' Margaret declared firmly, pushing Graves to one side with the tip of her walking stick and addressing Davenport directly. 'I'm tired, and my daughter is waiting outside in the car to take me home. I see no good reason for being held here against my will.'

Davenport rose.

'Of course, Mrs Hemshaw. You are free to go when you wish. In the case of sudden death, we like to ensure we do everything right. I wonder if you wouldn't mind answering a couple of questions before you go? It won't take a minute.'

'Oh, very well,' Margaret said, sitting on the spot Robert had just vacated. 'Be quick about it. My daughter can be very impatient.'

Davenport sat down and said, 'Can you tell me about the meal last night?'

Margaret ran through the previous night's events, ending when Mr Finney had kindly shown her to her room. She detailed everything she had eaten and drank and tried remembering what Max had consumed. She did not see Max eat or drink anything that another guest had not eaten or drunk. She fell asleep quickly and heard nothing until she rose for breakfast that morning.

'Thank you, Mrs Hemshaw. You've been very helpful.'

Graves helped Margaret get up and led her out of the office. He returned a few minutes later with Sanjay Chakrabarti.

Sanjay's story was much like Mrs Hemshaw's. It didn't deviate in the slightest. Max had seemed perfectly well in the moments before he retired to bed, if a little unsteady on his feet. Apart from that, he had appeared in good spirits. Once he had retired to bed, Sanjay had stayed there until the morning and never left his room. He had nothing more to add.

Gareth Black faced Davenport and smiled.

'It's hard to believe we were all chatting to the poor man just a few hours ago.' He remarked. 'Heart attack, I suppose?'

'We won't know until the autopsy.' Davenport said. 'Perhaps you could run through last night for us?'

Gareth had an eye for detail. He remembered everything everyone ate and drank and said that he didn't see Max consume anything that at least one other guest didn't. He gave an accurate time for when Mr Finney had escorted Margaret to her room and for when Max had been helped to his room by Gemma. She had been gone for no more than fifteen minutes. He noticed nothing untoward in Max's demeanour.

Sydney Fletch answered her questions in much the same manner as Gareth. She was matter-of-fact and detailed. She omitted no detail, however small, and could think of nothing Max had consumed that hadn't been consumed by someone else.

'I suppose, if it was food poisoning or something, at least one of us would have been ill, too?' Sydney asked.

'Yes. If it were bad enough to kill an otherwise fit young man, it would at least have made the next person very ill. And no one else has been ill.'

Sydney expressed her sadness at Max's passing and left the room.

'Make sure you have everyone's contact details,' Davenport said.

Sergeant Graves held a sheet of paper aloft. It contained everyone's telephone numbers, addresses, and email addresses.

Davenport glanced at her watch. There was one more person she wanted to interview.

***

She found Jack Finney standing at the door to The Larches in conversation with an elderly lady, who leant on an old walking stick for support. They both turned as Davenport and Graves walked down the path.

'This is the police, Grace. You must excuse us. I'm sure they have some questions for me!'

Grace smiled at the young police officers and gave Finney a knowing look. It was a look that told Finney that she would return later and that she expected details.

Davenport held out her warrant card.

'I know who you are, Detective Constable Davenport. Come in.'

'It's Inspector, now, sir.' She said, 'I'm surprised you remember me. This is Sergeant Graves.'

'Come in, come in!' Finney said, leading them into his little cottage and showing them both to a large settee where they settled in. 'Of course I remember you. I never forget a thing or a person. If I'm honest, I forget things occasionally, but never people. Congratulations on your promotion. I always knew you'd go far. Can I get you tea?'

A few minutes later, they were all sitting, drinking tea, eating biscuits, and reminiscing about the old days.

'I was very sorry to hear about your wife,' Davenport said delicately. It had been a few years, but she was sure it was still raw.

Finney lifted a picture frame on a coffee table beside his armchair. Caroline.

'That's very kind of you to remember her,' Finney said. 'It was hard, to begin with. I was angry that she had left me, but I've accepted it over the years. One begins to understand life the older one gets!'

Davenport sipped at her tea.

'I suppose you've heard about Max Wilde?'

Finney chuckled.

'There are no secrets in a village like Burnham-on-the-Wold.' Finney said. 'Gossip flies through villages like this before the truth has got its boots on. Sudden death, I suppose?'

Davenport said that it was.

'How come you were at the dinner last night?' She asked.

'Purely by accident.' Finney answered. 'I'd never met the man until a few weeks ago. I knew he lived here, of course. Had a few drinks at The Marlborough. Met his brother. Then I met Max at the summer fête he holds at his house. I came second in the Marrow growing competition. His gardener pipped me to the title, not unexpectedly, and that was where I met him. His assistant, Miss Collis, recognised my name. She knew all about the Painswick Poisoning case and introduced me to Max. He invited me to his dinner party, thinking his guests would find me interesting.'

'Can you tell me about last night?' Davenport asked.

Finney's statement was a carbon copy of everyone else's. They all told the same story.

'Once you left the party, you showed Mrs Hemshaw to her room and came home? You never saw Max after that?'

Finney shook his head.

'I'm afraid not. Sorry.'

Davenport and Graves made their way up the path from The Larches and walked back towards the Manor, passing The Marlborough. Several cars lined the narrow country lane, and Davenport recognised some of the journalists from the local papers. Bad news travelled fast. Within a couple of hours, the nationals would join them.

'What happened to his wife?' Graves asked as they walked up the long drive to Burnham Manor.

'It was just as the Painswick case cracked.' Davenport started. 'It had been ten years to the day when his daughter had died. I don't think the two of them ever got over it. I knew Caroline to speak to. She was a lovely woman. On the tenth anniversary of their daughter's death, she filled herself a hot bath, poured a glass of wine, and opened her arteries with a razor blade. Finney found her like that when he got home. He retired from the police a few months later and retired from Gloucester after that. He moved out here a few years ago. I'm ashamed to say we all pretty much forgot about him. I guess he's found his peace out here.'

She turned and looked at the oak trees as they swayed in a gentle breeze. It was peaceful, she thought and then turned to her sergeant.

'There's nothing more for us to do here. Let's get back to the station. We should know how Max Wilde died by Monday. Then we can put this to bed.'

***

'Everything all right, guv?'

DI Davenport had never fully understood how Seargent Graves had acquired his stripes. He was not known in the station for being the sharpest tool in the box, but he had something that most other officers lacked. Empathy. He had an uncanny ability to tap into the mood of the person he was with. It was a skill that worked wonders during interrogations and, like now, to sense Davenport's mood.

She had barely acknowledged it herself. It was nothing more than a lump in her throat. An uneasy feeling. A sense of something not quite right.

'I don't know.' Davenport replied. 'Something feels off.'

Graves remained quiet as he watched the turmoil pass the Inspector's eyes.

Davenport thought about Max Wilde and his guests. She thought about the menu, the drinks and the fugu. Fugu.

'You spoke to the Japanese bloke?' She asked.

'Yes. And his granddaughter. I have their statements here.'

Graves pushed a file over to Davenport. Davenport ignored it.

'Give me the bones, Seargent.'

'Mr Fukushima was on Max Wilde's show earlier in the year. Max invited him and his granddaughter to the UK to prepare fugu sashimi for his guests. They arrived last week and attended Max Wilde's dinner party last night. Mr Fukushima prepared the fugu, after which he and his granddaughter returned to The Marlborough Hotel.'

Davenport tapped the table with her index finger.

'And the legality of fugu in this country?' She asked.

'According to our legal experts, it is not necessarily illegal, although they have confirmed that it is possible to breed non-toxic fugu. The problem is that Max wasn't the only one to eat the fish.'

'So if the fish was poisoned, we should have more than one victim?'

'Yes.' Graves nodded. 'And that goes for all the other food on the menu. Everybody had a bit of everything.'

Davenport hummed.

'So Max Wilde did not die of food poisoning.' She declared.

Graves agreed.

'All the leftover food was recovered and is in the lab waiting to be tested. Just in case.'

'The elephant in the room, of course,' Davenport mused, 'is that did someone wish Max Wilde dead, and did they poison him?'

'If they did, it wasn't in the food.' Graves added.

'What about the drink?'

'Same issue.' Graves said. 'No one drank from a bottle that wasn't drunk out of by another guest. They all shared the same drinks.'

'Then why the hell do I have an anxious feeling in the pit of my stomach? What the hell is bugging me?'

'Perhaps it's all the celebrities?' Graves pondered. 'It's high profile. It's career-making stuff. Or career ending, if it all goes wrong.'

Davenport smiled.

'Thanks for that!' She joked.

Graves smiled.

'Sorry. But I'm glad you're leading this one. The whole country's going to be watching.'

Davenport sighed. He was right. If Max Wilde's death turned out to be anything other than natural causes, she was going to be front and centre of the spotlight.

'Can I get you a drink, guv? Tea?'

'A glass of water would be nice….'

Davenport sat bolt upright.

'Guv?'

'The water. The water's bugging me.'

'Why?' Graves asked. 'It's not unusual to take a glass of water to bed.'

'No. But I'm anxious, and the water is making me more so. We did bag it up, didn't we?'

'It's at the lab. They'll run it through some tests next week.'

Davenport reached over to her phone and dialled a number. It picked up on the second ring.

'It's Davenport. Yes. DI Davenport. Who's in the lab today? Good. Put him on for me, would you.'

There was a short pause.

'Afternoon Akim, it's DI Davenport. I take it you're running the show there this afternoon? Good. I've got a favour to ask. We sent a load of foodstuffs to the lab today from Max Wilde's place. Yeah, that's the one. Could you pop something at the head of the queue? It was a glass of water. Yeah, hang on.' Davenport looked up as Graves bore down on her with a list of evidence retrieved from Burnham Manor. 'Okay, it's bag number MW3816. Yeah. Full tox screen. I know that's expensive. Today, if possible. Okay. Thanks, Akim, I owe you one.'

Davenport hung up and settled back into her chair.

'Could take a few hours. How about some coffee?'

***

Gareth twisted the throttle on his Suzuki motorcycle and felt every part of its 1300cc engine grunt immediately to life. He found the twisty lanes of the Gloucestershire countryside much to his liking, although here and there, they showed signs of severe neglect. He had no particular plan, and he liked it that way. He had no home to speak of, just a cheap little flat on the south coast, which he returned to now and then when the fancy took him. It didn't take him that way now. He dropped onto the M6 and headed north, looking at the roadsigns for inspiration.

He was free-spirited, and it suited him. He went where he wanted, when he wanted, and he answered to no one. He enjoyed the nomadic lifestyle, and since his last book had gone through the roof, he no longer had to concern himself with money. What did concern him, as he pulled into services to re-fuel, was Sydney Fletch. She had got completely under his skin.

As they had left Burnham Manor that morning, the small collection of crime writers had exchanged numbers and email addresses. The death of Max Wilde had a strangely unifying effect on them. They had all become lifelong members of a unique clique whose numbers would only diminish and never increase. They had become the last people to have seen Max Wilde in his final moments, forever linked by the tragic circumstances surrounding his death.

Sydney had walked with Gareth to his bike and had implored him to take care. Bikes made her nervous. He assured her he would.

'Call me.' She said as he donned his helmet and fired up his bike.

'Try stopping me!' He joked.

He had watched her in his mirrors as her eyes followed him, riding down the sweeping, long drive to the gate and disappearing into the lane beyond.

Several hours later, he pulled up at an isolated inn on the edge of the Lake District and secured a room for the night. Tomorrow, he would dive into the mountains and go exploring.

He ate a light meal in a corner of the pub and drank a cool beer. He was entirely absorbed in people-watching when his phone buzzed, and he half expected to see a message from Sydney.

It wasn't from Sydney.

He read the message twice and was about to set his phone down, thinking it was a wrong number, when he received another message. Like the first one, it was anonymous. He read that one several times before closing his phone and wondered.

He finished his beer and ordered another. His plans for tomorrow had changed. Sir Arthur Conan Doyle once said, "There was villainy afoot," and he was curious to see where it led.

But first, he would ring Fletch.

***

Margaret Hemshaw was happy to be home. She liked home. She much preferred it to elsewhere, which often did not contain the things in life that gave her pleasure.

Pat had driven them back to her little home in silence. She seemed inelegantly grief-stricken.

'People die, Pat. Pull yourself together.'

So they had driven in silence, and Margaret listened to the radio as tributes were being paid to the celebrity chef and best-selling crime writer, who had mysteriously died during the night.

'Sycophants, the lot of them,' she declared as Pat pulled up in front of Lilac Cottage. 'Probably didn't even like the man when he was alive, and now they're all out to be a part of his death.'

'At least you made no secret of your dislike for Max.' Pat said as she helped her mother out of the car.

'I did not like the man, and I will not say I did, just because he's dead.' Margaret said. 'But I did not wish that for the man, though I daresay some did.'

Pat wondered who she meant.

It was a bittersweet day. What had started as a beautiful summer's day, albeit clouded by Max's death, had taken on an altogether different feel by evening. The wind had picked up, and dark clouds swept over the horizon, bringing a hint of rain. The weather seemed to reflect the mood in Lilac Cottage. It became dark and broody.

Margaret sat in her armchair and watched as raindrops gathered on the windows and began streaming down. Pat was absorbed in a book.

Margaret reached over and picked up her phone as it vibrated. She read the message that had been sent and ignored it. The second message followed swiftly on the first. This one piqued her interest. She looked up as Pat's phone made an awful noise. She, too, reached over and read a message. When the second one came, Pat looked at her mother and then sheepishly back at her phone.

'Is there something you need to tell me, Pat?'

Pat placed her phone on silent and dropped it face down on the arm of her chair.

'No.'

Margaret held her hand out.

'Show me the message you just got.' Margaret demanded.

'I won't.' Pat said defiantly.

'Patricia Hemshaw, give me your phone this instant!'

Pat knew at once the kind of mood her mother was in and knew there was no defying her when she was like this. It wasn't worth the trauma. She gave her mother her phone and waited. She didn't need to tell her the passcode. Her mother knew everything.

Margaret read the two messages Pat had just received. They were identical to the ones she had received.

I saw you.

And then:

Be at the Winterbrook River Cruiser, Wallingford, at 1 pm tomorrow. Non-attendance is not recommended.

'What's the meaning of this?' Margaret asked.

'I could ask you the same, mother. I assume you got the same message?'

'That's neither here nor there,' Margaret stumbled, momentarily forgetting that she had received the same message. 'Tell me what they saw. What did they see, Pat?'

Pat retrieved her phone and stood before her mother. For the first time, she looked down upon an old woman and felt her embarrassment subside. What could she do? More to the point, what had she *done?*

'You first,' Pat said. 'What did *you* do, mother?'

'I don't suppose it matters. I haven't done anything to reproach myself for, though I suspect you cannot say the same.' She looked at her daughter, and Pat began to wilt. 'We won't be going, anyway. It's just someone's idea of a sick joke.'

'Do you think it has something to do with Max?' Pat asked.

It hadn't even occurred to Margaret to think it had anything to do with anything else. She was about to reply when Pat's phone buzzed. She answered it quickly.

'Sanjay. Yes. You too? I don't know. I suppose so. Mum got one, too. It must be about Max, mustn't it? Okay, yes. I'll see you there at one.'

'We're not going.' Margaret insisted as Pat hung up.

'We might not be, but I am.' Pat argued, and she added extra defiance for good measure. 'Sanjay thinks it's a good idea if we went if only to see what it's all about.'

Margaret pondered her dilemma for a moment or two. She wasn't keen on letting Pat out of her sight for too long.

'Very well, then, I shall come along as well.' Margaret said. 'But, mark my words. No good will come of this. No good will come of this at all.'

***

Finney sat in his conservatory and listened to the rain as it hammered down on the roof. For a few brief seconds, the night sky was illuminated as a streak of lightning zipped across the horizon, and a rumble of thunder echoed in the hills around. He was about to pour himself another shot of whiskey when he heard his front doorbell ring, followed by a knock. It had just gone nine o'clock, and no one he knew would call at such a late hour. He walked through his small cottage and unlatched his front door. Beyond stood a damp Sydney Fletch beneath a large umbrella. Lightning flashed ominously behind her.

'Sydney.' Finney exclaimed. 'What on earth are you doing here?'

'May I come in?' Sydney asked.

'Of course, come in, come in!'

Finney closed the door behind her and divested the young woman of her raincoat. Sydney dropped her wet umbrella into an umbrella stand and looked at Finney. She wore a light grey hoodie and blue jeans, and when she smiled, Finney noticed that her face appeared to come alive. She was even more beautiful than he remembered her being, even if he had only last seen here the previous evening.

Finney offered tea and biscuits, and the two sat opposite each other in front of an unlit log burner.

'I'm sorry to drop in unannounced.' Sydney began. 'I wasn't sure of the right thing to do, and then, when Gareth rang me and told me that the others had got the message, I seemed to get even more confused. Then I thought of you.'

She waited as Finney digested what she had just said, then realised she must have been talking gibberish. She opened her phone and passed it to Finney. 'Read this.'

She waited as Finney read the message.

'You said the others had received the message,' Finney asked. 'Who, exactly?'

'Gareth and Sanjay. Gareth learned from Sanjay that Margaret and Pat Hemshaw also got the message.

Finney considered this.

'Pat is Margaret's daughter,' Finney mused. 'She wasn't at the dinner.'

Sydney shook her head. 'No. But we did learn something about Pat after you left.'

Briefly, Sydney filled Finney in about the scandal between Max and Pat.

'That would explain Margaret's hostility.' Finney said.

Finney sat quietly for a few minutes, considering this new turn of events.

'If I'm being honest, I would counsel caution.' Finney began. 'I wouldn't go. It's most likely someone's idea of a joke. A poor joke, for sure, and not funny.'

'But..' Sydney started, looking for the right way to express herself. 'It kind of implies that Max's death may not be natural, doesn't it?'

Finney had already considered that possibility.

'In a way, it does.' He agreed. He read the text message on Sydney's phone again. 'But it seems very vague. Deliberately so. *"I saw you."* But it doesn't say what they saw or why it might be relevant. It seems deliberately speculative.'

'I don't follow?' Sydney said.

'Well, we don't know that Max was murdered. There's nothing that I know of that suggests that might be the case. But somebody may have seen something, heard something, or witnessed something that didn't make sense at the time but does now that Max is dead.'

'Surely, if they had seen something, they would have seen the "who" as well?'

'Not necessarily. They may have witnessed the mechanics of murder but not the executioner. Equally, they may have heard snippets of a conversation but not those engaged in it. Not until Max's death, and sometime later, does what they have seen or heard make sense. But they still don't know who.'

Sydney took her phone back.

'So what does this mean?' She asked.

'It means someone's gone fishing.' Finney said. 'They're hoping that they're right and that one of those people invited via that message will give themselves away.'

'Blackmail.' Sydney said.

'Indeed. Blackmail. And a very dangerous kind. The kind that can get you killed. Murder is easy once you've done it for the first time. Blackmailing a murderer is a bit like sticking your neck in the lion's mouth at dinner time and prodding him in the ribs with a stick.'

Sydney laughed at the analogy.

'I think I'm going to go.' Sydney said forthrightly. 'Gareth will be there, and Sanjay. I think it might be fun.'

'You have a disturbed idea of what constitutes fun,' Finney joked.

They were interrupted by Finney's phone, which picked that moment to spring to life. He answered it on the third ring.

'Hello? Yes. Oh, hello. Yes, of course. No, no, that's quite alright.' There was a long pause as Sydney watched the expressions change on Finney's face. 'I see. Yes. That's kind of you to let me know. Yes, of course. Thank you. Good night.'

Finney hung up and stood up. He walked over to his whiskey bottle, poured two large glasses, and handed one to Sydney.

'Well,' he said, considering his words. 'That changes everything.'

He sat back in his armchair and took a long, slow sip of his drink.

'What is it?' Sydney asked. 'What's wrong?'

'That was DI Davenport.' Finney replied. 'I always knew she was a good copper. She has an instinct for it. She rang out of professional courtesy, given how I was present at Max's dinner party.'

Sydney waited patiently for what she knew was coming.

'He was murdered, wasn't he?' Sydney asked.

'They don't know for sure, but that's where the investigation is heading. They are pushing through with the autopsy. It'll be held tomorrow. It seems DI Davenport was a bit suspicious of a glass of water next to Max's bedside, which she had rushed through toxicology. She's just had the results.'

'Poison?' Sydney asked.

'The tests show the water contained a deadly amount of an alkaloid called Coniine.'

Sydney shook her head.

'I don't know what that is.'

Finney smiled, although Sydney detected no humour there.

'You heard it mentioned last night,' Finney explained. 'It's the main alkaloid in Hemlock.'

Sydney gasped. 'The Quail.'

'Indeed, the poisoned quail. They're testing all the food and drink that was eaten last night, but Davenport's convinced Max was poisoned via that glass of water. Besides, I remember several people eating quail.'

'That's right. You and I had the kebab. And so did Margaret. Sanjay, Gareth and Max all ate quail.'

'So, even if the murderer was poisoning a lot of Max's food to ensure he got a lethal dose, it couldn't have been in the quail. Besides, the glass by Max's bedside contained enough Coniine to do the trick.'

'I can't remember if Max ate or drank anything that someone else didn't share with him.' Sydney pointed out.

Together, they ran through what they could remember from the previous evening. Finney made notes. They determined, without a shadow of a doubt, that Max never consumed anything that at least one other person didn't also consume.

'The glass of water it is, then. Although I don't see why that is so important?' Sydney said.

'Because Max is unlikely to have poured his water before bed.' Finney mused. 'That means someone *inside* the house poisoned it.' He looked directly at Sydney. 'Tell me what happened after I left.'

Sydney ran through the events succinctly. She ended just before she kissed Gareth goodnight.

'So Max was taken to bed after I had helped Margaret to her room.'

'Yes.'

'And then, later, you all retired to bed at the same time.'

'Yes.'

'Who locked the house?'

'I assumed it was Gemma. She has her own cottage in the grounds.'

Two questions for Gemma, then, Finney thought. Was there a glass of water on Max's bedside when she helped him to bed, and did she lock up before she went home?

'Did you leave your room at any time during the night?' Finney asked.

'No.'

'Did you hear anyone else leave their rooms?'

'No.'

'Did you do anything that might have prompted someone to send you that text message?' Finney asked.

'Nothing. Nothing at all.'

Sydney waited as Finney's eyes glazed over, and he retreated within his thoughts.

'Is there anything else I should know?' Finney asked a few minutes later.

Briefly, Sydney described the day she shared with Gareth. She started with Gemma performing a sex act on Robert in the kitchen, followed by their tour of the gardens and the poison garden. Her description of Fenwick was colourful, and Finney remembered the grizzled old man he had seen as he had walked up the lane to Burnham Manor with Grace. Sydney described the maze, the argument with Margaret, Sanjay, Max's brother, and the strange young woman who performed a similar act on Max. Finney raised an eyebrow.

'Young women certainly love the Wilde brothers!' He exclaimed.

Sydney raised an eyebrow. They didn't do it for her. She thought of Gareth and felt her heart skip a beat. She needed to have a word with her body. It had a habit of reacting to thoughts of Gareth, with unexpected, if not unpleasant, results.

'That's a lot to work with,' Finney mused. 'I daresay there's more we don't know.'

Sydney took a long sip of her drink and relished the sharp assault on her tastebuds.

'I wonder why you didn't get a message?' She asked.

Finney smiled and nodded. He pulled a sweet from his tin and popped it into his mouth.

'You're a smart young woman, Sydney.' He said. 'I was hoping you would ask that. It proves to me that you have the makings of a detective. Question everything. Trust no one. As it is, I am an outsider. I have nothing in common with the rest of you, and we move in different circles. In truth, I suspect that whoever sent that message did not want professional eyes watching their every move. It may be easy to deceive some people, but I have a lifetime's experience in deception. I can smell it a mile off. It's akin to performing a magic trick in front of magicians. They're bound to see the sleight of hand.'

'Do you think I should go tomorrow?' Sydney asked.

'I do not. I think that someone is playing a dangerous game. Now that we know that Max may have been murdered, we need to consider another possibility. We need to consider that the person who sent that text message is the murderer.'

'But why?' Sydney asked. 'What could they hope to achieve by it?'

'Assuming that only one person is involved in the murder, everyone else is a witness. But what have we witnessed? Right this minute, there is the possibility that someone is sitting somewhere, wondering if they have gotten away with it. They know for sure that the police will discover that Max was murdered, and they'll want to be sure no one knows something they shouldn't. The only way they can do that, without raising suspicion, is to bring everyone together.'

'Another fishing expedition.' Sydney remarked

'Yes. A dangerous one. I would feel more comfortable if you didn't go. You may not know what it is that you know, and you may give yourself away to a killer. It's far too dangerous.'

'Then come with me.' Sydney said.

'I haven't been invited.' Finney countered.

'All the more reason to come.' Sydney argued. 'Only three people will know you haven't been invited. You, me, and the killer. If you're there, they'll likely get spooked and give themselves away.'

Finney swallowed the remains of his sweet and drained his glass. He got up, fetched the whiskey bottle, and poured two more large measures.

'I shouldn't,' Sydney protested. 'I have to drive.'

'I have a spare room,' Finney argued. 'If we're going to go hunting for a killer, we need to work together.'

'You'll come, then?' Sydney asked enthusiastically.

'Against my better judgement, yes. I'll come. I have a feeling that even if I didn't, you'd still go, and I'd feel guilty if you ended up being murdered.'

'Excellent.' Sydney said. She took the glass of whiskey and settled into her chair.

'I only have one rule.' Finney said. 'You must trust no one. And, I mean, no one. Not even young Gareth Black.'

Sydney felt herself begin to blush. Mr Finney missed nothing.

'And what about me?' Sydney asked. 'What if I'm the killer, and this is some bizarre challenge I have concocted so that we can play a deadly game of cat and mouse?'

'Then I accept the challenge.' Finney declared. 'Remember, everyone's a suspect. Trust no one, and doubt everything you are told. If you are the murderer, I will find out.'

Sydney raised her glass into the air.

'Well, I'm not. So here's to a successful hunting expedition.'

***

By the time morning broke, the storm had long passed over. Sydney sat in Finney's kitchen and drank coffee, and the two conspirators plotted a strategy.

'No one must know that we have spoken.' Finney insisted. 'If the invite is from the killer, they will know I haven't been invited. If they know that you asked for me to go, then your life will be in danger.'

'What about your life?' Sydney asked.

'Murderers are vain creatures, by and large. My presence will intrigue them but won't worry them unduly. They may be more cautious, so we must redouble our observations.'

They talked for an hour and mulled over several strategies. It was clear that whoever had sent the invites was worried that they had said or done something that would give them away. It may be something small and, on the face of it, innocuous. Between them, they needed to piece together their observations for the night of Max's murder and those of everyone else who was present. To do that, they needed to get people to talk.

'Easier said than done,' Sydney remarked. 'Writers write, we don't talk. We write, and we listen.'

'Then we must draw them out.' Finney said. 'I think they will open up to you,' he added. 'You're young and personable.'

And pretty, he mused.

Sydney glanced at the clock on the wall.

'I should go home and get changed,' she said, rising. 'We shouldn't be seen arriving together. I'll see you at one o'clock.'

***

The autopsy on Max Wilde was undertaken early tha next day.

DI Davenport and Sergeant Graves had watched the proceedings from the viewing platform that looked down over the laboratory. They watched as Max's body underwent a thorough and detailed examination. His body was photographed, and evidence was taken. The young doctor who carried out the autopsy gave a monotone running commentary and detailed his discoveries as he found them. When they had finished, Max's body was returned to the mortuary, and the young doctor and his assistant gathered their findings and gathered in Conference Room One.

'Good morning, DI Davenport.' Dr Akim beamed as the two police officers took their seats. 'Shall we have coffee?'

Akim directed the question at his assistant, who dutifully prepared coffee and sat them down in front of everyone.

'Sorry to get you out on a Sunday,' Davenport said, 'but the Chief Super thought it was important.'

'Death never sleeps.' Akim said. 'Although the bodies are not usually in any kind of hurry. Tomorrow would have sufficed, but as we are here, shall we begin?'

Dr Akim went through the formalities of confirming the deceased's identity, age, date of birth and address. None of that was in dispute.

'The body showed no signs of trauma. In terms of his health, I should say Mr Wilde was at the peak of physical fitness. We have examined the contents of his stomach, which does little more than confirm what we already knew he ate the previous evening. Given the rate of digestion, I should say Max Wilde died between one o'clock and two o'clock on Saturday morning.'

'Does that tell us anything about what time Max may have consumed the fatal dose of Coniine?' Davenport asked.

'Not really, no.' Akim admitted. 'It's not a quick-acting alkaloid if taken in a small enough dose. Socrates remained alive for several hours after taking a fatal dose of Poison Hemlock. He was able to record the effects that it had on his body as the poison gripped him. A small enough dose, taken early, may manifest itself in much the same way as alcohol. The victim will become increasingly unsteady on their feet and slur their words. A little while later, unconsciousness will follow, followed by death.'

'So if Max Wilde had taken the fatal dose at dinner time, death may still have occurred when it did?'

'Yes.' Akim agreed.

Davenport thought about that for a moment.

'Miss Collis said Max looked pretty intoxicated at dinner. She had to help him to bed. Could it be possible that Max was given the fatal dose then and not later, as we assume?'

'It's possible,' Akim agreed. 'But we've run a detailed toxicology report on the food and drink eaten that night, and we can't find a trace of it anywhere.'

'And Max Wilde definitely died from Coniine poisoning?' Davenport asked.

'He did.' Akim nodded. 'We've found a large quantity of it in the contents of his stomach and his bloodstream. It's definitive. Max Wilde died of Coniine poisoning.'

Davenport tapped her fingers on the table.

'Could Max Wilde have taken a fatal dose deliberately?' She asked.

Dr Akim smiled.

'As the detective, I must leave that question firmly in your ballpark.' He said.

Davenport didn't smile. She thought it incredibly unlikely that Max Wilde would have killed himself. He was in the prime of his life, with several successful careers and more money than most people could dream of. If it wasn't suicide, then it must be murder. If it was murder, then she had a glut of crime writers as suspects to investigate. But where to begin?

***

The Seven Dials Hotel and Restaurant sat on the side of a hill on the outskirts of Wallingford and looked down upon the river Thames as it meandered its way through the Oxfordshire countryside. Its landscaped gardens ran from beautifully adorned patios surrounding the Victorian coaching house down the hill until they folded gracefully into the riverbank. Here, an old boathouse stood looking a little tired and unloved, and besides that, berthed on the dock, sat the squat-looking restaurant cruiser, The Winterbrook. She was a wide beam narrowboat almost seventy-two feet long and twelve and a half feet wide, bobbing gently in the water.

Sydney drove into the hotel's car park and made her way down to the dockside. From a distance, she saw Margaret and a familiar young woman, who sat on a picnic bench beneath a colourful parasol, drinking from takeaway coffee cups.

'Pat said you'd be coming.' Margaret said. 'I wonder what *you* did.'

Sydney was prepared for Margaret's acid tongue, and she steeled herself against it. She could be quite brusque, she thought, as only older people could be, and she laughed it off.

'Margaret!' She joked coyly. She clutched her chest theatrically. 'I'm sure I don't know what you mean!'

Pat stood up and held out her hand.

'You must be Sydney Fletch,' she said. 'I'm Pat Hemsworth, Margaret's daughter.'

Sydney smiled sweetly and shook Pat's hand.

'It's lovely to meet you finally.'

'Lovely?!' Margaret exclaimed. 'What's lovely about it? A man's dead, and we've been summoned here by god knows who, for god knows what reason, and it's already a hundred degrees, and I don't like boats!'

Sydney watched as Pat gave an almost inaudible sigh.

'Are you here for the dinner cruise?' A female voice asked.

The three turned to see a smartly dressed young woman emerge from the boathouse carrying a clipboard and a sheet of paper.

They said they were.

'It's much cooler on the boat if you want to embark. There are cold drinks, too.'

Sydney helped Margaret step onto the boat. For an old woman who walked with a stick, she was as sure-footed as a workhorse. Sydney followed Margaret into the restaurant cruiser, followed by Pat. They sat together at the boat's bow, looking out onto the water.

The narrow boat was luxuriously laid out. A dozen tables were on either side, each for four people. An Art-Deco lamp sat in the centre of each table, and each place was laid with brightly polished cutlery. Crystal-cut wine glasses twinkled in the summer sun, and each table was set with a bottle of red wine and a bottle of white.

Margaret poured herself a glass of red and laid the bottle back on the table. Pat took the bottle and offered some to Sydney before pouring herself a glass.

'There's Gareth!' Sydney declared as a familiar figure strolled towards the boathouse. Sydney rose. 'Excuse me, I'll let him know we're here.'

Margaret watched the lovestruck young woman walk through the narrowboat and onto the dock. Sydney embraced the young man who approached. She watched them carefully. She didn't trust the Fletch girl any more than she trusted Gareth Black, and she was determined to get to the bottom of this ridiculous text message saga. It was clearly a joke, but at whose expense?

Sydney kissed Gareth on the cheek a little more enthusiastically than she intended.

'You should see who's with Margaret!' She giggled.

Gareth looked over Sydney's shoulder and located the Hemshaw women at the front of the boat. At first, he couldn't quite make out the figure next to Margaret, and then the sun caught her face and lit her up.

'No! It Isn't, is it?'

Sydney laughed.

'It is! It's the woman from the maze. The woman who gave Max a good time!'

'Well, I'll be damned!' Gareth exclaimed. 'Have you sought her out for any tips?'

Sydney dug him in the ribs.

'I'll have you know that I don't need any tips, thank you very much.' Then, she added. 'But you know what that means?'

'That if I play my cards right, I could be in for a good time?' Gareth said.

'If you're not going to take this seriously, I won't bother talking to you.'

He was being serious, if only about a different subject. His desire for Sydney Fletch was a serious matter.

'Go on,' he said, 'what does it mean?'

Sydney looked into Gareth's eyes for a sign of disingenuousness. She found none.

'It means Pat Hemshaw was at Burnham Manor and could have been there all day.'

Gareth thought about that.

'True. So that makes her a murder suspect.'

Sydney looked at Gareth and marshalled her facial expressions so they didn't give her away. As far as she was aware, no one knew that Max had been potentially poisoned.

'Murder?'

'You haven't heard?' Gareth asked. 'It's all over the news. He was poisoned.'

'Have you heard?!'

Sydney and Gareth turned to see Sanjay breeze into their presence.

'Someone poisoned the old sod. Murdered! That must be what this is all about. Who do you reckon did it? My money's on Margaret.'

They climbed on board the narrowboat and took up seats near the Hemshaws.

'Have you heard the news?' Sanjay asked, a touch indelicately. 'Max was done in. Probably by one of us.'

Margaret gave him a cold look. By the expression on Pat's face, they could tell that they knew. Pat was scrolling through her phone.

'They know all about us,' she cried. 'My god, how do they know all this? It says we're all suspects. It says we're all being investigated.'

'Put the phone down, Pat.' Margaret said. 'Of course they know. It's their job. This whole affair is either going to make us famous or infamous. Certainly can't hurt sales.'

'Mother!'

'She's right,' Sanjay said. He gleamed as he did so. 'Sales will go up. This kind of thing can only be good for a crime writer!'

They all turned as Gemma Collis embarked. She wore a light-fitting summer outfit and tied her hair tightly to the back of her head. She sat at Gareth's and Sanjay's table.

'I suppose you've all heard?' She asked.

The expressions on everyone's faces told her all she needed to know.

'Do they know how he was murdered?' Sanjay asked.

'I spoke to DI Davenport this morning. They're not saying much, only that it was something called Coniine. They found it in a glass of water by Max's bedside. Initial toxicology reports show a considerable amount of it in Max. She's officially opened a murder investigation.'

'I don't think I've heard of Coniine.' Gareth said.

Sydney knew, but she held her tongue.

'I suppose that's what the murderer would say,' Gemma noted without a hint of accusation. 'But it's the main alkaloid in Hemlock.'

'The quail!' Sanjay exclaimed. 'My god, I had the quail!'

'It wasn't in the quail, Sanjay. It was in Max's water.'

'Still, a bit of a coincidence, eh?' Sanjay said.

It was. The coincidence wasn't lost on anyone.

They were interrupted by Robert Wilde as he climbed onboard the vessel.

'So, you lot all got the message too?'

He sat on the table opposite Gemma's and didn't look at her. He poured himself a white wine and drank it in one fell swoop. He poured himself another.

'So which one of you fuckers murdered my brother?' He asked.

'Possibly none of them.' Finney said as he climbed aboard the boat. He took a seat next to Gemma and poured two glasses of wine. He handed one to Gemma and smiled.

'Perhaps you killed your brother?' Finney suggested.

Robert sat back in his chair and sulked.

'Have you heard the news, Mr Finney?' Margaret asked. 'Apparently, Max was poisoned.'

'I have heard, Mrs Hemshaw. I spoke with DI Davenport this morning. The investigation is in good hands.'

'Is that why you're here, Mr Finney?' Pat asked. 'Are you here to investigate us?'

Finney sipped his wine.

'I am here by anonymous invitation,' he said slowly.

Sydney surreptitiously watched everyone's faces as Finney made his statement. He had suggested that morning that someone might ask, and he had implored her to watch them carefully. Look for the little things. People can't control the hints and giveaways. Look for the "tell".

No one so much as blinked. What she did notice, however, was that everyone was regarding everyone else with suspicion.

The smartly dressed young woman, who had mysteriously appeared from the boathouse earlier, climbed aboard the boat and walked up to where her guests were sitting.

'Good afternoon, everyone, and welcome to The Winterbrook. My name's Cath and I'm your host for today.' She glanced at her watch. 'We were due to set off five minutes ago, but we're still waiting for one more guest to arrive. I'm sure it won't be much longer. Please help yourself to drinks. There's a fridge at the front with cold ones and some soft drinks.'

'Who's paying for it?' Sanjay asked.

'It's all included, sir. Please help yourself.'

Sanjay drained his glass and poured another.

'Ah, it looks like our last guest has arrived,' Cath said, greeting the young woman who had just climbed aboard.

Everyone looked up in surprise as an immaculately dressed Sakura Fukushima walked up the boat and sat beside Robert.

'Right, that's all of us,' Cath said. 'My husband is the skipper for today's little trip. We shall head upstream for a little while, where we will dock for half an hour, where you can take a picnic and enjoy the scenery. After that, we'll make a slow and leisurely return. The trip takes about three and a half hours in total. There is no smoking permitted on board, and if you vape, we kindly ask that you step out onto the bow of the boat to do so. There are lifesavers at the bow and stern in the unlikely event that we sink, and there are several floatation devices at strategic points outside the boat should anyone fall in. Any questions?'

'I have a couple.' Finney said.

Everyone turned to look at Finney. They all had questions but didn't want to ask them or didn't know how.

'Who booked this trip?'

Cath looked confused.

'I… I don't know what you mean?'

'It's a simple question,' Finney continued, applying his policeman's hat. 'Who made the booking?'

'The booking was made over the telephone. They didn't give a name.'

'And you accepted an anonymous booking?'

Cath looked uncomfortable.

'Forgive me,' Finney said, 'that sounded rude. Perhaps I should explain. We have all been invited here today anonymously.'

'Oh, it's a surprise party!' Cath said, and the relief in her voice was palpable.

'In a manner of speaking,' Finney explained. 'We are all either friends or relatives of Max Wilde.'

Cath looked uncomfortable again.

'My god, I'm so sorry,' she said. 'We heard it on the news earlier. Poor man.'

'Indeed.' Finney agreed. 'We are also all suspects in his murder, so we'd all very much like to know who invited us here today.'

Now Cath looked shocked.

'The booking was made over the telephone. We didn't get a name.'

'Was it a man or a woman?'

'I really couldn't be sure, one way or the other.'

'When was the booking made?'

'Yesterday morning.'

The day Max was found.

'You accepted an anonymous booking so late? You must already have had bookings?'

'We did. They offered an awful lot of money. Enough to offer all those with bookings a free dinner cruise some other time.'

'And have you been paid?'

'Yes. An envelope full of cash was delivered yesterday, shortly after the booking was made.'

'Did you see who made the delivery?'

'A boy from the town. He was given the envelope to deliver and a hefty tip.'

I see,' Finney said slowly. 'Entirely untraceable. One last question…. was the food and drink supplied to you, or have you sourced it all?'

Sanjay was midway through another glass of wine when he realised the nuance in Finney's question.

'We bought it all. We've prepared all the food today from our kitchens.'

Cath took Finney's silence as her cue to escape, and she disappeared into the stern of the boat. A few moments later, they felt the boat vibrate as its engines were started, and the boat pulled gently away from the bank.

The occupants of the Winterbrook sat in silence and watched as the Oxfordshire countryside floated effortlessly beside them. Everyone waited anxiously to see what would happen next.

***

'Right, then,' Margaret said loudly. 'I think this is an opportune moment for whoever sent that message to own up and tell us what this is all about.'

Everyone remained quiet.

'It's just some sick joke.' Robert growled. 'It's in bloody bad taste if you ask me.'

'But you came, nonetheless.' Finney pointed out. 'May I ask why?'

Robert fumbled with his glass of wine and looked at no one in particular.

'I wanted to see what it was all about.' He grumbled.

'I can't speak for anyone else,' Margaret said, 'but I came because Pat was coming, and Pat was coming because Sanjay was. It's someone's idea of a silly joke.'

'Maybe not.' Finney mused.

'What do you mean by that?' Sanjay asked.

'I mean, that the landscape has changed.' Finney explained. 'We all received the message yesterday evening, long before we discovered that Max was poisoned. It was fair to assume then that the text could have been an elaborate practical joke or a potential blackmailer looking for their mark.'

He paused and waited for those who hadn't thought of that to catch up.

'But now we know that Max was murdered and that, in all probability, one of us killed him.'

The sentence dropped into the small party like a bomb.

'I had no reason to see my brother dead.' Robert spat. He looked across at Gemma, who looked down at the table before her. Finney watched it play out and waited for Sydney to drop her bombshell.

'That's not exactly true, is it Mr Wilde?' Sydney countered.

Robert scowled at Sydney, and through the corner of his eye, he saw Gareth grow by five inches as he prepared to come to her defence.

'What the hell do you know?' Robert asked.

'Rather a lot. I know that you and Gemma were having an affair and that you were trying to keep it a secret from Max. I also know that Max was selling a majority share in your business and that you were unhappy about it. I'd go so far as to say that you were deeply unhappy about it, which is why you punched your brother in the mouth.'

Robert smiled, and the corners of his mouth twisted into a sneer.

'Brothers fight all the time. Max and I have done this since we were kids. There's nothing new there. It doesn't mean I killed him.'

'Who inherits Max's estate?' Finney asked.

Robert shrugged.

'I don't know the contents of his will.' Robert said, 'I imagine it's very complex. But, as it goes, as part of the agreement Max and I had, in the event of one of us dying, the other automatically secures the other's share of the business.'

Finney nodded.

'So, yesterday, you were about to lose control of your business, and today, you inherit the disputed other share. I'd say that's a powerful motive.'

'I can't argue with that.' Robert admitted. 'If I'm honest, I could have murdered the selfish sod, but I

didn't. I was nowhere near Burnham Manor Friday
night.'

'And where were you?' Finney asked.

'London.' Robert replied. 'We have a restaurant with
rooms above it for when we are in town. I went to see
my lawyer, who, incidentally, assured me we could
challenge the sale, and then I returned to the restaurant
and stayed there until the morning when I got Gemma's
call about Max.'

'Can anyone corroborate that?'

'Staff at the restaurant saw me go to my rooms in the
evening and again at breakfast.'

'And during the night?'

'I was alone.' Robert stated.

Gemma looked up and smiled. Robert started to thaw.

'Well, that's settled then,' Sanjay chirped. 'Robert
murdered his brother to save his restaurant. Case closed.
Who wants another glass of wine?'

'You seem pleased with yourself,' Margaret observed.
'Indelicately so, some might say.'

'I had no love for the man,' Sanjay countered. 'But I
didn't wish him dead or desire his death. I have no
motive.'

'You didn't seem happy with him on the day of his
murder,' Sydney argued. 'You were raging at him in the
maze. I'd say anger is a powerful motive. And revenge.'

'Anger? Revenge? For what?' Sanjay challenged.

'Max's deal with the BBC killed your television career.'
Gemma said quietly. 'Max knew you had ambitions that
way. He knew the BBC were desperate to sign him, and
he also knew that when they did, they would drop you.
He enjoyed the power that he had over you. It pleased
him.'

Sanjay fell deadly quiet.

'I suppose it's my turn next?' Margaret said. She watched Sydney carefully. The young woman was proving to be something of a nuisance. 'You saw me in the maze, too, didn't you?'

'I did.' Sydney admitted. 'I heard your argument with Max.'

'You're quite the little spy, aren't you?' Margaret said, 'That's very interesting. And yes, I had a heated discussion with Max. It involved Pat. I suppose Pat's small indiscretion last year is public knowledge? Yes, of course it is. That's human nature. People love to gossip. I warned Max off, and he assured me he had acceded to my request to stay away from Pat. It rather negates any need on my part for wanting him dead.'

'Except not long after you argue with Max,' Sydney said, 'Pat came into the maze and finished what she started last year.'

'Pat!' Margaret screamed, and her voice shredded the otherwise peaceful cruise.

'Oh, mother, don't be so shocked.' Pat said calmly. 'I'm a fully grown woman. I did nothing wrong. I'm over Max. I wanted to prove it to myself as much as to Max. It was my way of getting closure. I told him so at the time. It was a farewell meeting, nothing more.'

'Don't be so naive, child!' Margaret fumed. 'No one's going to believe that for one minute. Not only have you put yourself at the scene of a murder, but you have implicated yourself and me, to boot. Stupid girl.'

'Margaret, I think you can be very unkind to Pat,' Gemma said, rising to her defence. 'You are quite mean when you speak to her. I don't like it.'

'No one cares what you like.' Margaret seethed. 'If anyone has a motive for seeing Max dead, it's you. He was going to cut you out! You were going to lose everything.'

Everyone looked at Gemma.

'Is this true?' Robert asked.

'Yes. I rang my agent. Max had already appointed a new ghostwriter. Our publishers were looking for a way to remove me.'

'Had they found one?' Finney asked.

'Yes.' Gemma admitted. 'Margaret is right. I was going to lose everything. The contract Max and I had was a bad one. I had no rights to anything.'

'While he was alive.' Margaret added.

'Miss Collis?' Finney asked.

'Again, Margaret is well informed.' Gemma went on with no hint of animosity. 'On Max's death, I retain all rights to his books. In effect, what was already mine becomes mine in law.'

'You were also the last to see Max alive?' Finney noted.

'Yes. I took Max to bed.'

'Was there a glass of water by Max's bedside?' Finney asked.

'DI Davenport asked the same question.' Gemma mused. 'I'm afraid I can't remember.'

'She would hardly admit to it if there were, would she?' Margaret argued. 'Not if that's how Max was poisoned. It makes her the likely suspect.'

'Except that Gemma was also the one to find Max in the morning.' Finney remarked. 'If she had, indeed, poisoned Max's water, surely she would have removed the evidence and muddied the crime scene, leaving us to question how and when the poison was given to Max?'

Margaret fell quiet.

'One last question, Gemma.' Finney said. 'Did you secure the house as you left that night?'

'I think so.' Gemma replied.

Finney looked deep into Gemma's eyes and sought the truth in her statements. Slowly, his eyes left hers and fell on Sakura Fukushima's.

Sakura sat opposite Robert and looked at no one. Finney felt that she looked like someone desperately trying to blend in with her surroundings and appear invisible. She looked up slowly as she felt everyone's eyes watching her.

'Miss Fukushima,' Finney began. 'You have us all at a bit of a loss. I don't think anyone here expected to see you.'

'Someone did,' Margaret exclaimed.

Finney bowed to Margaret's observation.

'Of course, one person was expecting you. The person that invited you. I assume you received an invitation via text message, like the rest of us?'

Sakura shook her head.

'No,' she said quietly. 'I did not get a text message.' She delved into her handbag and withdrew an envelope. 'This was left for me at The Marlborough Hotel, where my grandfather and I are staying.'

Finney took the envelope and removed the letter. It was worded exactly as the text messages. He handed the letter to the others, watching as it made its way around the party.

'Can you think what the author of this note meant by "I saw you"?'

Sakura shook her head.

'Were you having an affair with Max?' Gemma asked. 'You're amongst friends, Miss Fukushima. We all know what Max was like.'

Sakura paused for a long time. She marshalled her thoughts.

'To begin with, yes.' She started slowly. 'Max and I began a relationship when he was in Japan. When he came to England, I followed him. We met many times.'

Finney watched the nervous young woman play with a ring on her left hand.

'When did you get married?' Finney asked.

Everyone fell into a stunned silence.

'Married?' Robert asked. 'That's not possible. He would have told me.'

'He wanted to.' Sakura said. 'He was going to. Soon. He said he had things to do first.'

'You can't be married.' Gemma stuttered. 'You… you can't be! I would have known. I know everything about Max. I knew his every move.'

'Not every move.' Sydney remarked.

Gemma threw her a look that would have melted diamonds.

'This complicates matters.' Finney said. 'For one, it gives you a motive for murdering Max. As his wife, you will surely be entitled to a great deal of money as his next of kin. Do you know if Max renewed his will after your marriage?'

'He was going to. I don't know if he did.'

'Robert?' Finney asked. 'Who would Max have used to draw up his will?'

'His lawyers are based in London. They're my lawyers, too. I'll ring them tomorrow and get an update.'

'What about me?' Gareth asked. 'It must be my turn. What motive do I have?' He asked.

Everyone looked at Gareth and realised they knew nothing about the man. He was a stranger to them all, including Sydney.

'No one?' He asked, appearing disappointed that he wasn't a suspect. 'Surely someone's got some dirt on me?'

Sydney threw him a warning look.

'Let me help you, then,' Gareth said, opening his phone. 'Since the news broke this morning about Max, and the Press named us all suspects in his murder, I have sold over two hundred thousand digital copies of my book. Given that I make nearly two quid from each one, that's almost half a million pounds in one morning. Pretty solid motive for slipping Max something deadly in his drink, wouldn't you say?'

'An excellent motive for murder.' Finney agreed. 'And also a good smokescreen for the real motive.'

Sydney sighed. She had tried to warn him.

'I think it's quite clear that Max was something of a womaniser, to use an old term.' Finney said. 'He liked his women, and he liked them young, and he liked them pretty. Young Sydney, here is all of those things, and much more. It is also clear that you hold something of a torch for her and were no doubt annoyed by Max's attempts, during the meal, to flirt with Sydney. I wonder if it isn't equally likely that Sydney fell for Max's charms that night and went to his room at his behest. Angry and filled with jealousy, is it not possible that you sought Max out afterwards and, in a fit of rage, dropped a lethal dose of Coniine into his bedtime drink?'

Gareth looked momentarily stunned. He hunted for the right words but found none.

'He just happened to have Coniine about his person?' Sydney answered, much to Gareth's relief.

'Did you not both walk through the Poison Garden on Friday? The day of Max's murder?'

'We did.' Sydney admitted.

Finney nodded.

'Am I also right in saying that in that garden, it is possible to find vials of poisons excreted from the plants?' Finney asked.

'You are.' Sydney agreed. 'Though I suspect they are fake.'

'Time will tell.' Finney said. 'DI Davenport is searching the property as we speak and will no doubt confiscate the vials of poison for further analysis. But my point is, anyone with any connection to Burnham Manor, including yourself and Gareth, had access to some very deadly poisons.'

'And why would I have wanted to kill Max?' Sydney asked.

'Perhaps you succumbed to his charms, despite yourself?' Finney argued. 'Or he forced himself on you, and you were unable to fight him off. Perhaps you returned later and dropped Coniine into his drink as some form of social justice?'

Sydney clapped.

'Bravo!' She cried.

'And what about you?' Margaret asked, directing the question at Finney. 'You were at the dinner and are here today. Why might you have murdered Max?'

Finney held his hands out.

'Perhaps I am the personification of Justice.' He decided. 'The long arm of the law. Perhaps I knew enough about Max to convince me that his passing would do more good for the world than for him to remain in it. I am Nemesis incarnate.'

They all sat and wondered, looked at each other, and wondered some more.

***

The party of murder suspects sat in silence for some time, each one consumed by their own thoughts. The calm waters of the river Thames swept beneath them as the narrowboat continued its slow chug upstream. The

English countryside had never looked so beautiful as it passed by. Fields of crop and pasture drifted alongside them, interspersed, here and there, by the odd cow that watched from the riverbank.

Their quiet reverie was broken by the return of their host, who walked cautiously towards them.

'In a few minutes, we'll arrive at our picnic spot, where you may disembark. We have set up several tables for you. Our staff will carry out your food and drink. It's a pleasant spot. Beautiful views.'

She turned on the spot and hurried away.

'I think you frightened her.' Sydney remarked, aiming the statement at Finney.

'Perhaps she's realised that if we are all suspects in the murder of Max,' Pat pointed out, 'she's also realised one of us is a probably murderer.'

'But which one, eh?' Gareth asked.

Everyone glanced at everyone else except Finney, who rolled his wine around his glass.

'Indeed.' He said slowly. 'Which one of us?'

The Winterbrook turned a small corner in the river, and the boat's landing point appeared. They all watched as the boat pulled up alongside. Beyond the dock lay a small meadow with several tables and chairs, and smartly dressed young waiting staff stood ready to serve.

One by one, they disembarked and drifted over to the tables. Robert was the last to leave and strolled along the riverbank deep in thought. Gemma watched the forlorn figure and felt her heart bulge. He looked so sad. She took a deep breath and steeled herself to say what must be said. She walked over to where Robert was strolling and edged into his line of sight.

'Robert...I...' The words failed her. She was a writer. She should have written them down.

She had half expected Robert to throw her the cold shoulder again, but he didn't. He held out his hand.

'Walk with me.' He asked.

Gemma took his hand, and the two walked away from the others, keeping close to the water's edge.

'Robert, I'm sorry.' Gemma stuttered. 'I should have told you what Max planned to do with your business when I found out. It was wrong of me.'

'I understand.' Robert said.

'I don't think you do,' Gemma countered. 'Not really. I was torn, you see. I thought I owed Max my loyalty when, in fact, I owed it to you. I love you. I never loved Max. He didn't deserve my loyalty.'

'You're not wrong there.' Robert stated. 'He didn't deserve your loyalty. But you did the right thing. It wasn't your place to tell me that sort of thing. Max was the one who betrayed me. Not you.'

'But then why did you run away? Why did you leave me?'

'I didn't, not really. I needed some time to myself—a bit of space. I'm afraid it got a bit noisy in my head. I had to go somewhere quiet to think.'

Robert turned and looked Gemma in the eye.

'Is it true Max was dropping you?' He asked.

Gemma nodded.

'Yes. It's true. His publishers were on board with it, too. They were going to cut me off and throw me out to sea.'

'And now you get to keep the books?'

'I do. Copyright reverts to me on Max's death.'

Robert paused.

Slowly, he said, 'And Max dies before he or his publishers can rip that contract up?'

Gemma nodded. 'Yes. But I didn't kill him, Rob, you must believe me.'

Without hesitation, he replied, 'I do. I don't think for one second you killed my brother. I know you too well, Gem. You couldn't do a thing like that.'

Gemma felt the tension drop from her shoulders. She had been so afraid that he wouldn't believe her.

'And I didn't kill him either,' Robert continued, 'though god knows I wanted to a few times. He could be a nasty sod. But the problem is, Gem, that we are quite clearly the prime suspects in this ridiculous drama. We need to stick together.'

'Yes, we do.' Gemma agreed. 'All three of us…' She added, carefully rubbing her stomach.

She waited while the penny dropped and watched Robert's face.

'You're pregnant?' He asked. 'You're pregnant? You're really pregnant?'

Still trying to figure out which way the conversation was leading, Gemma nodded vigorously.

'We're having a baby? I'm going to be a dad?'

Gemma watched as a smile stretched across Robert's face.

'Yes, you're going to be a dad.' She declared.

Robert threw his arms around her and squeezed gently.

'Oh, my god, I'm so happy.'

They stood at the river's edge for several long minutes, cuddling and squeezing one another. Slowly, Robert pulled away. His expression had changed. He looked confused.

'It seems wrong to be so happy the day after my brother has been murdered.' He said.

'I know. I wasn't sure if I should tell you or not. Not just yet, anyway. But life goes on, Robert, even in the midst of tragedy. We should celebrate life as much as we must mourn those that have gone.'

'Yes. You're right.' Robert agreed. He fumbled inside his trouser pockets for a moment, looking for something. Slowly, he pulled out a small box and flipped its lid open. A diamond ring peered from within and sparkled in the sunlight. 'Marry me, Gemma. Let's be a proper family.'

'How long have you been carrying that around with you?' Gemma asked.

'Quite a while. Things like this make me nervous.'

Gemma looked over her shoulder to where the others were milling about. No one was paying them much attention. She turned and faced Robert.

'Yes, Robert. Of course, it's a yes.' She placed a finger on the ring box lid and carefully closed it. 'But I won't wear the ring just yet. Not while all this is going on. It wouldn't seem right.'

Robert put the box back in his pocket.

'Don't bloody well lose it,' she joked, kissing Robert gently. 'What are you going to do about the other wife?'

They both looked over to where Sakura was stood. She looked lost and hopelessly out of her depth.

'Really depends on what the Will says.' Robert said. 'Max may have updated it to include her, so we probably won't need to do anything.'

'And if he has included her, to the exclusion of everyone else?'

Robert looked at his new fiancé. He had never known the contents of Max's Will and had never asked. He always just assumed he was a part of it.

'We'll cross that bridge when we come to it.' He said. 'There's no point trying to guess. Max has probably got a few surprises left for us, I'm sure.'

***

'Pat. Walk with me.'

Pat was deep in conversation with Sanjay and was about to assert what little confidence she had in rebuffing her mother when she saw the look on her face and decided that now wasn't the right time.

Pat took her mother's arm, and the two strolled away from the main party. Once they were out of earshot, Margaret began to talk.

'I am very disappointed in you, Pat.' She began, and Pat noted a different inflexion in her voice that she hadn't heard before. She sensed the disappointment was real and not some knee-jerk reaction that her mother was famous for.

'Mother, I'm a grown woman. You can't control me forever. I'm a free spirit.'

'Yes dear,' her mother said, 'but you are naive and not streetwise. There are things you can't possibly understand. I take full responsibility for that. It is my fault.'

Margaret stopped and turned to her daughter.

'I have mollycoddled you and wrapped you in cotton wool, and I fear I may have created someone who is not yet ready to face the world on her own. I did it for my own selfish reasons, and I'm sorry. It has served me well, having you near, but I have failed you.'

'Don't be silly, mother. I'm not going anywhere.'

Margaret patted her gently on the hand.

'I am frightened for you, Pat. I'm scared.'

Pat searched her mother's eyes for dishonesty but found only the truth.

'I didn't kill Max.' Pat assured her. 'I had nothing to do with it, I promise.'

Margaret turned and continued the walk along the riverbank.

'I know you didn't,' Margaret replied. 'But the shadow of suspicion falls on us all. Being at Burnham Manor on the day that Max was murdered darkens that shadow. It darkens us both.'

'I was only there for a short time. I didn't stay long. I only went for closure.'

'But you were seen.' Margaret said. 'You were seen with Max.'

'But I left straight after. I wasn't there when he was murdered.'

'What time did you leave?' Margaret asked.

'I can't remember. It was right after I met Max.'

'Did anyone see you leave?'

'No. I didn't think anyone had seen me there at all.'

'Where did you go afterwards?'

'I went home. I spent the day at home.'

'Did anyone see you there? Did you stop anywhere on the way home? Did you get fuel or food? Anything at all?'

Pat shook her head.

'No.' She lied.

Most of what she said had been true, but a young taxi driver from the village could give her an alibi for that night, should she need it. There was no point upsetting her mother when she didn't need to.

'So you have no alibi.' Her mother stated. 'And that worries me.'

'Mother, there is no need to be afraid. There can't be any evidence that I murdered Max because I didn't do it.'

'Yes, dear,' Margaret said, slightly exasperated. 'It's not like the British Justice system isn't littered with miscarriages of justice. We used to hang innocent people, Pat. Rather too often.'

Pat fell quiet.

'What about your alibi, mother? Do you have one?'

'I do not.' Margaret admitted. The kind Mr Finney showed me to my room, and I stayed there until the morning. It is not beyond the realms of possibility that I could have snuck out of my room, poisoned Max's glass of water, and returned to my room unobserved.'

Pat was about to ask her whether she did that but thought better of it.

'The problem is,' Margaret continued, 'that as you know, it doesn't matter what you do or how careful you are; someone always sees.'

Margaret turned them around and began walking back to the party.

Someone always sees.

The words caught Pat by surprise. She looked ahead of her at the motley collection of crime writers and solvers and wondered.

***

'You don't believe that Gareth dropped Max a deadly dose of poison just to protect my honour, do you?'

Sydney hooked Finney under the armpit and led him away from the party. She made her statement when they were out of range of the others.

Finney chuckled.

'No, I do not. But the man has a burning passion for you. I do not doubt that if someone dishonoured you in any way, Gareth would slap them in the face with a brick and quite happily clean the crime scene. But this is not a crime of passion. It is carefully considered and reasoned murder, planned and executed with precision. I believe Gareth is capable, as are we all, but the motive is not burning passion. At the moment, I cannot conceive of young Gareth's motivation.'

'Good. Me neither.' Sydney exclaimed. 'I wonder if you have conceived of mine?'

Finney chuckled again.

'You tease me.' Finney said. 'Not unlike how you tease Gareth Black, only for different reasons.'

'Do you think I tease him?'

'Yes, I do. He's besotted with you. And you know it, too, and you play with him like a cat plays with a mouse, tempting him with his heart's desires before slapping him down beneath your sharpened claws.'

'Mr Finney! You have such a low opinion of me!'

'On the contrary,' Finney argued. 'I have a very high opinion of you. I'm growing quite fond of you. You are intelligent, articulate, and talented, and you know all these things are true. And yet you toy with Gareth's emotions cruelly. You should let him go if you do not reciprocate his feelings.'

Sydney smiled.

'What makes you think they aren't reciprocated?' She giggled coyly. 'My virtue must be hard won. I won't just give it away!'

Now, it was Finney's turn to smile. He detected no hint of deceptiveness.

'I think I shall play with him a little longer.' Sydney declared. 'He'll appreciate it in the end.'

Finney watched as Sydney hopped back to where Gareth was sitting and pulled him to his feet.

'Come on, let's go for a walk!'

Finney stood and watched the young couple walk hand in hand across the meadow. He was joined in this by Sanjay, who appeared at his shoulder.

'Young love, eh.' Sanjay commented. 'Oh, to be young again.'

Finney looked at Sanjay. He took a sweet from his tin and popped it into his mouth.

'I couldn't think of anything worse,' Finney remarked. 'I wouldn't be young again if you paid me.'

***

Robert held out his hand and took Sakura's in his. She was incredibly beautiful, he thought. Elegantly so. She was petite with the darkest eyes, topped with a head of the glossiest black strands of hair he had ever seen. Her skin was almost translucent and flawlessly so. Her hand was soft and tiny in his, and he shook it gently.

'It's Sakura, isn't it?'

He knew it was. Gemma had just told him.

Sakura bowed.

'Yes. Sakura Fuku….'

She paused, unsure of how to continue.

Gemma pushed Robert gently to one side and hugged Sakura warmly.

'It's so lovely to meet you again,' Gemma said. 'You must forgive us, though. This is all a bit of a shock.'

'Yes. For me, too. Max spoke of you both often.' She looked across at Robert. 'You are his brother. He told me much about you.'

'Unfortunately,' Robert said, 'Max being Max, he told us nothing about you.'

Sakura looked guilty.

'I begged him to tell you about me, but he kept putting it off. He said there were things he needed to do first. He thought you would try to convince him not to marry me.'

'We didn't think Max was the marrying kind.' Gemma said.

'He wasn't.' Sakura agreed. 'I met Max last year when he visited Japan to research his new show. I knew all about him. His reputation preceded him.'

'It had a habit of doing that.' Robert agreed.

'Max always got what he wanted,' Sakura continued, 'but he hadn't met me before. I resisted his best attempts to convince me to become his lover, and I think it frustrated him. I think I was the first woman to say no to him. He extended his stay in Japan for another month while he worked on me but to no avail.'

'I remember,' Gemma said. 'I wondered what he was up to.'

'I think, during that time, he fell in love with me. I think I was the first person he truly fell in love with. We kept in touch and got together again this year while he was filming his show. Max declared his love for me and said that he never wanted to spend another day apart from me and asked me to marry him. I followed him back to England, and we were married.'

'And here you are.' Robert said.

'I'm sorry for your loss.' Sakura said. 'I didn't know what to do when Max died. I was very confused. I didn't know how to approach you. How to tell you. And then I got that letter.'

'Did anyone know about you and Max?' Gemma asked.

'I didn't think so.' Sakura replied. 'Even my grandfather doesn't know. I suppose I shall have to return to Japan.'

'No.' Robert said firmly. 'I mean, it's not going to be easy. We don't know what Max's Will says yet. And I don't suppose the immigration department will be easy to deal with. But we'll sort something out. One way or another, we'll take care of you.'

Gemma looked across at her fiancé, and her heart swelled.

'But you don't know me,' Sakura said. 'You don't owe me anything.'

'True, we don't know you,' Robert agreed. 'But we can fix that. I never thought Max would find anyone to fall in love with properly, but he did, and now you're part of our family. And you're right, we don't owe you anything, but Max was my brother, and I owe it to him to take care of you for as long as you need us to.'

Sakura smiled.

'Perhaps now would be a good time to tell you you're going to be an uncle?'

Robert's mouth dropped. Gemma slipped her arm around Sakura and pulled her close.

'Please forgive Robert. To be told to expect a niece or nephew on the same day he was told to expect a baby daughter or son has probably been too much for him.'

Sakura beamed.

'You too?'

Gemma nodded.

'But not a word to anyone just yet.' She begged. 'Not until this is all over.'

***

English summers have a unique way of announcing their end suddenly and without warning. One minute, cotton wool clouds float aimlessly across azure blue skies, and the next, they are chased over the horizon by darker brothers, laden with rain and thunder. The small party had returned to the tables and eaten a lunch of freshly made sandwiches packed with sumptuous fillings and feasted on all manner of locally grown foods, washed down with a modest serving of wine. The thunder ripped the air and rippled in the distance before small spots of rain began to fall. By the time they had all climbed on board the Winterbrook, the heavens had opened, and rain fell like stair-rods, causing the once peaceful river Thames to erupt in anger.

Sydney sat near the boat's bow and watched as her fellow travellers divided themselves into carefully defined cliques. Robert and Gemma sat with Sakura towards the centre of the boat, and the three of them chatted between themselves, to the exclusion of the others. Margaret took a table opposite and commanded Pat to sit next to her. Sanjay sat across from Margaret, and Sydney pondered the complex relationships she saw there. Was Sanjay in love with Pat? She thought so but she also thought that Margaret would be a stubborn thorn in their sides should the two ever decide to be together. Sanjay was much older and more experienced. Margaret would find him a difficult man to bully.

Gareth strolled along the boat with his usual carefree demeanour. Sydney found much about the man to admire. He was taller than her, dark-haired, and free-spirited. His shoulders were broad, and his arms thick. She watched as he approached her and sat beside her. She found an odd comfort in his presence. It warmed her soul and, not for the first time, roused her desires.

Finney climbed aboard the boat last and lingered there while it was turned in the river, and it began its slow journey back downstream. He moved slowly along the centre of the boat before he stood before everyone, his hands crossed behind his back. Gradually, everyones conversations ended, and they all looked up at Finney as he watched them all.

'I think,' he began slowly, 'that the time has come to address the elephant in the room.'

Everyone watched him as he spoke.

'Yesterday, Max Wilde was cruelly murdered. We have, all of us, since received a text message or letter inviting us to attend this cruise. A thinly veiled threat was made suggesting that it would not be in our interests not to attend. The writer has also indicated that they have seen us do something that would, perhaps, encourage our cooperation.

'To begin with, I didn't think much of the text. It seemed to be a vague, undefined threat and not one I would usually entertain. In my line of work, I have been threatened many times, anonymously and face to face. In every circumstance, I have ignored the threat, and nothing has ever come of it. I particularly take short measure with anonymous threats. They are spineless and weak, usually not unlike the sender.

'In this case, if I'm to be honest with you, I was intrigued. Who doesn't like a bit of mystery in their lives? I was graciously invited, as something of a curiosity, to one of Max Wilde's infamous dinner parties, attended by the great and the good of the crime writing world. For a man of my advancing years, it was a wonderful opportunity to mix in circles I could never hope to be able to mix in, and you have all made me very welcome.'

Finney glanced at Sydney and smiled.

'At first, I thought the text message was designed as a way for the sender to lure out the potential killer for blackmail, but I have since concluded that it is more likely that the murderer himself sent the message.'

'Him?' Margaret questioned.

'Forgive me,' Finney bowed. 'Or her. And let me be very clear,' he continued. 'I do not know who killed Max Wilde, but I am firmly of the opinion that any of you is capable of it and that one of you here today is the killer. One of you sent that message.'

'But why?' Sydney asked. 'If not blackmail, then what?'

'Perhaps it was blackmail.' Finney said. 'Perhaps, during this trip, the blackmailer and their mark have been identified, and the game is playing out beyond our sight. Now let me be very clear once again.' Finney went on, his face belying his fears. 'If I am right in this, then whoever you are, you are playing a dangerous game. Take whatever you think you know to the police and let them deal with it. This is not a game.'

He paused to allow his words to filter down to his audience.

'And if not blackmail?' Sydney asked.

'In that case, we can safely assume that the murderer has arranged this charade to see if they have got away with it or whether or not they need to act to stay safe. I must beg you all to take extra care. You may not be aware of what you know or have seen that interests the murderer. It may be something entirely trivial and of no importance, but it can be extremely damaging to the murderer when taken in context with whatever it is they are trying to hide. Murderers will not hesitate to kill again to keep their secrets.'

Once again, he paused to allow his words to register. He looked at everyone in turn and then sat next to Sydney.

'Is that it?' Margaret asked.

'What do you want?' Finney asked.

'Well, I don't know.' Margaret flustered. 'You're the bloody detective. Detect!'

Finney held his hands out.

'What can I do? I was a detective many years ago. But I am not anymore. I don't have the resources or, if I'm honest, the inclination.'

'But you do have the skills.' Sydney argued. 'You know what to look for. The right questions to ask. The right holes to poke around in.'

'Fletch is right.' Gareth agreed. 'You're certainly the right man for the job.'

'DI Davenport is the right man for the job.' Finney countered.

'Woman.' Margaret corrected.

Finney nodded in Margaret's direction.

'And she is perfectly suited to the job.' Finney said. 'She will find the killer.'

'And what if she doesn't?' Robert asked. 'You lot are bloody crime writers. If anyone can get away with murder, it would be one of you.'

Gemma shot him a stoney look.

'Tel me I'm wrong.' Robert pleaded.

Gemma smiled.

'No, you're not wrong.' She agreed. 'I'm pretty sure if I were going to commit murder, I have the skills for it. And the knowledge. I think I'd be a worthy challenge for the best detectives.'

'That's settled then, 'Pat said. She looked at Finney. 'Why don't we set our private bloodhound on the scent? He has a history of catching poisoners. I think it would be right up his street.'

'Seconded.' Robert declared.

Finney sank in his chair.

'I'm an old man.' He begged. 'I'm too old and too tired.'

'Then I'll do the leg work if you like.' Sydney said enthusiastically. 'I can be the Watson to your Holmes or the Hastings to your Poirot. What do you say?'

'More like the Laurel to his Hardy,' Margaret joked. No one laughed.

Gareth sat upright in his seat and leant towards Sydney.

'I could be the Tommy to your Tuppence?' He said.

Sydney smiled at the reference. She admired his knowledge.

'Why not?' Sydney said. She turned to Finney. 'Go on. Say yes. Let's do it. We'll help. It will be fun.'

Finney sighed. He looked up at Robert.

'Mr Wilde, this is your brother's murder. It is not a game. Do you want enthusiastic amateurs nosing around in it?'

'I do.' Robert said firmly. 'You're the man for the job. Find my brother's murderer.'

'Very well.' Finney agreed. He looked at Sydney and then at Gareth. He turned his gaze to Sanjay and then at Pat and Margaret. Slowly, he looked across at Sakura, Gemma and Robert. 'Just remember that you all asked for this. I cannot be held to blame for the result. I will find the killer. I will hunt that person down and reveal their identity, and I will not stop until I have done so.' He turned to Sydney. 'We'll start tomorrow.'

***

The rains had continued all that night and long into the morning. Finney made a strong coffee and sat beneath a large parasol in his courtyard. The ground was still wet, but the clouds had passed over, and a gentle August sun bore down on him and warmed him gently. He sipped his coffee and stared out into his garden. His mind had kept him awake most of the night, and it was engaged now, dipping back and forth from theories and musings until his head began to throb.

Sydney. Dear Sydney. She had stolen his heart from the first moment he saw her. She reminded him of his precious daughter, and the memory delighted him. Every time she was near, he felt his daughter beside him. It lifted his spirits and motivated him when age and weariness threatened to slow him down. Could it be possible that Sydney Fletch had crept across to Max's room in the depths of night to administer a lethal dose of hemlock? It was possible, of course. She was a capable young woman, but he couldn't quite determine a motive strong enough to warrant Max's murder. If Max had attacked her, he felt sure that Sydney would have left pieces of him all over Burnham Manor. No, poisoning would not have been Sydney's choice. There may well be another reason for Sydney wishing Max's death, but he couldn't think of it. Indeed, nothing strong enough to convince a murder investigation team to believe her guilt. No. It just didn't work.

He came to the same conclusion with Gareth Black. Poisoning didn't fit well with him, and had he exacted a terrible revenge on Max for Sydney's love, it would have been brutal and violent. No. Gareth Black didn't fit, either.

He was equally unsure of Sanjay Chakrabarti. There was something about the man he felt uncomfortable with, but he couldn't place his finger on it. Sanjay had appeared unhealthily happy at Max's passing, but this didn't make him a killer. Revenge was a powerful motive, and Max had caused Sanjay's budding career to falter. He felt sure that Sanjay was capable and he had a strong enough motive. As one of the guests at Burnham Manor that evening, he had the opportunity too. It was worth considering. Some elements could work, but they would need strengthening to convince DI Davenport.

He knew little about Sakura Fukushima, or Wilde, as she now was, and he reserved judgment. It would be interesting to see the results of Max's Will. It would be a powerful motive if he had changed it in her favour.

Gemma Collis had a strong motive for wanting Max Wilde dead, and he did not doubt that she was perfectly capable of it. She knew Burnham Manor well and could move about its corridors undetected. She had also been the last to see Max alive and had a perfect opportunity to poison his water. The problem, as Finney saw it, was that Gemma was also the one who found Max in the morning, and had she poisoned his water, she had a perfect opportunity to get rid of the evidence. It was a minor point but important. It provided Gemma Collis with a psychological alibi of sorts.

Without knowing the contents of the Will, it was hard to understand how strong Robert Wilde's motivations were. Certainly, he would have lost everything had Max followed through with his intention to sell his majority share of Wilde's restaurant business. But was that motivation enough to force Robert to act against his brother?

He knew very little about Pat Hemshaw save for the fact that she seemed to be at the mercy of her overbearing mother. There had been a scandal between her and Max, and she had no doubt paid a heavy price for it, but was that motive for killing him? It was certainly weak, but nothing could be worse than a woman scorned. But the poisoning element didn't work for him. If Pat had murdered Max, it would have been a crime of passion, and she would probably have killed herself at the same time. She was more Romeo and Juliet than a cold, calculating poisoner.

Her mother, on the other hand, was an entirely different matter. Everything about Margaret Hemshaw pointed to a cold, hard, calculating woman, perfectly capable of exacting a terrible revenge on Max Wilde. Yes, Margaret Hemshaw worked.

He was interrupted in his musings by Sydney, who swung open the iron gate to his garden and walked in. She was followed in her wake by her lap dog, Gareth, who closed the gate behind them and followed Sydney to where she had sat next to Finney.

'Good morning,' Finney said as Gareth took a seat. 'I thought we were going to meet at the Manor?'

As they had parted the previous day, they had made hasty arrangements to gather at the scene of the crime.

'We were going to,' Sydney explained. 'The front gate's completely blocked by reporters, asking some rather difficult questions. We decided we didn't want to answer them, so we came here instead.'

Max Wilde's murder had made headline news. The fact that several well-known crime writers were in the frame for it had whetted people's appetite for the gossip. There was nothing like a good murder to unite a country, Finney mused. It would be trial by social media. He was glad he was getting old. He didn't like the new world much and wouldn't miss it when he left.

He took out his tin of sweets, popped one in his mouth, and stood up.

'Right. Let's do this.'

***

Finney led them from his garden, around the side of his cottage, and out into the street. They were surprised to find Pat Hemshaw standing looking at them.

'Pat?' Sydney exclaimed. 'What are you doing here?'

Pat looked sheepish.

'Mother's gone up to London for the day. She suggested I join you.'

'Really?' Sydney said. She failed miserably in trying to hide her surprise.

'I know,' Pat agreed. 'That's what I thought. She's been acting odd for the last couple of days. I think Max's death has reminded her of her mortality. She almost said kind things to me this morning.'

'That doesn't sound like your mother.' Gareth remarked.

'She has a kind heart.' Pat said as if that explained it all.

'Well, you are more than welcome to join us.' Finney said. 'We're heading up to the house now.'

'I was going to meet you there,' Pat explained. 'I heard you talk about your plans yesterday. But there's a lot of journalists there, and then I remembered that you lived in the village, Mr Finney, so I came looking for you.'

'You did the right thing.' Finney nodded. 'There's no need for us to add fuel to their fire. I know of another way into Burnham Manor. I saw Mr Fenwick come out of a gate just the other night. Had I not seen it with my own eyes, I wouldn't have believed a gate was there.'

They followed Finney through the village, past the Wellington, and up the small hill towards the Manor. Just as they were about to turn the corner, Finney stopped and opened a cast iron gate in the stone wall.

'I must have walked past this gate a hundred times,' Finney told them, 'and I never once saw it. Isn't it odd how you often miss things that are staring you in the face?'

Finney opened the gate wide and beckoned them all through. They stepped into a small wooded area that marked the edge of the gardens and ran with the large stone wall throughout the entire circumference of Burnham Manor. Finney closed the gate behind them and pondered his next steps.

A well-worn path ran to the left, and they could make out Fenwick's small cottage in the distance. By the state of the path that led to his house, Finney deduced that he was a frequent drinker at The Marlborough.

A similar, but less worn, path ran to the right. Through the trees, they could make out Gemma's small cottage and the large iron gates holding the throngs of press at bay.

In front of them lay a third path, which ran straight through the trees to the garden's edge. They followed this path until they emerged from cover and made their way across the immaculately manicured lawn to where several cars were parked in front of the house. Finney recognised DI Davenport, who was in conversation with a young policewoman, and he couldn't help but notice the disapproving look she gave him as four of her main suspects approached.

'Mr Finney.' Davenport said. 'What are you doing here?'

Finney felt guilty. He hadn't been keen on opening a private investigation into Max's death, and his professional head thought he was stepping on Davenport's toes. However, he was also a suspect and didn't like that either. He was determined to furnish DI Davenport with a solution to the mystery that suited them all.

Briefly, he filled DI Davenport in on the events of the last twenty-four hours, including the anonymous messages and the cruise, finally explaining how he had come to be asked to look into the case by everyone who was most affected by it.

'I can't say I'm happy about it.' Davenport said. 'You should have told me about the messages.'

'I didn't think you would be happy. I wasn't sure what the messages meant, and I only went along out of professional curiosity. I can assure you we will not trouble you or ask you to disclose information that is not yours to disclose.'

'And if you discover anything else of interest to me or that may be pertinent to the case?' Davenport asked.

'I doubt we will discover anything you haven't already discovered, but you have my word that you will be the first to know.'

Reluctantly, Davenport nodded. She couldn't stop them, provided they didn't obstruct the official investigation. Having Finney's nose in the case might even prove helpful. So far, they had unearthed nothing, and her boss was beside herself with anger.

'May I ask where you are with the case at the moment?' Finney asked.

Davenport shrugged, and Finney could see the strain cross her face.

'If I'm honest, we're no closer to solving it than we were on Saturday morning.' Davenport explained. 'I spoke to Robert Wilde this morning. He's due to have a meeting with Max's solicitor shortly. He's coming here.

'I know about Sakura, Max's new wife, though god only knows what that means to the case. It's another suspect to muddy the waters. Our forensic analysts have determined that the vials of poison in the Poison Garden are real. Mr Fenwick and the late Mr Delancey distilled them over thirty years ago. Mr Delancey was certainly an odd character. If he weren't dead, I'd be investigating some of the things he got up to.'

'What about Fenwick?' Finney asked.

'He's an old man,' Davenport said. 'We could charge him with producing proscribed poisons, but what would that achieve? Robert and Sakura have agreed that we can pull down the Poison Garden. A team from the Chemical and Biological Warfare unit at Porton Down is coming to take it all away.'

'And you are no closer to understanding who put the poison in Max's water or why?'

Davenport shook her head.

'No. Anyone at the party that night could have done it. You all had the opportunity. Miss Collis can't be sure if she locked the house that night, which means anyone could have let themselves in. She remembers bumping into Mr Fenwick as he returned home from the pub, but she can't remember locking the front door to the Manor! As for Mr Fenwick, he can barely remember what he did this morning, let alone on Friday night.'

Davenport sounded frustrated. She looked up as she heard the growl of a powerful engine pull through the gates to the Manor. They watched a brand new Mercedes pull up in front of the house and a suited man in his early sixties climb out of the front seat.

'This must be Max's Will.' Davenport said. 'This should be interesting.'

***

'This is all most irregular…'

Max Wilde's solicitor had been shown through the doors of Burnham Manor and settled into Max's study. Gemma gave him a steaming cup of tea while everyone else took their seats.

DI Davenport and her sergeant took the two-seater sofa that Robert and Gareth had moved into position, facing the solicitor. Robert sat beside the solicitor beneath the large fireplace, and Gareth sat beside Sydney. Finney drew up a chair for Sakura and Pat, then found a comfortable chair nearby and lowered himself into it. They all waited for the solicitor to speak.

Mr William Constantine placed his briefcase onto the coffee table before him and took his cup of tea in hand. He sipped at it gently.

'Yes, indeed.' He continued. 'Most irregular.'

Mr Constantine was at least a hundred and six years old, Sydney concluded. What little hair remained upon his head was ghostly white, bordering on yellow. He had an aged, wrinkled face, pot-marked and freckled with liver spots. His eyes were the dullest grey, and when he spoke, his voice was tired and monotonous.

'Mr Wilde, as executor of your late brother's will, you have every right, in law, to know the contents of his Will before Probate. That being said, I am very uneasy at revealing the contents of his Will in front of such an audience.'

He looked up, and his eyes fell on the police officers. Davenport smiled.

'We can apply for a warrant if that pleases you?' She said.

Mr Constantine was about to say that it pleased him very much when Robert spoke.

'That won't be necessary.' Robert interjected. 'I think it's important that we know the contents of Max's Will, if only so we can determine how to proceed.'

Mr Constantine nodded.

'Very well.' Mr Constantine said reluctantly. 'Max's Will is relatively straightforward. Contracts and agreements already exist between him and Mr Robert Wilde regarding the future of their shared business interests, and similar arrangements exist concerning his business dealings with Miss Collis. Regarding his Will, he leaves Burnham Manor, its contents and grounds, to the National Trust so that they can maintain it as a tribute to fifty years of English Crime Writing. Mr Fenwick, the gardener, will continue to live in his home until his death, as specified in the Will of the late Mr Simon DeLancey. Miss Gemma Collis will receive the cottage where she currently resides and a sum of money amounting to twenty-five per cent of the remaining funds when all other matters have been resolved. His brother, Mr Robert Wilde, will receive the remaining seventy-five per cent.'

Mr Constantine sat back in his chair and drank more of his tea.

'May I ask how much that may amount to?' Finney asked.

'You may not.' Mr Constantine replied curtly.

'May I?' Robert asked.

Mr Constantine hesitated.

'As matters stand, the sum of Max's estate, before taxes and fees, amounts to approximately one hundred million pounds.'

Sydney felt the gasps from the people around her. Max's wealth had clearly been underestimated.

'How the bloody hell did he acquire that amount of money?' Robert asked. 'He was useless at everything.'

'Your brother may well have been useless at everything,' Mr Constantine explained, 'but he was very useful in surrounding himself with talented people who weren't useless. You, Mr Wilde, ran his restaurant empire while Miss Collis here took care of his writing empire. He had people taking care of his business needs, television career, and investments. If Max had one talent, it was drawing people in that could help him get what he wanted. He was the face. The name. The personality. People like Max are a magnet for money. He knew what worked and where to look for it, even if others worked out the detail.'

Sydney appreciated the analysis. Max was not a brilliant chef; Robert was. But Max's charm, drive, and intuition for what worked had pushed their business to great heights. He was no writer; Gemma was, but his image and name drove sales. He had great ideas for television and cooking shows and fronted them with style and panache while others did the legwork.

Robert looked across at Sakura and then at Mr Constantine.

'You may not know, Mr Constantine,' Robert said. 'But Max was married a short time ago to this young lady, Mrs Sakura Wilde. Are we to assume that he made no provision for her in his Will?'

'He did not.' Mr Constantine replied.

Everyone looked at Sakura.

'I did not marry Max for money.' She said. 'I do not want his money. I am happy to go home with nothing, which is exactly what I came here with.'

'We won't let that happen,' Gemma said, 'Max would have wanted you to be looked after.'

Gemma shot Robert a look.

'Gemma's right,' Robert agreed. 'We'll make sure you are well looked after. I owe it to Max.'

Mr Constantine coughed.

'Forgive me, Mr Wilde.' He said. 'I am fully aware that Max and Mrs Wilde were married. Max came to me a few months ago to tell me of his intentions and to employ me to help him sort out a few of the legal implications, particularly to manage Mrs Wilde's residency permit.'

Mr Constantine paused, and it was clear he was struggling with his thoughts.

'Perhaps, Mr Wilde,' he continued, 'we could talk in private?'

'That won't be necessary, Mr Constantine. I'd rather everything was above board and out in the open.'

Mr Constantine did not look happy. He sighed and put his cup on the coffee table.

'As you wish. As I said, I fully knew of Max's wedding and arranged as many formalities as possible. I am happy to say that I was also in attendance at the wedding and, despite my reservations, I am convinced that your brother married this young lady for all the right reasons. I have never seen a man so deeply in love, nor his love so emphatically reciprocated.

'Two weeks ago, Max and his new wife came to see me and instructed me to compose a new Will, which I did and was due to be signed here today in this very room.'

There was a long pause as everyone waited for Mr Constantine to continue.

'Obviously, the new Will remains unsigned due to Max's untimely murder.'

Or suitably timely, Sydney thought. She watched as the old solicitor opened his briefcase and withdrew a large Manilla envelope. He laid it down on the coffee table and tapped it with his index finger.

'The details of that new Will are contained within this envelope. As before, you remain, Mr Wilde, an executor to this new Will.'

'But surely that new Will means nothing?' DI Davenport asked. 'As it remains unsigned?'

'Not at all,' Mr Constantine replied. 'A Will is little more than a written document that confirms how the deceased wished his estate to be divided. A Will must show the true intentions of the deceased before their death. There are also provisions under the Inheritance Act for the protection of family members and dependants.'

Mr Constantine looked across at Sakura. Sydney saw the young woman nod in the lawyer's direction.

'I have been in contact with Mrs Wilde on this matter and must inform you that I represent her in this regard. It is my belief, for which I am prepared to swear in court, that the current Will does not and did not reflect Max Wilde's true intentions. I have advised Mrs Wilde that I believe she will successfully challenge the current Will, and Mrs Wilde has instructed me to proceed in this matter.'

So much for being happy to go home with what she came with, Sydney thought.

'What does the Will say?' Robert asked.

Mr Constantine cleared his throat.

'Mr Max Wilde's entire estate, the house, grounds and capital, become, on Max's death, the sole property of his wife, Mrs Sakura Wilde.'

***

DI Davenport and Seargent Graves followed the elderly solicitor as he left Burnham Manor. They were escorted to the door by Gemma Collis.

'I suppose the spotlight's on us now?' She asked.

'The spotlight's on everyone,' Davenport challenged as they watched the elderly Mr Constantine slide into the welcoming embrace of his expensive car, and drive away.

'I suppose it is.' Gemma sighed. 'We're sending down to The Marlborough for food, if you care to join us?'

Davenport declined.

'I'm afraid we have work to do,' she said, as three plain vans came up the drive in procession. 'This must be the scientists from Porton Down.'

Davenport and Graves made up the welcoming committe as the vans pulled up, and Gemma Collis disappeared back inside the Manor.

'DI Davenport.' Davenport said, her hand outstretched, as the man who looked like he was in charge got out of the lead vehicle and approached her.

He took her hand warmly. He was an older man who looked like he hadn't been outside in decades. His hair was a dusty grey and his skin was the colour of milk.

'Dr Makepeace.' He said brightly. 'Although that it has been argued that my name is something of a paradox!'

He gave a little chuckle, as though it were the first time he had ever made that joke.

It made Davenport wonder. Porton Down was the home of the UK's military research wing and, more recently, the home of the UK Health Security Agency. Most of what went on within its walls were top secret and hidden from public scrutiny.

'Better let the dog see the rabbit.' Dr Makepeace continued as he was joined by several other pale looking individuals.

'This way,' Davenport directed, and she and the mysterious men from Porton Down, crossed the garden and into the small coppice, where the walled Poison Garden was to be found.

'Do you get much of this sort of thing?' Davenport asked as she swung open the cast iron gate to the garden.

'Yes. I'm afraid the internet has made everyone an expert. You'd be surprised what people get up to behind closed doors.'

Davenport doubted that. Her career had exposed her to some of societies' strangest and most colourful people.

'Right. We'll just crack on, if that's okay.' Dr Makepeace said, as his team of scientists began spreading out through the garden. 'We'll let you know if we find anything interesting.'

Davenport and Graves left the gaggle of scientists to it and gathered on the lawn in front of Burnham Manor.

'What next?' Graves asked.

Davenport looked at the house before her.

'That's a lot of money to kill for,' she mused. 'I want a deep dive on Max's new wife. A full history and background check.'

'It would seem odd to kill Max Wilde before he changed his Will in her favour.' Graves pondered.

'It would,' Davenport agreed, 'but I want to know more about her. But Max dying before the will change does rather point the finger at Robert Wilde. He loses a lot when the Will changes, and he stood to lose everything if Max had sold his share of Wilde's Restaurant. I want a detailed background on Robert Wilde. Find out whether he really knew about Sakura and the Will change. And go hard on his alibi. Let's see where he was on Friday night.'

'What about Gemma Collis?' Graves asked.

'She has the second strongest motive for wanting Max Wilde dead. I want background checks on everyone. Find out Pat Hemshaw's movements on Friday night. See if we can put her near the scene of the crime.'

'What about Mr Finney?'

Davenport screwed her eyes up.

'We must count him as a suspect but treat him like a witness. The thing that bothers me most is this text message saga. What do you think that was about?'

Graves shrugged.

'Someone's idea of a joke?'

'It's more than that.' Davenport said, shaking her head. 'It tells me that a lot of thought and planning has gone into this. This isn't a crime of opportunity. We're going to need to be at our best. Get down to Wallingford and find out what you can from the owners of the river cruiser. Whoever set that up may have left some incriminating evidence. Get in touch with the service provider of the number used to send the text messages. There may be something there.'

Davenport gazed at the mansion house before her and thought about the people inside. It was likely that one of them was a murderer. But which one?

***

'That's quite some motive for murder.'

An early lunch had been ordered from The Marlborough's kitchens and laid out in the dining room. The French windows were thrown open, and warm summer air breezed in on the back of a light wind. Across the large oak dining table, immaculately constructed foods sat in dishes and bowls and emitted such a delightful smell that it proved hard for the guests to resist. They dived into locally cured meats, cheeses made from the milk of nearby dairy farms, and trout from a nearby fishery. Warmed new potatoes, seeped in rich butter and seasoned lightly with mint and pepper, formed a perfect accompaniment to the buffet. More tea was made, along with several cafetieres. Jugs of homemade juices were brought up and laid in the centre of the table.

Sydney followed Gareth around the table and then out onto the patio. They sat next to Finney, and Gareth said:

'That's quite some motive for murder.'

One hundred million pounds, Burnham Manor, its attendant grounds and properties, and god knows what other delights Max had collected over the years, all suddenly the property of one very lucky young woman. Sydney began to wonder about the mysterious Sakura Wilde.

'Do you think?' Finney asked.

Sydney looked at him. Finney had a way, sometimes, of making you question what you thought was bloody obvious.

'She's a very rich young woman.' Sydney argued. 'Not quite the empty hand she was happy to go home with.'

'And she was talking to the solicitors behind everyone's backs.' Gareth added.

'Interesting.' Finney said and then said no more.

'How so?' Sydney asked.

'Until yesterday,' Finney mused, 'no one knew Max was married or knew anything of his young bride. We had none of us met Sakura. As a foreign woman in a foreign land, I think it's not unreasonable to reach out to the only person she knew could help. An experienced and wise old man that Max trusted implicitly. Mr Constantine. Why would she share her knowledge of the new Will with us, complete strangers? Potentially, any one of us could be responsible for Max's death. Who could she possibly trust? No, I do not think it odd that she kept that to herself. Sakura has certainly become a very wealthy young woman, but then, had Max lived, she would have been extremely wealthy anyway. Burnham Manor would still have been hers, and I am sure she would have wanted for nothing.'

'So our investigation goes no further forward?' Gareth asked.

'On the contrary,' Finney said, smiling. 'Our investigation leaps forward much as I suspected it would. I firmly believe Robert and Gemma have the strongest motives for wishing Max dead. Under the terms of the new Will, they get nothing.'

'But they couldn't have known that? No one knew of the new Will or even that Max had got married.'

'So we are told.' Finney said. 'Is it beyond the realms of possibility that one, or both, of them, discovered Max's secret and acted swiftly in the execution of his murder to secure their inheritance?'

'If anyone could discover Max's secrets, it was Gemma.' Gareth agreed. 'She knew every detail of his life. I imagine it would have been quite hard to keep anything from her. She would have noticed him acting strangely.'

'And they were lovers.' Sydney mentioned. The image of Gemma and Robert going at it over the kitchen worktop still lingered in her mind's eye.

'They could have been in it together.' Gareth exclaimed. 'Gemma's a clever woman. I've read Max's books. Her plots are solid and well thought out. What if she left that poisoned water by Max's bedside on purpose, believing, as we do, that had she been the poisoner, she would have disposed of the evidence? With Robert conveniently in London that night, she's practically thrown the spotlight away from themselves.'

Finney nodded. They were good points. The water by Max's bedside had certainly confused the issue.

They let the conversation drop as Sakura and Pat came through the French windows and sat with them.

'What will you do now?' Sydney asked.

Sakura still looked like a lost puppy. She didn't look like a killer.

'My grandfather has returned to London. I will return with him later. He flies back to Japan tomorrow. I will stay in London until after the funeral, and then I shall go home too.'

'Nonsense.' Robert said as he walked through the French windows. 'You'll stay here, in Burnham Manor. Max would have wanted it that way.'

'Yes, of course you will,' Gemma agreed as she followed Robert onto the patio. 'Let's not worry about the Will today. Whatever happens, Burnham Manor is your home. Max wanted it that way.'

'What will I do in such a big house?' Sakura asked. She turned to Pat. 'Perhaps you would stay with me?'

'God no, mother would never allow it!' Pat said.

'What about Sydney?' Finney asked. He avoided eye contact with Sydney and threw the question at Sakura.

'Would you?' Sakura asked.

Sydney looked deep into Sakura's deep, brown eyes and puppy dog expression and scrambled around in her head for an excuse that would hold water. She couldn't find one.

'I suppose so,' she said reluctantly. 'I don't see why not. It could be fun.'

'Good, that's settled then,' Robert beamed. 'If you need anything, I'll be at The Marlborough and Gemma's just down the drive at Honeysuckle Cottage.' He glanced at his watch. 'I'm afraid I must love you and leave you. I have an appointment with the undertakers in an hour.'

Robert took Gemma's hand, and the two disappeared into the house.

Pat stood up and took Sakura's hand.

'Let's explore the house.' She said, and suddenly, it was just Finney, Sydney and Gareth on the patio.

'What the hell did you do that for?' Sydney asked. It was clear from how she said it that she wasn't happy. 'I don't know the girl from Adam and haven't got a thing in common with her. I can't think of anything worse than being stuck in this bloody great house with her.'

Finney fidgeted in his seat.

'I am afraid for her life,' he said slowly, 'and I don't want to be responsible for her murder. I want you here, where you can keep a watchful eye on her.'

'You think she's in danger?' Sydney asked.

'I do.' Finney said. 'If Gemma and Robert have anything to do with Max's murder, and they killed him to inherit his wealth, it's clear they knew nothing about the second Will. Now they know they stand to lose everything they have schemed for. If Sakura were to die before she could challenge the Will, then…..'

Finney threw his hands out and waited for his two young followers to catch up.

'Bloody hell.' Gareth exclaimed. 'I hadn't thought of that. Perhaps I should stay too.' Sydney noticed the twinkle in his eye. 'To keep an eye on you both.' He added.

'That won't be necessary.' Sydney countered. 'Sakura and I will be quite safe.'

Gareth deflated.

'Actually,' Finney began, and two sets of eyes looked in his direction. 'That's not a bad idea. I would feel more comfortable if Gareth were here, too. But discreetly. Later, when we all go our separate ways, come back under cover of darkness and let yourself into the house. Sydney, leave the back door, nearest the kitchens, open.'

Sydney was about to protest, but the look on Finney's face told her he wasn't joking.

'Okay.' She said.

'Good.' Finney continued. 'I think I'd like to go and look around the maze. Rather a lot seemed to happen there.'

***

They waited for Pat to catch up. She called for them as they walked across the immaculately manicured lawn.

'I think it's all got a bit too much for Sakura,' she said by way of explanation. 'She's gone for a lie-down.'

'A wife, a widow and a multi-millionaire in the space of a few weeks. I'm sure she's exhausted.' Gareth said, and the sarcasm positively dripped from his lips.

'That's unkind.' Sydney said. 'She could be perfectly innocent in all this. She could be just an innocent bystander caught up in a mess of someone else's doing.'

'Or a very smart and intelligent murderess.' Finney added.

The three young people who followed in the older man's footsteps looked at one another. Sydney sighed.

'So you don't believe she could be the next victim?'

The exasperation in Sydney's voice was not lost on Finney. He liked to mix things up. It amused him.

'She could be. I never said it was a fact. If it proves that Gemma and Robert are the villains in this particular drama, then she is in mortal danger. On the other hand, as Gareth has succinctly pointed out, she has recently become an inordinately rich young woman. I have not yet determined the solution to this particular problem, and one must keep an open mind.'

'So she could be a murderer?' Sydney asked.

'She could.' Finney nodded. 'She could indeed.'

'And you think it's a good idea that I should rattle around this big old house with a potential psychopath or, if she's not a psychopath, to rattle around this big old house defending her against potentially two other murderous psychopaths?'

Finney smiled.

'Yes. But that's why I want Gareth here, too. For added protection.'

'Oh. So you think Robert and Gemma killed Max for his money and may now want to kill Sakura to guarantee it?' Pat asked.

'In a nutshell, Miss Hemshaw.' Finney replied. He had forgotten she hadn't been there when they were discussing the new turn of events. 'But we must keep this all from the new Mrs Wilde. On the one hand, I don't want to alert her to the spies I have planted in her household or, on the other, to frighten her unnecessarily.'

'Spies?' Sydney asked.

'Yes. Spies.' Finney smiled. 'If there is any evidence to confirm who murdered Max, it's likely to be inside Burnham Manor, and if you are within Burnham Manor, it is likely you will discover that evidence.'

Sydney hooked her arm through Finney's and walked alongside him.

'You're quite sneaky.' She said.

'I am.' Finney laughed. 'Come on, show me where you and your young paramour hid.'

They had approached the entrance to the maze, and Gareth watched as Sydney and Finney entered. He hooked his arm through Pat's and held her firmly to his side. He would have preferred it to have been Sydney's arm, but any port in a storm. Pat looked at him as though he had lost his head. She wasn't used to men being so forward.

'The last time I was in this maze,' Gareth explained, 'Sydney left me there on my own, and it took me four hours to get out. If I'm going to get stuck in there a second time, I demand company.'

Pat relaxed and led them both through the entrance. The last time she had been in the maze was when she had last seen Max alive. It was a memory she would treasure.

They followed Sydney and Finney as they meandered through the hedges. Sydney was as sure-footed as a mouse in a field of maize, and she led them directly to the centre without missing a step.

'We hid here.' Sydney pointed to a small hole in the hedge that had allowed her and Gareth to stay unobserved.

A fine hiding point, Finney agreed. Anyone entering the maze would have been unaware of their presence. Equally, those within the centre or leaving the maze would have failed to see them.

'Where was Max during this time?' Finney asked.

Sydney walked over to where Max had been standing during their observations.

'Describe the timeline of events, beginning with the first person to enter the maze.'

Briefly, Sydney recounted what she and Gareth had witnessed.

Margaret Hemshaw had been the first. She had brandished her stick in Max's face and given him short measure about his relationship with Pat. Max had denied any recent impropriety, and Pat confirmed that was true.

'You told me that Margaret threatened Max?' Finney asked.

'I'm not sure it was a threat,' Sydney said. 'She said something about someone putting his lights out one day.'

'Meaning to kill him?'

'That's what I understood her to mean.' Sydney agreed.

'How did Max react?'

'He laughed in her face.' Gareth declared. 'He was very dismissive of her.'

'And then Sanjay came into the maze.' Sydney said. 'He was very angry with Max. They argued about Max's contract with the BBC and how it cost Sanjay his show, Death in the Raj. Max rather patronised him, if I'm honest.'

'How did Sanjay react?' Finney asked.

'He said something about actions having consequences and asked whether Max was ready to pay the price of his actions.'

'I see.' Finney said quietly. 'I wonder what he meant by that?'

'I'm sure he meant nothing by it,' Pat countered, and everyone noted the passion in her voice. 'He's not that sort of man. He's kind and considerate. He doesn't have a cruel bone in his body.'

Yes, Sydney thought. There was definitely something between Pat and Sanjay. She wondered if Margaret knew.

Finney deflected her emotions.

'And then Robert Wilde?' He asked.

'Yes. He was furious.' Gareth declared. 'He's a fairly well-built man, too. He didn't pull his punches, that's for sure. He laid Max out cleanly.'

'And they argued about The Marlborough?'

'They did.' Gareth said. 'Robert had just found out that Max was selling his sixty per cent share in the business, effectively forcing Robert out. Robert begged him to sell him his share, or at least his controlling share, so he could keep control of the business.'

'I wonder why Max owned a controlling share?' Finney pondered.

'They hinted at it during the row,' Sydney explained. 'There did seem to be some history there. Max used it to hurt his brother.'

'A question we must put to Robert.' Finney said. 'What happened next?'

'I did.' Pat said. 'I must have been next into the maze. I found Max clutching his bloodied nose.'

Finney turned abruptly and looked Pat square in the eye.

'Why did you come here, then?' He asked.

Pat looked sheepish. She wasn't ashamed of herself, far from it. She had fulfilled her heart's desire, and she had no regrets, but that didn't mean she wanted an audience.

'We're not judging you, Pat.' Sydney said, taking her hand in hers. 'I'm sorry we saw you. It was a private matter. I'd be horrified if I knew someone had watched me!'

Gareth fidgeted uneasily next to her.

'The truth is,' Pat said, 'that Max had completely broken me. I'd fallen utterly in love with him, and he used me. Mother had been apoplectic, as usual, and forbidden me to see him. She never let me out of her sight for a whole year. Not once. I had no way to get close to Max to try and understand what had occurred. I admit I was desperate. I can see that now. When Mother left to come to the dinner that day, I followed. It was my first opportunity to see Max. When I saw him in the maze, the bubble burst. Suddenly, I felt like I was the one in control. I was in charge of my emotions and my life. Max had been nothing more than a catalyst that drove the change in me. He opened my eyes, and they've stayed firmly open ever since.'

'What about your mother?' Sydney asked gently.

'Mother is something else.' Pat agreed. 'But something has changed recently. She's getting old. She may even have mellowed a bit. I wonder if she hasn't felt the bubble burst, too.'

Finney wondered.

'Right,' he said at last. 'Show me the Poison Garden.'

***

The Poison Garden was now a shell of its former self. In its present condition, it would have been hard for any of them to describe it as a garden at all. The building still stood, but it looked grey and old, and where once its contents had hinted at its dangerous character, now it felt empty and lacking substance. DI Davenport stood at the entrance, watching as figures dressed in chemical and biological warfare suits flitted about the garden's carcass, removing what was left of its shell. They carried plants in their arms and ferried them to waiting vehicles, where they would be removed for study or destruction.

Sydney felt a hint of sadness as she watched the slaughter unfold. She turned to say something to Finney and found Mr Fenwick standing beside her. She gasped and reached out for Finney's arm.

'Mr Fenwick, you made me jump!' She exclaimed.

Finney turned as he felt Sydney's hand grab his arm and saw the quiet-footed Mr Fenwick standing by Sydney's side. None of them had seen or heard him approach.

'Bloody criminal, what they're doing!' Fenwick said, and his displeasure manifested in a hard scowl that stretched his aged face.

Sydney didn't like Fenwick much and rarely made that conclusion about anyone. But Mr Fenwick had an air about him that she didn't like or trust, and from where she stood, she could smell the beer on his breath.

'Old Simon Delancey and I put that together over thirty years ago,' he reminisced. 'He wanted to know all about them, how to grow them, how to nurture them, how to isolate the poisons they contained. We spent a month distilling and refining our potions until we had a hundred of the deadliest poisons at our disposal.'

Fenwick reached into a dirty trouser pocket and retrieved a small vial. He held it out in front of him and let the vial roll in the palm of his hands.

'There's enough poison in this vial to kill a hundred people.' He declared. He rolled his hand closed over the glass. 'It used to give Delancey a buzz. Having that much power. Power over life and death. Just a small drop of this liquid in someone's tea or coffee.'

Sydney shivered.

'Do you think it's wise having that stuff in your possession?' Gareth asked. 'Probably isn't even legal.'

'It isn't,' Finney said sternly.

Fenwick dropped the vial into his pocket.

'Ain't used it in thirty years. Ain't going to start now.'

Everyone looked around as they heard footsteps approach. DI Davenport had seen them and was making her way over.

'That's us about done, here.' She declared. 'Who was that you were talking to?'

Sydney turned and realised Fenwick had gone almost as silently as he had arrived.

'That was the gardener.' Finney said. 'Mr Fenwick. He has a habit of appearing by your side like an apparition. One minute he's not there, and then he is; the next, he's gone again.'

Davenport recognised the description. She had bumped into him a few times during the investigation.

'Simon Delancey left him the gamekeeper's cottage?' She asked.

'He did. It's just over there through the trees.' Finney pointed to where a small cottage could be seen through the trees. 'Although I think he spends most of his time in his greenhouse.'

'He's an odd fella,' Davenport said. 'We may have a word with him about some of these plants and poisons he's kept in this place.'

'Seems a bit redundant.' Gareth said. 'Now that it's all gone. He's an old man. It's unlikely he's a threat to anyone.'

'Still,' Davenport pondered. 'I've heard some troubling things about Delancey, and I can't help but think Mr Fenwick has some dark secrets.'

Davenport looked across at the remains of the Poison Garden as she heard her name called out.

'If you'll excuse me,' she said, mainly to Finney, and she turned and walked back to her Sergeant.

'Sometimes,' Pat said, 'I often wonder if some secrets are best left unknown.'

The sentiment passed around the little group, and each of them nodded sagely.

'Let's go and chat to Mr Fenwick,' Finney declared. 'I feel he knows much more about what goes on around here than anyone else.'

***

Mr Fenwick did not look too pleased when the quadrant of amateur detectives filed into his small greenhouse. He sat in an old armchair surrounded by shelves full of gardening tools. A table sat to his right, and a glass of beer sat on it. Next to that was a packet of rolling tobacco and the burning embers of a recently extinguished cigarette. He reached over and turned down an old-looking radio just above his head.

'What do you lot want?' He asked. He reached out for his glass and drank the liquid within. He reached behind his chair, opened a small fridge concealed behind, and pulled out another beer.

Finney led the conversation.

'Do you know who I am?' Finney asked.

'Seen you about.' He answered gruffly. 'Ex-copper, I'm told.'

'I live in The Larches in the village.'

'I know where you live,' Fenwick interrupted. 'Like I said, seen you about.'

'You seem to see a lot,' Finney said. 'And know a lot about a lot of things.'

'I don't know much,' Fenwick countered. 'I know plants and gardens. Been doing it all my life. It's all I know. As for seeing things… People are not very good at staying hidden when they think they've not been seen.'

'Did you see anything the other night?' Finney asked. 'The night of the dinner party.'

'I saw people coming and going.' Fenwick admitted. He looked at Pat and then at Sydney and Gareth. 'I saw them all day and then into the evening. I saw you, too.' He said, looking directly at Finney.

'Yes. I was with Grace. She walked with me to the gate. You were on the way to the pub, I presume?'

'I was. I have a few pints on a Saturday night. As many as my pension will allow.'

'I understand you bumped into Miss Collis during the night?'

'I did. She was on her way home.'

Finney screwed his face up in concentration. He looked at the others.

'What time did the party break up, and you all went to bed?' Finney asked.

'I can't remember for sure,' Pat said, looking to the others. 'Gone one o'clock.'

'Closer to two,' Gareth said.

'Yes,' Sydney agreed. 'Closer to two.'

Finney looked at Fenwick.

'Pubs usually shut at 11. What time did the Marlborough close?'

Fenwick fidgeted in his armchair.

'I left the pub at twelve, or thereabouts.'

'And you were still wandering about Burnham Manor a few hours later? And why were you outside Gemma Collis's house?'

Fenwick took a slow drink of his beer and placed the glass on the table.

'I don't have to tell you anything.' He said firmly.

'Of course not,' Finney admitted. Sydney noticed the smile cross his face. 'Gareth, would you mind seeing if

Detective Inspector Davenport is still here? Perhaps Mr Fenwick would rather talk to her.'

Gareth turned to leave.

'Wait!' Fenwick cried. 'There's no need for the police. They stick their noses in where it's not needed.'

'Very well,' Finney said. 'Then why were you lingering about the grounds almost two hours after you left the pub?'

'I like to watch people.' Fenwick said slowly. 'And I like to be outside. This is my home, and I can walk where I please.'

'I don't disagree.' Finney admitted. 'But you have a rather disturbing habit of sneaking up on people without them being aware of your presence. A skill, I daresay, you have acquired over many years?'

Fenwick looked reluctant to say anymore. Finney turned to Gareth and nodded at him. Fenwick watched the interaction.

'Wait!'

Gareth paused.

'Mr Fenwick?' Finney pressed.

'Simon Delancey had a fondness for the darker side of humanity. It intrigued him and interested him. He used to have parties at the house, where all sorts of weird and strange people would come. I used to watch from the sidelines.'

'What sort of people?' Gareth asked.

'Girls, mostly. Sometimes boys. All paid for. They entertained him.'

'Underage?' Sydney asked.

'No. Never that.' Fenwick said. 'Young, for sure, but never kids. People like that disgusted him. They were all willing and legal.'

'And you watched them?'

Fenwick nodded.

'I did. I grew a taste for it. Simon Delancey knew, and it amused him. I think it excited him. We became friends through our love of the more interesting sides of human nature.'

'And you continue to watch today?'

'Not so much.' Finney admitted. 'But I don't sleep much anymore. Sometimes, I wander through the village and around the grounds. I hadn't intended to meet Miss Collis that night. It was a coincidence.'

'Thank you, Mr Fenwick.' Finney said. 'You've been very helpful.'

They gathered outside the greenhouse, and one by one, they followed Finney to where the hidden gate led out into the street.

'That was creepy.' Gareth said as he followed in Sydney's footsteps.

'Gives me the heebies.' Pat agreed.

'A dirty old man, for sure,' Sydney admitted. 'But I find myself strangely drawn to Simon Delancey. I want to know more about him and his predilections.'

'I think Simon Delancey understood the human psyche, to a certain extent.' Finney said as he opened the iron gate and stepped into the street. 'He seemed to have a deep understanding of what made people tick and what made them go wrong. His books certainly lean that way. It's no surprise he dabbled himself.'

'Where are we going?' Sydney asked.

Finney looked down the lane to where the Marlborough could be made out in the distance.

'For lunch.' He declared.

***

DI Davenport remained at the Poison Garden and watched as the scientists from Porton Down identified, tagged and bagged up everything within it. One or two were dressed in biological warfare suits with canisters strapped to their backs to help them breathe.

Dr Makepeace oversaw the operation and catalogued everything on a small tablet. He looked up as Davenport approached.

'Nothing too hideous,' he said, 'although there are one or two plants that could do you some serious mischief.'

'What will happen to the plants?' Davenport asked.

'Most will be destroyed. Some can give off fairly toxic fumes when burnt, so we'll pop them into one of our incinerators.'

'And the vials of poison?'

'They will be destroyed.' Dr Makepeace said. 'Some could still be quite toxic, even after all these years. You've got to wonder what they were thinking of when they made them. Bloody dangerous stuff, I can tell you.'

Davenport agreed. She thought of the strange Simon Delancey and the rumours she'd heard about him, and then she thought of Mr Fenwick.

She turned from the Poison Garden and headed towards Mr Fenwick's shed. It was time they had a word.

She held out her warrant card as she entered Mr Fenwick's greenhouse.

'I know who you are.' Fenwick grumbled. He took a swig from a bottle of beer he was holding and dropped it down on the table in front of him. 'What do you want?'

'I want to arrest you.' Davenport began. 'But I'm not going to. Not yet, at least. But I think you need to tell me about what you and Delancey thought you were doing creating all those poisons.'

Fenwick shrugged.

'It was Simon Delancey, mostly,' he began carefully. 'He was into all that stuff for his books. He took his research seriously. He asked me, once, if it was possible to grow his own plants to extract its poison. He didn't know how easy it could be, so we gave it a go. It turned out it could be quite easy.'

'That's where the poison garden started?'

'Yeah. After a while, we were growing all manner of plants. Some exotic ones, grown from seeds smuggled into the country by Mr Delancey, and some fairly common ones. The kind of plants you see growing in your average English garden. Mr Delancey found that fascinating. I think it made part of one of his bestsellers.'

'And you successfully extracted poisons from them?'

'Yes.'

'Even though it's illegal and extremely dangerous.'

Fenwick shrugged.

'People do illegal stuff all the time. No one got hurt. That was never the intention.'

'How do you know if the poisons you extracted were successful?' Davenport asked.

Fenwick smiled, and his crooked, blackened teeth broke out from between his lips. It looked more like a snarl.

'We didn't test them on people if that's what you mean. Although Delancey often joked about getting away with the perfect murder! No, it was rabbits and rats, mostly. Foxes, if we could catch one.'

'Tell me about Friday night. What did you do? Where were you?'

'I was here till about eight, then I went to the pub. Came back about eleven.'

'Did you see anything? Hear anything?'

'Saw lots of things. Heard lots of things.'

'Anything that might interest me?' Davenport asked.

Fenwick shook his head.

'Probably not.'

Davenport knew the type of man Mr Fenwick was and knew better than to harass him. She took a business card from her pocket and handed it to him.

'If you think of anything or remember anything, call me.'

She watched as Fenwick dropped her card onto the table.

'Probably won't.'

Davenport stepped out of Mr Fenwick's greenhouse and into the sun. It was hot and getting hotter. There was so much to think about and very little to go on. She sighed. The feeling that this would not be straightforward was beginning to haunt her.

***

There was a buzz inside the Marlborough as they stepped inside. Gareth led the way and strode directly up to the bar, and laid an appreciative eye along the beers. He ordered a local ale and turned to Sydney.

'What would you like?'

'I think I'd like to try what you're having.' She replied.

'A beer drinker as well? I think I'm falling in love.'

The words escaped his lips before he had time to engage the brake. He looked at Sydney in the hope that she hadn't heard, but it was clear from her bemused expression that she had. He felt the blood rise in his neck and sweat gather on his brow. Finney watched the exchange with some amusement, and it reminded him of his faltering first steps with his late wife.

'I should like to try that beer, too.' Finney said, relieving Gareth of some of his stress. 'Miss Hemshaw?'

Pat looked across the bar.

'Well, if you're all having beer, I'd like to join you. Mother disapproves of women drinking pints. She thinks it's demeaning.'

'Four pints it is then.' Gareth declared to the young bartender, who began pouring the second glass. 'Are we too late for food?'

The young lady behind the bar looked around the building as if to say, 'Do we look like we have room?' But said, 'We are very busy. All our tables are fully booked. It's been like this since Mr Wilde was… you know… murdered.'

'That's okay, Ella, I'll look after these people. Please bring the drinks and some menus to table thirteen.'

Robert Wilde stepped into the bar from a door in the corner, where a selection of boxed snacks were stored.

'I saw you on the cameras,' he said. 'I've been trying to get on top of some paperwork. Come through to the lounge.'

He stepped out from behind the bar and led them through the pub. The public bar was filled with lunchtime drinkers, and they had to squeeze their way through to the more relaxed lounge, which encompassed the remainder of the ground floor. It was almost four times the size of the public bar, and Robert meandered his way across the room, over uneven floors and under low-hanging beams, until he turned beside a huge open fire, which, in turn, led to a small inglenook. Gemma sat on one of the large, comfortable-looking leather chairs in front of the fireplace, drinking a coffee and reading from a tablet. She looked up as they descended on her.

'Oh, hello.' She said. 'Have you come for lunch? Please, sit down.'

Gareth sat beside Sydney on one of the two-seaters surrounding the old oak table. Finney sat in an armchair by himself, and Pat shuffled in next to Gemma. The young bartender set a tray of four golden beers on the table and fanned several menus in front of them. She began to speak the script they fell into when taking food orders, determining to point out the specials, the soup of the day, and which fish were on the menu when Robert interrupted her.

'That's okay, Ella. They're my guests. Could you get a bottle of the Chateau Philipe? On my tab, please.'

'We don't mind paying our way,' Gareth interjected.

'Nonsense,' Robert said firmly. 'I won't hear of it. Besides, I want to hear how your investigation is going.'

Robert took the last armchair and fell into it.

'Perhaps we should order food first?' Finney suggested. 'I am quite hungry.'

'Excellent idea.' Robert enthused. 'If I may make one or two suggestions…'

After a few minutes, food was ordered, a bottle of Chateau Philipe was opened, and several glasses were poured. Gareth sank his pint quickly while the others relished the silky flavour momentarily before turning to the wine.

'So,' Robert asked, 'are we any closer to the truth?'

Everyone turned to look at Finney, who placed his pint glass on the table and turned and looked at them all in turn.

'No.' He said. 'We have discovered that Simon Delancey was a man of colourful character, and Mr Fenwick is a man of dubious moral integrity.'

'Really?' Gemma asked. 'Do tell!'

Sydney relayed the knowledge they had acquired from the horse's mouth.

Gemma sat back in her chair, disgusted and slightly bemused. She was disgusted because voyeurs were a special kind of weird and intrigued because the writer in her wanted to know more.

'Oh. You don't think he was perving on me, do you?'
She asked as the realisation dawned on her.

'I see no other reason for him to be in that part of
the garden at that time of night.' Finney said. 'I think he
is too old to be of any danger to you, but even so, I
think it would be best if you locked your home securely
at night.'

Gemma shuddered.

Finney turned to Robert.

'Tell me about you and Max,' he asked.

Robert shrugged.

'Not much to tell that hasn't already been well
documented,' he said. 'We grew up here. This place used
to belong to our parents. I'm fourteen months older than
Max. I grew up looking after him, making sure he didn't
get into too much trouble, and punching the bullies
when they went too far. When we were teenagers, we
started working in the kitchens here. I loved it. It's all I
ever wanted to do. For Max, it was something to do
while he was looking for something better. That was who
he was. He always thought there was something better
and was always looking for it. He couldn't stay with
anything for long before the urge to move on engulfed
him. I'm afraid he was like that with women, too. He was
never happy with what he had.'

'But he became a chef?' Finney asked.

'After a fashion.' Robert replied. 'I qualified first and
started working in the kitchen here. Max followed
because he couldn't decide what else he wanted to do.
After a couple of years, we took over the pub from our
parents and started a new venture together. Max had
some excellent ideas, but he never had the staying power
to see them through or, if I'm honest, the skill. He was a
chef, for sure, but not a good one.

'When we were kids, we used to go scrumping in old Delancey's place. Everyone told us not to go there. I think people were a little bit scared of him. Now I'm older, I realise that people didn't want children hanging around the home of a man like that. Our parents must have heard some of the rumours about him. I never saw anything myself, but Max used to come back telling some tall tales. Delancey intrigued him. When he was about fifteen, Max bought a copy of one of his books and became obsessed with crime fiction. He said that one day he would become a bestselling crime writer.

'Then, after a few years of running this place, we started opening restaurants further afield. We started to get a bit of a name for ourselves. Wilde's became the name on all good food writers' lips. Max went off to run one of them by himself, but typically with Max, it didn't last long. He got bored and careless, and the business suffered. One day, I was asked by a television company to feature on one of their shows, but I wasn't particularly interested, so Max went instead. They loved his segment and invited him back. Before long, he had his own cooking show, then a quiz show, and then his novels. Crime and food. Max found his niche. When Delancey died, he bought the house. Everything Max had ever wanted fell at his feet. He barely had to work a day in his life.'

Robert paused as a selection of starters were laid on the table.

'If you were a partnership,' Finney began, 'and I assume you were equal partners, then why did Max own a controlling stake in Wilde's?'

Robert nodded.

'I wondered when someone would ask.' He looked at Gemma, who smiled lovingly at him. 'The truth is I was a bit jealous of Max and his success. The backbone of

Max's career was food and crime, two things he wasn't particularly good at. I crafted the menus and Gemma his novels. Max got all the glory. I started to gamble. Not much to begin with, but after a couple of years I had fallen into considerable debt with some particularly nasty characters. I had to go to Max, cap in hand, to beg for his help. It cost me my pride and the controlling stake in the business.'

'Which hurt the most?' Sydney asked.

Robert fell quiet, and Gemma threw her a look that, in normal circumstances, would have melted steel.

'My pride, to begin with. Max took the controlling share to hold it over my head to show me that he was in control and had all the power. I never thought he would ever sell it. When I found out, my pride took a battering for a second time.'

'Fortunately,' Sydney pointed out, 'the contract between you held that, in the event of one person's death, the other would acquire the remaining share.'

'What the bloody hell are you implying?' Gemma spat, and Sydney saw the venom in the whites of her eyes.

'She's implying,' Robert said, 'quite rightly, that I'm the number one suspect in Max's murder. Of course I am. I gain the most.'

'Well, I think it's rude,' Gemma added, taking an angry sip of her coffee.

They finished their starters in an awkward silence. The plates were carried away, and the servers returned with more food. Robert ordered a second bottle of wine.

'I also gain considerably,' Gemma said after some time had passed. 'Am I a suspect?'

'Of course you are.' Sydney said, relishing Gemma's discomfort. 'I should say you are suspect number two. But then again, we are all suspects.' She added, looking around the table. 'Every one of us.'

***

They stepped out of the pub into the early afternoon sun.

'Well, that was fun.' Gareth said.

Sydney ignored the comment.

'I think it was enlightening.' Finney said as he turned out of the pub towards his cottage.

'You do?' Sydney asked.

'I do.' Finney replied and said no more.

Pat looked at Sydney, who raised an eyebrow. Sydney looped her arm inside Finney's and walked next to him.

'Do tell.' She implored him.

Gareth and Pat stepped in behind. Once they were clear of the pub and away from prying eyes and curious ears, Finney began to talk.

'First of all, Gemma is pregnant.' He declared.

No one said anything.

'I remember my dear wife when she first fell pregnant with our daughter. They have a look. A sense of something I can't quite put my finger on but which I've seen in many expecting mothers since. On top of that, she didn't drink during the night of the meal. Not a drop.'

'That's not true.' Sydney declared. 'She had a drink. I saw her.'

'Yes, she had a drink. Or, at least, she had a glass with liquid in it. But she never drank from it. Not once. Not for the entire night. I watched her. And then, during the cruise, and now, during lunch. She hasn't drunk a drop of alcohol.'

'That's hardly a reason to think she is pregnant.' Pat said.

'Very true,' Finney agreed. 'Not drinking alcohol does not automatically preclude pregnancy, but continuing to accept alcoholic drinks while not consuming them is suspicious in itself. It assumes the person is attempting to continue a show of normalcy when their position is anything but.'

Gareth nodded.

'Yes. That makes sense.' He agreed. 'Do we think it's Robert's?' He shot Sydney a look. He felt strangely jealous that she had Finney's arm and not his.

'We do.' Finney said.

'What does that mean for the case?' Sydney asked.

'I don't know,' Finney admitted. 'Robert and Gemma's motives for wishing Max dead were strong to begin with. As Sydney pointed out, they are suspects number one and two. With a child on the way, Gemma's maternal instincts will be strong. If she is our murderer, I think it is even more likely she will kill again to protect herself and her unborn child. The danger has never been greater. Sakura is in great danger.'

They had strolled through the village as they had talked. They came upon Finney's small cottage and gathered at his gate.

'I should go back to Burnham Manor, then.' Sydney said.

'Yes, I think you should.' Finney agreed. Turning to Gareth, he said, 'You should leave the village. Ride your bike far away from here and don't return until after dark. I will leave my garage door open. Park your bike there and make your way to the Manor. Sydney, leave a door open at the back of the house. Gareth can enter there under cover of darkness. Remember that Mr Fenwick is as quiet as a mouse and as observant as an eagle. Try not to be seen.'

'What should I do?' Pat asked.

'Go home.' Finney said rather more abruptly than he had intended. 'Your mother needs you. She will certainly miss you if you're not there.'

Pat agreed. 'Yes, you're probably right. You'll keep me posted, though. With everything?'

'I have your number.' Sydney said. 'I'll create a WhatsApp group. We'll update you through that.'

Finney and Sydney waited while Pat got in her car and drove off. Gareth fired up his motorbike, nodded in Sydney's direction, and rode away.

Finney turned and took Sydney's hand.

'Be careful,' he begged. 'Trust no one, see everything and miss nothing. The answer to the puzzle stares us in the face. And if you truly have feelings for young Gareth, you must give a little, or he will walk away, and you'll never see him again.'

The words rang in her ears as she walked back through the village, past the Marlborough and through the wall to the grounds of the Manor. As she passed the pub, two pairs of familiar eyes watched her. Robert and Gemma. She had come to dislike Gemma for no other reason than she didn't like her. Beyond that, there was no valid reason. She also regretted winding her up at lunch. If she was a killer, that probably hadn't been a wise decision.

Sydney walked through the gate and stepped into the gardens. She looked around and could see nothing, but she felt uneasy and couldn't explain it. Was she being watched? Was Fenwick watching her? Or someone else?

She made her way across the lawn and through the French windows, which had been left open. She closed them behind her and locked them. She walked over to the drinks cabinet, found a crystal cut glass and poured herself a whiskey. The amber liquid burned her throat and warmed her soul.

'Hello.'

Sydney jumped.

Sakura appeared in the doorway behind her.

'I'm sorry!' She said, 'I didn't mean to scare you.'

'That's all right,' Sydney said, clutching her chest theatrically. 'I'm feeling a bit jumpy for some reason. I helped myself to a drink. I hope you don't mind?'

'No. Please make yourself at home. It is still all very strange to me. There aren't many houses like this in Japan. It is so big.'

'It must be tough for you.' Sydney agreed. 'Do you know what you plan to do?'

Sakura took another glass from the cabinet, and Sydney poured her a whiskey. They sat down on the sofa and sipped at their drinks.

'I will stay for the funeral, and then I will return to Japan. My family is there. It's where I should be.'

'What about the Will?' Sydney asked.

'The lawyer is determined to act on my behalf. He thinks I have a good claim, but I don't want the money. I want to go home.'

Sydney looked across at the cute young Japanese woman with a flawless complexion and the darkest hair she had ever seen and felt a pang of envy. She was beautiful, young and wealthy and could land herself any man she desired. But then, so was she, albeit not as rich, and she knew she could have any man she wanted. But did she want Gareth? He was a few years older but still good-looking and adventurous. Doubt clouded her thoughts. She didn't want a puppy. She wanted a man. But was Gareth that man?

'You should allow the lawyer to challenge the Will.' She said suddenly. 'Max would have wanted you to have it. He married you and wanted only the best for you.'

'Yes, but it will cause trouble. I don't want trouble.'

Sydney leant forward in her seat.

'I shouldn't tell you this, but Finney thinks Robert and Gemma are the prime suspects in Max's death. He's worried for your safety..'

'Of course,' Sakura agreed. 'If they have murdered Max for the inheritance, and now they are in danger of losing that inheritance, they may kill again. They may want to kill me.'

'You've thought about it?' Sydney asked.

Sakura nodded.

'Of course. I've thought of nothing else. Why would two strangers invite me, the one who stands in the way of a great fortune, to stay in this big house? I don't trust them. I don't trust anyone.'

'You can trust me.' Sydney stated. 'And you can trust Gareth.'

Sakura smiled.

'I've seen the way he looks at you. You play him like a piano. He's in love with you.'

Sydney sat upright. That was the second person who had said she was playing with Gareth, and it suddenly hit home. She was playing with his emotions, and it wasn't fair. She would talk to him later. Make it right.

'Gareth's coming here tonight, after dark. I'm going to let him in through one of the back doors. He's coming to protect you.'

'Me? What about you? Is he coming here to protect you or make love to you?'

'I haven't decided yet.' Sydney said. 'For the first time in my life, I'm not sure what I will do!'

Sakura drained her glass and poured herself another. She reached over and refilled Sydney's glass.

'He's cute.' Sakura said. 'In a very English way. You should at least go for a test drive.'

Sydney laughed.

'Is that how you caught Max?'

'Of course. I knew his reputation, and he could be charming and attentive. But I made him wait. I kept him at arm's length, and it only increased his passion. Much like you are doing with Gareth. When the time was right, I let him taste his heart's desire, and he only wanted more! Once you have trapped them, you must let them enjoy some of their spoils!'

'I'll bear that in mind!'

'I've put you in the Blue Room.' Sakura explained. 'I can't bring myself to sleep in Max's room. It seems disrespectful. I've taken the one next door. It's far enough from your room that you won't be overheard!'

Sydney smiled and wondered. What was she going to do with Gareth?

***

Pat drove north for over an hour. The glass of wine at lunch had made her light-headed and a bit sleepy. It had also made her bold. She composed the text message while sitting in a lay-by, drinking strong coffee from a takeaway cup. She waited in the lay-by and wondered what she would do if he said yes. As the alcohol wore off, her determination and confidence decreased. She started to doubt herself and regret her haste. Her passion faded, and her desires were replaced with a sense of unease. Worst of all, what if he said no?

He didn't.

She sat in the driver's seat and watched as the world continued around her. She needed to make a decision. In the end, it was an easy decision to make. In reality, she had already made it. Now, she had to follow it through.

She put the car into gear and followed the road until it reached a junction. Birmingham lay ahead of her, home to the south of her. The postcode he had given her pointed north, and she steered the car in that direction.

She was determined not to lose her nerve. He had said yes. She had not been rejected. Her mother's angry and disappointed voice fell quiet in her head.

An hour later, she pulled into a residential street and found the house number she was looking for. She rang the doorbell and waited.

Sanjay opened the door and beamed.

'Pat. It's so lovely to see you again.'

He stepped aside, and Pat walked into his home.

'I was surprised to get your message.' He said, closing the door behind her.

Pat hesitated.

'I'm sorry..' She began, and the words failed her. Gathering her resolve, she walked up to Sanjay and planted her mouth on his. She felt him respond, and his arms reached around her and drew her closer. They kissed passionately for several minutes before Pat broke away.

She looked him in the eye and searched for a clue as to what to do next. In front of her, she saw a man totally in love.

She took his hand and led him upstairs.

'Which room?' She asked.

Sanjay opened the door to his bedroom, and they stepped inside. Pat walked over to the windows and drew the curtains closed. She turned and began to remove her clothing. When she was entirely naked, she moved closer to Sanjay and began removing his clothes. Sanjay paused.

'Are you sure this is what you want?' He asked.

'I've never been more sure of anything in my life,' Pat replied as she removed the last item of his clothing and reached out for her desire.

They entwined within each other's arms and fell as one onto the bed. Pat relaxed as Sanjay climbed between her legs and began to make slow, passionate love to her.

When they had finished, she lay in his arms and wanted the world to end. It could never get better than it was right then, and she wanted it to last forever.

***

DI Davenport sat at her desk and listened as Sergeant Graves gave a detailed account of his day.

He had been to Wallingford and interviewed the owners of The Winterbrook River Cruiser. The booking had been made over the telephone to one of the owners, Mrs Catherine Fisher, who couldn't be sure if the caller had been a man or a woman. The voice had been slightly muffled. It was unusual to have a last-minute booking like that, particularly as they had already been fully booked. Still, the caller had made a substantial financial offer, which more than made up for the inconvenience. The money was given to a young man in the street, who delivered it to her as she spoke to the caller on the phone. She could hardly refuse the offer. The payment had been made in cash, and she didn't know who the young man was. Probably a tourist.

Davenport despaired.

'Nothing there then?'

Sergeant Graves shook his head. Still, it did tell her that some considerable forethought and planning had gone into it. Max Wilde's murder had not been opportunistic.

Sergeant Graves was still waiting for a contact in the Tokyo Police Department to return his messages. Given the time differences, they would have to wait and see if Sakura Fukushima had any questions to answer.

He had scoured the Police National Computer for information on Pat Hemshaw but had drawn a blank so far. She had driven to Burnham Manor on the Friday preceding the murder, and there was nothing to suggest that she hadn't gone straight home after her encounter with Max. Equally, there had been nothing to indicate that she hadn't stayed that day and murdered Max in the evening. Despite scouring CCTV and traffic cameras, he couldn't categorically confirm where she was, which left her firmly in the frame.

Sergeant Graves had contacted the agents for Gemma Collis, who confirmed her contract with Max Wilde's estate. Without giving specifics, they said that the contract, while it was still honoured, was worth at least half a million pounds a year to Miss Collis. A generous amount indeed. Now that Max Wilde was dead, Miss Collis could expect upwards of five million pounds a year from sales and film and television rights to her work. Miss Collis would have lost everything had Max Wilde not died.

Sergeant Graves' deep dive into Robert Wilde's movements on the night of his brother's murder had yielded nothing more than a confirmation of what Robert Wilde had told them. Transport For London confirmed that his car was caught on one of their cameras entering the city around five o'clock on Friday evening and again at four-thirty the following morning as his car headed out of the city. Staff at Wilde's in the West End corroborated his story and confirmed that he had stayed overnight in one of the rooms above the restaurant.

'Can anyone confirm that he stayed in his room all night?' Davenport asked.

'No. They saw him go in that evening after having a drink at the bar, and one of the staff saw him leave the following morning at around four o'clock. He was taking a fish delivery that morning.'

'Could it be possible for Robert Wilde to leave the restaurant unobserved, take a train or taxi back to Burnham Manor, kill his brother, and then return to the city before his absence was noted?'

Graves had already done his homework.

'It is eminently possible.' He declared. 'I'm getting CCTV of all the stations out of London to Gloucestershire, and I'm trying to get as many taxi and Uber companies to report any visits to Burnham-on-the-Wold that night. It's a long shot, but we may get lucky.'

Davenport shook her head. There were too many variables. If that was what Robert Wilde had done that night, it was unlikely they'd be able to pin him down.

'What about the others?' She asked.

'Nothing doing.' Graves said glumly. 'Everyone's as clean as a whistle. Not a blemish on their characters. Sydney Fletch has a few family members whose rap sheets are as long as your arm, but nothing from her. Gareth Sebastian Black has never crossed swords with the Justice system, and neither has Margaret Hemshaw. I'm still waiting for Mumbai to reply, but I imagine the same can be said for Sanjay Chakrabati.'

Davenport leant back in her seat.

'What about the telephone number of the phone used to make the text messages?'

'It was an EE Sim,' Graves began, 'and they've confirmed that it was a Pay and Go, topped up with a credit voucher you can buy in almost every shop and garage forecourt in the country. Chances are, it was paid for in cash. Completely untraceable.'

'A burner phone.'

Graves nodded.

'I'm still waiting for an email from EE, which should narrow down where in the country the texts were sent. It would have logged on to a cell tower somewhere. It's been switched off since Saturday evening.'

Davenport held out little hope that tracing the phone would bear fruit. It would tell you where but not who. If the sender was clever, they'd have found a way to automate the sending of the text messages or paid someone over the internet to do it for them. She would be surprised if the guilty party were anywhere near the phone when the messages were sent.

Someone had planned this very carefully.

***

The lights of Gareth's motorcycle broke through the early evening dusk and lit the country lanes ahead. The heavy machine growled and purred as he expertly manoeuvred it along the twists and turns of the darkening lanes. He passed the sign welcoming him to Burnham-on-the-Wold and followed the street until The Larches appeared before him. True to his word, Finney had left the doors to his garage open, and Gareth rode straight in.

Finney heard the bike as Gareth pulled into the street, and he waited within the small garage until man and machine were fully inside and closed the doors behind them.

Gareth dismounted and slipped off the rucksack that was strapped to his back. He unclipped his helmet, placed it on the floor, and removed clothes from his bag.

'You're later than I expected.' Finney said as Gareth began to change out of his safety gear and into more comfortable clothes.

'I got a bit held up.' Gareth explained.

'Sydney will be expecting you.' Finney said.

He watched as the young man in front of him draped a dark jacket over his shoulders. He wore dark trousers and black boots and looked every bit the secret agent he wanted him to be. It was imperative he got into Burnham Manor unseen.

'Don't enter the grounds of the Manor through the gate we used today,' Finney implored him. 'Go the other way and follow the edge of the property as it edges out of the village. You should be able to find a way in up there. It will bring you down near the back of the maze. There's nothing much up there, which probably means Mr Fenwick won't be sniffing around.'

Gareth zipped up his coat and looked at Finney.

'You really think they're in danger?' He asked.

'I hope not.' Finney answered. 'I also think Miss Fletch is capable of looking after herself, but I would feel more comfortable knowing you were there to look after her.'

Gareth smiled. Sydney was a fiercely independent young woman and would have appreciated that appraisal of her skills. He didn't doubt it, either.

'What if I'm the killer?' Gareth asked.

Finney opened the door to the garage for Gareth to exit through.

'You're not.' Finney declared with certainty. 'Besides, you are in love with Miss Fletch and would die for her. Of that, I am certain.'

Gareth stepped into the evening light and heard the door shut behind him. He was thinking about the young Sydney Fletch as he followed the edge of Burnham Manor until he found himself outside the village. Fletch's youthful figure and alluring eyes beckoned him until he found a way into the property and slowly reached the edge of the maze. Sydney had been the focus of his thoughts almost from the first moment he met her. He struggled to think of anything else. The way she talked, the way she walked, the way she spoke. Every little thing about the young woman tugged at his heartstrings and stripped him entirely of reason. He would die for her, too. Twice, if such a thing was possible.

He stayed in the shadows as he approached the house. It wasn't easy to do, as the house, and most of the gardens were bathed in light. Even the huge cedar tree in the centre of the lawn was lit up. Notably, however, there were few lights on inside the house. A room was lit up at the top of the house and one at the bottom. Gareth guessed that the one on the ground floor was the lounge, where he would no doubt find the source of his emotional turmoil. He felt his heart skip.

He kept close to the building as he walked around, ensuring he remained unseen. He stopped every few yards to listen for the sound of Mr Fenwick approaching. He heard nothing. The first door he tried fell open to his touch, and he stepped inside. It was pitch black, and he closed the door behind him and felt the walls for a light switch.

***

Pat swung her car into the drive of Lilac Cottage, and her headlights lit up the house briefly before she turned away and parked up. Her mother was waiting for her as she went into the house, and she felt certain she would be able to smell the sex on her. She could smell it herself. It was all she could smell. Sanjay and her as one person. They had enjoyed each other's company that afternoon, and Pat had to tear herself away so her mother wouldn't get too suspicious. As she approached her mother, she was sure she could smell him.

'Where have you been?' Her mother demanded to know.

Pat leaned over her mother, who was sitting in her favourite chair reading a newspaper and kissed her on the cheek.

'You know where I've been, mother. I've been with Mr Finney and the others at Burnham.'

It wasn't a lie. It just wasn't the whole truth. Her mother could tell a lie before it had even been spoken.

Margaret looked at her daughter and raised an eyebrow.

'All day?' She asked.

'Most of it.' Pat said. 'We had lunch at The Marlborough.'

Pat sat on the sofa next to her mother and filled her in on the day's events whilst carefully avoiding her afternoon with Sanjay.

'That's very interesting.' Margaret said as Pat fell quiet. 'Very interesting indeed. I wouldn't wonder if that gardener didn't know more than he was letting on. I wonder what else he saw that evening while stalking Miss Collis.'

'It makes you think.' Pat agreed. 'I think he's a bit weird. It wouldn't surprise me if he turned out to be the killer.'

'A killer, certainly.' Margaret mused. 'But not Max's killer. Somehow, that doesn't fit.'

Pat wondered what she meant.

'I'm going for a bath.' Pat declared. 'Do you need anything?'

Margaret said she didn't and watched as her daughter rose and left the room. She wanted to say more to her, but the words turned to dust in her mouth. She had so much she wanted to say, but she couldn't bring herself to say it. She knew full well that Pat hadn't been at

Burnham the entire day, and she wondered if Sanjay had treated her daughter with the respect she was due.

She was too old to fight. Too old and far too tired. She didn't have the strength. She didn't have the time, either. Time was not her friend. Time was running out.

***

He had stumbled into a utility room of sorts. There was an old, dirty sink at one end and an ancient-looking clothes' dryer next to it. Boots and shoes were scattered across the floor, and a dozen coats hung from the walls. Gareth made his way through the room to the door at the far end and opened it carefully. Confident that no one was about, he stepped out and closed the utility room door behind him.

'You're late.'

It wasn't an accusation or a reprimand but a statement of fact. Sydney sat on an easy chair surrounded on three sides by shelves of dusty old books. She had one of the books in her hands and closed it shut as she spoke.

'We never set a time.' Gareth argued.

'True. But still. I've been waiting.'

Sydney stood up and placed the book back in its position on the bookshelf.

'A Delancey first edition.' She said. 'I read a couple a few years ago. They're very dark. Come on, I've got a bottle of wine open.'

Gareth followed Sydney as she tripped lightly through the old house. She opened a large oak door and held it open for Gareth as he walked inside.

It wasn't a room he had been in before, and part of his brain reasoned that there must be quite a few of those in Burnham Manor. Unlike Max's office/lounge, this room was smaller and less formal. It also had less of the "I'm entertaining" vibe of the room that hosted part of the dinner Gareth had attended the other night. He followed Sydney as she walked over to a small sofa and sat down. She patted the seat next to her, and Gareth obliged. By the time he had settled, Sydney had poured him a glass of wine.

'Were you seen?' Sydney asked, handing him the glass.

'I don't think so.' Gareth replied. 'I'm pretty sure I wasn't.'

'Good,' She said as she took a large mouthful of wine. 'I've told Sakura you're staying here. She's put you in the same room you were in before.'

'You told her?'

'I did. She's a very sharp and intelligent woman. She's painfully aware of the danger she's in, and I think she's a little relieved that there's someone here to look out for her. I also didn't want her to stumble on you unprepared.'

'Where is she?'

'She's gone to bed. I think the stress of it all is getting to her.'

'I can imagine.'

Gareth sat back into the arms of the sofa and sipped at his wine. He wanted to reach over to Sydney and kiss her and tell her he loved her, but doubt and fear held him back. He got mixed signals from her and certainly didn't want to ruin his chances by making an ill-informed move on her. His life was full of ill-informed manoeuvres, and while some of them had ended happily, some had ended disastrously. He didn't want it to end that way, not with Sydney. Sydney was different.

They sat for some time, drinking wine and chatting like old friends. By the time midnight rang out from several of the clocks in the house, they had dusted off two bottles of wine and chased them down with a single malt.

'I'm going to bed.' Sydney declared as the last gong sounded. She finished her whiskey and stood up. 'Good night, Mr Black. I shall see you in the morning.'

Gareth watched as his chance slipped away and left the room. He finished his drink and sighed. Maybe she wasn't as into him as much as he was into her? It was always possible. She was quite a few years younger than he was. Perhaps he was kidding himself? Perhaps she was too far out of his league? Maybe it was worth making a determined move on her if only to see how she truly felt.

Thoughts on how that might be managed and achieved filled his mind's eye as he went to his room. The alcohol made him light-headed, and his feet weren't as sure-footed as they usually were. He paused by her room and made as if to knock on it. Doubt hit him again.

Now was not the time. They were relying on him. He needed to be there for them both. He turned and opened the door to his room. He closed it behind him and fell back on it while his conflicting emotions battled it out for supremacy. It was the right thing, he told himself. There'll be other times.

He heard a faint knock on the door. He opened the door and found Sydney there. She had already changed for bed, and Gareth's eyes stuck firmly to hers while his peripheral vision took it all in.

Sydney stepped up to him and kissed him passionately. Her lips were soft and gentle and they danced with his as he felt her tongue gently explore his mouth. She moved closer to him, and he could feel the contours of her body touch his, and he felt his ardour rise.

She broke off suddenly and stepped back.

'I didn't want you to think I wasn't interested.' She said, and her voice cracked with the effort. 'I wanted you to know there was hope and perhaps to give you a little taste.'

He could taste her all right. Now, he wanted to taste even more.

'I'm afraid I'm one of those who revel in the chase. Are you up to the chase, Mr Black?'

Gareth watched as the beautiful Sydney Fletch smiled at him, bade him good night, and danced lightly back to her room.

He closed the door to his room and smiled. He would take care of himself for tonight, but tomorrow, the chase was on.

***

From his bedroom at The Marlborough, Robert Wilde had a commanding view over the village of Burnham-on-the-Wold. He stood at the window and watched as the village slowly came to life and its residents began their day. He sipped at his freshly brewed coffee and watched as the postman drove his distinctive red van up through the village and along the main road, passing the entrance to Burnham Manor. Beyond the gate he knew would be closed, he imagined Gemma's small cottage set back among the trees and smiled.

Gemma. The first woman he had ever truly loved. He had fallen for her the moment Max had brought her back to the house and had continued to fall in love with her ever since. The fact she had dallied with Max made no difference to him. Women had mainly been playthings of his brother, and he knew that he had an hypnotic hold over many of them. Gemma's fling had been momentary and insignificant, and he often wondered if Max remembered that they had even been together.

It didn't feel awkward to be with Gemma. It had only ever felt right, and now she was pregnant with his child, it felt even more right. He couldn't find the words to express his emotions, but he knew his heart was full and ready to explode.

From his vantage point, he saw an older figure appear on the road. He had stepped out from a gap in the wall that surrounded Burnham Manor and strolled towards the village centre. John Fenwick. He had never liked the old gardener, and the more he discovered about him, the less he liked him.

He followed the old man as he entered the Village Stores and Post Office. A few minutes later, he came out with a loaf of bread and a pint of milk and began the slow walk back up the hill to the Manor.

Robert mused that something needed to be done about Mr Fenwick. And someone needed to do it soon before it was too late. He didn't want a man like that anywhere near Gemma. He was determined to do something about him.

***

Gemma saw him, too. She had taken her first cup of tea of the day outside, sitting beneath the lee of an old oak tree that dominated her garden. She enjoyed her morning routine and spent the first few hours drinking tea and reviewing yesterday's work.

She heard the creak of his front door as he left his house and, a few moments later, saw his head as he moved along the small footpath that led out of the gardens. For once, he didn't see her, or at least he made an effort to show that he wasn't watching her, and

Gemma felt grateful for that small mercy. Knowing that the dirty old creep enjoyed watching her had made her feel uncomfortable, even if the psychology of it intrigued her. She wanted to learn more about the man but didn't want to be anywhere near him. It was a paradox that confused her emotions; her pregnancy had already exacerbated that.

She laid a hand on her stomach and thought of the future. She hoped it would be a boy. Robert would love that. Or a girl. Girls always stole their father's hearts.

A few minutes later, her daydream was broken as she heard the iron gate open and John Fenwick return. He didn't look her way. Instead, he turned and went straight to his small cottage.

He was a strange man, she thought. Very strange indeed.

***

'Mother? Why are you up so early?'

Pat found her mother in the kitchen, drinking tea and staring idly out the window. The sun had risen, and golden rays soaked everything in a fresh, warm light.

'I have an appointment in town.' Margaret replied.

'You didn't say,' Pat said, turning on the kettle.

'Do I have to tell you everything?' Margaret said. 'I'm sure you don't tell me everything.'

Pat resisted the urge to turn and look at her mother. There was no one in the world like her mother who could elicit the truth from her with a simple raised eyebrow. Pat knew the only way to resist this simple interrogation was not to face her mother. She had tried it before, and it never worked. Don't look at her. Change the subject.

'Will you be out for long?' Pat asked.

'A few hours. I have some business that needs tidying up.'

Pat stirred her tea and took a seat opposite her mother.

'Would you like me to drive you?' She asked.

'No. I have a taxi booked. He should be here any minute. I think this might be him now.'

Pat heard the familiar sound of tyres on the stones in front of the house. Margaret stood up and gathered her things from the table.

'What will you do while I'm out?' Margaret asked.

Pat thought of Sanjay. She could still feel him inside her, and it warmed her. But Sanjay was a long drive away, and she'd never make it there and back in time. Not if her mother was only going out for a couple of hours.

'I have some ideas for our next book. I'm going to try and straighten them out.'

Margaret smiled. Perhaps she hadn't been so wrong in her treatment of Pat. Perhaps she had given her the opportunity she needed. She would make an excellent novelist in her own right.

But first, there were things she needed to do. Important things. Things that couldn't wait. It was the right thing to do; she knew that. And it had to be done, and it had to be done today.

'I think I may stay in town tonight.' Margaret said. 'A kind lady from The Guardian wants to interview with me, so I think I'll take her up on it. Would you book me a room at the Savoy?'

Pat tried not to look too keen for her mother to stay away for the night. She didn't do it often, which was a rare treat for both of them. Pat was only ever left alone when her mother stayed at the Savoy. It was a thing she did when she needed a pick-me-up. It gave them both a break.

'Of course. I'll ring them right away.'

Pat watched as her mother collected her coat from the hallway and opened the front door.

'I'll see you tomorrow,' she said, closing the door behind her.

Pat reached for her phone and sent Sanjay a message. His reply came back swiftly. Pat smiled.

Things were beginning to work themselves out. Everything was going to be just fine.

***

Sydney showered, changed quickly, and knocked on Gareth's door. When no reply came, she knocked again.

Perhaps he was an early riser, she pondered, when still no reply came. She had spent the night wondering and thinking and mulling things over. She had resolved to stop playing with him and was determined to give up a little more freely than she had already done. When Sydney Fletch resolved to do a thing, she did it and to hell with the consequences. Besides, he had tasted quite nice last night, and she wanted more. The feel of Gareth Sebastian Black in her arms, his body so close, had stirred something within her.

Disappointed that he wasn't in, she went down the staircase and into the lounge. The patio doors were open, and she could see Sakura on the patio beyond.

'Good morning,' Sydney declared brightly as she stepped outside.

Sakura wore a thin, white dress that held gently to her shoulders and hugged her figure. Sydney thought she had the figure of a teenage girl, and she felt a little jealous. Her skin was flawless, and her hair was shiny, black, and well-tended. Max certainly knew how to pick his women.

'Good morning,' Sakura said. 'I have made tea and toast. I have laid the table for us.'

Sydney looked down at the table and saw it laid for three people. She had forgotten that Sakura knew that Gareth had stayed the night and was about to ask why she had laid for three when the realisation dawned on her. More than that… something else.. something she couldn't quite grasp. Now, what was it?

'Morning.'

Gareth appeared on the lawn below and took the small steps to the patio.

'Everyone okay? Excellent. Tea. Shall I be mum?'

He took one of the chairs and began pouring. Sydney remained standing. She was staring out across the lawn.

'Syd?' Gareth asked.

Sydney looked at Gareth and then at Sakura. Something tugged at her from a place deep within her memory, but it was fleeting and soon lost. A figure briefly appeared in her line of sight, far out across the lawn. Mr Fenwick.

You seem to know a lot. And know about a lot of things.

And then, mysteriously:

I don't know much… As for seeing things… People are not very good at staying hidden when they think they've not been seen.

Yes, of course. If anybody had seen anything on the night of Max's murder, it would have been Mr Fenwick. He saw everything. And everyone. What was it Mr Fenwick had been hinting at?

'I'm going to speak to Mr Fenwick.' Sydney declared and bounded down the steps and onto the lawn. She strode purposefully across the grass and headed to the gardener's sanctuary, where she guessed he was heading.

Gareth and Sakura watched with some bemusement as Sydney disappeared from view.

'What do you think that's about?' Gareth asked.

Sakura shrugged.

'I don't know. She looked like she had seen a ghost.'

Sydney walked with purpose as all the questions gathered on her lips. She saw the gardener's greenhouse appear before her and opened the door. It took a second to take in the scene.

Mr Fenwick was convulsing in front of her. A bottle of beer had fallen from his hand and was dripping its contents onto the floor. Sydney stepped over the prostrate figure and moved him so he was more comfortable. He had begun to foam at the mouth.

She considered getting up and calling for the others. In her haste to speak to Mr Fenwick, she had forgotten to bring her phone. As she wondered what to do next, Mr Fenwick's convulsions began to slow. She watched in horror as his breathing slowed, too.

She leant over the old man's face and slapped him to try and rouse him. Unsure of what to do next, she opened his mouth and made as if to perform mouth-to-mouth.

She felt strong arms engulf her and pull her away. She struggled and swore at her attacker.

'Get off me. We need to help him!'

'If your lips touch his, you'll die.'

Sydney turned and found Gareth holding her. Sakura stood behind him, holding her hands in front of her mouth in horror.

'Smell it!' Gareth shouted.

Sydney relaxed in his arms. She leant towards Mr Fenwick's body and smelt the faint aroma of almonds.

'Cyanide.' She said quietly.

'There's nothing you can do for him.' Gareth said. 'Come away. We need to call the police.'

***

Detective Chief Inspector Davenport took a back seat as Scenes of Crime's officers did their business. They were impressively efficient. She watched as men and women in white suits and shoes covered in blue plastic covers moved about the greenhouse, photographing, recording and itemising everything that was there. One leant down next to the small refrigerator and shone a small torch between it and the wall. A second later, she stood up and dropped a glass vial into a plastic evidence pocket. She handed it to Davenport.

Sydney Fletch had described the scene she had witnessed and then recalled that Mr Fenwick had shown her a bottle of something that he said contained enough liquid to kill a hundred men. *Just a small drop of this liquid in someone's tea or coffee….* Or beer, Davenport thought. A bottle of beer still lay on the floor next to Mr Fenwick.

The initial search of Mr Fenwick's body had failed to produce the bottle of poison, so Davenport ordered a fingerprint search of the greenhouse. She held up the evidence bag and examined the vial. Nothing was written on the label, but it showed signs of recent spillage, indicating that some of the contents had been poured out. She handed the bag to her sergeant and instructed him to enter it into evidence. She stepped out of the greenhouse and looked across the lawns to the house.

'Right,' she said out loud, but to no one in particular. 'Let's go and have a chat with our witnesses.'

She found Sydney, Sakura and Gareth in the drawing room. They had each taken a seat and waited patiently for Davenport to come and talk to them.

'Would you like tea?' Sakura asked.

'Thank you,' Davenport said. She sat near the others and waited while Sakura poured tea from an antique-looking teapot. 'Tell me about this vial of poison that Mr

Fenwick showed you.' She asked, looking directly at Sydney.

'Have you found it?' Sydney asked.

'We have,' Davenport admitted. 'I don't suppose you remember how much liquid was in it?'

'It was full.' Gareth declared.

'Yes.' Sydney agreed. 'It was. Mr Fenwick said something about never having used it and never needing to. I think it made him feel important.'

'And how many people knew of this poison vial?'

'It was just Sydney, Pat and Mr Finney at the time.' Gareth explained. 'But I expect Fenwick showed it to a lot of people. It was like his party trick.'

'You're probably right,' Davenport agreed, and it pained her to admit it was likely to prove very true. She turned and looked at Sydney. 'How did you come to find Mr Fenwick?' She asked. 'Why did you go there?'

Sydney chose her words carefully. There was still a great deal she didn't understand.

'I saw him when I came down for breakfast. It occurred to me, after everything we have learned about Mr Fenwick, that he may have seen something important on the night of Max's murder. He has - sorry, had a nasty habit of creeping up on you without you knowing he was there. I wondered if he had seen the murderer that night and maybe didn't realise its significance. It seemed like a good opportunity to find out.'

'And he was already convulsing when you found him?' Sydney shuddered.

'He was. He was foaming at the mouth. I was going to give him mouth-to-mouth when Gareth stopped me.'

Sydney shot Gareth a grateful look. She had been so close to making a devastating mistake.

'Was it cyanide?' Sydney asked.

'It seems the most likely culprit, based on what you have told us, but we won't know for sure for a couple of hours.' Davenport turned and looked at Gareth. 'What made you follow Miss Fletch to the greenhouse?'

Gareth shrugged.

'Curiosity. Sydney seemed distracted by something, and I wanted to find out what.'

'And I followed him.' Sakura added.

'And how closely behind Miss Fletch were the two of you?' Davenport asked.

'A few seconds.' Gareth declared.

Sakura agreed.

'That will do for now,' Davenport said, standing up. 'I'm going to send my sergeant in to take your statements. While the memory's still fresh.'

Davenport closed the door behind her, and the drawing room fell quiet.

'How many people do you think knew about Mr Fenwick's little vial of poison?' Sydney asked.

'I imagine everyone knew of it. You, Finney, Pat and I heard about it from the horse's mouth.' Gareth pondered. 'Robert and Gemma have known the man for years; he must have bragged about it to them. Pat could have told Sanjay and her mother. I suppose Sakura is the only one who didn't know.'

Sakura giggled.

'In mystery books, that would make me the prime suspect!'

Sydney laughed, but there was an element of truth to it. What did Sakura know? And where had Gareth been that morning when she had called on him? And why did nothing make any sense?

She caught Gareth watching her.

'What?' She asked, and her words came out more abruptly than intended.

'You know something.' Gareth accused her.

Sydney said, 'No, I don't,' but she didn't convince herself, let alone Gareth. Something was bugging her, but she couldn't pin it down.

'Come on, spill the beans.' Gareth said. 'I thought we were a team?'

Sydney smiled. She wanted that. She'd never been in a team. She furrowed her brow.

'There's something. You know that feeling you get sometimes when something's making you anxious, but you don't know what? That's how I feel. Like I've seen or heard something that didn't make any sense, but I can't for the life of me think what it is.'

Gareth laughed. He knew the feeling well.

'It'll come to you. Have more tea.'

***

'What do you think, guv?' Graves asked as Davenport and he walked slowly back across the lawns of Burnham Manor.

'I don't know. I think Miss Fletch is a smart young woman. You should read her book. She's very clever. I think she is right about Fenwick. The old man must have seen something on the night of Max Wilde's murder that put a marker on his back. The problem is, he could have seen any one of a number of people who were at the Manor on Friday night. But why would that be suspicious? They were all supposed to be there.'

'Not all of them,' Graves disagreed. 'Robert Wilde was supposed to be in London and Pat Hemshaw at home in Wiltshire. There were at least two people who shouldn't have been here that night.'

'Agreed.' Davenport said. 'So if either of them were here that night and Fenwick had seen them, he would have information on them that they wouldn't want to be made public. Of course, Fenwick wouldn't necessarily have known their alibis, so wouldn't have made the connection. But, once it was clear that he was prowling the gardens of Burnham Manor that night, our murderer is living on borrowed time. They would have to deal with Mr Fenwick sooner rather than later. One slip, and their alibi is done.'

'Prime suspects One and Two.' Graves said.

'One and Three.' Davenport corrected. 'Robert Wilde and Gemma Collis are close, and both stood to lose everything if Max Wilde lived. Gemma is number Two.'

'You think they're in it together?' Graves asked.

'It's possible.' Davenport paused for a moment. 'We need to break an alibi. Go hard on Robert Wilde. I'm not loving Pat Hemshaw as a prime suspect. My money's on Robert Wilde.'

✳✳✳

News of Fenwick's death made a pass of the village almost before the man's body had gone cold. By the time the undertakers had removed him to the mortuary, the news had done a tour of the country and returned once more to Burnham-on-the-Wold in the form of more reporters. They arrived in the village in their dozens and filled the small country lanes with their vans and satellite dishes. Max Wilde's murder was taking on a whole new form and was the leading feature on nearly all the national news reports.

The internet had also proved to be a fertile ground for the development of an army of amateur detectives who, with no previous experience in anything of

277

importance, began to fill the digital highway with their fanciful and, often, libellous theories. Within hours, Burnham-on-the-Wold had become the Mecca for these detective tourists, and the small village buckled under the weight of numbers.

'Come to Lilac Cottage,' Pat declared during a hastily convened Zoom call.

Mr Finney's house had been swamped by journalists begging for an exclusive interview, and he had sought refuge at the Manor. Robert and Gemma had also found themselves besieged at The Marlborough, and they, too, fled to the security of Burnham Manor.

'I think it would be easier if you came here,' Gareth declared. 'I don't suppose you've heard from Sanjay?'

Pat could still feel the results of Sanjay's lovemaking on the inside of her leg, and she smiled. As soon as she had been sure her mother was safely tucked away in London, she had called Sanjay, and he travelled down to Lilac Cottage, where the two of them had spent the day exploring each other's bodies. When the news of Fenwick's murder reached them, Sanjay had hurriedly dressed and raced back to Birmingham. Her mother had cancelled her stay at the Savoy and was returning home that evening.

'I wonder if coming here wouldn't be better?' Pat said. 'There must be a lot of journalists there?'

'She makes a good point.' Sydney agreed. 'It would give us all a chance to escape from this fairground attraction we've all become.'

'Yes. Do that.' Pat implored. 'I'm afraid the house isn't particularly big. We could put a couple of people up, but there's a nice farm nearby with luxury pod things. I know the owner. I'm sure he'd give us a good rate for a few nights.'

'That's settled, then,' Robert agreed as Gemma nodded in his direction. 'We'll wait until it gets dark and make our escape. I know a few secret routes out of the Manor. They won't even know we've gone.'

'Okay. I'll talk to my friend and make sure he's got somewhere for you. I'll see you all later.'

The refugees made themselves comfortable and wasted time as best they could. Gareth followed Sydney into the drawing room, and they sat together on a small sofa. Sydney lifted Gareth's arm and leaned in for a cuddle. They sat like that for some time, and every few minutes, Sydney sighed deeply.

'The problem about getting a glimpse of something,' Gareth said softly, 'is the harder you try to focus on it, the more obscure it becomes. Whatever you think you may have seen or heard, forget about it. It will come to you when you least expect it.'

'Easier said than done.' Sydney said. 'It's like an earworm you can't get rid of. It just plays in a loop in your head.'

He hugged her tightly, and she revelled in his strength and warmth. Slowly, she closed her eyes and the loop broke, and she drifted off into a light sleep.

Robert and Gemma spent the late afternoon fielding phone calls and emails. Eventually, they both gave up and silenced everything. The house fell desperately quiet.

'When is Max's funeral?' Sakura asked. She had sat quietly on an old armchair and watched as everyone went about killing time. Robert had forgotten she was there.

'I meant to talk to you about that,' Robert said. 'I've booked a preliminary date at St Mary's in the village. It's in ten days. Max had already bought a plot in the churchyard, so he'll be buried there.'

Sakura nodded.

'What will you do after that?' Robert asked.

'I want to go home.' Sakura said, and Robert could see the pain and homesickness in her eyes.

'Will you come back?' Gemma asked. 'We'd like you to. This should have been your home. Our babies will be cousins.'

Sakura smiled. She hadn't made her mind up yet. There was still so much to think about.

'Maybe.' She replied in the most non-committal way she could muster.

Finney wandered about the gardens and watched as the sky began to darken. The garden took on a new look as the sun sank towards the horizon. Shadows grew beneath the big cedar tree in the centre of the lawn and stretched their arms towards the house. He wandered beneath its magnificent overhanging branches and marvelled at its majesty. He walked slowly around the edge of the perfectly manicured lawn and amongst the herbaceous borders that were in full bloom around it.

He removed a sweet from his tin and dropped it into his mouth. He followed the borders as they circumnavigated the property. Eventually, he returned to where he had begun, beneath the majestic branches of the old cedar tree.

It was almost time, he thought, as the dark skies chased the sun from view.

'It's beautiful here, isn't it?'

He turned to find Sydney standing before him.

'It certainly is.' He agreed. 'If tarred by tragedy.'

'I wonder if a little bit of tragedy and mystery don't add to the character of a place like this?' She asked.

'That would be the writer in you,' Finney laughed. 'But, yes. I'm sure it does.'

'They're getting ready to go,' Sydney explained. 'Apparently, we're going to sneak out the back like a troop of escaping criminals. Robert's hired a taxi driver friend to meet us in the lane. It's all rather exciting, don't you think?'

She was always finding things exciting, Finney mused. Perhaps that was her youth? It was refreshing to see someone enjoying their life, even under such strange circumstances. Life had long ago ceased to be exciting. It had almost worn him out. Being in Sydney's company changed that, if only while she remained in his company. Her zest for life was infectious.

She slipped her arm through his and led him towards the house.

Gemma switched off all the lights within the house, save for a couple in the upstairs rooms and some in the drawing room, to give the illusion that they were all still at home. She locked the front door and met them all at the back. Under cover of darkness, they followed Robert as he plodded across the gardens, through the allotments at the back, and out through a gate at the furthest end of the grounds. It was the same gate Gareth had used just the other night. In the lane beyond, two cars were sat with their lights ablaze. Robert greeted one of the drivers with a solid handshake, and the escapees piled into the vehicles. Within minutes, Burnham-on-the-Wold was long behind them.

∗∗∗

Pat met her mother as she stepped into Lilac Cottage and divested herself of her summer coat.

'So someone's done the old gardener in, have they?' Margaret asked as Pat dropped her overnight bag onto the stairs.

'So it seems. Cyanide, apparently.'

Margaret shuddered. It was a most unpleasant way to die, if mercifully quick.

'I wonder how they administered it?' Margaret pondered. 'And when did we first start using cyanide? Is it an old thing? Can we use it in one of my books?'

'Absolutely we can,' Pat enthused. She had been researching the stuff for weeks. 'The Emperor Nero used it in Roman times, and Napoleon urged his troops to dip their bayonets in it during the Prussian war. Its properties were well known during our period of interest. I've actually started plotting a murder that uses it for our next book. Would you like to take a look?'

Margaret waved her away.

'God, no, not now. I'm far too tired. I just want to sit down and have a glass of brandy.'

'Of course, you must be exhausted,' Pat said. 'How was the interview?'

'What interview?' Margaret grumbled.

'The one you went to London for.' Pat replied. If that's where you were, she thought. 'The journalist from the Guardian?'

'Oh, that. Nothing doing. She cancelled. Complete waste of time.'

Pat followed her mother through to the lounge, where she took a spot on her favourite armchair and stretched her tired legs out.

'Pour me a brandy,' she commanded, and Pat dutifully obliged.

'I rang earlier,' Margaret said, watching her daughter's expression carefully.

Pat felt the colour rise up her neck. She had forgotten to divert the calls to her phone.

'I must have been outside.' She explained.

'I rang several times.' Margaret countered and saw the guilt writ large across her daughter's face.

'I mustn't have heard it.'

'You do know it's portable.' Margaret argued. 'Next time, take it outside with you.'

'Of course, mother.'

Pat handed her mother her glass and poured a small one for herself.

'Since when have you drunk brandy?' Margaret asked.

Pat smiled. She had been secretly pouring herself a small glass of brandy since she was a teenager. She had grown quite a taste for it.

'Oh, not long,' she lied.

'Well, see that you don't drink too much. Strong liquor is not for girls.'

Pat was about to argue the point that she was no longer a girl and then decided it wasn't worth it.

'I've invited the others over to stay for a while.' She said.

Margaret gave her a stern look.

'What others? Who, exactly?'

Pat listed them all.

'Well, they can't stay here. We haven't the room. And why can't they stay at Burnham Manor?'

'Because it's become difficult for them, what with the press coverage and everything. They all need somewhere quiet to stay until it all quietens. And I've spoken to Mr Bennet over at Cobham's Farm. He's got a couple of pods free that they can use. They're quite posh. I think they'll be very comfortable.'

'Hmm. Seems quite the imposition. I suppose Sanjay will be coming?'

Pat tried to keep the indifference in her tone of voice.

'Not tonight, no. I think he'll be coming down tomorrow. I thought we could do a big lunch for everyone.'

'You seem to have thought of everything.' Margaret said, and Pat noted the accusatory inflexion in her voice.

'You don't mind, do you?' Pat asked. 'They're friends, after all.'

Margaret looked at her daughter and felt the tension in her shoulders subside. Pat had few friends. Perhaps this lot wasn't too bad. They all had something in common, and Pat needed friends.

'I don't mind, but you'll have to do everything yourself. I'm too old for hosting lunches.'

Margaret swallowed the last drop of brandy and rose from her chair.

'I'm going to bed. Don't stay up too long.'

Pat watched her mother as she left the room. She was beginning to move slowly, she thought. Age was starting to tell.

Pat poured herself another glass of brandy and sat back in her chair. She wondered where her mother had been that day and then remembered what she had been doing, and nothing else seemed to matter.

***

'The pods sleep up to eight people.' Mr Bennet explained. He handed the keys to Robert. 'Pat said you'd probably want two; these are the best I have. They're fully equipped with gas, water and electricity. Each one has a log burner, not that you'll be needing it, and a hot tub at the back. Pat asked me to fill your fridges with some bits to keep you going for tonight. I hope you enjoy your stay.'

Mr Bennet turned and disappeared into the night.

'Girls to the left, boys to the right.' Robert declared. He handed Gemma a key.

'Shame.' Gareth said quietly so that only Sydney could hear. 'I was rather hoping to bunk up with you.'

Sydney dug him in the ribs.

'I'll have you know I'm not exactly quiet.' She teased. 'I wouldn't want to keep everyone up all night!'

'All night?' Gareth asked. 'I can't wait to find out how true that is!'

'It seems you may have to wait a little longer,' Sydney giggled. She grabbed her hold-all and followed Gemma and Sakura into the pod, turning at the last minute to give Gareth a sultry smile.

The pods turned out to be less pod-like and more cabin-like. They were luxuriously fitted out, with a communal lounge area at one end, a kitchenette at the other and doorways leading to bedrooms dividing them. Once they had settled in, Sydney raided the fridge and found several bottles of champagne and a note from Pat. It simply read, "Enjoy!"

Sydney and Sakura changed into swimwear that Pat had fortuitously left for them, grabbed a bottle of champagne and retired to the hot tub. Gareth had already taken the plunge, and they found him sitting at the back, enjoying the bubbles.

'I trust you have shorts on in there?' Sydney asked.

She felt Sakura stifle a giggle. Despite knowing she had a good, well-proportioned figure, she still felt a little self-conscious next to Sakura. She was unbelievably pretty with immaculate skin, and Sydney watched Gareth's gaze as she stepped into the tub. Respectfully, Gareth held Sakura's eyes, and Sydney was pleased to see that his gaze wandered a little more freely as she stepped into the water.

Gareth opened the champagne, and the three chatted and gigged like old friends.

Finney joined them a while later but remained outside the tub. Several rattan chairs with cushions for comfort were laid nearby. Robert joined him, and Gemma soon joined them both.

'I must say, Pat's outdone herself here.' Gareth said.

'Indeed.' Finney agreed.

'Did she leave you all swimwear?' Gemma asked.

Robert nodded.

'She did. She got the sizes right, too.'

'Then why don't you join us?' Sydney asked. 'The water's beautiful.'

Robert felt uncomfortable. He never wore shorts, even in the summer. He wasn't keen on showing his legs.

'I..I… I don't know, perhaps later.'

Gemma looked at him. She was painfully aware of how shy he could be.

'I'll go if you do,' she dared.

Ten minutes later, Robert dropped into the hot tub next to Gemma. He took a glass of champagne from Sydney, and Gemma declined one.

'Is there something soft?' She asked.

'How's the pregnancy going?' Sydney asked abruptly.

Everyone fell quiet.

'I suppose I shouldn't be surprised you know,' Gemma said. 'It's early days yet. We wanted to keep it quiet until all this was over.'

Sydney nodded. She appreciated the sentiment.

'I think I would like orange juice, too.' Sakura said.

Sydney looked at her.

'You too? I didn't see that coming!'

Finney relayed back and forth from the kitchen, topping up orange juice and champagne when necessary. In the case of Gareth, Sydney and Robert, it was more often than he hoped. In a couple of hours, four bottles of champagne had been consumed.

'I think I'm drunk.' Gareth declared at last and stood up. Sydney was relieved to see that he was, indeed, wearing shorts. She was also relieved that age had not yet approached his body. He was lean and well-built, with well-defined muscle lines and strong pectoral muscles that twinkled in the light. She felt her emotion stir.

'I'm going to bed.' Gareth declared, and he struggled to get out of the tub. Finney came to his aid and held his arm as he made ground fall.

'I shall walk this young man back,' Finney said. 'I'll see you in the morning.'

'Yes. I think bed's a good idea.' Sydney declared.

She stood and wobbled. Sakura took her arm, and together, they climbed gently out of the hot tub and returned to the pod. Robert took Gemma's arm and helped her out of the tub. He was more sure-footed than the others, but even he felt his vision swim. He kissed Gemma as she opened the door to her pod.

'Goodnight,' he mumbled. He kissed her and stumbled back to his pod.

'It will be all right, won't it?' Gemma asked as he went. 'Everything will work out, won't it?'

Robert turned and smiled.

'It will be all right.' He said. 'Everything always works out in the end, one way or another.'

Yes, Gemma thought. One way or another.

***

Pat opened the little gate at the bottom of the garden and smiled as she saw Sydney walking hand in hand with Gareth. It was about time, she mused. The sexual tension between them had been palpable from the very first moment she had met them. She liked Sydney. They weren't too dissimilar in age, and she hoped they would become close friends.

'Morning Pat,' Sydney greeted as she stepped through the gate.

The lane they wandered along had once been an old route through the hills to London, back when horse and cart ruled the road. It had fallen into disuse in the Twenties and was now a popular destination for walkers and horse riders. During the hours of darkness, some of the more colourful elements of society took to its shadows in search of random encounters with other like-minded souls. Pat blushed at the memories that flooded to mind. Mother would not approve.

'Morning,' Pat responded cheerily. 'Go on up to the house. Mother's put some tea on.'

Finney held out his hand and gently took Pat's. He leaned in and kissed her on the cheek.

'Good morning, Pat,' he said. 'We all owe you a debt of gratitude for coming to our aid. You outdid yourself. You really did.'

Gemma agreed. She stepped in as Finney let go of Pat and hugged her.

'Those pods are to die for!' She gushed. 'You must tell us how much we owe you for everything.'

'Really, it was nothing,' Pat replied, blushing. She was unused to getting compliments. Mother could usually be found moaning at her.

She held the gate as Robert followed Sakura through. Together, they walked across the gardens to where Margaret was laying cups on a table.

'Here you all are.' Margaret said, not disguising her displeasure for a moment. 'I suppose you'd better sit down.'

Margaret sat at the head of the table beneath a large parasol strategically placed to deflect the early morning sun. She poured herself a cup of tea and sat back in her chair.

It's very kind of you to invite us to your home, Margaret.' Finney said, taking a chair next to her. 'Very hospitable of you.'

'Hmm,' Margaret mumbled.

The others took up positions around the table and poured tea.

'I see Sanjay isn't here.' Margaret said.

Pat blushed again, and Sydney caught the look in her eyes. So, she'd bagged Sanjay, had she? Good on her, she thought. Everyone deserved a little fun in life, especially Pat.

'He'll be here in a while, mother.' Pat said, and the frustration was evident in her voice. 'Please help yourself to food,' she continued, addressing the table. 'I've made a selection of sandwiches and pastries. I didn't know what you'd all want to eat!'

'It looks wonderful,' Sydney enthused.

'And tastes divine,' Robert gushed as he took a bite out of a pastry. 'Please tell me this isn't shop-bought?'

Pat shook her head.

'No. I made everything myself.'

Robert's eyes toured the foodstuffs laid out in front of him. There were mounds of it.

'All of it?' He asked in amazement.

'She got up early.' Margaret said abruptly. 'God knows why. She could have bought all this stuff from the supermarket.'

'Well, I'm glad she didn't.' Robert countered. 'This is delicious food, Pat. I could do with a chef like you at Wilde's!'

'She has enough to do here!' Margaret argued.

'Oh, mother, I'm sure he was only joking.'

'I was not.' Robert said firmly, selecting another pastry from the table. 'Honestly, these are some of the best pastries I've ever eaten.'

Pat blushed some more.

'I've been cooking since I was a child. Mother was always so busy.'

Margaret scoffed.

'They taste pretty normal to me.' She grumbled.

'Well, I won't be told otherwise,' Robert said. 'We must talk recipes when you have the time.'

'She won't.' Margaret sniffed.

'Perhaps I can email some to you?' Pat suggested. She was careful not to aggravate her mother. She had been in a funny mood since she had returned from London yesterday, and it hadn't improved much overnight.

'Pat tells me the gardener chap was murdered.' Margaret said. She addressed the comment to Finney.

'Indeed, he was.' Finney admitted. 'I spoke with DCI Davenport this morning before we came out. They've confirmed that it was cyanide. The working theory is that someone poured a fatal dose into one of his beers and re-sealed it. He took a swig, and it was enough to kill him.'

'A strange coincidence.' Margaret pondered.

Everyone watched the elderly woman and waited for the punchline, but none followed.

'What do you mean?' Finney asked.

'Well, if someone dropped a Mickey Finn into one of his beers in the hope that, eventually, the old sod would get around to drinking it, it surprises me that Miss Fletch just happened to be there at the same time. A coincidence, don't you think?'

'Just that.' Finney agreed. 'A coincidence. The word was invented for just such an eventuality.'

'Hmm.' Margaret mumbled, and never had a single "hmm" carried more baggage.

'But, actually,' Finney continued. 'Not so much a coincidence as a simple chain of events that can be followed from the beginning to its natural conclusion. We can safely assume that Mr Fenwick entertained himself at the local pub the previous evening, as was his habit. It is unlikely that he would have returned to his greenhouse for a drink upon his return. That place is his sanctuary. A place he goes to that isn't home, his garden or the pub. That evening, he would have returned home to either continue drinking or to sleep.

'It's safe to assume, then, that the poison was added to his beer overnight. The following morning, he followed his standard routine and left for the local stores, returning a short while later. I believe several people saw him doing this. After breakfast, he visited his greenhouse, poured himself a beer and settled into his chair for the day. Sydney has seen Mr Fenwick on his way to the greenhouse and decides to confront him about what he may have seen on the night of Max's murder. It is no coincidence that she arrived at the scene when she did, the last event in a chain of predictable events.'

'But why?' Margaret argued. 'Why then?'

'I think it's clear to us all, now, that Mr Fenwick knew more than he was letting on.' Finney said. 'It was a conclusion I had been working on, but Miss Fletch got there first. A tribute to her powers of observation, wouldn't you agree?'

Margaret's face said that she disagreed, and her mouth moved as if to say the words to confirm it, but Gareth got in first.

'Absolutely. First rate deducting!'

'I think we could make a good detective out of young Sydney Fletch.' Finney beamed.

A general murmuring of praise passed the lips of those sat around the table, but Margaret remained impassive.

'I don't suppose the brilliant Detective Davenport is any closer to working out who did it then?' Margaret asked.

'DCI Davenport now has two live murder cases to investigate.' Finney explained. 'That's no mean feat, I can tell you. Her first task will be to try and find a link between the two.'

'A link?' Margaret snorted. 'Of course they're linked. Any idiot can see that!'

'Any idiot can,' Finney agreed. 'But Davenport is no idiot. Davenport is a professional detective. She needs evidence and proof. Speculation is for amateurs.'

Margaret sat back in her chair, deflated.

'You must have some theories?' Gemma asked.

Finney took his cup of tea and sipped at it.

'I have theories, of course,' he admitted. 'But I don't have to prove them. Davenport does. In this case, DCI Davenport has no shortage of suspects or opportunities. What she lacks is a significant motive. Take me, for example, as DCI Davenport must do. What motive do I have? Until recently, I didn't know Max Wilde. I had never met him. I had the opportunity, of course. I had plenty of opportunity to commit both murders. But why would I?'

'You have the knowledge too.' Gareth pointed out. 'And the expertise. If anyone could get away with this crime and commit it perfectly, it would be you.'

Finney smiled.

'Good.' He said. 'You're beginning to think like a detective. Everything you say is true. But the motive is lacking. One must have a motive!'

'So, who, then?' Gemma asked.

'I am not the only one with the skills and the knowledge to perfect this crime.' Finney said, looking slowly around the table and at all the faces that stared back at him. 'Apart from Robert, you are all experienced and knowledgeable crime writers. And each of you has a motive…

'Let's start with Margaret, shall we?' Finney turned and looked at Margaret Hemshaw. 'There was no love lost between you and Max Wilde. You made no secret of your dislike of the man and even speculated that someone may one day put an end to him. You are clever and not without your guiles. I believe you would happily kill to protect your daughter. Max Wilde behaved terribly with Pat, and I believe you would happily have murdered the man for it.'

'True.' Margaret admitted. 'I only wish I had.'

'And then we come to Pat herself.' Finney continued. 'You tell us that you visited Max on the day of his murder for closure, but we only have your word for that. It's entirely possible you felt betrayed by Max. Hurt. Scorned. We all know the adage about a woman scorned. I can see a passionate woman like you murdering a man like Max. It wouldn't be the first time.'

Pat laughed. 'I suppose that's all true. But I didn't kill him.'

'And then there's Sydney.' Finney went on. 'Here, I find the motive week. Max played with Sydney during the meal, but I saw a strong young woman deflect his best efforts. Max may have become annoyed and frustrated at his lack of progress and possibly even gone to Sydney's room later that night to force himself on her. And, if that happened, I could make a case for Sydney murdering Max for revenge, but somehow, none of that sits well with me.

'To begin with, there's Sakura. We didn't know it then, but Max was married, and, I think, happily so. I believe he flirted with Sydney that night because it amused him, but I don't see him going to her room to take what he wanted. And if he had, Sydney would have fought him like a lioness. If Max had died that night at Sydney's hand, he would have died hard and violently, and Sydney would have been covered in his blood. But that's not how Max died.

'Which leads us to Gareth, Sydney's lovesick puppy.'

A lighthearted giggle lifted the table's spirits.

'I suppose that's an apt description.' Gareth laughed.

'There's certainly a case for you, the snubbed paramour, taking out a love rival, but I have to say, as motives go, it's a poor one. I see you more as the kind of man who would meet his enemies face to face and punch them in full view of the world.'

'It was certainly tempting.' Gareth agreed.

'And then there's Sakura, a suddenly very wealthy young woman. But here, too, I struggle to find a good enough motive.'

'You don't think inheriting a huge amount of money is good enough motivation for murder?' Margaret snorted.

'In this case, no.' Finney answered. 'You see, by marrying Max, Sakura had already secured a vast fortune. She didn't need to kill him. Killing him essentially cut the head off the goose that was laying the golden eggs. That's why I'm fairly certain Sakura did not murder Max.'

'What about Sanjay?' Pat asked.

'He's not here to defend himself,' Finney noted, 'but we all know Sanjay was furious that Max's deal with the BBC scuttled his ambitions. It's certainly motive enough.'

'But not as strong as mine?' Gemma asked.

Finney turned and addressed her.

'Indeed. Yours is one of the strongest motives. Max's deal with his publishers would have destroyed your career. You would have been left with nothing.

Everything you have worked for and created would have been lost. Max would have destroyed you.'

'I can't argue with that.' Gemma agreed. 'Max dying saved me. But even if he had lived, I would have survived. It's what people do. I would have had Robert by my side, regardless.'

Robert took Gemma's hand in his and squeezed it gently.

'And yet, Max dying saved Robert too.' Finney said. 'Robert was about to lose everything as well. His is the strongest motive. Actually, the two of you, united, had a great deal to lose if Max had continued on his path. The fact he died before he could finish what he started merely enhances that. Together, you may well have plotted Max's death. It was a mutually advantageous killing.'

Silence descended on the table. It was broken by a doorbell ringing in the distance. Pat stood up.

'That will be Sanjay.' She said and disappeared into the house.

'We are back where we started.' Robert commented. 'Motive's all right and everything, but there isn't an ounce of proof anywhere.'

'Agreed.' Finney admitted. 'And that, in itself, is very odd.'

Pat came back out of the house with a noticeably lighter foot. Sanjay followed close behind, carrying a box of chocolates wrapped in a pink bow. He handed them to Margaret and kissed her on the cheek.

'I'd love to take credit for them,' he explained, 'but they're not from me! I found them on your doorstep.'

'That happens all the time.' Pat said. 'Fans get nervous coming to the house, so just leave gifts on the step and run off!'

'I do wish they'd stop leaving chocolate.' Margaret complained as she pulled the plastic wrapping off and opened the box. 'I only like the strawberry creams.'

Margaret took the only strawberry creams in the box and passed the rest to Pat.

'Which is good for me!' Pat laughed and handed the box to Finney, who selected a chocolate and popped it into his mouth. The box of chocolates made a brief pass of the table.

'We were just talking about motives for killing Max,' Sydney told Sanjay as she bit into a chocolate truffle.

'I see,' Sanjay said, taking a seat and retrieving a cup from Pat. 'I suppose we're all under a shadow with old Mr Fenwick?'

Margaret coughed.

'Any news on that?' Sanjay continued.

Margaret coughed again.

'Are you all right, Mother?'

Margaret coughed and struggled to form words.

'Mother?'

Finney stood up and moved closer to Margaret.

'Margaret, are you all right?'

She wasn't. She clutched her throat and gasped for air.

'Pat, get some water. Someone call an ambulance.' Finney said, but it was too late. Margaret began to fit, then tensed suddenly and dropped to the table.

Finney felt her neck for a pulse.

'I think she's dead.' He said.

'We should try CPR. She may be having a heart attack.' Sydney said, moving to Margaret's side and carefully dragging her to the floor.

'Wait!' Gareth shouted. He had seen a heart attack first-hand, and this didn't look like that. Margaret's face had twisted in agony, and her lips had gone blue. Of the four strawberry creams that Margaret had taken from the box, only one remained.

'No one eat any more chocolates.' He commanded, and the realisation of what he meant stunned them all.

***

DI Davenport pondered the man who sat across from her. The identification lanyard that hung from his neck suggested he was Detective Inspector Meadows, Criminal Investigation Department, Wiltshire. His face, on the other hand, suggested he was Tom Meadows, schoolboy, and he had no business being a policeman.

He spoke like a policeman, he walked like a policeman, and his ID said he was a policeman, but Davenport considered the lack of a five o'clock shadow at five o'clock in the afternoon an indication that he hadn't fully grown up.

'Sorry to have kept you,' Meadows said as he pulled up a chair and sat down. He held a folder full of files which he opened and spread out on the table. 'I think I have everything we need.'

Cause of death had been attributed to a lethal dose of cyanide poisoning, and a detailed investigation determined the source of the cyanide to have been a selection of chocolates given to Margaret Hemshaw by Sanjay Chakrabarti. In particular, strawberry creams.

'We took detailed witness statements from everyone who was at the house at the time of Mrs Hemshaw's death.' Meadows continued. 'Our initial focus was on Sanjay Chakrabarti. He gave Mrs Hemshaw the chocolates and was clearly a prime suspect.'

Davenport disagreed but didn't say so. She didn't think Mr Chakrabati would have been so stupid as to give Margaret Hemshaw a box of chocolates he had poisoned himself.

'According to Pat Hemshaw,' Meadows continued, 'fans were apt to leave gifts for her mother on the doorstep. Often chocolates, sometimes small teddy bears and the like. We conducted a thorough check on all cameras located on the street outside the house, and we obtained a lot of footage from doorbells and CCTV cameras. Apart from delivery drivers and postmen, there were no unusual visitors to the house in the twenty-four hours prior to the chocolates being found. We did catch Mr Chakrabati on a neighbour's doorbell as he made his way along the street to the house. He wasn't carrying anything, so we're pretty sure the chocolates were left before he arrived.'

'What about the chocolates?' Davenport asked.

'One of the most common varieties you can buy. Pat Hemshaw attested to the fact that her mother was partial to the strawberry creams, and it had become something of a tradition in which no one but her mother ever ate them.'

'So by poisoning those particular chocolates, you could almost guarantee that no one else would eat them?'

'Exactly so,' Meadows agreed. 'No other chocolates in the box were poisoned. Everyone who was at the lunch knew that Mrs Hemshaw would demand the strawberry creams. It was one of those things that people did.'

Davenport contemplated that for a moment. It was a risky strategy for a murderer to adopt, but she had to admit it was almost foolproof. She had met Margaret Hemshaw. If she wanted the strawberry creams, it was unlikely anyone else would get a look in.

'Why did her lunch guests come through the back gate to the house instead of through the front door?' Davenport asked.

'Everyone in the party, except Sanjay Chakrabati, had stayed at a local luxury pod site nearby. It is actually the more logical route into the gardens. It would have been more suspicious if they had all entered through the front.'

'Anything else?' Davenport asked, more in desperation than hope.

'There is one thing.' Meadows said. He selected a file and passed it over to Davenport. 'Mrs Hemshaw was dying. She had cancer. I've spoken to her doctor, who confirmed it. She had refused treatment. Best case scenario, she would have lived for a few more months. Her doctor tells me it would have been a devastating assault on her body. He suggested, albeit subtly, that it was almost a blessing that she had been murdered when she had. It saved her and her daughter an awful amount of suffering.'

Davenport read the report.

'Any suggestion of suicide?' She asked.

Meadows rubbed his head.

'No. Mrs Hemshaw's doctor suggested the opposite was true. She had a zest and a passion for life and was a stubborn old girl who would have taken it on head first.'

Davenport nodded. That was a fair appraisal.

'Do you think all these deaths are linked?' Meadows asked.

Max Wilde, hemlock poisoning. Motive unclear. John Fenwick, cyanide poisoning. Possible removal of a witness. And now Margaret Hemshaw, cyanide poisoning. But why? Had Margaret Hemshaw seen or heard something? Did she come to her end because the killer was desperate to hide their tracks?

'I'm certain they're linked.' Davenport said. 'Proving it is easier said than done. The trouble is, has the killer finished, or is there more to come?'

Davenport sensed the cloud that hung over Lilac Cottage as she walked slowly up the small path. The driveway and approach to the front door were carpeted in wreaths of every size and colour imaginable. It had been over a week since Margaret Hemshaw had died, and the line of mourners that stretched away from her front gate seemed to get longer by the day.

Davenport had rung ahead, and she found Pat Hemshaw at the door as she approached.

'I've had to disconnect the house phone,' she said as Davenport stepped inside. 'They won't stop calling.'

'I can get some uniform up here if you like,' Davenport said. 'Encourage them to move on.'

'It's not so bad.' Pat sighed. 'It reminds me how much my mother was loved and how much she'll be missed. It's the journalists. They're relentless.'

They sat in a small room at the back of the house. Pat made coffee for Davenport and poured herself a large red wine.

'Any more news on mother?' Pat asked.

Davenport relayed to Pat the information that DI Meadows had passed to her.

'So she was poisoned then?' Pat asked.

'She was.' Davenport said. 'Did your mother say anything to you about the case? Any suspicions she may have had?'

'We talked about it, of course.' Pat admitted. 'But I don't think she had any specific suspicions. If she did, she certainly didn't speak to me about them.'

Perhaps she did, Davenport thought, only maybe she didn't realise that Pat was the killer and, by doing so, had signed her own death warrant.

'Did you know your mother was sick?' Davenport asked.

'Mother was never sick.' Pat said. 'She refused to be.'

Davenport paused. She waited as Pat absorbed the question more fully.

'Did you find something in the autopsy?' She asked.

Davenport searched her face for some hint of dishonesty. She found none.

'I'm afraid your mother had a terminal illness. It was unlikely she would have lived for more than a few months.'

Pat gasped. She looked genuinely shocked.

'I..I.. I didn't know.' She stuttered.

Davenport believed her. Genuine emotion was hard to fake, and she had seen a lot of fakers in her time.

'Do you think your mother may have taken her own life?' Davenport asked.

'Absolutely not.' Pat said firmly. 'No. Never. She'd have fought to the bitter end and made my life miserable! Oh, that sounded callous. That's not what I meant. Not like that.'

'But it's true,' Davenport agreed. 'She would have made your life hell. More so. That's a fair motive to murder someone.'

'I see.' Pat said. 'Yes. I see. You think I killed Max Wilde and the gardener, and you think I killed my mother to finally be free of all the people who had betrayed me and made my life a misery.'

'It's a possibility. You have no alibi for the time of Max's murder, and you could easily have placed a lethal dose of cyanide in Mr Fenwick's beer. Of all the people in your mother's life, you have the strongest reason for wanting her dead and the best opportunity for putting the chocolates on your doorstep.'

Pat smiled, although it was cracked with emotion. She placed her drink on the side and got up. She found a pad on an easy table nearby and wrote something on it. She handed it to Davenport.

'What's this?' Davenport asked.

'I can't prove I didn't poison Mr Fenwick's beer or the chocolates which killed my mother, and I'm grateful for the fact in English law that you must prove I did, not the other way around. However, I can prove I didn't kill Max Wilde. On that paper is the name, address and telephone number of a rather cute young taxi driver who spent the afternoon of Max's murder with me on the couch you are sitting on, and he didn't leave until the following morning. I would be grateful if this information were kept between us.'

Davenport looked back at Lilac Cottage as she left the house and made her way back up the drive. The evening was chasing the day away, and clouds were gathering. She'd get Graves to follow up on Pat's alibi in the morning. If Pat was telling the truth, and she had no reason to suspect she wasn't, she could probably eliminate her from the list of suspects.

It wasn't nearly enough. In every case she had worked on, there came a point at which they arrived at a critical moment when the case finally broke. She felt like they were nearing that point now. All she needed was a lucky break. But where was she going to find that?

Dessert

Delicious Death
Chocolate cake, of course!

Coffin Cake
Cherry and almond loaf cake

I-Screams
A selection of ice creams

Rancid Rhubarb and Custard
A celebration of Rhubarb and Custard

Guilty Pleasure
A sticky date pudding with salted caramel sauce and a pistachio praline

After the Funeral

Detective Inspector Davenport watched as the raindrops gathered on the windscreen and began rolling down. It had been threatening for days, and it seemed fitting that it chose that moment to begin.

She was parked on the main road that snaked through Burnham-on-the-Wold, opposite the Marlborough Hotel and next to the small Village stores into which Sergeant Graves had recently gone. Ahead lay the small church of St Mary's, and she and Graves had watched as the funeral procession arrived and made its sombre way into the church.

Graves had taken celebrity spotting to new highs and had been unusually excited as the great and good of the literary and television world appeared and subsequently vanished into the hallowed walls of St Mary's. When the mourners stopped arriving, a horse-drawn hearse rumbled past them, followed by Robert Wilde, Gemma Collis and Sakura Wilde. As they waited outside the entrance to the church for Max to be carried in, the heavens had opened, and the dark day turned even darker.

She turned as Graves opened the door and climbed back in. He carried two cans of cola, crisps, and a sharing bag of sweets. He handed Davenport one of the cans and a bag of crisps and looked out of the windscreen.

'Have I missed anyone?' He asked.

Davenport cracked her can open and took a swig.

'Pretty sure I just saw Florence Pugh.'

Graves almost choked on his drink.

'Really?'

'No.' Davenport said abruptly.

They sat in the car in silence, their only soundtrack the constant beat of raindrops on the car. After about an hour, the church bells began a monotone tolling, and the mourners filed out under black umbrellas to the graveyard. The coffin containing Max Wilde's body followed soon after.

'Should we pay our respects?' Graves asked.

'No.' Davenport said. 'I don't like getting wet.'

***

Gemma took Robert's arm in hers and followed the pallbearers as they carried Max's coffin from the church. The bells tolled a steady beat, and the rain rattled the old roof tiles of the church.

Robert took an umbrella from an usher at the door and opened it for Gemma and Sakura to shelter under.

'It was a good service.' Gemma remarked.

'Max would have been pleased.' Robert agreed. 'What time is it?' He asked.

Gemma fished her phone from a pocket and fumbled as her phone dropped unceremoniously to the floor. She heard it crack.

'Shit.'

She picked her phone up and wiped the rain and dirt from it. Her screen had fallen face down; now, it was nothing more than a spider's web of cracked glass. She tapped the home button, but nothing came on.

'Fuck.' She said, a little louder than she had intended. She looked behind her to see if she had been overheard and was relieved to find she hadn't.

'It's okay.' Robert said. 'I've got a couple of spare phones at home. You can have one until we get you a new one.'

They walked slowly behind the coffin as it snaked its way through the old graveyard until they arrived at Max's final resting place. The mourners had gathered to one side and allowed the pallbearers to carefully place the coffin into position next to a freshly dug hole. Max and Gemma stepped in beside the vicar and waited for the committal to begin. Sakura stood nearby, unsure of the etiquette.

Robert was pleased to see so many of Max's peers and friends had made the journey for his funeral. They all waited beneath large black umbrellas that swayed in the wind. He noted poor Pat, too, her arm linked inside Sanjay's. He nodded a solemn hello, and she attempted a smile in return. Next to her were Sydney and Gareth, suitably dressed in black and with arms entwined. Mr Finney was next to them. He wore a large black overcoat and an old fedora. It suited him, Robert thought. More people should wear hats.

Robert's eyes landed on the plot next to Max's. Their parents had gone to their final reward several years ago, barely months apart, and Max had bought the plot next to theirs for when his turn would come. No one had expected it to be so soon.

The vicar began the committal ceremony, and Max was lowered carefully into the ground. Robert and Gemma threw a small amount of soil onto the coffin and said their goodbyes. Sakura followed suit and then followed them out of the churchyard.

The three of them waited by the lychgate and shook hands with the mourners as they slowly left the churchyard. Robert invited them all back to The Marlborough for drinks, and most accepted, although one or two claimed other commitments and left.

The Marlborough had been closed for the day, although the staff had been kept on to serve the mourners.

Gemma shook the rainwater from her coat and slipped it over the back of a chair. She took her phone from her pocket and dropped it onto the table.

'You may need to charge my phones. They're probably flat.' Robert said. 'Would you like me to do it for you?'

'No. Stay here. These are your guests. I'll go. Where are they?'

Robert didn't know for sure, but he had a small nook upstairs where he often went to read. There was a small desk there, which probably had them.

'Get me a coffee, would you?' Gemma asked. 'I won't be long.'

She found the door to the rooms upstairs and typed the four-digit code into the lock. Although The Marlborough was once a small hotel, the upstairs rooms were now purely residential. Robert had turned the rooms into his own luxury accommodation. Gemma had stayed there often, more so in recent weeks.

She found the small nook and rifled through the drawers of the desk. She found two phones, one of which looked like it had seen better days, and selected the other. It had no power. Gemma found a charger in the drawer and plugged it in. She'd return for it in an hour and swap the sim cards.

***

Graves offered a sweet to Davenport, which she declined. He had a mouth full of sweets when his phone began to chime.

'Hello?' He said in a muffled voice. 'Hang on a sec.' He took a couple of bites and then swallowed the sweets down. 'Say that again. When? Are you sure? Where? Okay, thank you.'

Graves hung up, and Davenport noted a smile stretch across his face. Graves rarely smiled.

'What?' Davenport asked.

'The phone used to send the texts inviting our suspects to The Winterbook has just been turned on.'

Davenport looked at him in stunned silence.

'I asked the phone company to monitor the number and call me if there was any activity.' Graves explained. 'I've got to admit; I didn't think it would get turned back on.'

'Where is it?' Davenport asked.

'They can only be sure to within a few meters, but their best guess is inside the Marlborough Hotel.'

Davenport looked across at the pub. There must be at least two hundred people in there, she mused. But on the other hand, there were only a few suspects. It had to be on one of them.

'Come on.' She said and stepped out into the rain. Graves followed, and they crossed the road and entered the pub. 'When I give the nod, ring the number. Let's hope it's not on silent.'

Robert held out his hand as Davenport and Graves approached.

'Good afternoon, Inspector.' He said. 'Can I offer you a drink?'

'No, thank you.' Davenport replied. 'I'm afraid we're here on business. New information has come to light.'

'Can't it wait, Inspector?' Gemma asked. 'This is a wake. Surely it can't be that important?'

'It can't wait.' Davenport said quietly. She nodded discreetly at Graves, who opened his phone and rang the number.

Finney watched the interaction with interest. Davenport was on to something.

'What's going on?' Sydney asked. She had watched Davenport and Graves enter the pub and grabbed Gareth's hand. They arrived just as Graves dialled the number.

'They say they have new information.' Sakura said.

'Can't it wait?' Pat asked. She, too, had seen the police officers enter the pub and came over to see what was going on. Sanjay followed.

'Does seem a little insensitive.' Sanjay agreed.

'Murder is a very sensitive subject.' Davenport said. She looked across at Graves, who shook his head. Damn. If the thing were on silent, they'd never find it.

'Is there somewhere we could talk?' Davenport asked, throwing the question at Robert. 'Somewhere quiet.'

She was convinced Robert was her man, but how to prove it? Despite all her efforts, they couldn't find a hole in his alibi. If the phone was on his person and it was on silent, they needed to get him somewhere quiet to listen out for the vibration.

'Of course. We can go to my rooms.'

Robert led them to the door to his quarters and entered the four-digit security code. Davenport and Graves followed him up the stairs into a large living room. As they entered, Davenport nodded at Graves.

'What's this all about?' Robert asked. 'You do realise I've just buried my brother?'

'I'm well aware of that, Mr……..'

She stopped as a phone began ringing nearby. Davenport left the living room and followed the noise. It led her to a quiet corner of the building, where she

found a comfortable-looking armchair and a small desk.
A phone was ringing on the desk. With a gloved hand,
Davenport picked the phone up and looked at the
screen.

'Are the last four digits of your number 1754?' She
asked as Graves appeared next to her. He had followed
Robert as he had followed Davenport.

'It is.' Graves said.

Davenport turned to Robert.

'Robert Wilde, I am arresting you on the suspicion of
the murder Max Wilde. I am also arresting you on
suspicion of the murders of Jack Fenwick and Margaret
Hemshaw. You do not have to say anything, but it may
harm your defence..'

'Robert! What's going on?' Gemma asked as Graves
turned Robert around and slipped handcuffs over his
wrists. Gemma had waited a few seconds after Robert
had taken the police officers upstairs before deciding she
didn't like where it was heading. Finney and the others
had followed.

'There's been some kind of mistake. This is
ridiculous!' Robert cried.

'Not another word, Robert.' Finney ordered. 'Do not
say another thing until you have your lawyer present.'
Finney turned to Davenport. 'Do you care to explain
this?' He asked.

'No.' Davenport said.

'Right.' Finney nodded. He turned to Gemma. 'You
and I will follow them to the station. Which station will
you be taking him to, Inspector?'

'Gloucester.'

Finney turned to the others.

'The rest of you go back to the Manor. Lock the
doors. Make sure the gates are locked, too. As soon as
they take Robert through the pub and out into the street,

the whole world will be on their way here. Wait for us there.'

The pub fell silent as Robert was led through and out into the street. Robert was marched across the road and into Davenport's car. Everyone who owned a phone was recording and taking pictures.

A marked police car pulled up alongside. Graves had called ahead. Crowd control in Burnham-on-the-Wold had now turned into a search party.

Davenport barked her instructions. 'Get everyone out of the pub. No one goes upstairs. Get some more uniform down here and turn that place upside down. Robert's our man. There'll be more evidence in there. Find it.'

Finney took Gemma's hand as they watched Davenport drive Robert away.

'Come on. Let's see what this is all about.'

***

'I can't believe they've arrested Robert,' Sydney said.

'It's ridiculous,' Sanjay agreed. 'Bloody nonsense.'

Gareth slipped his arm around Sydney and drew her towards him. They were sitting on a large sofa in the lounge of Burnham Manor, where they had all escaped after Robert's arrest. Finney had been spot on with his analysis of what would happen once the police had dragged a shackled Robert Wilde through the public bar. Stunned faces were quickly replaced by intrigued ones, and one or two made hurried phone calls to journalists of their acquaintance. By the time the five had returned to the Manor, journalists were already beginning to set up camp outside the gate. Some had been filming outside The Marlborough when Robert was driven away and were lucky enough to catch the spectacle in time for the five o'clock news.

Pat stood up and paced the lounge restlessly. It had been nearly five hours since the arrest, and no one had heard from Gemma or Finney.

'No news is good news.' Gareth had said, and the cliché burned his soul.

'Perhaps we should ring them?' Sakura said.

'It'll be no good.' Sanjay said. 'They won't know anything yet. We just have to wait.'

'It's the waiting I hate.' Pat said. 'What if he did it?' She said suddenly.

'Pat!' Sanjay exclaimed. 'You mustn't think like that.'

'Mustn't I?' She replied. 'Why not? If the murders are linked, and we all think they are, then whoever killed Max killed my mother.'

There was silence as everyone accepted what they knew was true.

'And what do we know of Robert? I mean, really?' Pat continued. 'I don't think I'd met him before this year. What about you, Sanjay?'

Sanjay shook his head in the most non-committal way possible.

'I'd met him a couple of years ago, briefly. At another of Max's get-togethers. I didn't know him, to speak of.'

'Sakura?' Pat asked.

She shook her head. 'I don't know him. But I like him. I don't think he killed Max.'

'Neither do I.' Sydney challenged. 'I don't think Robert killed his brother.'

'Despite the inheritance?' Pat argued. 'The multi-millions of pounds he would get? And if Max hadn't died when he did, he would surely have lost his career, too. He would have lost everything.'

'It's a hell of a motive.' Gareth agreed.

Sydney sat up, and Gareth's arm fell from her shoulders.

'You don't think he did it, do you?' She asked.

'If I'm honest, I don't know. I don't want to rush to say he did or didn't do it until I have all the facts. Speculation does us no good at all.'

'Here here.' Sanjay said. 'We should wait until we hear something.'

As he spoke, Sydney's phone began to ring.

'It's Finney,' she said as she pressed the green handset on the screen. 'Hello?'

Everyone waited as Sydney stood up and began muttering single-syllable words on the phone.

'Okay, I'll call you back in a bit.'

'Well?' Pat demanded as Sydney hung up.

'They're on their way back. They haven't charged Robert with anything yet, but they're going to hold him for twenty-four hours while they continue searching The Marlborough.'

'Can they do that?' Sakura asked.

'They can hold him without charge for twenty-four hours, longer if they need to, but they'll need something solid to go on to apply for an extension.' Gareth said. 'Do we know why they've arrested him?'

'Apparently, the phone the murderer used to summon us to the cruise was found in Robert's flat above the pub.' Sydney replied.

'That's not enough.' Gareth said. 'They'll need more. Fingerprints or something.'

'But the phone was in his flat!' Pat argued. 'What more do they need?'

'Well, I don't know about anyone else,' Gareth said, 'but I know the code to Robert's private quarters.'

Everyone looked at him in astonishment.

'One-Eight-One-Five, followed by the star button.' Gareth said triumphantly.

'How the hell do you know that?' Sydney asked.

'I'm a crime writer.' Gareth said. 'Things intrigue me. I watch people. I watched Gemma earlier as she went up to Robert's flat to see if I could catch the numbers to the lock. I do it in all the pubs and shops I go into. You'd be surprised how lax people's security is. Gemma gave no thought to covering the pad, and I saw her type the numbers in. I just haven't forgotten the numbers yet. So, you see, if I could do it, and if someone wanted to deflect attention from themselves, it would be quite simple to set Robert up.'

Sydney smiled. She liked that.

Pat didn't smile. It wasn't enough. Gareth was right.

'Anyway, why were you going to call Finney back?' Gareth asked.

'Oh, yes. I almost forgot. They're going to pick up a takeaway on the way home. There's a good Thai place on the way. I said I'd take a food order.'

'Do you know, I am hungry.' Sanjay said. 'With all this going on, I hadn't noticed.'

'Right, I'll google the restaurant and get a menu.' Gareth said.

A few minutes later, Sydney had texted over their food order.

Sydney held her hand out for Gareth's.

'Come on, help me look for plates and stuff.'

They left the lounge and walked across the entrance hall to the kitchens. Gareth set about rifling through drawers and cupboards and pulling out plates and cutlery as he found them. Sydney walked over to one of the preparation tables and hopped up.

'Do you remember the last time we were in this kitchen?' Sydney asked.

Gareth stopped rifling. He looked up to see Sydney swinging her legs back and forth and smiling at him. He walked over, and she parted her legs and drew him near. She looked into his eyes and then kissed him passionately.

'I remember Gemma seemed to enjoy herself.' Gareth joked.

'I want you.' Sydney said, and she joined her legs behind him and squeezed tightly.

Gareth enjoyed the contact. He felt his blood rise. He had never been so close to his heart's desire.

'Here?' Gareth asked.

'No. Not here. Later. Come to my room. Come to me.'

Gareth rested his forehead on hers and smiled.

'I thought you'd never fucking ask.'

***

Nobody spoke much when Gemma and Finney returned to the Manor, and food was laid out on a coffee table set between two sofas. Sydney and Gareth carried the plates to everyone and placed one spare plate on the table. They had overcounted. Or they had counted Robert by mistake.

Sydney paused as she was about to take her seat. She stood looking abstractedly at thin air while a thought crossed her mind. It was odd. It confused her. She frowned.

'Syd?' Gareth asked.

Sydney said nothing. She carried on standing, looking at nothing in particular.

"We're waiting for one more person to arrive."

The cruise. The Winterbrook and Sakura's late arrival. *"We're waiting for one more person to arrive."*

Sydney shook her head. It wasn't possible. She couldn't have known. *Could she?*

If she did know, how? How did she know? The only way she could possibly know was if…

Sydney looked down at her friends, who were all watching her with interest.

'Is everything okay, Sydney?' Gemma asked.

'You know that feeling you get when you're on the cusp of a great idea, but you can't pin it down?' Sydney explained. 'Like it's almost fully formed, except you can't quite grasp the detail?'

Finney didn't have a clue what she was talking about, although he suspected the other writers in the room probably did. 'Drinks?' He asked.

Sydney stood vacantly, looking at the plates as they were slowly filled with food. Finney made a quick pass and delivered drinks back to the party.

'Can I help?' Sakura said, rising.

'Not at all,' Finney insisted. He sat Sakura back in her seat and pressed her drink into her hand. 'Drink up.' He stood back and watched as the party got stuck into their food and drinks. He walked over to Sydney and put a glass of red wine into her hands. 'You should sit down, Sydney. You're making the place look untidy.'

It was something his late wife often said to him. Repeating it made him feel closer to her.

Sydney turned and looked at Finney. The glass of wine slipped and fell to the floor, spilling its contents onto the carpet.

Finney smiled.

'I thought if anyone were going to work it out, it would be you,' he said.

Sydney shook her head.

'I don't think I have, not really. Not all of it.' She turned and looked at the others. 'What did you put in their drinks?' She asked.

Everyone had fallen quiet. They had slumped over and rested where they fell.

'A sedative.' Finney admitted. 'Quite a strong one. I needed to be sure that man of yours was put out quickly. I was hoping you would have drunk yours, too. It would have saved us both a lot of bother.'

Sydney watched as Finney reached into his jacket and pulled out a gun. He pointed it at Sydney.

'Sit down.'

Sydney sat at the edge of the sofa.

'I don't like guns,' Finney said. 'They've always made me nervous. When I retired from the force, I had a lot of contacts, not all from the right side of the law. You can buy anything these days if you know who to ask.'

'You were going to shoot Max Wilde because he killed your daughter.' Sydney said. 'And because ten years after her death, your wife killed herself. And you blamed Max Wilde.'

'Well done.' Finney nodded. 'Very well done, indeed. I always said you had the making of a good detective. And yes, I was going to shoot Max Wilde, and I didn't care if I were caught. It made no difference to me.'

Finney paused, and his eyes glazed over. The pain came back. Sydney watched as the darkness engulfed him.

'She was twelve years old.' Finney began. 'We took her to dinner as a birthday treat. I can remember the day like it was yesterday. We booked weeks in advance and arranged for a cake to be brought to the table. We knew she had allergies. We always carried an Epi-pen, just in case. We were assured that no ingredients in her food were likely to disagree with her. We were very careful. We were very specific. No peanuts. We were very, very clear.'

Finney's face twisted in grief.

'But we didn't know Max Wilde. He had a habit of changing menus and ingredients on a whim and not telling the staff. He did it that night, and my baby girl died because of his flippancy and carelessness. We tried to save her. The paramedics kept her going until we got to the hospital, but it was no good. She died in my arms that night on her twelfth birthday.

'I don't know how we survived. I'm not even sure we did. The best part of us died with her. We threw ourselves into our work and pushed on. They say life continues, but it doesn't. It didn't for us. Our lives ended that night. We just got older with every year that passed.

'Ten years to the day that my baby girl died, Caroline took her own life. I don't think she could bear the suffering anymore. I was angry, to begin with. I was angry with her for leaving me. Now, I had to suffer again. All because of Max Wilde. All I could think of was revenge. I had served justice all my life, and it failed to serve me when I needed it most. Every time I turned on the TV, there he was: Max Wilde, celebrity chef, television presenter and best-selling writer. He was living a hundred privileged lives, whereas my daughter wasn't able to live one. I wanted to kill him so badly.'

Sydney looked at Finney, who continued to point the gun at her.

'They made me retire. So I came here, to where I knew Max Wilde lived, and plotted my revenge.'

'That was years ago.' Sydney said. 'What happened?'

Finney shrugged.

'I lacked opportunity. I wandered around the village, hoping to bump into the man one day. I carried the gun with me at all times. I would have done it, too. Gladly. Unfortunately, our paths never crossed.'

'Until this year?'

'Until this year.' Finney agreed.

Sydney watched Finney carefully. She didn't doubt for a minute that he'd use the gun and kill her. She needed a plan, and she needed one quickly. Unfortunately, Finney was stood between her and the door. If she could get the other side of that, she'd stand a chance.

'Max Wilde's arrogance made him invite me to his little party. If I'd known it was that easy to get an invite, I'd have entered that bloody competition sooner. Once I knew I would be in his company for an extended period, another plan began to form.

'Everyone in the village knew of Simon Delancey's poison garden and the poisons that still resided there. Fenwick couldn't resist telling people of his stash of vials. I'd overheard him several times in the pub, bragging about them to those who would listen. He was an unpleasant man, not unlike Simon Delancey. I broke in once and stole a few vials of various poisons. He had quite the collection.'

'Fenwick saw you.' Sydney said. 'But it wasn't until Max died that he realised what you would use them for. I remember he said, *"I saw you too."* He was telling you he knew.'

'That's what I thought too. I thought I'd covered my tracks quite well. No one said anything of concern on the little cruise, and I was entirely certain I'd got away with it until I spoke to Fenwick. I must admit, I hadn't foreseen that. But you can't think of everything; the trick is making sure you act swiftly when your errors have been highlighted.'

'So you murdered Fenwick.'

'I did. But I'm curious,' Finney said. 'What gave me away?'

'The cruise.' Sydney said. 'I'd always assumed that when I turned up on your doorstep on the night we got the text messages, you hadn't got one, too. But I now think you did get them. You sent the text messages to yourself so that you could be on the cruise, but when I showed up, you decided to act differently.'

'I did.' Finney admitted. 'Like I said, I always thought you'd make a good detective, so I decided to muddy the waters and confuse things, if only in your head. But that doesn't explain how you knew it was me?'

"We're waiting for one more guest to arrive."

'The lady on the cruise said she was waiting for one more person to arrive before setting off. If you hadn't been invited, as I thought, she should have been waiting for eight people. Me, Gareth, Gemma, Robert, Pat, Margaret, Sanjay and Sakura. When she said she was waiting for another person to arrive, there were already eight people on the boat. She had been told to expect nine. So, if you had been invited, why did you lie to me? As soon as I uncovered the lie, it all started to fall into place.'

Finney nodded. 'I'm afraid I clichéd myself. I tried to be clever. It was silly of me.' Finney gripped the butt of the gun harder. 'It's not going to happen again.'

'But why?' Sydney asked. 'Why are you going to kill us? What will that achieve?'

'Because you're all so damned over-privileged and arrogant. Why should you lead your lives when my daughter can't? What right do you have to live? And I want Robert Wilde to suffer. He should have controlled his brother better. He's as much to blame as Max. I want him to suffer. I'm going to kill him the way I died. Slowly and over many years. He will forever live with the knowledge that he was in jail when his girlfriend and his unborn child were murdered. He could do nothing to save his sister-in-law, his niece or nephew, or you lot. He'll have to live with that for the rest of his life or do what my dear wife did and release himself from his pain.'

'And what will that achieve? You'll spend the rest of your life in prison.'

Finney smiled, which erupted into a laugh.

'No, Sydney. I won't. When the bodies are found, they'll find mine, too. They'll find an unused gun and no fingerprints and seven syringes, all with traces of a lethal mixture I put together myself. Unfortunately, that's in the boot of my car, which is outside, so I really need you to go to sleep while I get it.'

'And if I refuse.'

Finney shook the end of the gun.

'One way or another, you die. I would rather it was neater. I like you, Sydney; I don't want you to die like that.'

Finney kept the gun aimed at Sydney and walked over to where he had left the bottle of wine. He poured a glass and then dropped a sachet of what Sydney assumed was a sedative into the glass. He returned to Sydney and placed it on the table before her.

'Drink.' He commanded.

Sydney took the glass and drew it to her mouth.

'They'll prove it was you. They'll prove it.' She said. She looked up at Finney and saw the door in the corner of her eye. By pouring her drink, he had opened up her escape route.

'I don't care.' Finney said. 'Drink!'

Sydney launched the drink, glass and all, directly into Finney's face. She felt the air part as a shot rang out, and a round thumped into the sofa. She was at the door in seconds, eternally grateful that it wasn't locked, and was

the other side of it as another shot rang out, and a piece
of the doorframe exploded into splinters.

The entrance hall was a big ask. Finney was old but
fit. She mentally assessed her chances of reaching the
door and then from the door to safety and realised she
couldn't do it. She bolted left and shot up the stairs,
almost halfway up, when a third and fourth shot rang
out.

The third round she heard flick the air to her left and
pound into the stairs. She didn't hear the fourth. It
slammed into her shoulder and rendered her arm useless.
There was almost no pain, merely a sensation, but try as
he might, she couldn't lift her arm. Her feet kept
pounding at the stairs until she reached the top. The fifth
round whistled by harmlessly, and the sixth ripped a hole
in her leg a few inches from her hip. She ran on as
several more rounds whipped through the air like
desperate hornets. She didn't know what to do or where
to go. No plan formed. She opened the door to one of
the rooms and fell in behind it. There was nowhere to
go. All she could do was sit there and wait. The title of
an old book came to mind. Death Comes As The End.
She had never fully understood its meaning. Until now.
Now she understood.

Finney stood at the bottom of the stairs, the gun held
down by his side. He was sure he had hit her, but she
hadn't fallen. She was a tough cookie, of that he had no
doubt. In a way, he was pleased. He did like her, even
though he was going to kill her.

'Come out, Sydney.' He shouted. 'Let's not do it like
this. You have nowhere to go. In a few minutes, the pain
is going to start, and the blood loss will overcome you. It
will end my way, whatever you do next. Be smart. Let's
do it the easy way.'

Sydney lifted her arm, and the pain raced through her body unabated. She stifled the scream that gathered on her lips and bit her lip until it drew blood. She could feel the adrenaline lose its grip on her faculties, and she began to feel dizzy. Finney was right. She didn't have long. She needed to do something. She had to try something.

She pulled herself from the floor and gathered her senses. Her left arm was shattered and useless, and blood was pouring from her fingertips. With her right hand, she lifted her arm and slipped her hand between the buttons of her blouse. She found some fabric nearby, which she made into a sling, and carefully tied her arm up. That would stem the flow for a bit. She walked over to a mirror and investigated the wound in her leg. Her jeans were darkening with the blood loss, but it didn't look too bad. It hurt like hell, but she could still walk. She took a deep breath and composed herself.

Finney waited for a reply, but none came. He could have followed her up the stairs, found her, and shot her, but he didn't want to do that. Besides, knowing Sydney, she would be prepared for that. He might be walking into a trap. She was a feisty, determined young woman, and he was a slow, old man. He turned and strode out the front door to the Manor, where he had parked his car. He opened the boot and retrieved a small bag. He had no fears that Sydney would try to escape while his back was turned. He was confident the shots he had landed would have slowed her down sufficiently. He closed the boot of his car and returned to where the others were still lying.

He waited.

Slowly, he opened his bag and began removing the contents. He laid seven syringes out on the table.

He turned as the door behind him opened, and Sydney staggered in. He still gripped the gun in his hand.

'Sydney, my dear, I'm so sorry. I didn't mean for that to happen.'

He looked shocked at the sight of so much blood. He waved the gun towards the sofa.

'Sit down.'

Sydney walked slowly past Finney while maintaining eye contact with him the entire time. She was banking on the fact that he didn't want to shoot her. That bought her some time. But time for what? She needed to work something out quickly. Time was not on her side.

'Do you think this is what your daughter would have wanted?' She asked. 'Is this what Sarah would have wanted as her legacy?'

The darkness fell over Finney's eyes.

'Don't even mention her name.' He screamed. 'Don't say her name.'

'Sarah?' Sydney challenged. 'I don't think this is what she would have wanted.'

Finney gripped the butt of the gun and pointed it at Sydney's face.

'Stop!' He spat. 'Not one more word.'

'You're betraying Sarah's memory.' Sydney said calmly. 'You're disgracing her!'

Finney raged, and Sydney watched the anger overwhelm him. He took five paces and pressed the gun to Sydney's forehead.

'Say her name again!' Finney cried. 'I fucking dare you!'

Sydney had no intention of repeating her name. She had grown up in a house full of boys and knew that you couldn't fight someone until they were within thumping distance. She couldn't fight Finney while he was five feet away from her. Now, he wasn't.

Finney saw the danger too late. Sydney used her good arm and swung it up and around so that it caught Finney's and pushed the gun away from her head. Finney lost his grip, and Sydney heard the weapon fall to the ground. She had levelled the playing field. Without pausing another second, she stood up quickly and planted the tip of her head onto Finney's nose. She heard it crack and watched Finney fall to the floor, clutching his face.

She stood there for a moment, stunned and unsteady. The blood loss was beginning to tell. She watched as Finney quickly regathered himself and stood up. Blood poured from his nose. She watched as his anger consumed him.

'I'm going to kill you.' He spat, and his eyes located the gun on the floor.

Sydney watched as he began to walk over to where it lay. She felt the blood rush from her head and the darkness approach. In the corner of her eye, she saw Finney bend down to retrieve the weapon. She was unable to move.

'Not on my fucking watch, you don't,' a familiar voice said from behind her.

Gareth rose from the sofa and launched himself at Finney. The two fell to the ground and fought for what felt like an age. Sydney began to recover her senses.

She saw Gareth launch several well-aimed punches at Finney, but he took them well. He used the butt of the gun on the side of Gareth's head, and he fell to one side in a heap.

Finney stood up and composed himself. He was still holding the gun. He pointed the gun at Gareth's body.

'Wait!' Sydney screamed, but there was no stopping Finney now. He squeezed the trigger.

It felt like a dream. There was so much noise. It all happened at once.

They came in through the door, screaming at the tops of their voices. Five men, dressed in black, carrying automatic weapons. The noise was disconcerting. It surprised them all.

'Police!'

'Drop the gun!'

'Drop the gun!'

'Drop the gun!'

And again, 'Drop the gun!'

So much noise. She didn't know where to look.

She turned and watched as Finney looked at her and smiled. He slowly turned the gun away from Gareth and slipped the tip into his mouth.

Then the noise stopped.

***

Sydney woke to find herself in bed. There were light curtains on the windows, and a soft, late summer sun shone through them. She took a moment to take in her surroundings and surmised, rightly, that she was in hospital. Gareth was sitting on a chair next to her, reading a paper.

'Morning, sleepy head.' He said.

'How long have I been asleep?' She asked.

'They rushed you into surgery last night.' Gareth explained. 'They've patched your shoulder up as best they could, but you'll probably need it fixed properly. I'm afraid the bullet smashed your shoulder to pieces.'

'What about my leg?'

'Bullet went clean through.' Gareth said. 'They've stitched you, but I'm afraid it will leave a scar.'

Sydney closed her eyes. Finney's face came to her. He smiled. Then, the gun.

'Finney?' She asked.

Gareth shook his head.

'He died instantly.'

'What about the others? Are they okay? What about their babies!?'

'Everyone's been given the once over and a clean bill of health. They'll all be here later.'

'Thank god.' Sydney felt the relief. She looked at Gareth. 'What the hell happened? How come you weren't drugged?'

'Because I didn't drink his little potion, that's why.' Gareth said. 'I saw you stood there, beginning to work it out. You had that look like fictional detectives do on the telly as the story works itself out in their heads. So I tried to see what you saw but couldn't see it. Then I watched as you looked at Finney, and I saw the look on his face. I still didn't get it, but I saw him pour some powder into the drinks he was handing out, so I pretended to drink mine. While you and he were having your little chat, I dialled DI Davenport and left my phone open so she could hear everything happening. When you made a break for it, and Finney started taking potshots, I spoke to Davenport to ensure she'd heard everything. I was going to take on Finney then, but Davenport ordered me to stand down and wait. She said Armed Response were only minutes away. So I went back and waited. I only went for Finney when no one came. I was trying to buy us some time.'

'He nearly killed you!' Sydney said.

'He nearly killed you too,' Gareth answered, 'and I bloody well wasn't having that. I'm still on a promise, remember?'

Sydney blushed. She remembered.

The door to the room opened, and Pat and Sanjay came in. They carried flowers and chocolates. Pat sat on the edge of the bed and kissed Sydney.

'We owe you our lives.' She said.

Sydney blushed again.

'It's true,' Sanjay agreed. 'We owe you a debt I fear we will never be able to repay.'

'Don't be silly.' Sydney gushed. 'But I could do with a decent coffee. The stuff in these places is usually awful. I don't suppose you and Sanjay would go out for some, would you?'

Gareth and Sanjay took their leave and disappeared. Sydney took Pat's hand and held it firmly.

'I know you killed your mother.' Sydney said.

She watched as conflicting emotions engulfed Pat, who suddenly burst into tears.

'Oh, my god, the guilt is killing me.' Pat cried. 'I've wanted to talk to someone so badly. I didn't know what to do. How did you know?'

'I didn't,' Sydney replied. 'I guessed.'

Pat sighed, and Sydney watched the relief lift the weight from her shoulders. 'Sanjay asked me to marry him. I suppose that's over now. What will you tell DI Davenport?'

'I'm not going to tell Davenport anything.' Sydney said.

Pat look confused. Sydney gripped Pat's hand firmly.

'I don't approve, Pat, I don't approve at all. You shouldn't have done it, but I understand why. Your mother was a powerful, controlling woman who could be unkind to you. I get it; I do. You wanted to live your life and couldn't do it while your mother was around. The irony is that she didn't have long to live anyway. I suppose, if that wasn't the case, I might feel differently, but I can't help but think you saved your mother from an awful lot of suffering.'

'I don't know what to say', Pat stuttered.

'You don't have to say anything. Promise me that you'll make Sanjay the happiest man alive and make pretty children. If ever you feel the need to confess to him, don't. Call me. We'll talk. Sanjay might not understand.'

They were interrupted as the door swung open, and several people entered the room. Gareth led the way.

'We found this lot in the corridor.' He explained. 'They had other ideas.'

He held aloft two bottles of champagne.

Robert and Gemma approached Sydney and kissed her on the cheek. Sakura followed and whispered her eternal thanks. Gareth popped the cork from one of the bottles, and Sanjay held out seven glasses, which were soon filled to the brim with sparkling liquid.

Gareth took centre stage. He held his glass in the air.

'Here's to the future,' he began, 'a bright future of good food, good wine, better friends and where all the murders occur within the pages of a good book. Hopefully written by one of us!'

A ripple of laughter gripped the small party.

'Cheers!'

9 781399 987837